Deal with the Billionaire

The Maid and the Billionaire

Lana Stone

The Billionaires of New York 3

Copyright © 2023 by Lana Stone

All rights reserved.

No portion of this book may be reproduced in any form without written permission from the publisher or author, except as permitted by U.S. copyright law.

Dedication

As always, I dedicate this book to the love of my life.

***

1

Dana

Swinging open the double doors, I entered the luxury suite on the forty-eighth floor of the Royal Renaissance Hotel, the first choice for the wealthy when the Four Seasons wasn't glamorous enough.

Although time was pressing, the panorama made me pause for a second as the floor-to-ceiling windows offered a fantastic view of downtown New York and Central Park.

Don't dawdle, Dana! My schedule was tight and Beccs, my best friend, had to show up any second.

I scurried under the Murano glass chandelier, which cast sunlight in thousands of facets on the white marble ceiling, directly into the master bedroom.

To the left of the bed, which was large enough to turn a small car around on, was a walk-in closet whose open doors offered me a glimpse of exquisite evening gowns and fine everyday clothes by Prada, Chanel and Dior. On the dressing table next to the door, diamond jewelry glittered in the daylight, attracting me almost magically. The precious jewelry set consisted of a necklace, earrings and a bracelet made of high-carat diamonds.

Carefully, I lifted the chain by the clasp and held it against my cleavage. My light blue eyes sparkled in the mirror, with the diamonds around my neck. A dreamy smile spread over my lips, while I posed in front of the mirror and blew an unruly curl, which had come loose from my braid.

The necklace flattered me, which could not be said of my outfit; this dark gray, knee-length dress had never flattered a figure.

But what wouldn't I do for my seven-year plan? Yep, I even wore that awful, monotonous one-piece suit, just like the other eighty-eight maids at the Royal Renaissance Hotel. Really all the girls looked a bit shapeless in it, even me with my petite figure, as well as Beccs, whose curves I secretly envied. My assistant manager, Shannon Williams, probably wouldn't have stood for anything else.

But I didn't have to hold out much longer. If I kept up my strategy, I'd have my own hotel in six years. I had already completed my bachelor's degree in business management the previous year, and now I was gaining experience at the best hotel in town. I wanted to get to know all areas from the ground up, and for that, I was happy to forego the higher starting salary that I would have been entitled to with my degree.

I dreamily looked at my reflection in the mirror; the time would come when I would be able to afford such a wonderful piece of jewelry.

"Gotcha!"

Heavens!

I flinched guiltily, almost dropping the necklace in shock.

"No harm done, Beccs," I replied hastily. I immediately put the jewelry back and raised both hands above my head like a criminal in front of a gun.

The thought that I could have damaged the chain made me dizzy. It certainly cost as much as a car, maybe even as much as a small apartment. Heck, the number of diamonds was probably worth more than I would ever earn in my lifetime.

"Dana Swanson, you are incorrigible." Rebecca sighed as she raised her left eyebrow.

"Nothing. Happened," I repeated. But Rebecca continued to look at me reproachfully as she crossed her arms and leaned against the doorframe.

Of course, I knew that I had to keep my hands off the guests' property, but I hadn't rummaged through a suitcase, I'd just had a bit of a fun with a fantasy. When jewelry lay out in the open on a dresser, I simply could not resist. It was almost an invitation, an appeal to dream, and surely it was no crime to dream a little. Was it? I was no thief, and by all that was sacred to me, I pushed all my temptations away.

Rebecca remained silent, her reproachful looks burning through my crumbling facade. I couldn't stand that look much longer. Fortunately, I knew my best friend well enough to know how to get her mind off things.

From my side pocket, I pulled out a pack of jellybeans and poured a good dozen onto my hand. I picked out the yellow ones myself, then held the remaining candy right in front of Rebecca's nose.

"Want some, too?" I asked, chewing.

Gosh, I loved snacking more than I should have, so I always had a considerable supply of sweets in my pockets. Of course, only those that weren't in danger of melting: gummy bears, Smarties, Skittles, nuts, dried fruit. I had something on offer for every mood.

Rebecca looked at me and kept her lips open a bit, as if she wanted to immediately start another rebuke. Beccs always looked at her daughter, Emma, with exactly the same look when she had done something wrong.

I took the opportunity and put a green jellybean in Rebecca's mouth.

"Dana!" Rebecca glared angrily at me but immediately began chewing. There was nothing like the taste of a green jellybean.

"That's why you shouldn't stand around with your mouth open," I said dryly.

Rebecca gasped and then burst out laughing.

"Don't tell me Vincent McMiller is still chasing you, Dana!"

"No, McMiller doesn't haunt me anymore – just his finger in my mouth!"

I thought back to the momentous first day of high school, when I had yawned unexpectedly and suddenly had the finger of Vincent McMiller – heartthrob, football player and my biggest nemesis – stuck in my mouth. Since then, I've been manic about holding my hand over my mouth while yawning.

To get rid of the memory of the taste of McMiller's finger, I put another handful of jelly beans in my mouth. Beccs, meanwhile, had begun to pull the satin sheets off the four-poster bed, and I came to her rescue.

Because it was an impossibility to cover these giant beds alone without leaving wrinkles or creases, the maids for the suites were divided into teams of two, which made the monotonous work a lot more bearable.

"Your obsession with the guests' luxury toys is going to cost you dearly someday," Rebecca said with a worried expression. She pulled the satin cover off the blanket and let it fall to the floor.

"I'm not doing anything. I'm just daydreaming," I replied as I pulled off the pillowcases.

Rebecca paused with her work for a moment and looked at me urgently.

"Williams will shred your daydreams to pieces if she gets wind of this."

I blew a strand of hair out of my face. Gritting my teeth, I had to admit that my best friend was right, but did I really have to change? At the moment, my dreams were all I had, and I would be extremely reluctant to bury them.

"You're probably right. Our boss would fire me."

"But before that, she'll have you tarred and feathered and then chase you through every single floor."

We chuckled, even though the situation was no laughing matter at all. Shannon Williams was the most petty personnel manager imaginable. Among us maids, she was known only as the Guardian of Limbo. Of course, I recognized my boss's good intentions, but Ms. Williams enforced her rules and demands so doggedly and aggressively that she lived up to her reputation. Despite this, or perhaps because of it, she had recently been appointed assistant hotel manager.

Since then, the maids suffered even more from her than before, because now she could also implement her crazier ideas.

"You know what's a much bigger problem in my life?" I asked rhetorically. "I'm too nice!"

And burned out. And always hungry. And the thing with my love life ... oh, we'd better leave that alone.

Giggling, Beccs threw her head back, her natural red highlights shimmering in the sunlight within her blonde hair.

"What's that supposed to mean?" I asked, shrugging my shoulders.

"I wouldn't call that nice, I would call that shyness-level ten thousand."

"Well, now, don't get carried away, Beccs."

"I've told you a hundred-million times that I never exaggerate!" To back up her playfully serious voice, she put her hands on her hips. Then she took a deep breath and leaned over to me with a conspiratorial expression.

"But seriously, you should speak your mind more often, you're our spokesperson to management and, since the tips were cut, there's been quite a bit of resentment."

On the same day that Ms. Williams was promoted, she had banned the acceptance of tips. Anyone who violated this rule was terminated without notice.

"I know. It's terrible that we've had to fill as many positions in a month as we normally do in a year," I sighed. I had known every single one of the fired maids personally. Good, nice girls who really couldn't help it. Some guests insisted on the tip and didn't let up until we caved in.

"And I miss Mr. Moore," I continued to whine. Jack Moore was the former deputy with whom I had a really good rapport. He had played a big role in my seven-year plan, and he had been something of a mentor to me in the early days. That is, until he had gotten a job offer as a hotel manager at a posh place near Madison Square Garden. His replacement had been none other than Shannon Williams.

"We all do. But you need to talk to her about it, Dana."

"I know. But I don't want to put her in her place, nor do I want to lose mine. I can't help it; I just can't confront her."

Maybe it was because I was afraid that I was making things worse for all the maids, or maybe it was just because of my boss's icy stare that I never contradicted her lately.

"We didn't choose you to be our spokesperson for nothing, you're helpful and smart. You just need to show more confidence, that would improve your life and our situation at the hotel, too."

I nodded. "You're right, Beccs. But with Mr. Moore, everything was so much easier..." I began, but my best friend cut me off.

"And you need to have sex!"

"Rebecca!" I snorted in shock at my friend's directness. Even though she wasn't wrong, I pushed away thoughts of the disastrous dates of the past few months and took the sheets to the laundry cart. Beccs followed me and pulled out fresh sheets. The scent of cinnamon and vanilla wafting up to me.

Not wanting to have to talk further about my non-existent love life, I quickly changed the subject.

"Does Emma still talk about her birthday every day?"

"First thing every morning, she asks if today is the big day. She can hardly wait to turn six," Rebecca enthused, beaming with maternal pride. In fact, Emma's big day was just under three weeks away.

"How cute." My heart sank, because Emma was just about the cutest little girl in the world.

Together we made the bed, making sure that the clean sheets did not touch the floor at any time, or we would have had to get fresh ones.

"And what about Disneyland?" I gasped as I shook the wrinkles out of the blanket. Rebecca sighed heavily and ran the back of her hand over her forehead.

"Well. The missing tips ... But maybe I can manage a few more events. A party here, a wedding there. You know."

The disappointment on Rebecca's face was impossible to miss, and my heart broke a little bit.

"We'll figure it out." I smiled confidently. I would have given my best friend everything I had saved without hesitation, but I had no reserves. I usually collected the tips I had received so far in a canning jar in my kitchen and donated them once a month to a different charity each time. The money was not nearly enough for my dream of owning my own hotel, but it was enough for a hearty meal, a warm jacket or medicine.

"Do you have any concrete suggestions?" asked Rebecca dejectedly, pulling the blanket taut so that even the last wrinkles disappeared.

"We could stop climate change, then Ms. Williams would get too cold and go back to hell."

We laughed so hard that we had to stop arranging the pillows for a moment.

"Don't say that too loud, Dana. I can well imagine that she's listening to us," whispered Beccs, holding her hand over her mouth.

I looked down at the radio that was in my fanny pack.

"Yes, she's crazy. But not that crazy."

"Well, I think so."

Admittedly, I had also thought about whether the radios were recording all conversations, but then Ms. Williams would surely have intervened by now. When we worked together and there was no guest around, we almost always talked to each other, just like the other maids.

"Maybe she's a little overambitious, you know what I mean? An initial euphoria that subsides with time." I had no idea why I was defending my boss, possibly because I hoped she would really relax over time, which would make all of our lives much easier.

"A little?" repeated Rebecca. "She may have good principles, yet she pushes everything to the extreme. That's how it looks."

"Okay, you win."

Like a diva, Rebecca put her hand to her forehead and howled loudly, "And then Fashion Week, too."

During Fashion Week, the Royal Renaissance Hotel was in a state of emergency, at no other time were so many people with strange preferences.

"Who was your favorite last year, anyway?" I asked curiously.

"Definitely the guy from Eastern Europe who checked the entire room with a Geiger counter beforehand, including us. Every single time we entered the room. And yours?"

"I think the artist who had covered the entire floor with sod, and you could only walk on it barefoot."

"That was awesome too!"

Yep. There were no unfulfilled wishes at the Royal Renaissance Hotel – that was not just a saying, but reality.

"By the way, I heard that the forty-ninth floor has been booked for quite a while by a single guest, a super-rich one. I can't wait to see how he's going to keep us on our toes," I said with a grin. Before Rebecca could answer, my radio crackled.

"Daaanaaa! In Room 2811, a guest is not satisfied with the cleaning of his shirt," Shannon Williams' voice rattled from the device.

"I'll get right on it," I radioed back.

"You do that." The crackling stopped; the guardian of limbo had disappeared from the line.

"Why does she always call you for extra requests, anyway? Surely there are other maids on the twenty-eighth floor. And that's really more for the front desk, if you ask me."

"I wonder about that, too. I don't know. Maybe because I'm too nice, after all?"

"Or because you're the only one whose name she can remember."

"I think it's because I'm so accommodating!"

Rebecca gave a short laugh. "Well, then I guess it's thanks to your obliging nature that you'll soon have to split in two to get everything done."

"Can you manage on your own, Beccs?"

"Yes, I'm grown up. That bed is made. I can handle the vacuum cleaner by myself, and we are good friends."

"Well, I'll see you later," I said with a smile. As I moved toward the door, Beccs called after me, "Oh, before I forget, I'm hosting a karaoke contest tonight. Do you want to come?"

"Karaoke? That's not really my favorite thing to do."

"Oh, come on, you don't have to sing! The contestants are all set, I bet it'll be pretty fun."

When Rebecca hosted the show, it was definitely funny. She didn't mince words during her events and always had the right joke in store.

"Come on, Dana. Please. If the evening goes well, I'll be able to host the program there more often, and that'll get us a lot closer to Disneyland. I need you to be my mental support."

I simply could not refuse my best friend's wish. Especially not when I imagined Emma's big, shining eyes in front of me, in which Disneyland was reflected.

"Okay, you've convinced me."

2

Connor

The limo stopped and, without looking up, I knew I was at my destination – the entrance to the Royal Renaissance Hotel.

I hadn't been in the city for a while, but New York hadn't changed; the city never did. Loud. Hectic. Pulsating. Exactly my taste. No other city in the world could match that dynamic. I'd been around a hell of a lot in recent years, but neither Moscow nor Paris nor Tokyo could keep up with New York.

"Sir, I can check in for you," my chauffeur offered politely, his voice deep. It made the petite, gray-haired man seem stronger. Although we had talked the entire ride, I didn't know the man. He was one of Dad's chauffeurs for the Lancester Company, my father's business. I held a considerable amount of the company's stock but preferred to concentrate on my own business.

"No, I'll do it myself, John. Just drive the car into the garage."

I had spent the last few weeks in England developing a new type of beer in my brewery. There, I had the best brewers in the UK teach me the art of brewing. Although I had many British business connections, classic Oxford English was unfamiliar to a man from the East Coast. There was a rough, pragmatic tone there that could come across as hectic or aggressive to some, by no means as noble as an Englishman who came from the southeast of the island. That's why I was looking for conversations almost everywhere today. I had held conference calls throughout the flight and, during the drive, chatted with John, the chauffeur.

"With pleasure, sir."

I pulled a one-hundred-dollar bill out of my pocket; I never carried smaller bills.

"You can take a cab and go home to your wife. I'm not leaving the hotel today."

"Thank you, but that's not necessary," John politely declined.

"I know. Take it anyway. Attend the next Boston Beasts game or take your wife out to dinner."

Smiling gratefully, John took the bill.

"Thank you, have a pleasant day, Mr. Lancester."

After I got out of the car, I tugged the sleeves of my tailored Armani suit and adjusted my cufflinks. I looked nostalgically after the sporty car, which turned slowly into the next side street to the hotel's underground parking garage.

The sleek model was a real feast for the eyes and rarely seen in the inner city. Such a beast wanted to tease and chase high-speed over the highway. In the dense New York city traffic, a Bugatti was a real waste.

In front of the glazed revolving door, set in gold, a bellboy came to greet me. The boy was barely of age, but he had the serious expression of an elder, like all the staff I encountered at the Royal Renaissance Hotel.

"Sir, may I take care of your luggage?"

"Thanks, but it's already in my room."

I entered the huge reception hall, which seamlessly merged into a bar. Undoubtedly, a few very select drops were served there, but the rough smell of ale still hung in my nose.

I walked purposefully to the reception desk, my footsteps echoing across the expensive, brightly polished marble floor. Behind the reception desk worked three employees with identical dresses, hairstyles and facial expressions. Two of them were documenting something, a third was talking quietly on the phone, taking notes as she went.

Even before I reached the table, one of the receptionists greeted me with a smile as she continued to look at her paper. Her businesslike smile turned into a genuine one when she looked me in the eye, which I almost took as an attempt at flirtation. I didn't take her eyelash fluttering any further seriously; she wasn't my type, in any sense of the word.

"Welcome to the Royal Renaissance. What can I do for you?" she asked, smiling broadly. She was still grinning, but the laughter would soon be gone when I mentioned my name. Things always went the same no matter where I was.

"I'd like to check in," I replied, bracing myself against the cool tabletop. "I'm Connor Lancester." I smiled to lessen the impact of the words at least a little. Three. Two. One...

The smile disappeared and her face turned chalky white; instead, gasping breath set in, and the young woman hammered away frantically at the keyboard.

"Mr. Lancester, of course! I'm really very sorry, I should have known," the receptionist stammered. I had never understood why my mere name sent most people into a state of emergency, but sometimes, mischievousness took over and drove me to savor it a bit.

"How could you have known?" I eyed the confused woman with a serious look. On the one hand, I felt sorry for her, but on the other hand, I just couldn't deny myself this joke.

"I ... um ..." she stammered awkwardly before putting on a business-like expression again, her flirtatious look gone.

Of course, everyone knew my name – my father's name – but almost no one knew my face unless they read Forbes magazine. I valued my privacy, which is why I kept the public away from my private life as much as I could.

"It's okay," I said with a wink, then read her name tag. "Tell me, Caroline. Is my suite ready? The flight was tiring, and I have another business meeting tonight."

"Of course, your luggage has already been taken upstairs."

Caroline rifled through some paperwork, picked up an electronic key card, and placed it on a small black box. It beeped briefly, then the receptionist nodded with satisfaction. She walked around the reception desk and led me to an elevator away from the others.

"This is your personal elevator," Caroline explained to me further. She held the card on a marked area on the left door frame and the elevator doors opened silently.

"May I escort you to the suite and familiarize you with everything?"

My cell phone vibrated in the pocket of my jacket, and I already had an idea who was on the other end of the line.

"Thanks, I'll be fine." Reluctantly, I pulled my smartphone out of my pocket and looked at the screen, which confirmed my fear. My mother.

"I hope you have a pleasant stay, Mr. Lancester." The receptionist nodded politely at me and hurriedly returned to the front desk.

I took the call, got on the elevator, and hoped that all the metal made for radio interference.

"Hi, Mom."

"Connor? Did you get here okay?" My mother, Diana Lancester, was the most caring woman I knew. Yes, she had a lot of love to give, and most of all, she loved having dozens of grandchildren around her. I loved my family, but I was far from wanting to start my own.

"Yeah, I just checked in."

"Fine, fine. I'm very glad your flight went well," she purred into the phone. Then there was silence. I pressed the button to the forty-ninth floor, and the doors closed silently. The elevator moved so quietly that I could have built a house of cards in it.

"Mom?" I asked. "Why did you call? What's on your mind?"

"What, nothing! Surely, I can check with my son to see if everything is all right?" Her voice sounded shrill and reproachful. Still, I knew exactly why my mom was calling me. I leaned against the wall and pulled my Gameboy out of my jacket pocket. I'd been playing Tetris on it since I was a kid, every chance I got. When I turned it on, I immediately heard the typical Tetris melody, which hung in everyone's ears for hours as soon as they heard it.

"Connor! Are you playing Tetris while we're on the phone?"

Yep, that's it.

"No, that's the elevator music."

"Ah," my mother replied suspiciously. She didn't let it bother her for long, though, because there were more important things she wanted to hear from me. "Then I'll let you sleep now. I'll see you at the wedding, okay?"

Of course, it was about the wedding of a distant acquaintance, for which I had to come back from London a week earlier because I still owed her a favor, which she was now calling in. Actually, it wasn't really a wedding, but rather a gathering of billionaires and investors who were using a festive occasion to make new business connections. Events that I only attended for the sake of my family.

"Oh, now that you mention it, Connor."

"Yes?"

"You had mentioned someone would accompany you!" Her voice quivered with anticipation of future grandchildren.

"Yes?"

"She will come, won't she? I really want to meet her!"

"I think so," I lied and was struck with a guilty conscience. There was no companion, there was no girlfriend and certainly no serious relationship! I could do without that, well and gladly. I took care of that with the help of women from a very discreet escort service.

Too bad that the same woman - the only one who was eligible for the job - had to cancel her appointment because she had eaten spoiled oysters.

Thanks to the escort service, I had managed to escape my mother's persistent matchmaking attempts over the last few celebrations.

"Oh, I'm so excited! It's really time for you to have a deep relationship and get married, son, I want you to be happy."

"No, Mom. You want grandchildren," I corrected her with a grin.

"One doesn't preclude the other, after all."

"I think having kids is more for Max, don't you think?"

My mom sighed audibly. Yes, my little sister was a case – cheeky, impetuous, and wild.

"You know how she is. But I'll definitely introduce her to the Bradfords' son. He'd be a good choice for her!" Just thinking about how Maxine reacted to the Bradfords' youngest offspring made me laugh out loud.

"Good luck with that, Mom! Good luck!"

"You're not making it easy for me, you know that?"

Ping. The elevator reached the forty-ninth floor, and the doors opened.

"Mom, I have to hang up now. I'll see you at the wedding."

"See you soon, Connor. I'm really looking forward to seeing you."

"Me too."

Sighing, I left the elevator, turned off my Gameboy, and entered my suite. As announced, my luggage had already been brought upstairs, my custom-made weight bench was right next to the balcony door. I needed fresh air when working out; it was the only way to push myself to my limits – and beyond. Stuffy rooms were the death of any training session.

To relieve my impending headache, I went to the bathroom, splashed cold water on my face, and took an aspirin. The transatlantic flight had exhausted me.

That damn jet lag every time.

The bedroom on this floor was bigger than many apartments. The bed was huge, and the closet that held my clothes was even bigger. All my suits were neatly placed on hangers and shelves, free of wrinkles, and looked almost a little lost in the vast emptiness. One garment, however, definitely looked out of place, a handmade silver dress.

I was in the Royal Renaissance Hotel. There was no question that this was an accident. In the most exclusive hotel in the whole city, probably even in all of America, no mishaps happened. I took the dress off the hanger and looked at it more closely. There was a paper knotted to one of the wide straps with a cord, which I untied to read the card.

You're welcome, Max.

"Great," I growled. Then I crumpled up the paper and dropped it, along with the dress, carelessly on the floor next to me. Maxine, that little beast, really never missed an opportunity to tease me. No way were we going to end this little mad sibling war. I needed an alibi, that much was certain. Just as certain as the fact that I didn't want to disappoint my mother.

But where could I quickly find a woman who fit my criteria? She had to be stylish, polite and not stand out in high society. Ninety-five percent of the available ladies fell through this grid alone. Finding a discreet escort company was another problem. And on such short notice, I certainly did not run across a woman who met all my criteria.

Fuck!

3

Dana

The Irish Oak Pub was packed when Beccs and I entered, loud voices mingling with modern pop music.

Now I understood why some guests preferred to stand outside the bar with their drinks to talk in small groups. Only in the niches that were integrated into the corner was there some quiet.

"I'm really glad you came along," Rebecca yelled over the noise, patting my arm.

"Sure thing," I yelled back. When I thought about it, it was definitely nicer to go out with my girlfriend than to have to spend the evening at home. Alone. With a bag of chips and a season of Big Bang Theory.

Sometimes I envied my best friend, because Rebecca's husband Tom was great, and Emma made their happiness perfect.

Rebecca pushed her way through the room, I made an effort to follow her as we squeezed through the dense crowd. Step by step we came closer to the bar, which announced itself with the typical smell of beer and peanuts.

"Is this place always this busy?" I asked breathlessly when we finally reached the bar.

"I don't know," Rebecca replied, shrugging her shoulders.

I often accompanied Beccs at her events and functions, but preferred rather small birthday parties, weddings and other celebrations. The main thing was that I could hide in the crowd without attracting attention, unlike my best friend, who loved her second job and liked to put herself in the spotlight.

At the edge of the bar, I grabbed a free seat, which I immediately claimed for myself. Since the competition began in a few minutes, Rebecca remained standing next to me.

She tapped me on the shoulder and said, "I guess it's busier today because there's a contest. They're very popular, especially if there's prize money."

"There's prize money?" I was astonished.

"Yes. Five hundred and fifty-five dollars. A good start, I think."

"I agree." I nodded with conviction. "I'd put the money in the form of chocolate or ice cream as a reserve for my erotic swinging hips, you know." I laughed as I braced my hands at my sides and gyrated my hips like a – somewhat awkward – exotic dancer. Rebecca laughed along, then her face became a bit more serious again.

"If everything goes smoothly, I get to host here weekly," Rebecca enthused.

"That's great!"

"Yes, it would be a real financial boost, and I could put some money aside for Emma's college."

To mentally support my best friend and world's best presenter, I gave her a hug. "You'll be fine, Beccs. You're the best event manager I know. The evening should be fun, and I bet there are a lot of really good singers!"

"How many event managers do you know?" asked Rebecca, eyeing me with a critical gaze.

"Enough to form an opinion," I replied, without elaborating on her question.

Rebecca looked at the clock, then beckoned one of the three bartenders who were drawing beer from various taps or mixing cocktails in a chord.

"What'll it be, ladies?"

"Drink whatever you want Dana, it's on me."

"Well, if that's the case, I'd like the best bottle of scotch."

Rebecca and the bartender exchanged uncertain glances, which I enjoyed for a moment before laughing out loud.

"Just kidding, a Bitter Lemon please."

"Sounds good, I'll take it too."

The bartender smiled kindly before asking, "I have a beer, something very special and free for all the beautiful women today. How about it ladies?"

I wondered if the bartender picked up many women with this scam, but kindly declined. Rebecca also clearly shook her head: "Your boss will kill me if I start slurring my words on stage. Speaking of the stage, I have to go. There's a little more organizing to do." She pulled a five-dollar bill from her purse and thrust it into the bartender's hand.

"You'll be fine, Beccs, no matter what. I am and will always be your biggest groupie," I cheered on my best friend.

"You're a sweetheart. Wish me luck anyway!"

"If you have talent, you don't need luck."

I winked at Beccs, then crossed my index and middle fingers for a symbolic, knowing how superstitious she was sometimes. I wasn't really superstitious – that was bad luck.

Beccs disappeared into the crowd, leaving me alone with the bartender, who maintained eye contact with me and leaned over the counter.

"The beer is really pretty good and it's free," he tried again.

He was persistent, but so was I. "I'm not a beer drinker."

"Then just sip it for a bit, but please taste it. It's important. My boss wants me to give away a total of two hundred bottles throughout the evening!"

I sighed. On the one hand, I felt sorry for the bartender, but on the other hand, I really didn't want a beer. But the pitying look, which reminded me of a little kitten in distress, made me go along with it.

"Okay, okay. Give me that beer!"

"Coming right up!"

Not a second later, an open bottle of beer stood in front of me. Lancester Light was written on the label in curved letters. Visually, the beer looked very stylish, but I didn't drink any of it, just wiped at the drops of condensation running down from the neck of the bottle, my gaze gliding around the room.

Garlands, streamers and posters in the colors of the Irish national flag hung everywhere, announcing the karaoke competition. Earlier, as a little girl, I had desperately wanted to be a singer, but I had quickly discarded the dream when I couldn't get a single note out at an event in front of the entire junior school.

Rebecca was standing with two men at the back of the stage, talking to them. Her arms were folded in front of her chest and her expression became more and more serious. Judging by their suits, they were the sponsors of the competition. The longer the conversation lasted, the more dissatisfied all three seemed.

The two men walked off the stage, leaving Rebecca alone. She took a breath, put on her professional face from the Royal Renaissance Hotel, and went to the mixing desk that was at the side of the stage. At the push of a button, the big stage lights came on and the music quietened down. The pub quietened down as well, and the first conversations fell silent altogether. Rebecca grabbed one of the radio microphones and stood in the middle of the stage.

"Welcome to the Irish Oak! Are you ready for karaoke?" Rebecca opened the event. There were cheers and restrained clapping here and there, and the crowd slowly became aware of Rebecca. There was no longer any sign of her discontent. I knew this work face well enough myself, as a maid you always smiled, no matter how miserable you were or how rude the guest was.

"I asked if you guys wanted to do karaoke!"

"Yes!" the crowd cheered louder.

"Very good! In total, there will be..." Rebecca hesitated briefly. "Ten contestants! I don't want to give too much away, but they're going to rock this place!"

The cheering got even louder.

"But before we get started," Rebecca began, then waited for the cheers to die down, "a huge round of applause for our main sponsor. NYC Music FM! Representing the station, Billy from the morning show is here."

The crowd went wild, glasses were raised, the alcohol level rose by the second and the bartenders picked up the pace.

"And also, let's hear it for Jonathan Murphy for hosting the karaoke contest!"

Again, the guests applauded, whistled and shouted, and Rebecca had to wait until the volume died down.

"Before I explain the rules, one more teeny-tiny thing." Rebecca held her fingertips close together, and her voice rose with each word. I knew my best friend, and I knew this wasn't a teeny-tiny thing. Whatever the problem was, it was anything but teeny-tiny.

"Unfortunately, one participant had to cancel at short notice, he is ill."

The guests commented in unison with an 'Ohhh' before Rebecca continued.

"So, if there is anyone else among you who wants to take his or her chance, he or she should scream here now."

Rebecca scanned the pub with a desperate look. Briefly, her gaze hung on individual guests, appearing to plea that someone immediately jump up and shout *here*, but it remained silent. I looked around at everyone's faces. There were a few indecisive expressions, but no one spoke up.

"Okay, you guys must be pretty shy," Rebecca winked. "Never mind, I'll be here at the mixer all evening in case anyone does want to enter the contest. After all, there's five hundred and fifty-five dollars in cash to be won!"

The enthusiasm was great, almost as if Rebecca had just promised the guests all a free beer. Of course, that was already being done.

"Okay!" Rebecca made herself heard again. "The rules are simple! You are the judges, and each and every one of you! After each song, we're going to measure the volume with this little device – a decibel meter. Me here, Billy in the middle, and Jonathan at the bar. The person with the loudest applause wins. To make it a little more exciting, we won't reveal the volume until the end! Let's go with our first singer, Kimmy, who will sing an Amy Winehouse classic. A big round of applause for Kimmy!"

The crowd welcomed Kimmy, a young brunette, with a big applause. Kimmy walked onto the stage, took the microphone from Rebecca, and waited for the music to start. Her friendly face was shyly turned to the floor, and she seemed to want to hunker down in her oversized college jacket. But only until the music kicked in and she sang Back to Black by Amy Winehouse in her powerful voice.

I swayed along to the beat of the music, and when the last note was sung, everyone cheered and clapped loudly, I also gave thunderous applause. The other contestants would definitely not have it easy.

Rebecca appeared back on stage and took the microphone from Kimmy to ask the next singer to come on stage.

Meanwhile, I continued to stare at the beer bottle in front of me, which had met a bad fate with me.

Well, a little sip can't hurt.

Carefully, I put the bottle to my lips and tried a tiny sip. I was amazed. Was that really beer I was drinking? Perplexed by the delicious taste, I took a bigger sip, looked at the label, and drank again.

This beer was damn tasty! While I wondered why I had been abstinent from beer for so long in the first place, I felt like I was being watched. Not in a creepy stalker way, but I felt the stares nonetheless. In the crowded pub, however, I had no chance of finding my observer, if he existed at all.

Don't get paranoid!

I was in a room full of people, of course one or the others' glance brushed over me.

When the rocker on stage sang Last Resort, all my paranoid thoughts were forgotten. All that mattered now was the anthem of my youth, which set the mood throughout the Irish Oak.

Quietly, I sang along with the song, nostalgically thinking of my high school days when the song was played up and down at every frat party.

The applause at the end of the song was so loud that I covered my ears while cheering as loud as I could myself. Come what may, this song was my favorite.

It took quite a while for Rebecca to announce the next singer, and when the song was intoned, she left the stage with a worried look. The closer she came to me, the darker her look became.

"A vodka on the rocks," Rebecca ordered a drink from the bartender, to whom she had explained ten minutes ago that she didn't want to drink alcohol. It really had to be super-serious.

"Is it really that bad?" I asked worriedly.

Rebecca sighed, drained her vodka on the rocks, and said, "One of the contestants dropped out, so yeah!"

"Yeah, you said that already, but what's the problem?"

The atmosphere was great, and the singers heated up the mood even more. I couldn't begin to count the amount of beer and how many dozens of cocktails had gone over the counter during the last song alone. It was a wet dream of every bar owner.

"There must be eleven contestants." Rebecca pointed to the poster above the stage announcing eleven contestants, handpicked from dozens of preliminaries.

"The sponsor wants a snapshot number. For Facebook and the newspapers. That was the condition for the prize money, eleven entrants for five hundred and fifty-five dollars, or they won't pay."

"How mean! Exceptions don't work? The event is already on!"

My best friend could hardly hold back her tears. "What do you think will happen here if the prize money is not paid to the winner! Then there will be a huge shitstorm coming at the Irish Oak because of false promises and cheap marketing methods."

"And it's all going to come back to you. Right?"

Rebecca nodded and ordered a second vodka.

"The guy said he'll give us until the last official singer to find a replacement, but so far it doesn't look like anyone else is coming forward. Slowly, people are getting way too drunk for the stage, too. God, this is a huge disaster!"

I would have loved to take Beccs comfortingly in my arms, but there was just too much crowding around us. If no one could be found to stand on the stage, that was it for Beccs' career as a presenter; word got around quickly. No more side jobs also meant no Disneyland for Emma. I knew that these fateful words were costing me more than I wanted to pay, but I spoke them anyway.

"Is there anything I can do to help?"

Crap. Rebecca looked at me with wide eyes and nodded vigorously.

"You could sing!"

"No, absolutely not! You know I would do anything for you, but not that!"

"But you can sing, very well in fact!"

Yes, at home in the shower when no one was around. But Rebecca alluded to the one evening when I couldn't stop myself because of a song from Frozen that Emma had been listening to in an endless loop all evening. After what felt like the hundredth time, we stood together in the living room, with brooms and remote controls misused as microphones, and warbled along exuberantly to the Disney hit. Who could suppress the reflex to sing along with this song? That's right, nobody.

"Yes. In front of you and Emma, not a thousand people!"

"Oh come on, that's maybe two hundred."

"Beccs, I can't do this. I really can't," I tried to squirm out, like an eel out of water. "Maybe someone will come forward after all."

I really couldn't, self-confidence wasn't exactly my strong point. I had failed at junior high, I definitely didn't need that feeling a second time.

The song was coming to an end and Rebecca had to go back to the stage. "Yeah, I hope someone else comes forward, too, or I'm screwed!"

Beccs brought one singer after another on stage, all singing mixed repertoire, most of the women choosing classic pop songs, the men more rocky stuff. Nevertheless, there was also an outlier who sang a song from the well-known musical Phantom of the Opera and a young woman – Annie – who tried her hand at rap. When the first notes of Bodak Yellow rang out, the audience went completely berserk. Then, when she started twerking to the beat, it was all over for the male audience members. Women getting down on their knees and shaking their butts was a new but persistent trend that permeated all clubs and bars where snappy music was played. The men whistled and shouted so loudly that their voices were almost inaudible.

When the beer was finished, I ordered another Bitter Lemon and a bag of bell pepper chips, which I nibbled to the beat of the music. A young, handsome man with a dark complexion squeezed through the crowd and leaned over to the bartender.

"Hola, I would like a special blend. Would that be possible?" the man asked with a Spanish accent.

"Sure, what?"

"Just take a glass and pour in two-thirds Lancester Light, one-third Spicey Dream of Havana and a shot of Blizzard Boiled Bourbon, sí?"

I frowned and concentrated on keeping my features from completely derailing. What kind of combination was that? The bartender was also puzzled but immediately complied with the unusual request.

"It's about a bet," the Spaniard explained to me with a grin. Then he accepted the full glass, paid the bartender and disappeared into the crowd again.

Wow. What the hell had just happened? My curiosity about what the creative bet was all about was piqued. Out of the corner of my eye, I watched the crowd part toward a small alcove. The Spaniard sat down on an empty seat, the opposite side of which was covered by densely packed people.

Stop stalking strangers!

There were more important things, like the fact that while the crowd was getting more boisterous with each song, at the same time the likelihood of Rebecca finding another singer was dwindling, and the more the show drew to a close, the paler she became. Her natural summer tan had completely disappeared.

What a bummer.

I was in a bind, and I hated myself for watching my best friend go down. But I also couldn't just sing in front of so many people! What if I sang off-key? The previous singers had prepared for this competition and had hit every note perfectly.

Heavens, this wasn't really a karaoke competition, but a world's best singer battle. I never stood a chance against that, and in the worst case

I made Beccs' situation even worse by driving the karaoke competition up the wall.

The last singer was called on stage and delivered a terrific Michael Jackson imitation, including the typical outfit with wide shirt, tight pants and polished shoes. But compared to the other participants, the applause was rather restrained. Maybe because it looked too much like a professional act?

Rebecca looked like she was about to faint.

Jesus, Beccs! You really owe me for this one!

I pushed myself off the bar with gusto and literally stormed the stage when the Michael Jackson clone had left it. I almost made a detour to the girls' restroom to hide, but my sense of duty as a best friend reminded me that if our roles had been reversed, Beccs would have bailed me out, too.

I consciously focused only on Rebecca and not on the audience to my left. Rebecca blinked a small tear of joy out of the corner of her eye, and her lips formed into a silent thank you, then she continued to moderate.

Let's hope this doesn't end in disaster.

"And now we come to our last contestant, Dana! She will..."

"Let it go!"

"Let it go from *Frozen*! A big round of applause for Dana, please!"

Rebecca handed me a microphone that weighed a ton. The crowd went wild, and I was forced to turn to the audience, because at the other end of the room was the TV on which the song lyrics were displayed, but which the other singers had never needed. Sure, they were prepared, unlike me, but I had only the desire to be swallowed by the ground. The audience stared at me expectantly.

Oh. My. God. All terrific singers ... and then me.

I stared stubbornly down, because as long as I saw only my own feet, I could halfway block out the audience. The music started, I took a deep breath and sang the first notes in a delicate, almost inaudible voice. Through the speakers that stood to my left and right, I heard my own voice, which Beccs readjusted at the mixing console to give the audience the best possible sound, just like the last singers. Of course, completely without autotune or other manipulations. She only adjusted the volume of the voice so that the singers could hear themselves better.

My heart was hammering so loudly that I could barely hear the music, yet I mustered all my courage and got louder and louder. And surprise! I liked it, because the acoustics reminded me of singing in the shower, only now there were about two hundred people listening to me. No one ran away, a good sign. I dared more and more and when the chorus started, I even went so far as to look at individual faces in the audience. No critical looks, only guests who were having fun and singing along, even some of the men got infected by the rousing chorus.

Suddenly I understood why my predecessors had felt so comfortable on stage, the atmosphere, the energy that was there on stage was great. The audience sang and celebrated with me. There was no stopping now. I sang the song full of emotion and unafraid of crooked tones, just like in the shower.

Take that, Junior High! I rock the fucking house!

Heavens, I felt like I was tripping after a caffeine overdose.

Then the song ended faster than I had thought, the time had passed incredibly quickly. Thunderous cheers followed. Whistles. Some stood up or applauded with their hands raised high. An incredible feeling! But with the music, my just-found self-confidence disappeared again, and I wanted to get out of sight of the other guests as quickly as possible.

Stop, no! Stay there! I barely understood Rebecca's signals but enough to remain in place.

"Let's hear it for Dana!" Rebecca cheered the crowd on even more. "We're going to take a short break to evaluate our measurements, then we're going to crown the winner or the winner."

Only slowly did the cheers die down, and even when I left the stage, there was no end in sight. Touched and smiling, I retreated back to the corner of the bar, and grabbed an unattended bowl of peanuts. In my safe little hiding place at the edge of the bar, I could take a breath. And nibble. Some of my friends even claimed that I was a real pro at destroying munchies; I would describe myself as more of a stealthy and hungry amateur.

My heart was still hammering violently in my chest.

I had to let this strange situation sink in. Unbelievable! I had really stood on this stage, in front of this huge crowd and had sung loudly without any blackout or nervous breakdown!

Rebecca consulted with the two organizers in the background. It didn't take long until all values were compared and added up, nevertheless the audience and the participants slowly became impatient. Of course, it was well after midnight and most of them had to go to work tomorrow. Jeez, just thinking about how overtired I was and that I have to work tomorrow made my temples ache.

Beccs and the two suit guys were welcomed on stage with thunderous applause.

"We have a result for you!"

Cheers.

"But to make it not quite as long, we're only going to pick the three podium finishers."

More cheers.

"Thank you to all the singers who participated, you were all great!"

More cheering, then silence.

Rebecca opened a folded paper and read it aloud.

"At a volume of one hundred and twenty-four decibels, which is the equivalent of a jackhammer or a thunderstorm roar, you cheered David onto the podium with Last Resort!"

David came on stage. Hands were shaken, then he was presented with a champagne bottle and a certificate. Of course, I also applauded loudly for my personal favorite of the evening.

"In second place, at a volume of a full one hundred and thirty-eight decibels, you were cheering for Annie with Bodak Yellow! Guys, you were as loud as a car race!"

Thunderous applause, and when Annie came on stage, part of the audience rapped the first lines of the song again, she also got a bottle of champagne and an envelope.

"And now we come to first place! One hundred and forty-six decibels were measured. That's louder than a fighter plane!"

Wow. I wondered who the winner was? I'd had the feeling that my favorite had been the loudest, but perhaps only because I had cheered so loudly, directly after came Annie, who had appealed mainly to the men with her dancing, but the applause had not been louder for any of the other participants, at least not in my opinion.

"First place is ... drum roll!"

Heavens, Rebecca knew exactly how to keep her audience on tenterhooks. I was jiggling around in my chair. The entire audience had fallen silent.

"Daaanaaa! Congratulations!"

Applause started and, out of reflex, I applauded along before I faltered. *Wait a minute ... Dana, that's my name.* Stunned, I looked for my friend, who beckoned me to join her on stage. My legs became as heavy as lead, and at the same time, I ducked down so as not to be seen by anyone. God, I was as embarrassed as when I had spent my birthday with Beccs at the bowling alley and suddenly everyone sang Happy Birthday to me.

"Come on, don't be shy, Dana!"

Immediately the audience joined in – "Dana! Dana! Dana!"

It didn't help, I had to get back on stage. As if in a trance, I went up the steps, shook hands with the two men whose names I had forgotten, and hugged Beccs, who gave me a bottle of champagne, a trophy, and fanned out five hundred and fifty-five dollars.

I hadn't had that much money in my hand in a long time! The crowd cheered and raved, a few photos were taken for the press, and then the bar owner announced the last call. When I left the stage, I immediately aimed for the exit, because now that the event was over, most of the guests would want to leave the pub in a hurry.

Again and again, I was stopped by partly drunken guests and praised for my singing skills, which caused a strange feeling in me.

When I finally reached the exit, I greedily breathed in the refreshingly cool night air. I stared awkwardly at the wad of bills in my hand, which was still trembling slightly with excitement. Although the area was rather quiet, I felt uncomfortable with so much cash.

I still couldn't believe that I had just won so much money! I wonder if Beccs had anything to do with it? No, the other two organizers also had a meter.

Now I asked myself what I wanted to do with the money. Invest it? Save it? No. I had a much better use for it.

"Dana, you were amazing." Rebecca hugged me from behind. I usually didn't hear those words often.

"Do you have the permanent job now?" I asked curiously.

"Yay, thank you! I really owe you for that."

"Yeah, right, you owe me at least three favors for that," I said with a serious face and a suppressed grin.

"Okay. If you ever get married, I will host everything from the engagement party to the wedding night. Everything!"

"Like I'm ever going to get married! I don't even have a boyfriend or anyone."

"You're twenty-four-years old, you definitely have plenty of time to find Mr. Right, don't worry."

I yawned loudly. "Man, I'm really looking forward to my bed!"

My bed was in a not-worth-mentioning, teeny tiny studio apartment that was only furnished with the bare essentials. As little time as I spent at home, decorations and frills had somehow never been necessary. I was either at the Royal Renaissance Hotel for work, or with Beccs and her family.

"Me too! Hopefully Tom will be here soon." Rebecca looked at her watch. "Oh dear, so late already? It's almost not worth sleeping anymore."

"Almost. But I'm cheap, and I'll take all the sleep I can get."

As a large white van turned the corner, Rebecca relaxed. It was Tom, driving toward the pub in her work van. Rebecca transported decorations in that van for the parties she hosted. Colorful fairy lights, candles, cloth tablecloths, balloons, rose petals and... and... and... It was a mystery to me how she was able to pack all that stuff into the back of it.

"Do you need a ride?"

"No, that's all right. I'll take a cab." My apartment was in the opposite direction. Tom drove closer and closer, and we hugged goodbye. As we did so, I placed the trophy, my purse, and the bottle just behind me on the window sill of the pub.

"This was a fantastic evening. Thank you," Rebecca said.

"Wait a minute, this is for Emma's birthday," I said, handing Rebecca the bundle of prize money. "For Disneyland."

"No, I can't accept that. You're crazy!"

"You don't have to accept it, either, it's a gift for Emma from her godmother."

"Thank you!"

Rebecca was close to tears, again, only this time they were tears of joy. Tom parked the car right next to the bar on the street, he remained sitting in the car, but waved to me.

"I'll see you tomorrow, okay?" asked Rebecca, opening the passenger side door.

"Of course I'll see you tomorrow. I'm already excited to see what new ideas Ms. Williams has for bankrupting the hotel."

Rebecca laughed out loud and got into the car.

"Yeah, we shouldn't miss that. Good night."

"Good night."

When a cab passed the pub, I quickly grabbed my purse and waved for it to stop.

4

Connor

Another cancellation.

Frustrated, I threw my phone on the bed and stared reproachfully at the silver dress across the room.

Now, I had called every reputable escort service I knew but none had a suitable girl for me in such short notice. Normally, I booked discreet evening escorts months in advance, because these events were always announced very early. Too bad that I had believed my presence in London would be enough of an excuse to use on my mom. Even more frustrating was my organized date still having a bad stomach upset.

Was an emergency at my newly acquired British brewery credible? Definitely, if it were to happen. But perhaps there were problems in my other businesses that required my presence. Unfortunately not, the grapes for the wine of my two Italian wineries were far from ready for harvesting and, at my schnapps distillery in Switzerland, the production processes had only been perfected this spring.

My phone rang. It was Gordon Griffith, the production manager at my brewery.

Speak of the devil. Admittedly, I would have preferred the callback of an agency, but I was no longer picky and took any excuse I could get.

"Yes, please?"

"Hi, I just wanted to let you know that the beer arrived at JFK Airport. We're still checking, but I'm in good spirits that all the bottles survived the transport well." Gordon sounded upbeat, his typical British accent impossible to miss, even though the noise volume in the background was enormous. Loud announcements, a babble of voices and other typical airport noises mingled.

"Very good," I grumbled.

"Where do you want us to deliver the beer?"

I had actually wanted to have the beer tested in a few pubs in England before it was released for sale, but Max had spread me wide to actually show up at this wedding, so I had improvised.

"I'll get the address to you. Thanks Gordon."

"No problem."

"Oh, could you still take care of the protocol and the allowance? I'm busy elsewhere and haven't had time to do that yet."

"Will do."

"Thank you. Great job."

I ended the call and sent the address of the Irish Oak to my production manager. This was the pub closest to the Royal Renaissance Hotel, so I could walk to it without any problems and breathe in the New York night air.

A short beep announced an e-mail.

Damn, the next cancellation.

Now there were only two requests left, and they hadn't turned me down yet. Hell, I didn't want to disappoint my mother, nor did I want to be set up with half the women's company. I needed a freaking Plan B, but even more desperately, I needed a short break from it all. Since arriving at the hotel, I hadn't allowed myself any rest yet, alternating between taking care of business or potential evening companions.

I poured myself a Lancester bourbon in a wide crystal glass. I usually never opened a bottle before a reasonable hour, but special times called for special measures.

I sat down in the upholstered armchair with genuine leather covering and swirled the amber liquid thoughtfully while inhaling the smoky, pungent aroma. The bourbon came from my father's distillery, and I always had a bottle with me on my travels – a little bit of home to take home. Funny thing was that I enjoyed the aroma, but I didn't drink alcohol.

For a second I leaned back and closed my eyes. My endless drive was now taking its revenge. Thinking was difficult for me, and a solution to the evening companionship problem became a distant prospect.

At such an exclusive event, I couldn't show up with a simple prostitute, that would do lasting damage to my family's reputation. Staying away from the event was also out of the question, because my mom, full of motherly pride, had told everyone that I appeared with my sweetheart, if I didn't come, it would break her big heart.

The ringing of my cell phone hit me so unexpectedly that a jolt went through my body, and I dumped half my bourbon on my pants.

Damn!

Cursing, I put the wet glass on the table, then took the phone call.

"Yes?"

"Senor Lancester?" asked a man with a Spanish dialect.

"Yes, on the phone."

"Very good. Justino Olivera here. Do you have time for a quick meeting? I know it's very spontaneous, but I'm only in town today and when I heard you were also here..." Mr. Olivera, speaking in broken but easily understood English, left the end of his sentence open.

Who was Justino Olivera again? I had to collect myself for a moment and sort out my thoughts until my memory kicked in.

He belongs to the Olivera Distillery.

"Of course, Mr. Olivera. I would be very happy if we could finally talk in person," I replied, pleased because I had been waiting for a call from the Oliveras for quite a long time.

I considered pushing our meeting ahead of the beer tasting, but one look at my handmade watch made me shudder.

"And tomorrow, you'll be back in Cuba already?"

"Sí, señor."

Damn.

For weeks, our co-workers had been writing or phoning each other. Our schedules and time zones always overlapped so inconveniently that it had never come to a meeting.

I had big plans with Olivera Distillery, but I couldn't postpone the sales launch of my beer if I cancelled the tasting. Either ... or?

"Mr. Olivera, how would you feel about a very relaxed business meeting, in a casual location?"

There was a brief, thoughtful silence, then the Cuban replied, "Sounds good to me."

"Very well, then I'll have the address sent to you."

"Gracias, hasta entonces – see you then."

When the call was over, I sent the Irish Oak's address to Mr. Olivera, then took care of my bourbon-soaked suit.

I traded in my tailored suit for a pair of dark, much more comfortable jeans and a matching shirt from Versace.

In a good mood, I left the hotel and headed for my business meeting. The prospect of finally doing business with the Oliveras made me forget my escort problem.

Deeply, I inhaled the fresh night air that blew towards me. Even after dark, the city and its inhabitants were still wide awake. Joggers ran in small groups through Central Park, bike messengers took advantage of the calmer traffic, and students in a celebratory mood streamed past me. Even in my many trips to Europe and Asia, I had not discovered a city that could reflect the New York zeitgeist.

I stopped in front of the pub and waited for my business appointment, who got out of a black limousine a short time later. Justino Olivera was also wearing casual clothes, which were more appropriate for a pub than a tailored suit. I considered it a good sign when my potential business partners placed more value on their abilities than on their outward appearance.

"Senor Lancester, it gives me great pleasure to finally meet you in person."

"The pleasure is all mine," I replied.

"This is a truly extraordinary place for a meeting," Olivera noted, looking around. Although Justino Olivera was barely over thirty, he possessed the facial expression of an old, experienced businessman. Beneath his businesslike poker face, he undoubtedly made tough decisions. I could see that at first glance.

"I'm having my new beer tested here right now, as a last resort before it goes to market," I explained my unconventional but well-working strategy.

"Ah, I see. An interesting method, a bit too fancy for our operation, I guess."

Olivera's family had been among the largest rum producers in South America since the 1960s, and there was no doubt that Olivera Distillery would also become one of the most profitable alcohol producers in the world within the next five to ten years.

I could have lectured for hours about why my unconventional method gave much better information about the beer than the standard testing methods, but I left it at one short sentence: "Where else can I get such honest, authentic feedback about beer than in a store where people like to drink beer?"

Olivera nodded thoughtfully. "Good, good."

After a quick handshake, we entered the interior of the well-attended pub. The exuberant mood pulsed through the room together with the cheerful music.

In a small alcove reserved for my business meeting, we both took a seat. From there I had a good view of the bar and the guests, quite a few of whom had a bottle of my beer in their hands or on the table. Judging by the contents of the bottle, most of the guests liked it. A good sign. On the stage was a large poster announcing a karaoke contest that was due to start any moment.

A good-humored waitress took our order.

"Two Lancester Light, please."

The broad grin disappeared from her face. "I'm sorry, sir. But it's only being tested by very specific people today, and we can't make exceptions."

These very specific people were women today, so I only had to observe half of all the guests, and tomorrow my Lancester Light team would document the reactions in men.

"I'm sure you'll make an exception for me. I'm Connor Lancester, the principal." I winked at her conspiratorially. Alternately, the waitress looked back and forth between me and her notepad, then found her smile again.

"Coming right up!"

I watched the waitress until she disappeared into the crowd, then turned my attention back to the businessman across from me.

"So, Mr. Olivera, what exactly are you interested in?"

"Olivera Distillery is looking for another backer to expand."

While Justino Olivera went into more detail, I watched the women at the bar. One woman in particular caught my eye. She was young, radiated a natural beauty and had beautiful blonde curls. With a shy smile, she chatted with a friend and the bartender, kept shaking her head, but finally gave in and accepted a bottle of Lancester Light.

I grinned. The bartender must have taken handing out the free beer pretty seriously. The blonde's girlfriend disappeared briefly into the crowd and then reappeared on stage – as the evening's host. There was toasting and dozens of beer bottles from my brewery were lifted into the air. Nevertheless, I only had eyes for the blonde beauty, who kept stroking the condensation along the neck of the bottle with her slender fingers. The young woman's thoughtful gaze was directed at the stage, where singing was now taking place.

Every fiber of my body wanted to go to her, brush a blonde curl from her face, and ask what her name was and why she didn't drink a drop of beer.

What's your name, beautiful?

Actually, I should continue listening to Olivera, but my brain just stopped when she put the beer bottle to her full lips. Olivera had completely faded out. There was only her, me and all the things I wanted to do with her.

Beauty, growled my beast within.

I tried to pay attention to every reaction of the unknown beauty, after the first sip she looked surprised at the label of the beer bottle, then she drank another sip and smiled so adorably that she infected me.

"How do you see it, Senor Lancester?" asked Olivera.

To be honest, I had absolutely no idea what the businessman wanted my opinion on.

"I am optimistic," I replied confidently. A standard answer that was often used, but rarely had a real message.

"We feel the same way."

Lucky.

Olivera took the beer bottle in his hand in front of him, said, "Salud!" and toasted with me. While I put my bottle down again, the Spaniard took a big swig.

"I don't know anything about beer, but it tastes good," Olivera said.

"Thank you." I let my gaze wander over the guests, who were talking animatedly, singing along, or even dancing. That's exactly what I had tried to capture with my beer, and as it seemed, my beer fit perfectly into the scene.

Well, I may have caught the mood, but Beauty's glow caught me. She swayed along to the beat of the music but did her best not to stand out in the crowd. Why? Although Beauty tried to hide her beauty and suppress her glow, I had peeked beneath the surface. My beast would break through her surface without any problems.

Heck, my mind was wandering in a direction I didn't like because I liked it too much.

Not now. Not today.

"Don't you even want to taste the beer?" asked Olivera. There was suspicion in his voice.

"No, I don't drink alcohol," I answered dryly. It was hard for me to take my eyes off Beauty.

Justino Olivera laughed out loud, thinking it was a joke, so I smiled along briefly before explaining myself. "I know it's a bit unusual for a man who grew up in an alcohol dynasty from childhood and makes his living from it not to drink alcohol."

"Sí, señor. But then how do you decide which drop makes it to market?"

"With a classic tasting. Just because I don't particularly like the taste of alcohol doesn't mean I don't enjoy the smell. I have a very reliable sense of smell."

"I understand." His voice was filled with suspicion and doubt, which Olivera could not mask even with a smile, but I was used to that as well.

"How about a little demonstration?"

"Fine by me."

"Good, now go to the bar and order something, whether it's beer or bourbon. The main thing is that the drink is in a glass that I can swirl."

I had been involved with bourbon since childhood, and over the years my interest in the other alcohol processes had grown as well. I had been right in every single demonstration, and without exception, I was confident now, too.

Olivera nodded, stood up and fought his way through the crowd to the bar. He was standing right next to Beauty. The realization that she would be a perfect companion for me hit me like a blow. Not only did she attract me on the outside like moonlight attracts a moth, but her character seemed respectable as well, her smile told me. Perhaps she was a bit too shy for my taste, but that was not an obstacle for me, rather a challenge.

Sighing, I rubbed my temples and discarded my plan at the same moment. Picking up women in bars was not my thing, somehow too weird and not very stylish.

Still, I continued to watch the beauty, and each time her full lips settled over the rim of the beer bottle, my beast inside growled loudly.

Olivera came back. His upper body blocked my further view of Beauty. In front of me was a large tumbler of dark liquid. "Salud - cheers, Señor Lancester."

When Justino Olivera faced me again, Beauty had disappeared.

Damn! I didn't believe in soul mates, but what if I had just lost my soul mate? I skimmed the celebrating guests, looking for her enchanting face, her golden curls, and her radiant smile, but to no avail. She had disappeared.

Jesus, what was wrong with me? Nostalgic feelings over a stranger? That didn't sound like me at all, Connor Lancester, heir to the Lancester dynasty and eternal bachelor.

My subconscious wanted to reassure me that she was too shy for me anyway. Beauty would not withstand my beast for a single second.

Sighing, I lifted the glass up and looked at the alcohol, which looked like liquid amber, next I smelled it. Spicy and smoky. A bit tart with a sweet final note. With the first breath I filtered out almost all the nuances until I smiled in victory.

Did Olivera really think I wouldn't recognize my own alcohol? Without a doubt, the glass contained a mixture of Lancester Light and a stronger alcohol. Rum or bourbon, perhaps a dark liqueur. I smelled a second time, this time paying attention to the smaller notes. Caramel? And something else. Cinnamon.

Thoughtfully, I let my gaze wander around the room, then I spotted her again. Beauty. There, where I would have expected her last, namely on the stage.

She sang a song that even seasoned men hummed along to softly, and the crowd went wild. Her voice was soft and gentle at the first notes, just as I had imagined her being. But her insecurity still dominated and covered her radiant beauty.

"So, what did I put in front of you, Senor Lancester?"

"My own beer." I took one last whiff. It smelled sweet and fruity. Peach? Apple?

Now Beauty's voice became louder and more powerful, her whole posture changed and suddenly a fire burned in her crystal clear blue eyes that I usually only saw in one place, my playroom.

I could hardly concentrate on the scent of alcohol, just a moment ago the smell had been dominant and so easy to recognize, as if I only had to see colors, but now in my head there was only Beauty.

"A blended rum," I said. "I'm guessing about four to five years old, at that time the caramel note was very popular."

Olivera nodded but continued to be silent. There was a third liquid, but the only thing I could think of was how Beauty sounded when she moaned, screamed, sighed with pleasure.

It almost blew my mind that I didn't know what Olivera had put in front of me. Another beer? Another bourbon? Juice or water? Actually, I should be ashamed of my miserable performance, because I could do better. Much better, in fact!

"The last ingredient is tricky," I confessed.

"That's right," Olivera grinned.

"It's a sweet rum. Reminds me a bit of your original Sweet Havana," I said thoughtfully. The song ended and the crowd cheered. I set the glass down for a moment and joined in the applause before refocusing on my business partner and our bet. With half an ear, I also paid attention to the presenter, because I was dying to know what Beauty's real name was. But the pub was so loud that I couldn't understand anything.

"No, I have to disappoint you, senor. Close, but wrong. Still quite an achievement, two out of three ingredients were right, I couldn't even tell my own rums apart."

"Thank you," I growled discontentedly.

Beauty walked off the stage and disappeared into the crowd. Again. Immediately, my beast wanted to lie in wait, stalk and hunt, but I had obligations. If I wasn't so interested in this secret Olivera Distillery process, I would have opened the hunt for Beauty long ago.

I looked expectantly at my future business partner. "So far, everything sounds pretty good, and I'm willing to invest, on one condition."

Now I had Olivera's full attention. The Cuban leaned forward a bit to listen better.

"I want to brew a thousand liters of rum using your secret process."

Olivera smiled, then shook his head. "You know I can't do that. I can't just give away all our family secrets."

Beauty was still invisible, obscured by dozens of patrons standing around the bar. I wonder if she was still there at all.

"Don't. I'm only interested in the process itself. I have no interest in a rum empire."

Actually, I wanted only one thing at the moment: Beauty. I wanted to keep watching her, then seduce her, and then ship her off to my hotel room where we would both spend lots and lots of time.

"You don't seem that way either, Senor Lancester, but rule is rule."

"I understand," I thoughtfully ran my hand over the rim of the tumbler. "That's my only condition, but it's essential to our deal."

The presenter was now announcing the winners of the evening, and I knew time was running out. After the awards ceremony, most of the guests would surely leave the pub. Probably also the unknown beauty, whom I stalked obsessively.

"Regrettable. I'll talk to my father and the board again, but I don't think they'll change their minds that quickly, it would take a really good offer."

"Of course, just let my people have an answer. And now that the business is done, we should enjoy the evening," I ended the business talk.

"No offense, but I should go. My schedule for tomorrow is very full, and my flight back to Cuba leaves very early."

"All right, nice to meet you, Mr. Olivera."

"También – likewise, Señor Lancester."

We shook hands, then Justino Olivera left the Irish Oak.

Now that I could fully focus on Beauty, I found the deal falling through less unfortunate than I should have.

Beauty, like all the other guests, looked expectantly at the stage. The presenter made it exciting, but when she announced the winner of the evening, Beauty turned pale. Cute.

When the winner did not enter the stage, the presenter encouraged the audience to shout her name. Dana.

Uncertainly, Beauty bit her lips, then stood up and walked on stage. Beauty – Dana – was beaming with surprise and joy but being so celebrated by the crowd seemed uncomfortable for her. I would have loved to take her protectively in my arms and drag her off to my most private rooms, thus protecting her from her fears.

After Dana was cheered, there was a large, confusing crowd, with almost half of the patrons leaving in one fell swoop.

Dana talked to the presenter while I held the tumbler in both hands and ran my thumb along the rim of the glass, as I always did when I was thinking. The crowd at the exit grew larger and larger, reminding me of an elephant squeezing through the eye of a needle. Then, from one second to the next, I had lost sight of the beauty that had been taking my mind – and costing me a bet – all evening.

I rose so that I had a better view of the room, but it was useless. Beauty had disappeared and, with her, my chance to throw Beauty to my beast.

Sighing, I grabbed my glass and went outside to get some air. Perhaps the slim hope of seeing Dana again also drove me out. Outside, in the cool night air, my thoughts quieted. The sidewalk was deserted, with only a single couple walking arm in arm along the opposite side of the street, giggling.

What a strange effect Dana had on me throughout the evening. No single woman had ever triggered so much fascination in me, much less so much confusion!

I was looking for a clue as to where she had disappeared to, even a tiny sign would have been enough. Something that reinforced my suspicion that I needed to see Dana again, but nothing happened. No damn sign that the feeling of defeat could outweigh.

Thoughtfully, I looked into the alcohol mixture that was swirling back and forth in the tumbler, then held the glass under my nose one more time. Now I had deciphered the weight of the nuances, almost as if the solution were in the liquid. The smells were now as easy for me to recognize as ABC.

Two-thirds Lancester Light, one-third Spicey Dream of Havana and a shot of Blizzard Boiled Bourbon.

I smiled, because my skills hadn't betrayed me after all, I had just lost my focus for a short time. As my smartphone vibrated, I set the tumbler down on the windowsill, right next to the trophy for the first prize of the competition, which I took in my hands with a laugh.

A sign.

To read my messages, I put the cup back on the window sill. One message was from my sister Max, who wanted to make sure once again if our appointment tomorrow still stood – and it did. There were also refusals to both requests from the escort agency, another sign in my eyes.

Smiling with satisfaction, I put my phone back in my pocket and took the trophy.

My beast wanted to hunt Beauty, no doubt, but the rest of me was looking for Cinderella, who had lost her trophy. I had to find her again!

5

Dana

Yawning, I moved onto a new down pillow.

"Tired?" asked Rebecca. She took the pillow from me and arranged it on the king-size bed.

"Tired as a dog!" I replied, then yawned again.

Today, Beccs and I were assigned to the luxury suites on the thirty-eighth floor.

"It's your own fault for taking a city tour in the middle of the night," Rebecca said with a grin, giving me a reproachful look.

"You're mean, Beccs, I just wanted my trophy back."

"Didn't work out so well, did it?" Rebecca laughed gleefully. "That trophy was worth a whole eight dollars, so if you want, I'll buy you a new plastic one after work."

I snorted indignantly. "It's not about the material value, it's about the symbolic value! I've never won anything, never! Even at the lottery booths at the carnival, there were only losers."

"Dana Swanson, you are the most pitiful creature in the whole world."

"Well, I guess I'll have to carry the burden," I replied, sighing theatrically.

"How did the meeting actually go?" asked Rebecca.

"Don't ask. If this keeps up, someone else can be the spokesperson."

"Why is that?"

"Because I don't want to keep spreading bad news, obviously logical arguments aren't enough to overturn Shannon Williams' plans." Frustrated, I bit my lips. I had really tried, in my polite and thoughtful way, but to that the assistant executive director was immune. Someone had to speak plainly to her, that much was clear. What wasn't quite so clear to me was whether I was the woman who could do it. Admittedly, I was far too afraid of saying the wrong thing, which is why I often said nothing at all. The fact that my future was in the hands of my limbo boss didn't make it any better, because she decided the course of my career. Whether I wanted to or not, my seven-year plan stood or fell with Shannon Williams.

Rebecca groaned softly. "Do I even want to know what new thing she came up with?"

"She wants to equip all rooms from the thirtieth floor up with pagers."

"Wait, what?"

"Yes, exactly. Each maid gets a room-specific pager and then gets to play gofer for things that guests can easily order through the front desk right now."

"Unbelievable. Then we get called in for all kinds of things we're not even responsible for."

"Exactly."

Beccs angrily stuffed the pillows into the covers and couldn't stop shaking her head. Because she was really hitting the down pillows, I had all the trouble I needed to shake the pillows fluffy again. After all the misappropriated punching bags were back in place, I went to the cleaning cart and got the feather duster. Slowly, Rebecca's anger had subsided enough for me to tell her how the conversation continued.

"I said the same thing, including that we wouldn't be able to do our actual job if we had to run all the time, but she wouldn't relent."

"I hate that we have to make up for the mistakes that others make."

Me too, Beccs, me too.

Rebecca gathered up all the sheets and covers and carried them outside while I carefully cleaned the dust off the door frames.

The vacuum cleaner sounded from the large living area, swinging back and forth energetically, a clear sign that Beccs was still in a rage. The poor vacuum cleaner had never done anything to her, yet it kept falling victim to her foul mood.

As I passed over the edges of the mirror on the dresser, my eyes caught on a large jewelry box; inside were dozens of bracelets, rings, and earrings. God, there was more money in that box, which was the size of a shoebox, than I would make in my entire life. A pair of earrings caught my attention: two small diamonds set in filigreed gold. I could have sworn that my grandma had worn exactly the same ones.

Just take a very, very quick look.

Carefully I took out the earrings and looked at them more closely, yes, my Granny had also worn such earrings. In the past, my grandparents had run a small, beautiful boarding house in New Orleans, where my parents and I had visited them every vacation. Wonderful, but long gone memories haunted my mind.

Unfortunately, the boarding house no longer existed; like thousands of other houses, it had been destroyed in a devastating storm years ago. My grandparents had not been able to cope with the loss until the end, which is why my parents had moved to New Orleans to support them, while I had stayed behind in New York to start my studies.

Lost in thought, I turned the small earrings in my fingertips, then my hands moved as if by themselves, and suddenly the earrings were on my earlobes.

Heavens, I looked just like the Granny in her younger years that I knew from old photos. The same blue eyes, the same narrow chin, only my curly blond hair was not open, but braided.

Okay, enough dreaming!

Carefully I took off the left earring and put it back into the box.

"Daaanaaa!"

I winced in shock before pulling the radio out of my pocket.

"Yes?"

"The penthouse suite on the forty-ninth floor is available! It needs to be cleaned immediately!"

Frowning, I looked in Beccs' direction, who continued to take out her frustration on the vacuum cleaner. Neither she nor I were assigned to the presidential suite, only the thirty-eighth floor, which we had our hands full with. Still, I couldn't disagree with my boss again, once a day was the maximum breaking point of our business relationship. I had no other choice, because what she said was law.

"Of course, Ms. Williams."

"Immediately!"

Yep, I got that. I rolled my eyes.

"I'll be on my way directly," I repeated, rolling my eyes again. I went straight to the living room and stood in front of Beccs, who understood the signal and turned off the vacuum cleaner.

"Beccs? Are you going to be okay here? I'm supposed to go to the top."

"Sure. Shoo, shoo – before anyone else gets the idea of hiring slave drivers, or better yet, electric collars with radio control."

I giggled. "Don't say that too loud. I'll probably see you in the next room or the one after that, I'm not sure what's coming."

"See you next week!" joked Rebecca further.

Without detours, so as not to lose precious time, I went to the top floor, which was not visited quite as often as the other suites. Logically, who would spend twenty thousand dollars for a single night in a hotel?

Twenty thousand dollars!

Okay, granted – the suite was two stories, encompassing more than eight hundred square feet with ten rooms, private pool, its own movie theater, two dedicated elevators to the reception and underground parking, and a private wine cellar, but did a single person really need such luxury?

I had to wait briefly both in the elevator and at the room door. My key card alone was not enough to open the door. Security for absolute privacy, the entrance areas and private elevators were monitored with cameras. The release was done by a separate security service, which of course was also committed to secrecy. Expensive security measures for expensive clientele.

The suite was deserted. I got right to work, or at least I wanted to. Except for the four-poster bed in the Master Bedroom, the guest didn't seem to have taken advantage of anything else. Neither the movie theater nor the liquor cabinet. Nothing. Relief spread that the guest had not celebrated a wild house party overnight, but the sight of the four-poster bed still made me sigh.

Actually, the beds were the reason why maids worked in teams of two, but the silk-covered bedspreads were not on the floor, which was good because it meant that the guest did not want new comforter covers because a few small wrinkles and creases did not bother him.

I was just getting the bed ready when I noticed a silver fabric lying on the floor in the open dressing room. So that I did not forget to fix it, I immediately took care of it. I picked up the soft, supple fabric, this beautiful dress must have cost a week's wages! The hand embroidered sequins, around the top of the dress, glistened in the daylight. The back of the dress was low cut, while the fabric was tight around the bust and waist.

Admittedly, I envied the woman who was allowed to wear this noble dress. Did she feel like a princess in it? Certainly not, otherwise she wouldn't have thrown it so guilelessly on the floor and left it there.

Dreaming, I held the dress in front of my body and imagined that I was this enviable woman to whom the dress belonged. I imagined myself being invited by a handsome prince to the fairy-tale ball, where I would have been, without a doubt, the happiest woman of the evening.

I hung the dress on a hanger again and gave it the care it deserved. In the process, I noticed that the dressing room otherwise contained only tailored suits, stylish and expensive. Whoever these suits belonged to had broad shoulders and a handsome figure.

I literally forced myself out of the dressing room to make up the bed, because I just couldn't help but indulge in my musings as I pulled the comforter taut, then carefully smoothed each wrinkle with my hand as best I could.

Although I had a lot to do with smoothing the blanket, the dress just wouldn't let me go. It was almost as if this dress was calling me. Louder and louder, until it screamed.

No, absolutely not!

Over and over again, I heard Beccs' voice in my head talking about anger, termination, and other punishments. I knew my best friend and my inner voice were right, but I still weighed the options as I stuffed a handful of jelly beans into my mouth at a time. I couldn't think straight on an empty stomach.

I gathered the facts. The suite had been deserted for about ten minutes, so chances were good that it would be quite a while before the guest returned. Besides, the suite had been assigned to me, so there was no one from the house who could see what I was struggling with. Should I take the chance, as long as my boss's surveillance mania didn't escalate to the point where there was video surveillance even in the bedrooms? Secret cameras in book spines or houseplants? Listening microphones in the fire alarm? In any case, I wouldn't be surprised if such plans were already in the deputy manager's drawer. Privacy and dignity were foreign words for my boss, as was her trust in her own employees.

Looking at my watch, I was pleased to find that I had cleaned the suite in less than seven minutes, with twenty-five minutes allotted for the top floor, which was also adjusted upward depending on the situation. The floor would take another ten minutes, so I had at least eight minutes left where no one missed me.

Heavens, it tickled my fingers like never before. This shimmering dress was just too magical to ignore.

Okay, one more time, just once. For one second!

I went back to the walk-in closet, to the most beautiful dress I had ever held – or would hold – in my hands. I gave myself over to my daydreams. Of princes and fairy tales, while I looked at myself in the mirror.

Without thinking about it, I took off my one-piece and slipped into the silver, floor-length dress. Hard to believe, but it was made for me, because it fit perfectly! I looked like a real lady, elegant and stylish, the low-cut back added sex appeal without looking cheap. Whoever had made the dress knew exactly what he was doing.

Again and again, I turned in front of the large mirror and looked at the dress from different angles. Each one flattered my slim figure and my feminine curves.

I was startled when the front door opened, then closed again. Oh God.

Please, let it be just Rebecca!

6

Connor

Ping.

With a typical signal tone, the elevator announced that I had reached the first floor. I walked unerringly to the reception desk, and a freelance employee whose face I did not yet know jumped out at me. She was about my mother's age and had her graying brown hair tied back in a tight bun. All in all, the woman looked like the strict governess of a girls' boarding school.

"Good morning, Mr. Lancester."

The word quickly got out about who I was, and by now all the employees certainly knew about me.

"Good morning, was there a courier here for me?"

"Yes sir, just a moment please," she excused herself and left the front desk.

Very good! I had actually forgotten the souvenirs from London for my sister on the jet because I was engrossed in my business talks. I leaned against the reception desk, but when I put my hand in my pants pocket, I reached into the void.

Damn. I had forgotten my smartphone in the room, but when I felt the Gameboy in my jacket pocket, I had to grin briefly. I had never forgotten my Gameboy anywhere, but I left my smartphone somewhere all the time.

Too bad I was waiting for a call from one of the agents I had put on Beauty. There had not yet been any newspaper articles that told me more about the identity of the fascinating beauty.

I knew exactly three things about her. Her name – Dana – that she drove me out of my mind, and third, my beast in a suit would not rest until I found Beauty.

The receptionist came back and held out a small purple bag to me.

"Here you go, Mr. Lancester."

"Great," I thanked him and looked into the bag, which contained a box of handmade chocolates, a bottle of my home-brewed beer, and a snow globe, with Big Ben inside.

Sighing, I returned to the top floor and faltered briefly when I saw the cleaning cart at the entrance to my suite.

The maids at the Royal Renaissance Hotel were really snappy. I heard soft noises from the bedroom, apparently the maid was still here.

"Don't mind me, I just forgot something," I called out loudly as I walked through the suite.

"All right," the maid replied softly. Somehow, I had the feeling that I had heard her voice before, but since I had already met dozens of maids and other staff in the hotel, I didn't think about it any further.

In the master bedroom, I retrieved my smartphone from the top drawer of the nightstand. Loud sighs came from the walk-in closet.

"Is everything all right?" I asked.

"Yes! Yes, everything is fine."

This voice is so familiar to me ...

No matter, as much panic as resonated in the girl's voice, all was certainly not well. Concerned, I opened the door. The sight that presented itself to me almost took my breath away.

Am I dreaming?

In front of me was Beauty, desperately trying to get out of the silver dress for the wedding. Unsuccessfully. She looked at me with big blue eyes while I couldn't help but eye her. I don't know why she wore the dress, but it fit like a glove and perfectly accentuated her feminine curves.

I wonder if Beauty knew she was in the lion's den right now.

"What are you doing?" I asked.

"I'm cleaning the room," Dana replied uncertainly as her cheeks continued to color.

"This outfit is a bit over the top for cleaning even for the Royal Renaissance Hotel, isn't it?"

"Oh God, please, I just couldn't resist. I'm so sorry!"

I took a step towards the beauty that had been on my mind since yesterday.

"That dress looks pretty good on you."

She answered nothing, but only bit her lips. What thoughts might be behind this beautiful facade? What else was she hiding beneath her beautiful surface? A profound interior?

Her blue eyes shone and reminded me of the sparkle of the sea at sunrise. She looked so innocent, so shy, so vulnerable. Like a fawn.

Inevitably, this girl triggered in me a protective instinct, and at the same time the absolute opposite – my hunting instinct. I took another step towards her.

"Aren't you going to thank me for my compliment?"

I didn't take my eyes off her, because I wanted to see every little emotion in her face.

"Thank you, sir." Her voice was barely audible. There had to be a tremendous amount going on in her head right now. I couldn't deny that I was enjoying this quite a bit. I loved it when I provided racing thoughts. I loved it even more when I drove women out of their minds.

When Dana looked at me with her big, innocent eyes, I realized that I was a whole head taller than her. Her chest rose and fell every second.

I sucked in her scent. She smelled like a sweet spring day. God, I loved how innocent she looked, she even smelled like sweet innocence. Dana didn't move, I had her captivated with my gaze.

"So, Dana, what do we do now?"

"Please, sir..." Dana's voice broke.

I was almost weak at her breathy, reverent voice. Even without being naked on her knees in front of me, Dana had such a submissive attitude that I would have loved to put her over my knee right away. Just like that, simply because I could.

But was she the right one for this? Dana seemed so delicate, so fragile, but on stage she had shown that she also had strength. And there was also a little bit of craziness in her, otherwise she would never have dared to put on that dress.

But should it really come to the point that she would become my sub, I had to sound out her limits exactly. In any case, Dana looked like she didn't know her own limits.

I shook all thoughts away from me. How did I even get the idea that this girl liked something of what I wanted to do with her? Just because I had found her now, didn't mean that she would get involved with me.

Men like me just knew what girls like Dana needed. Besides, I knew she would be the perfect companion for tonight, because her natural charisma was stronger than the insecurity she was struggling with.

I would have loved to look at her like that for hours, but I had no more time, I was already late for my meeting now.

"What am I going to do with you, huh?" I asked another time.

"Please, don't tell my boss. I'll do anything for it, really anything!"

Oh Dana, you're almost making it too easy for me.

Dana's curiosity had solved my two biggest problems in one fell swoop: finding her and the wedding escort problem.

"Do you like the dress?"

The question seemed to surprise her. Hesitantly, she answered, "Yes. It's the most beautiful dress I've ever seen."

"What do you think of that, Dana?" I pronounced her name deliberately slowly, drawing it out with relish. "I consider this situation our spicy little secret, and you consider the dress a gift from me." Dana sighed in relief, but when she realized I had more to say, she held her breath. "But in exchange, you have to accompany me to a little event tonight."

She bit her lower lip thoughtfully.

God, not much longer and I lost my temper if she kept biting her lower lip so seductively.

"Sir, I can't accept that."

"Why not?"

"It's forbidden, sir."

God, if Dana addressed me as Sir one more time, I would fuck her right now. My questioning look was enough to elicit an explanation from Dana.

"It is forbidden for all employees to talk to guests in the hotel..."

"To fuck?"

Dana nodded sheepishly. "I would have called it something else, but yes."

Damn, there had to be a true force of nature hiding beneath that shy surface, I was sure of it. Dana was a diamond in the rough that had to be polished first to bring out the inner beauty, but under my experienced guidance I would refine her, ennoble her and turn her into something perfect.

Okay, I definitely needed a sub again, in the last weeks and months my work had taken me so much that I came to almost nothing else. The evening with her would decide, not only whether Dana wanted to go such a way with me at all, but also whether she could go such a way.

"In that case, there is no problem. The party is outside, and we are invited guests. Besides, you're hardly planning to seduce me, are you?"

Dana's cheeks turned red, she shook her head and I had to grin.

"Are you really not going to tell anyone what just happened here?"

Shaking my head, I brushed a loose strand of hair back behind Dana's ear. The sparks that flew between us could not be overlooked.

"No, it remains our secret. It was a mistake, and mistakes happen."

She sighed with relief. "Thank you, I will never forget this!"

"So? Do we have a deal, and you'll join me tonight?"

"But I don't have any shoes to match." She looked down at her black, unadorned pumps, a model of the ugliest kind worn by all the maids in the hotel.

"I'll take care of that, don't worry," I reassured her.

"Hmm."

Dana couldn't admit it yet, but she had long since decided to spice up this boring, formal celebration a bit. I estimated that Dana broke in one, two minutes at the most.

Very well. So, I had found a woman for tonight after all, who accompanied me to the wedding – and already at first sight I knew, this woman had potential for more. More than I was willing to admit.

"And I have to work until eighteen," Dana quickly added.

"That long? It's now," I looked at my gold watch, "nine o'clock."

"Yes, it's always a state of emergency here during Fashion Week." She smiled and blew the unruly curly strand out of her face that I had recently tried to tame. Now Dana already seemed much less shy than before.

"That sounds awful." I was a workhorse too, but most of the work was in my head; Dana's body, on the other hand, had to hurt like crazy after Fashion Week ended, and in a way that no one liked.

"That's my job," she replied politely.

Good answer.

"So, do we have a deal?"

"I don't. I don't think I'd be good company."

"I'll decide that." My gaze became more serious, and along with my somber look, my eyes turned darker. I gave her a small taste of what she could expect.

"Okay. What time should I be here?"

Good girl.

"Right after your shift ends. The sooner, the better."

"All right. And in return, don't tell anyone what happened here." It was almost a commanding tone she used to make sure what the deal was. I grinned, not showing any teeth, because she placed such a high value on the contract details.

"Of course, I'm a man of honor."

Dana held out her hand to me. Her delicate hand seemed tiny in mine.

"Deal?" she asked with an expectant look.

"Deal," I replied.

Then there was silence, but not an uncomfortable silence, I thought. It was more like a thoughtful silence. Shyly, Dana scratched the back of her neck and angled her gaze downward. A high-carat diamond earring gleamed on her right ear.

"Fancy earring, where's the second one?"

"What?" Dana's hands darted gropingly to her ears, and all color drained from her face.

"Oh dear, the earring! Excuse me, I have to go," Dana said in a fluster. She started to move, trying to squeeze through the door, but I blocked her path, so she slammed into me with all her might. Her delicate body, meeting my massive muscles, faltered, but I was on the spot and caught her feathery body. Our eyes met, Dana's eyes deep as the ocean. For a brief moment, time stopped until Dana cleared her throat.

"Thank you."

I helped her up, she sorted her blonde strands and then squeezed between me and the door frame.

"Didn't you forget something?"

Dana thought for a moment, then looked down at herself and grabbed her temples. "Oh, God. I'm all messed up."

Yes, she obviously was, surely the lost earring meant a lot to her. Dana squeezed her slender body past me a second time.

"I need to change."

Of course, I understood the hint, but I ignored it. Her body was beautiful and undoubtedly flawless. There was nothing Dana needed to hide and nothing she should be ashamed of.

If she was my girl someday, I would drive this naughtiness out of her first. The beast would already see to it that Beauty recognized her beauty herself.

"Go ahead." I stretched my arm invitingly toward her uniform.

Dana bit her lips. "Alone, please."

"Okay. But only because you asked so nicely."

I was serious, with a nice request you could achieve a lot with me. When I left the room, I remembered that I still had Dana's cup.

"One more thing, my dear." I went back into the bedroom and got it out of the drawer, after all, Cinderella needed her lost glass slipper back, just as my ice princess needed her trophy back.

Dana watched me intently. When I held her trophy in my hands, her eyes grew huge.

"That's my trophy!"

"True, and you've earned that one, too."

Dana's cheeks turned red, and she looked down at the floor in embarrassment. "Oh dear. You heard me yesterday, didn't you?"

"Yes."

I was deliciously amused that Dana was more embarrassed to be heard than to be caught wearing someone else's dress.

"I'm afraid I can't take the trophy now," Dana sighed.

"Then we'll leave it here and you can take it later," I offered her.

"Thank you, sir."

In order not to lose my senses, I looked at the clock. A quarter past nine. Now I had to leave urgently to meet my sister.

"See you tonight," I said goodbye As I walked, I looked at Dana one last time, then left the suite.

Incredibly, I had really killed two birds with one stone. First, I had found Beauty faster than expected, and second, now I had an evening companion and would be able to continue to save face in front of my family.

And maybe I have a new sub.

7

Dana

Do not panic! Breathe deeply! Keep calm!

Easier said than done, yet I forced myself to stay calm. Everything felt so surreal, so unrealistic. Today was a chain of terrible coincidences and stupidities. It was as if I were the protagonist of a bad comedy of life, with fate as the director.

How could I have forgotten to take off the second earring?

Shannon Williams had radioed me at the moment I had just messed with the earrings, and everything just melted in my brain at that shrill voice. Self-preservation instinct.

Even worse, the forgotten earring was just a drop in the bucket considering what had just happened to me.

I had put on a guest's dress – a no-no. Even worse, I had been caught doing it, and suddenly I was the date of a billionaire guy who was also outrageously good-looking.

God, my legs softened again, thinking of those dark brown eyes that had sparkled at me. Dim and eager. How could a single glance of his have so much power over me?

He had the energy of a wolf, dangerous and unpredictable, at the same time he seemed to have been focused and controlled. Incredible how calm he had remained. Deep inside I had to admit that I had liked it. Yet he hadn't even introduced himself. My goodness, I was adoring a man I didn't know at all!

I wonder what was going on behind that flawless, striking face. I would have loved to read his thoughts at that moment. Perhaps his thoughts would have given me peace.

Damn you, insecurity!

My heart fluttered when I thought of how he had murmured my name, so animalistic and demanding. A sharp contrast to his cheeky grin when he'd rubbed my trophy in my face. I still couldn't believe he'd heard me in the pub. Heavens!

Today is the worst day of my life!

With deep breaths, I tried to calm myself. In the dressing room, I had only had eyes for the billionaire, for his focused gaze and broad shoulders. His dark eyes had catapulted me completely out of the here and now.

Heavens, that look! This self-confidence!

Only men who knew what they wanted possessed that kind of self-confidence, and I was smart enough to know that was the most dangerous kind of man there was. These men took what they wanted – because they could. And now I was dating just such a man. I really had to watch out, because no matter how careful you were, no matter how many chains, deadbolts and security locks you protected yourself with, they opened one lock after another with determination, charm and a smile. It was never allowed to get that far on my date tonight.

If only I had left that damn dress alone, none of this would have happened. Okay, almost none of it. The thing with the earring still existed, strictly speaking that was even my bigger problem. At worst, I joined the long line of maids who had been fired by Ms. Williams for various – often unfair – reasons. But if my resignation said theft, that was it, because that meant I'd never find another job. Then my dream of owning a small hotel was finally dashed, and even the best seven-year plan in the world didn't help.

As quickly as I could, I changed my clothes. There was a small chance that the guest was not yet back in the room, and I could just put the earring back.

As if nothing had happened. Easy peasy.

Or not. Beccs was already on the next floor and the guest was back in the room, which elicited a heavy sigh from me.

This can't all be true.

I felt like the victim in a great cosmic drama. But today I also magnetically attracted all the problems. Maybe fate was lying on the couch with his buddies with popcorn, waiting anxiously to see which flaw I would put my foot in next.

What now? I couldn't just breeze into the room and shout, "Ta da, here's the borrowed earring!" No, I couldn't do that; I needed an excuse to get back into the room. Thoughtfully, I walked up and down the long hallway, stopping short in front of the elevators. A small side table separated two elevators, on it was a vase of flowers with roses. Bingo.

I took the vase from the table and went back to the apartment. I swore to myself a hundred times that I would never, never again touch even one piece of jewelry that was in the rooms. Never again, and especially not clothes! Today had really done me in. Future dates with guests were just as taboo for me from now on, no matter how sexy or charming they might be.

With a racing heart, I knocked on the room door. "Room service."

"Come in." The stern voice belonged to an elderly lady. I opened the door with my key card, meanwhile balancing the vase of flowers in my left hand.

"I bring you a vase of flowers, courtesy of the house."

"That's nice." Her voice was cold and emotionless; there was even less emotion in her expression. The woman could be the clichéd, strict governess of a gloomy children's home. At least she looked the same. Her hair was tied back tightly, her eyebrows were two thin, angular strokes, and her lips pressed tightly together. The additional facial rigidity from Botox reinforced this prejudice.

"I'm sure the flowers will look wonderful on the dresser in the bedroom," I said, and immediately set off.

"No, just put them here on the table. Thank you."

Great. And now? Immediately, Shannon Williams' very first and most important rule flashed up: In this house, the guest is always right, no matter how wrong he may be.

"I'd love to." I clenched my teeth, my brain was in chaos. I desperately searched for a way to sneak my way into the bedroom after all, but there was no way. My thoughts raced, overflowed, and left nothing but emptiness. No, not quite. Little kittens from a video Beccs had played this morning traipsed around in my head, unfortunately those cute kittens wouldn't help me now. Concentration!

Then finally the saving idea came to me, it was neither creative nor particularly good, but better than nothing.

"Do you mind if I take a quick look at the en suite bathroom?"

"Why is that?" It looked like she was trying to raise an eyebrow.

"There was probably a problem with the plumbing on the floor above this one, they just want me to make sure the surrounding rooms aren't affected."

I held my breath tensely, because I was the worst liar in the world. The tip of my nose quivered, and my cheeks reddened as soon as I even thought of a fib. What could I say? I just didn't like lying, which I didn't find reprehensible.

"If that's the case, go ahead."

Yes, you can rely on the good old water pipe burst.

"Thank you." I relaxed and literally ran into the bedroom to put the earring from my little side pocket back to its twin. Then the next shock, arriving at the jewelry box, there was no trace of it.

That. Can. Not. Be. True.

Now where the hell was the other earring? Was there a hidden camera? Or some shock therapy from Beccs? I sighed loudly. Hadn't I put it back in the box? I couldn't remember it one hundred percent.

"Is everything all right?" the guest called from the living room.

"Yes, everything is fine." Don't!

In tears, I took the earring back. It was definitely more noticeable when a single earring was lying there than when both were missing, in those tons of jewelry. It certainly wouldn't stand out as long as I found both earrings again. Hopefully!

And if it did ... no! I couldn't and didn't want to think about that yet, not everything was lost yet, the twin couldn't be far.

With eagle eyes, I skimmed the floor around the table, back to the living room; I just had to go back the same way I had come. Maybe the earring had caught on my dress and fallen down on the way to the suite on the forty-ninth floor.

"Is there anything else I can do for you?" I asked as I inconspicuously scanned the floor of the room.

"No, I don't think so."

"Fine, if you do, just call me, I'll be happy to help," I said with a sugary smile. "Have a great time at Fashion Week."

"Very thoughtful of you, thank you."

Actually, I had hoped to learn through a short conversation how much time I still had until departure, but the dialogue was so wooden that it passed as smoothly as a boat. The chances were good that the lady would stay until the end of Fashion Week. Otherwise, she would have told me, right? Now the only chance I had was to check the system inconspicuously, but first I went back the way I had come, step by step. Inch by inch, I combed the Persian carpets and the marble floors. My gaze darted from left to right and vice versa, as if I were watching a tennis match.

I made poor progress on some of the very light carpets, a diamond on a light carpet was like a needle in a haystack, almost invisible to the naked eye.

I was so focused on scanning the floor that I forgot everything around me, until I almost ran into the assistant director.

Yes, it's official: the universe hates me.

"Dana! You can't just wander the halls here lost in thought and expect guests to avoid you!"

"Yes, I know, sorry! It won't happen again."

"I hope so. What are you doing here anyway?" asked Shannon Williams with a critical look.

"I'm looking for a guest's earring that went missing." I tried to tell the truth; I might still be able to swindle a guest, but my supervisor, with whom I had worked for years, was not so easily dazzled.

"Well, um..." She searched for the right words. "Go ahead with that but watch out for guests! I have to go; one of the maids wants to leave early because of an illness. I can't believe it. Vacation during Fashion Week! Some people might get ideas. Maybe I should cut the Christmas bonus for that kind of action?" Shannon Williams rushed past me toward the elevators. If I couldn't talk to Beccs right away, I was going to burst. Maybe my best friend could bail me out somehow?

I just had to find the earring, literally my entire career hung on that earring.

Please, please, please!

8

Connor

As yesterday, the limousine parked right in front of the entrance to the Royal Renaissance Hotel. John, the chauffeur, politely opened the driver's side door first and let Maxine out, then I left the car.

Immediately, a bellboy came and, together with the chauffeur, cleaned out the contents of the trunk. I had used the meeting with my sister not only to talk to her about the past trip and business, but also to go shopping. Three pairs of beautiful high heels in four different sizes each, as well as over four thousand dollars' worth of blush, powder and eye shadow. Also, underwear, perfumes and scented lotions. Just what a woman needed as a guest at a wedding, according to Maxine.

Of course, I liked to surround myself with beautiful women, but I had had no idea how many different layers of makeup were on a natural-looking woman's face. My mind drifted back to Dana, who was clearly beautiful without a ton of makeup. Without a doubt, Dana possessed that kind of natural beauty that some women spend hours in front of the mirror to achieve.

As we entered the lobby, I let my sis go first, and two bellhops grabbed all the shopping bags to take them to my suite.

"Fancy, fancy," Maxine said, spinning once on her own axis. As she did so, her summery white dress blew sweepingly. "A little bulky, though."

"Well, what did you expect from the most expensive hotel in town?"

"I don't know." Max shrugged, her gaze analyzing the lobby in minute detail. Occupational disease, Max would say to that. No matter where she was, in her mind she was moving furniture around, putting up different vases, laying different floors, hanging different paintings, and different lamps. How did I know this? Because Max let everyone in on it, always without exception, but I loved my sis anyway.

"Maybe a little more color, more gold, and maybe other warm tones. All the white marble with the black leather furniture and roses all over the place, it looks more like the red queen's throne room."

I had to grin. Now that Maxine had brought it up out loud, I actually felt reminded of Alice in Wonderland.

"I could arrange to talk to the executive director if you'd like. He wanted to talk to me anyway," I suggested.

"Sure, right now I have my hands full, but I'm always open to projects like this."

"And where is your beloved now?" my curious sister abruptly changed the subject.

"Good question. I guess it's around here somewhere."

"Uh-huh."

Serene, knowing that my evening companion was really here somewhere, I put my hands in my pockets and gave my sister a serious look.

"So, you don't believe me that a beautiful woman will accompany me to the wedding today."

"That's right," Maxine grinned cheekily. "Because you're Connor Lancester, you can't last ten minutes in the same place, let alone with the same people, plus all your previous girlfriends never showed up a second time."

Yes, that's how you could describe me in a few words.

"So, what did I buy all this stuff for?"

"To have an alibi, and then, all of a sudden, she's sick, or she's a doctor and she has to go back to her charity in Africa. I wouldn't put it past you to play the my-girlfriend-is-Batman card that's needed in Gotham City."

I put on a second, winning smile. "You can believe me, I'm not going to show up alone tonight, but with a very enchanting girl."

"Are you paying her for this?" Maxine's look was serious, but her eyes sparkled mischievously.

"No, I'm not paying them to do it. Who do you think I am?" I asked innocently.

"Someone who will do anything to avoid mom's matchmaking tactics."

"You mean more like matchmaking disasters."

"Yeah, or something. Maybe you should just listen to Mom's intuition and see who she introduces you to?" She shrugged and rested her head on her shoulder at an angle.

"The same goes for you then," I replied even more triumphantly. Because today's conversation with my mother had shown me that her puppy status was crumbling.

Looking at the clock, I growled softly, because in twenty minutes I was expecting Dana in my suite.

"I have to go, I'm expecting my evening companion in my suite soon, would you like to join me upstairs for a drink?"

"Granted, you seem very credible, Connor, but I still don't believe you. Anyway, I can't. I still have to get dressed."

"Then I'll see you at the wedding, sis."

"Ditto, brother dear. By the way, mom and dad are dying to know who you're going to bring with you."

"All right, I'll see you there then."

"Oh, and thanks again for the snow globe. It's perfect."

Smiling, I hugged my sister and gave her a brotherly kiss on the forehead.

"Only the best for my sis."

Maxine loved snow globes and it had become a tradition for me to bring her a snow globe from every country and major city I visited. She had a pronounced fear of flying, which is why she rarely left the country.

"See you later," Maxine smiled and walked toward the exit. Halfway there, she stopped, turned around again, and asked, "What's your date's name, anyway?"

"Dana," I answered without thinking.

Maxine bit her lips. "Hmm, maybe you really do have a real date?"

I winked at my sister.

"You better make sure you bring an escort yourself. Otherwise, mom will take care of it."

"Oh, come on. You're kidding," Max chuckled. Still.

In my suite, I carried the shopping bags into the bedroom and arranged creams, makeup, and perfume in front of the large mirrored dresser. I had never been interested in how a woman put on makeup, but with Dana, I had the feeling that I absolutely had to watch her.

I dropped into the wide leather chair, pulled my Gameboy out of the side pocket, and started it up. Next to me was a glass of Cabernet

Sauvignon de Música; its fruity sweet scent was my first ever wine creation. Not many knew the meaning of the pun, because I had dedicated this wine to the theme song of Tetris, which accompanied me throughout my life – Music A.

Before the first block had even cleared the bottom row, there was a soft knock on the door. I literally jumped out of my chair to open the door for Dana before she could use her key card to do so. Just for giving me some peace from the single-woman world, she was sure to get my attention.

"Glad you're here. I appreciate you being on time Dana."

"Thank you." Dana smiled shyly at me, and I held the door open for her.

"Must have been a busy day, huh?"

She nodded. "Oh yes, and what a day."

"Did you find your second earring again?"

"No," Dana sighed heavily. "But I'll be fine." She smiled her defeat away bravely, then her eyes fell on the dress on my bed. Her pained expression gave way to a glow. Christ, I could hardly take my eyes off Dana already, even though she was wearing the most hideous one-piece in the world. What effect would it have on me once she wore a dress worthy of her?

"I never thought I'd wear a dress like this."

"You already have," I teased her, even though I knew what she meant. Dana grinned back, then her face became serious again.

"I'm not sure what to ... call you?"

"Simply Connor, you are my evening companion. You don't need a sir for that."

In the bedroom it is.

"Okay, Simply Connor, let me get ready." Her blue eyes shone brightly. She had already lost some of her shyness. I hoped the rest fell away from her as well.

"We still have some time. You can shower in peace if you want."

"Really?"

"Really. When was the last time you had a relaxing hot shower?"

Her eyes grew big and lit up. "That was way too long ago!"

"Go ahead, the bathroom is free." I pointed to the open en suite bathroom where she disappeared. Only a second or so later, the water started, and I sat back in the chair.

My fingers clawed at my Gameboy as I struggled to control myself. Every fiber of my body wanted to follow her into the bathroom and do unspeakable things to her that she might like better than she would admit, but I remained seated. Dana was different, definitely, her effect on me was almost frightening, but the same rules applied to her as to all the other women I allowed to come close to me.

With Dana, I had the uneasy feeling that she might be the first to really touch me in the process, but all in good time.

Although Dana's feet were still wet, she flew silently, like an elf, across the floor, while her voluminous blonde curls, despite the wetness, bounced along with each step.

The fatigue was washed out of her face, leaving behind her soft, fair skin and bright blue eyes, small freckles around her nose made her flawless skin seem more alive. When she saw me, she paused, like a deer in shock that was caught in my headlights gaze.

"I didn't expect you to still be here," Dana admitted quietly.

I know. "Don't let me bother you," I said as I admired her shapely body under the tightly wrapped towel.

I pointed to the dressing table in front of her.

"Oh, okay." Still puzzled, yet nodding, she sat down in front of the mirror and skimmed the thousand makeup items my sister had fired into the shopping basket like one possessed.

Of course, I didn't want to conjure anything up, but I was kind of grateful that Dana's gaze was roaming over things as forlornly as mine, plus I loved her natural complexion.

Again and again, our eyes connected in the mirror.

"Connor? What do you expect me to do as your escort? I've never done anything like this before, and I don't want to embarrass you."

"Actually, all you have to do is smile nicely and drink enough champagne, then you won't stand out at all. Besides, you're there with me, they'll leave you alone, I'm sure."

"Why do you want to be left alone? Aren't such events for drinking expensive champagne together with friends?"

I laughed. "Actually, such parties are just for making new contacts. You rarely make friends at these events, and I've already done business with most of the guests – or never would."

"That sounds like a high-quality company."

"It is, believe me, the quality company you have in mind can only be found in Hell's Kitchen."

"Hmm, I don't know, I find the sharpened knives behind the back almost worse than the visible gun at the ready." She took a deep breath. "Oh God, sorry, I didn't mean to ... judge."

"Yes, you did," I replied. It wasn't often that someone shared their honest opinion with me. "But I value honest opinions and interesting views. You have no idea how rarely anyone disagrees with me."

"Yes, I do, I have some idea about that, I know the other side of the coin."

Her eyes remained focused on her reflection, her movements seemed purposeful, but every now and then she took a brief moment to return my glances in the mirror.

"Say, Connor, what do you need me for anyway? If all you want me to do is smile, and you don't want to socialize?"

Yes, how could I explain the situation without offending her?

"I need you because if I don't, my mom will sic the entire, female elite on me."

Dana grinned broadly. "I don't think these women need the lure of your mother, as attractive as you are."

After Dana realized that she had just flirted with me, her grin gave way, and she distracted herself by drawing on an eyelid. So much innocence packed into this incredible body was a dangerous mix for me. My beast was pawing with his hooves, and the more time I spent with Dana, the more willing I was to let him off the chain.

"My mom really wants a house full of grandchildren, so she's just grasping at any straw she can get."

"And you're grasping at any straw to get away from the grandkids."

"Yes, you could call it that."

Attachments, staying in one place, and regularities just didn't find a place in my changeable lifestyle.

"A life on the run is only half a life," Dana said thoughtfully.

"Oh, with all I've been through, that's enough for five lifetimes."

"It's still not worth anything if you don't have someone to share it with."

I did not say anything, but I thought for a long time about the truthfulness of her words.

Dana, meanwhile, took an oval brush and combed through her damp curls, not exactly gentle. When Dana noticed my critical look, she said, "There's no chance of loosening the knots by tenderly coaxing them."

Dana gathered her wonderful hair, but I told her, "Stop. You should wear your hair down."

Dana nodded and spread her semi-dry hair evenly over her back and shoulders.

"Done." Dana stood up, and I was relieved to see that she had not used even half of the things that were on the table. Dana had not lost any of her natural beauty due to the makeup, on the contrary, she looked like a real lady, like a princess of the world.

She is my princess.

Uncertainly, she stood in front of the bed on which the dress lay.

"What are you waiting for?" I asked.

"Here's to being able to change."

"Go ahead, you can." My look was serious, and my emphasis was somewhere between a request and a command. I was giving her a little taste of what could follow if she decided to turn herself over to me.

Dana's cheeks flushed, she said nothing, but her look was clear.

Okay, I really had to drive this insecurity out of her if I wanted to deal with her longer. Slowly, in small steps. But that was too much for my beast. Dana's shyness was just found food. And right now, my beast was pretty hungry. I would have to shake her entire worldview, maybe even destroy it and rebuild it, but she really had to be ready for that, and she wasn't. Not yet.

Damn, I just had to muster all the self-control I had not to fuck Dana on the spot with these thoughts. Painfully, my erection pressed against my suit pants.

If I had had more time, I would have made her take off all her clothes for me.

Voluntarily ... and full of excitement.

But we didn't have any more time, in fact we were already too late, but I didn't want to deprive Dana of the rain shower with massage jets on the wall, which washed away all tiredness at high pressure. Not that anyone at the wedding would mind if we were late – least of all the bride and groom themselves, who had long since set off on their honeymoon.

I cleared my throat and stood up.

"You should get dressed. We still want to catch something of the celebration, don't we?"

"Yeah, right."

"But next time I'll watch you do it." My voice left no doubt that I meant it. Dana said nothing, but the gleam in her eyes as she got a taste of my dominance was delicious.

I turned away from her so she could put on the silver, floor-length dress.

"Done."

"Turn around!" I ordered. This morning I hadn't had a chance to look at her as a whole, which I wanted to make up for as quickly as possible now. It was as if the dress had been tailored for her, as if it would bring out her perfect curves in a stylish way. Paired with the silver heels, whose straps were adorned with gold buckles, she looked incredible. Definitely Dana would be the most beautiful woman of the evening, and every single damn guy at this event would be looking her up, no question about it.

In her left hand, she held a small black bag with gold embellishments, the same design as her heels.

Dana didn't even know how incredibly beautiful she was, otherwise, she certainly wouldn't be so reserved and insecure, but once I had convinced Dana of her beauty, there was no stopping her – for either of us.

"Good girl," I praised her.

If Dana allowed me, I would show her own beauty to her, her strength, and a whole lot more.

Smiling, Dana curtsied, her eyes falling on the towel on the floor, which she picked up and hung neatly.

Shaking her head, she came back. "Sorry, force of habit. Sometimes you just can't get out of your skin."

"I know that all too well." My voice was smoky and resembled a growl. I didn't quite know if it was me or my beast who had answered, which made my understanding of their problem clear.

"Come on, we should go!" I said. Because if we didn't now, my beast would attack Dana, that much was certain.

9

Dana

Overwhelming.

That was all I could say about this event. The size of the ballroom alone left me speechless, as it felt like Central Park would fit in the room!

"May I have this dance?" Connor asked me charmingly. He held out his arm to me, and I grasped it gratefully. Connor was a true gentleman, even though I couldn't help but notice his somber looks. I clutched the small black bag in my hand tighter, as if it were my life preserver. Inside was a handkerchief, a pack of forest honey gummy bears, and the twin of the lost earring. Why? I didn't really know myself, perhaps because I didn't want to leave the evidence of my crime in the hotel.

"If I may note, you are the most beautiful woman of the evening."

I smiled sheepishly. "Thank you."

Unbelievable! This morning I thought the biggest event of the evening would be a pack of Ben & Jerry's and a Carpool Karaoke marathon, and now I was with the most charming bachelor in the world and going to a wedding that cost more to host than a single-family home! Somehow, I felt like I had missed something in the fine print, but there was no fine print, no hidden contracts, and no clauses. Just his offer that I just couldn't refuse. The deal of a lifetime, which was ironic because turning him down would have cost me everything I cared about. Although, the longer I knew Connor, the more certain I was that he would have kept our secret no matter what.

Connor led me down the length of the room, past dozens of round tables covered in fabric and decorated with beautiful bouquets. At the edge was a huge buffet full of macarons, tarts, creams filled in jars, and other sweet pastries. Everything looked almost untouched, and not a single person stood in front of it, what a waste! Was I the only one in this room whose stomach growled at the mere sight of it?

"How do you like it?"

"It's just amazing," I marveled. "I'm afraid Beccs won't believe any of this unless there are proof photos."

"You have the dress, that should be enough proof, right?"

"Right." I felt my cheeks redden.

We walked past a string quartet playing Pachelbel's Canon in D and the dance floor filled with more and more couples.

"Let's go over there," Connor offered, and I nodded. In one fluid motion, Connor casually brushed my hand, his warmth leaving tingling goosebumps that kept spreading.

Heavens, it's hard to believe what such a delicate touch could trigger in me. Had he done that on purpose, or had it been a coincidence, and Connor didn't even know about the effect of his gestures? No, when I looked into his deep brown eyes, I felt that he knew exactly what he was doing.

We stopped in front of a large, curved window that offered a view of the decorated garden. From here I also had a good overview of the huge hall, in which there must have been five hundred people. It must have cost a fortune to set up everything. All of it was perfectly arranged and decorated in bright, warm colors. Thousands of flowers and wreaths, vases and bouquets left a delicate summer scent in the air. Nevertheless, the sight of the company made me shiver.

"Are people always so ... cold with each other?" I asked. Arrogance and snootiness competed with each other, women waged contests for the most high-profile jewelry on their bodies, men compared the horsepower of their sports cars and stock growth.

No conversations that, in my opinion, belonged at a wedding, but which I nevertheless heard to the left and right of me. But the strangest thing for me was the absence of the bride and groom.

"As I said before, these events are for business. There's no exuberant splashing around in the shark tank."

Connor spat that word out like it was bile bitter, and I knew exactly what he meant. Most of the guests reminded me of the Royal Renaissance Hotel.

"If you block out these conversations, it's still beautiful. We should enjoy it," I said, spinning around like a ballerina. Connor didn't let go of my hand, on the contrary, he elegantly pulled it back and I landed in his strong arms, giggling.

"You're right, especially with such a graceful companion, it should be easy for me to enjoy this evening to the fullest."

His scent was dreamlike, masculine and tart, sandalwood with a slight hint of caramel. For a moment I paused and enjoyed the moment.

Who would have thought that I, of all people, would date a gorgeous billionaire? That's right, no one. Not even in my dreams could I have imagined it. And to top it all off, Connor was not only outrageously handsome, but also so accommodating and nice, quite unlike most of the other super-rich people I had contact with at the hotel.

"Would you like something to drink?" asked Connor.

"Yes, I'd love to."

Connor beckoned to one of the many waiters, who balanced a tray with dozens of glasses. Champagne flutes with the finest champagne or freshly squeezed orange juice. Connor took two glasses and handed me the glass with the champagne, while he preferred the orange juice.

"Cheers."

"Cheers."

Carefully, as if it were boiling hot liquid, I sipped it. I had never drunk champagne in my life, especially not in this price range. It surprised me how fruity and tangy the drink tasted, no comparison to the party champagne from the store around the corner.

"Why don't you drink champagne?" I asked curiously. Anyone who had their own chauffeur definitely didn't have to worry about alcohol and blood-alcohol levels, but Connor had mentioned during the drive that he didn't drink alcohol. Ever. He had also mentioned a few things about his family in passing, so that I wouldn't be embarrassed later on if the conversation got out of hand.

"I don't like the taste," he replied with a smile.

"And what about your own alcohol?"

"What about it?" He raised his left eyebrow, a mixture of rebuke and curiosity that caused me to go weak in the knees.

"Well, it's like a chef who doesn't taste his own food, or a composer who doesn't listen to his finished piece."

Connor looked at me as he pushed a blond curl out of my face with the back of his hand. Then he stroked my cheek with his fingertips, down to my neck.

"There's more than one sense in which to enjoy something." His murmur sounded like a somber promise. And there it was again, that dark gleam in his eyes. That fateful desire that I could hardly resist.

Stop! You hardly know him, I reminded myself to be careful. Quite apart from that, I was only his alibi, which I was only too happy to suppress, but nevertheless could not forget if I wanted to come out of the matter with a sound heart.

Connor took another step closer to me, his focused gaze holding me captive. He leaned forward and whispered in my ear, "You'd be amazed at what your senses could perceive."

Oh, wow.

The tingling in my abdomen spread throughout my body in a split second, followed by a shiver that coursed through every single nerve, through every cell of my being, all the way to the tips of my hair.

But before I could say anything, Connor took a step back and shook the hand of a man who came up behind me before giving him a brotherly hug. He was about the same age as Connor, wore a plain but expensive-looking tuxedo, and seemed genuinely pleased to meet Connor. Next to him stood a young woman in an elegant satin gown. The sparkle in her eyes was only matched by the incredibly beautiful jewelry she wore, which was definitely handmade. The many filigree details and ornaments testified to great passion.

"Josh, what a surprise," Connor greeted the man. "And Sam, you look adorable." Connor put his arm around my shoulders. "Dana, I'd like you to meet. Josh and Samantha Anderson."

"Hi. Nice to meet you."

I smiled, but all the fuses were blowing in my head because Connor hadn't mentioned them. Geez, I had no idea what to say if I got caught up in a conversation. Smile nicely, nod, and hope it stuck to questions about the weather?

Connor seemed to sense my insecurity, because my body became as hard as a board. Every single muscle in my body had tensed so much that it reminded me of the density of granite. But at the same time, my stiffened back and granite muscles were joined by soft knees, thanks to Connor's arm wrapping protectively around my waist.

"I really wasn't expecting you two, what are you doing here?" inquired Connor.

"We're here for Fashion Week," Sam replied with a smile, I could hear a faint Eastern European accent coming out that I found quite charming.

"But surely not to look at the latest shoes or hats, right?"

"No," Josh replied this time, his accent also seeming charming. "This time we're exhibitors, too."

Wow.

The two of them didn't look at all like they were designing for Fashion Week in my eyes, they seemed much too down to earth, friendly and above all too normal for that.

"It's about time." Connor turned to me and explained, "Josh is one of the most talented jewelry makers in all of Europe."

So, then the jewelry Sam was wearing came from Josh, how romantic!

Josh thanked him with a nod, then took a champagne flute from a passing waiter as well.

"How's the beer coming?" he then asked.

"Great, really great. If you want, I'll have a keg sent to you."

"I insist." Josh cleared his throat briefly, then asked, "Did you finally find a designer for the bottles?"

Connor shook his head. "No, not yet, but so far the Lancester Light has some testing going on before it hits the market, so if you'd still be interested, we can talk about that."

The type of beer made my ears prick up, because I had drunk a bottle of Lancester Light yesterday. It was the first beer that I had tasted.

"Maybe. A big job that was scheduled after Fashion Week fell through, so I'd have time."

Sam butted into the conversation. "Dana, what do you say we enjoy the festivities while the men talk business?" She held out her hand to me. I cast an appraising glance at Connor, who nodded at me with a smile.

"I'd love to." I was only too happy to accept Sam's invitation, because I felt uncomfortable getting involved in Connor's business conversations. It felt like they were private matters that were none of my business.

Still, I wondered if I would have learned more about Connor if I had stayed. He seemed so mysterious and secretive, as if he had a secret that should never see the light of day. The longer I was with Connor, the more questions there were to answer.

As I walked, Sam euphorically pulling me down the hall, I turned to my charming date one last time.

"Don't worry, dear. I'll find you again."

Hopefully.

Confidently, Sam bypassed most of the wedding party.

"Shall we take a closer look at the desserts?" asked Sam, who was already pulling me there.

"Who can resist those tempting cupcakes?" I replied anyway. Sam leaned over to me and said in a whisper, "Very good. I've been wanting to snack the whole time, but it looks awful standing there alone."

I giggled. "Yes, but now there are two of us."

Determined, we made our way to the desserts, which looked quite wonderful even from a distance. The closer we got, the better everything looked. Every single part was perfect.

"Hmm. This all looks so yummy," Sam sighed.

I did not even know where to start with this wonderful buffet, because I would have loved to try everything. First in the order in which they were served and then again alphabetically!

I was in sugar heaven.

"How lovely and detailed the decorations are," I gushed.

"It's rare that someone still has passion for what they do," Sam replied, proudly stroking her necklace. Then we grabbed two plates and began our calorie battle. Sam opted for a big slice of blackberry chocolate cake, and I shoveled more macarons onto my plate than was good for my hips.

But it tasted so divine that every single bite was worth it.

"How long have you two known each other?" asked Sam, trying to encourage a casual chat. The question came so suddenly that I almost choked. If Sam knew what the situation was really like, she probably would have choked.

"We just met a little while ago."

"Oh, nice, then everything is still fresh and exciting, with butterflies in your stomach."

"Yeah, you could call it that." I bit off a pistachio macaron.

"I can still remember when I met Josh, in the beginning everything was so ... business and I was incredibly shy and suddenly, bam! Overwhelming feelings and an attraction that continues to this day, growing stronger with each passing day." Sam's eyes lit up, and there was a gentle smile on her lips. I envied their perfect relationship.

"That sounds wonderful."

"Yes, it is, but I don't think Fashion Week is doing him any good."

"Why is that?"

"Because he hasn't made jewelry in weeks, he's just been hanging over paperwork and files. Fashion Week just makes people go crazy!"

"Tell me about it, it's no different at the hotel," I sighed. Sheer chaos also broke out at the Royal Renaissance Hotel as soon as the first posters for the fashion event were distributed.

"So, you come from the hotel industry? How exciting!"

Damn, Sam was a good listener, and I was knee-deep in my first faux pas.

"Yeah, something like that," I said slowly, feverishly trying to figure out how to wriggle out of this situation. "So, Josh makes the jewelry himself, right?"

"Yes, after he rediscovered his passion, he was hard to get out of his workshop." Sam smiled and subconsciously grabbed her necklace. An idea came to me.

"Say, does Josh make earrings by any chance?"

Sam tilted his head. "It depends, why?"

I bit my lips, because what I was about to do seemed almost forbidden, but it was my only chance to make up for the biggest mistake of my life.

"I'm a little embarrassed, but I'm pretty clumsy sometimes." I shrugged and smiled awkwardly. "In a nutshell, I lost an earring that meant the world to me. I looked and looked … but never found it."

Actually, I had wanted to ask Beccs for help, but she had had to leave the hotel in a hurry because Emma had fallen in the kindergarten. I hadn't even noticed at first, and when Rebecca had sent me a short message from the hospital, I had been on the verge of a heart attack. Fortunately, nothing bad had happened, nothing that a motherly kiss on the forehead and a rainbow unicorn plaster could not have cured.

"Oh, I'm really sorry about the earring. Josh is pretty busy right now, but I'm sure he'll have time after Fashion Week."

"That's too late!" it burst out of me before I could stop myself. Whoops.

"Is it urgent?"

"Without going into the specifics: Yes. It's super urgent."

Lordy, I was ashamed of my cryptic statements, but I could hardly confide in Sam that they might have become accomplices in covering up my unintentional theft.

"I see, if you send me a picture of the other earring, I'll squeeze it into his schedule somehow. Come to think of it, probably tomorrow."

My heart leapt for joy.

"I don't have a photo, but I have the other earring with me."

"What a happy coincidence."

Yeah, what a coincidence. Not.

More like a reminder not to do anything else stupid. I gave Sam the earring, which she, like a real expert, examined from different perspectives.

"It's a beautiful piece. I'm almost certain Josh will make time for it soon, as the design is definitely in line with his preferences."

A huge stone fell from my heart.

"That's great! How much is this going to cost me?"

My future annual salary? Eight additional jobs? My soul? Hard to believe, but that stupid earring really almost made me want to sell my soul to the devil.

"Nothing at all." Sam smiled warmly.

"No, that would be unpleasant for me," I answered honestly. I would rather scrape together the money with dozens of side jobs than swindle any luxury from gullible people.

"This earring," Sam held it up in front of my face, "is my one chance to enjoy some quiet moments with Josh, he's been so busy all this time with the planning, the models, the special requests from the other organizers, that we kind of fell short, and this buys me some time. The time with Josh is the most precious thing to me, more precious than any diamond, so it's a fair deal."

I was speechless and envied the two of them for their intense love.

"Okay, that sounds fair. Do you think I could get the second earring back this week?"

That was the deadline until the owner of the earring left again, I found out.

"I think so, yes. I'll take the earring with me and take good care of it, is that okay?"

"Of course. Thank you so very, very much! You doing this for me really means a lot."

Yes, I was really relieved, finally something went well! Now I could enjoy the evening and what might follow.

Behind Sam, Connor and Josh emerged, relaxed as they strolled through the party, laughing after Connor cracked a joke. When they reached us, Connor asked with a smile:

"So, are you enjoying the party?"

"Yes, very much so." I looked conspiratorially over at Sam. Not only had she solved my biggest problem, but she had also shown that there were definitely nice people at parties like this. "So how are your business meetings going?"

"Very good," Connor said, grinning at Josh, who in turn grinned back, then looked at Sam. "Sam? Do you mind if I kidnap Dana? I'd like to introduce her to my parents."

I swallowed.

Take a breath. It's just his parents!

10

Connor

I led Dana through the wedding party, hoping that my mother would hold back a bit. With her bright personality, she got everything off her chest, and Maxine was her exact match. I, on the other hand, took more after my father - quiet, thoughtful, workaholic. But I didn't think Dana would get to meet him today, because my dad hated these kinds of events even more than I did.

"Don't worry, my family is nice."

"I'm sure," Dana answered excitedly. Her nails dug deep into my arm with excitement, but I didn't let it show.

"The women in my family are a little forward sometimes," I explained. "Just don't take it personally."

"Okay." A waiter walked past us, and Dana grabbed a champagne flute as she walked, downing it in one gulp to build up some courage. "I can't believe I'm actually doing this."

Mom and Maxine stood at the edge of the dance floor. Both eyed the dancing couples with the same critical gaze. Maxine had on a gold silk knee-length dress, my mom wore the same design, with a braver cut that reached to her ankle.

"There they are in front. Just smile nicely and nod and you'll be fine," I said casually.

Dana nodded, then flashed me a grimacing, hideous grin.

"What an adorable smile." Dana giggled, and the grimace turned into a genuine smile. I stopped short and pushed a blonde curl out of her face. "Just be natural."

My fingertips stayed longer than necessary on her cheek. Dana's skin was so soft, so warm, that I just had to touch her and couldn't get away from her.

With big blue eyes, Dana looked at me. "What if they don't like me? Or I blab my mouth off? What if I embarrass you? How will you look then?"

I put a finger on Dana's lips, silencing her.

"You're beautiful as a picture, enchanting and kind, maybe a little too shy for my taste, but trust me: they'll find you lovely."

"I hope so." Dana forced herself to smile, then took a deep breath and nodded.

"When it comes to women, I'm always right."

I noticed Dana's questioning look but ignored it; I would answer her that question soon enough.

When Mom saw us, she almost dropped the champagne glass on the floor with joy.

"Connor!" she called out to me, waving. As if we were at a train station or airport and not at an elite wedding.

Dana's body tensed, but when I gently stroked her back with my right hand, her posture relaxed again.

"Hi, Mom. You look great." I broke away from Dana to hug my mother.

"You really need to visit more often!" she reprimanded me while we were still hugging.

"I will, I promise."

I gave my sister a kiss on the forehead, as I always do. "Hey, Max."

With a critical look, Maxine looked over at Dana.

"Don't you want to introduce us to your companion?" she asked curiously.

I put my arm around Dana's shoulder and pushed her one step further forward. There was more resistance in this delicate body than I had suspected, it cost me more strength than expected to push Dana another step forward.

"Don't be shy!" I said. Then I turned to my family. "Meet Dana."

Mom's eyes lit up, her eyes already reflecting two dozen grandchildren with angelic curls and bright blue eyes. "Pleased to meet you! Diana Lancester."

"Nice to meet you, Mrs. Lancester." Dana shook her hand.

"Oh, please call me Diana," she offered. She leaned forward and whispered, "I feel so old here anyway!"

"Mom, it's just because Dad locked himself in the bar with half the really old people," Maxine replied. "Dana? I'm Maxine, nice to meet you."

Yes, my dad couldn't stand such events, so he locked himself in a private bar with a few other men until the festivities were over.

I was hoping that my family would now talk about the coming rain, the benefit gala, or my trip to London, but I was actually expecting a hard-hitting cross-examination.

My mother looked Dana up and down and sighed comfortingly, "That dress fits you like a glove, it's beautiful!"

"Thank you, I've never worn such a wonderful dress," Dana replied. "I feel great."

Mrs. Lancester pounded my chest, "She's so magical!"

"Yes, she is," I replied, smiling proudly at Dana.

She is really magical.

"I must confess that I had thought you were a myth," Max interjected.

Dana laughed and then looked at me.

"No, I'm not a myth," Dana winked. Although I could feel under my hand how tense Dana was, she seemed more confident on the outside. She was one hell of an actress when it counted.

"Where did you two meet, anyway?" Maxine sipped her champagne, her gaze continuing to rest on Dana.

"At the Royal Renaissance Hotel," Dana replied with a smile.

"And how exactly?" Now Max looked at me.

"I remember very well how she suddenly stood in front of me, in a beautiful dress, with big eyes she had looked at me, and I just had to ask her out."

Maxine's critical expression softened, and my mother looked back and forth between me and Dana with delight.

"Oh, how romantic," Mom enthused.

"Plausible," Maxine said. "Okay, I believe you."

Irritated, Dana frowned.

"Is there any reason not to believe us?"

"Oh, no. Connor just hasn't brought anyone for a long time," Max said with a shrug.

I cleared my throat, my hand sliding from Dana's back to her waist. She had the perfect shape, the perfect grip ...

"It's just hard to find a suitable woman for me."

I was serious about that. Quite apart from the fact that I was on the road so much that I hardly made any female acquaintances, the women I inevitably met didn't match my type at all. Arrogant, in love with luxury, too little brains, too much Botox and no passion. And then there were preferences that wanted to be fulfilled ... a desire that few women could satisfy. My beast was picky, and there were few women who could appease my beast in a suit.

Dana's eyes lit up with joy at my sincere compliment.

Mom took another step closer. "Tell me, Dana, would you like to have children someday?"

"Mom!" I sighed, because she really didn't miss a beat.

"What? It's just a normal question among women," Maxine defended Mom with a grin.

"How much did Mom pay you to say that?"

"Nothing. But you know I'm the good kid." Maxine winked cheekily at me. With that, she opened the next round of our perpetual sibling war.

"If you were the good kid, you'd have offspring by now," I countered calmly.

"Touché."

"Shh!" interrupted Mom, who had put on her sensationalist face. "So, Dana?"

"At some point, definitely. When I see how happy my best friend is with her daughter, my heart sinks."

"Yes, it's quite wonderful. And you know what would also be quite wonderful? If you both came to our gala."

And the prize for the worst transition went to ... drum roll! Mom.

Dana turned pale. "A gala?"

"Yes! We host a small benefit gala every year and raise money for a good cause."

You really couldn't call my parents' events small. The entire elite from the East Coast gathered once a year at the Lancester estate to outdo each other with their donation bids.

"You definitely have to come," Maxine teased. Sometimes my little sister really was a beast.

Before I could say anything, Dana replied, "That sounds great. It's great that you're advocating for others, but I'm afraid that I ... may have other commitments, my schedule is pretty full in the near future."

True regret could be seen in her face.

I wanted to say something, but I held back, after all, I didn't even know what the next morning looked like, let alone the next month or where the gala was!

Of course, I felt that there was something between me and Dana, a tender attraction and clear desire. And then there were moments when this feeling disappeared again - displaced by Dana's insecurity.

It was probably better not to rush into anything and just wait. I couldn't force Dana to make the first move, but she had to, it was the only way I could make sure she had freely decided to do so.

"That would be a real shame," Mom said with a regretful tone.

"Yes, I would think so too," I winked. "We'll see, maybe it will work out."

"Yeah, maybe," Dana replied sheepishly.

"I'd be happy. It's not so easy to find nice company here," Maxine said. She toasted first Dana, then me.

I smiled. Not that I would place any value on my sister's blessing, but it was obvious that Maxine liked Dana, and that pleased me. Like our mom, she didn't mince words and said what she thought. No matter what kind of reactions she could provoke with it.

Maxine looked around, "I really need to talk to the organizer more, these bouquets are wonderful!"

"My sister is one of the best interior designers in the world; she also hosts my parents' parties."

"And other events. But also private apartments and hotels," Maxine added proudly.

"That sounds great. I think it's nice to be able to pursue your passion."

Dana's look became all dreamy and I wondered what her heart was beating for.

"Right. What do you say to these bouquets, Dana?"

I was more than curious about Dana's answer, because when Maxine asked questions like that, she wanted to embarrass the person and put them through their paces.

"I think they are beautiful. But for a gala I would use fewer pink flowers, more yellow and purple. And definitely snow white tablecloths. Shell white takes so much color away from the flowers."

Maxine was obviously impressed by Dana's answer. She nodded and looked thoughtfully at the decorated tables. "Yes, you're right. Snow-white tablecloths would look much better. Do you work in the business?"

Dana flinched noticeably.

"No, but my best friend, she talks a lot about her assignments."

"Your girlfriend definitely knows what she's doing," Max winked.

I butted into the conversation, "Now if you'll excuse us? I'd like to ask Dana to join us on the dance floor."

"Sure, go ahead," Max said, "Come on, Mom, we were still going to see the gardens. It was nice meeting you, Dana. I'd really like to see you again."

"Oh yes, very nice indeed!" replied Mom as she walked.

"It was nice to meet you too," Dana called after them, then I took a deep breath.

The conversation had gone better than I had hoped. Much better. For a moment it had even felt as if Dana had been more than just a companion.

I had to remind myself that Dana, however, was not actually more. We had a clear deal, which was fulfilled with the end of the celebration.

At midnight, my Cinderella will disappear into the night ...

But just because she wasn't my girlfriend yet didn't mean she couldn't become one, right?

"So, may I ask you to dance?"

Dana hesitated. "I can't dance."

"You don't have to be able to do that either, it's enough if the man can. I'll guide you."

"Sounds tempting, but..."

She did not finish speaking. There it was again, Dana's uncertainty.

If I ever got the pleasure of Dana getting down on her knees in front of me, my beast would definitely knock the insecurity out of her. Dana stood in her own way and slowed herself down. In my eyes, standing still had no reason to exist.

When I heard my name, I sighed softly.

"Connor? What a surprise to see you here."

Even before I saw Deborah Landry, I had smelled her. She had been using the same perfume since I met her fifteen years ago at a brunch for investors in the Lancester Company.

"Deborah, nice to see you."

I greeted my old friend with a hug.

Deborah wore her platinum blonde, chin-length hair loose, and around her neck was a heavy gold necklace adorned with emeralds that perfectly matched her green dress with a plunging neckline. As always, Deborah had paid a lot of attention to her appearance.

"Let me introduce you to my escort. Dana." First, I pointed to Dana, then to Deborah. "Dana? This is Deborah Landry, an old friend."

"Nice to meet you," Dana said, extending her hand, which Deborah ignored.

"Yeah, me too, sweetie. So, Connor? How was England?"

"Great. The new beer is going to be really good. Testing is still going on, but it will go to market in two to three months."

"Exciting," Deborah said monotonously. "You'll have to give me a tour of the brewery sometime. Or better yet! Through your Italian vineyards. Sicily must be beautiful this time of year."

"Of course, if the opportunity ever arises."

"I'm sure there will be a good opportunity for that," Deborah grinned.

"And how is your cousin? I heard he had a fall at the Derby."

"Yes, terrible thing! But he's back on his feet, I guess. We don't keep in close contact." Deborah sipped her champagne flute and checked her beige painted fingernails. "Anyway, I think it's nice to run into you here. It's been way too long!"

I nodded. Actually, I had run into Deborah at every major party, which wasn't surprising since our parents used to have many projects together. Not to mention, this kind of company wasn't as big as you might have thought.

Dana watched the action silently, but then grabbed my hand and said, "I'd like to dance now."

With all her strength she pulled me towards the dance floor, but at the same time she looked as graceful and delicate as a real lady.

"Sorry, Deborah. But you don't deny a lady a wish," I said, shrugging my shoulders. "I'll see you later."

Angrily, Deborah looked in Dana's direction. "I'm sure," she replied sweetly.

The small orchestra played a jaunty version of Johann Strauss' most famous waltz: *At The Beautiful Blue Danube*. A conceivably bad song for a dance beginner, but Dana allowed herself to be led softly and light as a feather under my hand. No doubt she had a natural feeling for my movements and the melody.

"What made you change your mind?" I asked, although I knew the answer long ago. No idea why, but my old girlfriend had the same chilling effect on almost all escorts.

"Dancing is nice after all."

"Didn't you just say you couldn't dance?"

"I can't either. It must be your leadership personality," she smiled.

If you only knew...

I gave Dana a serious look.

"I rather think you were jealous."

"Me? No. To whom, anyway?" replied Dana innocently. I almost believed her.

"I'd like to know that, too. Deborah is just an old friend."

"Who likes to flirt with you, huh?" She blew a blonde curl out of her face.

"So, you are jealous after all."

"Would you wish that?" Her question sounded sincere. Immediately, the grin disappeared from my face as Dana looked at me expectantly with her big blue eyes.

11

Dana

I leaned back in the comfortable leather upholstery of the limousine and closed my eyes. I couldn't have stood much more; to dance in these forbidden high heels had been death for my feet.

"That was a wonderful evening, Connor."

"True. And you were an adorable companion."

I had felt like a real princess. All the beautiful ball gowns, the wonderful music and the enchanting decorations – every girl dreamed of such an event. Nevertheless, the evening left me somehow unsatisfied. No, it wasn't the evening, but Connor, who hadn't answered my question. I was almost bursting with curiosity!

Connor signaled the driver, and the limo drove off. Of course, I knew our deal was done, yet I clung to the idea that I was still his escort.

I bit my lips to avoid saying anything rash, eager to hear his response. Connor's smile haunted me.

His silly, beautiful would-you-wish-I-were-jealous smile.

What kind of answer was that? None!

And why was I even bothering about it? We had spent a single evening together, that was the deal. Nothing more, nothing less.

I threw my high heels off me as if they were hot potatoes, and the stinging pain of my ankles immediately subsided. Moaning with pleasure, I massaged the cramped muscles of my legs.

"Heavens, I have no idea how I'm going to get through the day tomorrow."

"Just take the day off?"

"During Fashion Week and other, big conventions, we're not allowed to take vacation. So whatever special requests you come up with, I will accommodate."

"While smiling?" Connor growled softly. Something had changed in his expression.

"Of course."

"Admittedly, I like knowing that tomorrow you will think of me with every single step you take."

The look he gave me was dangerous as hell, because it said: I know what I want – you.

I could only think of two very opposite ways to deal with this situation. First, I smiled nicely, accepted everything and saw where it led me.

Or two, I put Connor in his place.

Yes, he was a billionaire and yes, he was damn attractive. He smelled good, his raspy voice catapulted me into other spheres, and he was the best dancer in the world. But did that give him the right to embarrass me like that?

Heavens, yes, I would think about Connor all day tomorrow, and definitely the day after. Probably even after that. But I didn't want to rub that in Connor's face at all. I didn't want him to know how fascinating I found him, besides, I wanted to protect my heart from this dangerous man who could steal it without any problems.

I decided to repay like with like, he owed me an answer, so I owed him one too.

"Would you like me to think of you every step of the way?" I asked, confident of victory.

"Yes," Connor replied seriously.

Damn.

I had not expected that. Connor had left me speechless with a simple, honest answer, with a single yes.

Nevertheless, I allowed myself to continue getting my hopes up. Of course, the illusion at the wedding had been charming, I had allowed myself to dream for a brief moment, but the dream was over, because the evening ended.

And what about Cinderella?

Well, Cinderella was probably the lucky exception. The minimal, possible probability in a statistic that was so small that no one paid any attention to it.

Cinderella was the zero-point-zero-zero-zero-one percent mismatch in a universe full of matches.

What was the probability that I was as lucky?

That's right, too small to even be worth mentioning.

The closer we got to my apartment, the more oppressive the mood became, at least for me. Connor sat quietly next to me and watched me. I couldn't read anything in his face, no movement betrayed what he was thinking about. He seemed like an open book, written in a foreign language.

"What else are you going to do today?" I asked after I couldn't stand the silence anymore.

Geez, after I said my question out loud, it seemed silly. The only possible answer was to sleep. But Connor didn't seem tired. Admittedly, neither was I, because I was far too exhilarated to sleep a wink right now.

"What I'm going to do or what I want to do?" he asked.

He gave me a serious, somber look. Clearly, I should only ask my question if I was ready for the answer, but how could I resist Connor? The answer was simple, I couldn't, I couldn't resist him.

So, I took a deep breath.

"I want to know both."

Oh, wow. Even before he answered, his gaze made my abdomen pulsate.

"I will take the most beautiful woman of the evening home, like a gentleman. But I would much rather take her back to my suite and do things to her that no gentleman would ever do."

My breath was taken away!

God, how could I resist such a look, such words?

Thoughtfully, I tried to interpret Connor's facial expression.

"I believe you are a gentleman through and through."

"Then you are sorely mistaken, Dana. I am a wolf in sheep's clothing, a beast in a suit."

His gaze was serious, his eyes gleamed darkly. I was caught in his gaze, yet I didn't feel lost, because things were clear at that moment as they rarely are in life.

I wanted to be proven wrong, because I really wanted to see the wolf and summon the beast. A teeny tiny part of me was still rebelling and didn't want me to, for fear that my sensitive heart might break. Uncertainty and curiosity fought a razor-sharp battle inside me.

"What is it?" Connor just about challenged me, "do you want to find out?"

"Yes, I do." My curiosity won out.

"Are you sure?" Connor's voice was deep and rough like thunder.

"Yes," I answered in a firm voice. I sounded more confident than I felt. Heavens, what I was doing right now was pretty exciting! My whole body was tingling with it.

"Good, I'm sure you won't let me down," Connor murmured.

I didn't know what Connor's cryptic statement meant, but I was sure I was about to find out. He pressed the long-distance phone that was connected to the driver's cab.

"John, please take us directly to the hotel, to the underground parking garage."

My whole body shook.

"You know that men like me ... for women like you, are dangerous as hell, right?"

"Yes," I sighed in a trembling voice. I knew all too well how dangerous Connor was for me. He made my principles shake, because of him I had broken dozens of rules – and the worst part was, I had enjoyed it.

This man was driving me crazy, and I wanted to lose myself in his madness. That was absurd, wasn't it? Others would call it passion.

Connor brushed my cheek, clasped my chin with his thumb and forefinger, and turned my head in his direction.

"You don't have to be afraid. I'll take good care of you, believe me."

"I know."

Connor's gaze rested gently on me. His thoughtful manner suited him well and triggered something like basic trust in me. As if there were a hidden bond between us, strong and indestructible, which I only had to discover.

"I've found you irresistible all evening, Dana."

I smiled shyly. Yes, I found Connor in his dark tuxedo attractive, too, because his eyes seemed even more somber and deeper than usual in this outfit. I had found it beautiful to be led through the dance hall in his strong arms, it had almost felt like flying.

His hand continued, over my cheekbones, neck, to my collarbone.

A low moan escaped from my throat. His hands roamed over my upper arm and the crook of my arm, up to my wrist. Every single inch of my free skin he touched, as if there were letters on my skin that he could read with his fingers like a blind man.

Through the tinted windows I saw the underground parking of the hotel, shortly after the car stopped.

"I'm going to fuck you tonight like you've never been fucked before," Connor said. At these sudden, clear words, my abdomen contracted. He almost brought me to orgasm with his words alone.

"But you have to do something for me first."

"What?"

"You'll see in a minute. Come now," Connor urged me. He opened the door, got out and held his hand out to me. But without those high heels, I found getting out significantly easier than before. I carried the shoes together with my handbag in my left hand, then I started walking.

"Wait a minute. Are you going to walk barefoot to the elevator?"

I responded to Connor's uncomprehending look with a shrug.

"Sure, I won't walk another step in these shoes, ever again."

"Understandable. But you're not going to walk around here barefoot."

"Don't worry, the Royal Renaissance Hotel is so clean you could eat off the floor anywhere," I reassured him.

"Don't argue. You'll learn soon enough that it's better not to contradict me."

He grabbed me by the waist and threw me over his shoulder as light as a feather. I screamed and giggled in equal measure in shock as he carried me like this to the elevator.

"Put me down now!" I ordered him and drummed my fists against his back. When he didn't respond, I additionally kicked my legs, trying to somehow kick myself free, but Connor didn't let me get away.

"Will you hold still?" His voice was reproving, and his grip on my body tightened. With his free hand he gave me a slap on the butt, which only strengthened my resistance. Just then, I forgot all about my insecurities. It was just Connor, me, and this degrading situation.

"I'm not a little kid, put me down already," I tried again.

"Oh, no? That's how you're acting right now," Connor countered calmly. "Be a good girl and hold still."

When I realized my lack of chances, I stopped resisting. Connor was simply much too strong. Besides, he advanced so much faster, which would surely shorten my degrading position on his shoulder.

"There you go."

I didn't begrudge him any form of satisfaction, so I kept silent. As my gaze wandered through the empty underground parking garage, my heart stopped for a moment. All the garage decks, elevators and corridors were equipped with surveillance cameras. Not that I thought security would take much interest in our goings-on, but safe was safe. I nestled my face tightly against Connor's back so that only my wild curls hiding my face could be seen on the videos.

Heavens, he smelled so incredibly good sandalwood, so masculine!

The private elevator was on our level, so the doors opened the same second Connor pushed the button.

After sending the elevator to the top floor, he let me slide off his shoulders.

"Finally." I strained to sound defiant, then sorted through my wild curls. There was also a camera in the private elevators, just above the emergency button, but it only activated when someone was using the elevator. For safety, I pressed myself so hard against the wall that my back covered the camera behind me.

Connor grinned at me and seemed to be taking full advantage of the moment.

"What, no thanks for that?"

"For what? For the humiliation?"

Connor raised a brow, his face growing more serious.

"Believe me. There are plenty of women who would love to thank me for even more humiliating things."

Yes, I had heard of these things, but actually had no idea about them. My love life consisted of a Sex and the City series marathon and a family stash of Ben & Jerry's.

"I believe that, but I'm not one of them."

"I think so, you just don't know it yet."

I could see myself in his dark eyes. His serious, determined expression was a sharp contrast to my uncertain expression reflected on his irises.

"Is that what you want me to do?"

The elevator braked gently, and the doors slid open silently. Soft light from a few small table lamps fell on us.

"No. Come with me." Connor took my hand and led us back to the Master Bedroom.

The bed had been freshly made in my absence. There was hardly anything more beautiful than a freshly made bed! Would the other guests appreciate it as much as I just now?

Connor led me in front of the large mirror, which showed me from head to toe. Then he took two steps back and circled me like a wolf circles its prey.

What was he up to? My abdomen tingled with excitement, only my insecurity hesitantly raised an objection.

Jesus, what is Connor doing to me?

He stopped right behind me. So close that I could feel his hot breath on my neck. His masculine scent ensnared me. In this moment, it surrounded me.

Over the mirror that faced us, he looked me straight in the eye.

"You had the opportunity to undress in front of me, to drive me crazy with your beautiful body, drive me out of my mind, but you didn't."

I bit my lips. "I'm not ... like that."

"I know. You're too insecure, too shy for that. But I want you to get over yourself today to give up some of your insecurity. You have no idea how much potential you would have if your insecurity didn't slow you down so much."

I smiled shyly at him. "If you say so."

Deep inside, I could feel that his words had hit the mark. There were so many situations in which I wished I had been more confident, but that was easier said than done.

"I know it takes courage," Connor spoke to me sympathetically. "Show me your body."

Where his breath met my skin, it left a tingling sensation.

"But what if you don't like me?" I looked down at myself, and my gaze lingered on my bare feet.

"I've never understood why the most beautiful women have the most doubts." Connor breathed a kiss on the back of my neck, then continued, "Your body is perfect. There's nothing to be ashamed of."

My gaze was still lowered, but there was true sincerity in his voice. Surely Connor recognized every little emotion in my face via the mirror.

I wonder if he knew what kind of battle I was fighting inside right now.

"Tonight, you belong to me. Show me your body. Show me all that you have to offer. Show me that you want me, show me that you want to be mine."

His hand grazed my neck as he lifted my chin. So, I was forced to look him directly in the eyes.

Connor looked at me questioningly. "Will you be mine tonight?"

"Yes."

It was surrounding me. His seduction skills were incredible. Never in my life would I have thought of answering his question with no. Connor made me feel wanted – an incredible feeling. I loved the illusion that the two of us had created together, I loved this version of us.

I liked that I belonged to him. Yes, sure, probably only for one night, but I allowed myself to enjoy it while it lasted.

Connor grasped my wrists and ran his fingertips up my arms until he reached the strap of my dress. Slowly, he slipped the wide straps over my shoulders and pulled the fabric down.

Connor fixed me, his eyes magically attracting my gaze. If I had wanted to, I could have held onto the dress. It would have been easy to push his arms away and yell stop, but I didn't. With pleading looks, I begged Connor to keep doing what he was doing. I wanted more of that belly tingle, more of his looks, and more of him. Absolutely!

Although the situation was foreign to me, I felt safe with him. Connor was my lifeline in an unknown world.

"Good girl," Connor whispered in my ear.

The fabric brushed over my breasts, my belly and finally fell in gentle waves to the floor.

I was now standing naked in front of him. Okay, almost, I was not completely naked, but still wore a champagne-colored, almost transparent panties, whose edges were framed with fine lace decorations.

Connor gave me time to get used to the new situation. A gentle breeze blew through the room through the open window, leaving tingling goose bumps in its wake.

"Look at yourself," Connor ordered. He smiled at me over the mirror, and I returned his smile. The warm light of the table lamps flattered my body.

"You look like you're carved out of marble," Connor murmured as he stroked my skin. There was a seductive grin on his lips and his dark eyes sparkled like black stars.

"See? There's nothing to be ashamed of."

Connor grabbed my wrists and guided them to my sides. From there, he directed my hands down over my womanly waist. He used my hands to touch me. Trying to stifle a moan, I bit my lips.

"You have nothing to be ashamed of, Dana. Neither for this, nor for your beautiful breasts."

He guided my hands over my breasts, whose curves stood out clearly from my upper body. My buds had already become stiff and sensitive with arousal. Moaning, I leaned my head back against his shoulder and felt Connor's strong upper body behind me. In this way, he continued to touch my body until I almost lost my mind.

Connor buried his face in my hair.

"Say it!" he commanded softly.

"I have nothing to be ashamed of," I whispered.

"Louder."

"I have nothing to be ashamed of!"

"You're a good girl who certainly doesn't have to be ashamed of that perfect body," Connor confirmed my words. Then he pushed my hands even further down until they reached the hem of my panties. Piece by piece, my fingertips slid under the fabric.

Jesus. I gasped for air and then sighed with pleasure. It relaxed me immensely to feel that Connor knew exactly what he was doing and how I would react. My ass pressed firmly against his hard erection, which was clearly pushing through the fabric of his pants.

Connor pressed my hands harder against my pubic area while he rubbed against my ass. All the while he looked me in the eyes.

"There is no finer compliment to a woman's body than a fucking hard cock," he said in a raspy voice.

I felt my own lust. My abdomen quivered, and I could hardly hold myself on my trembling legs, every single cell of my body was tingling. It was overwhelming – and probably only the foreplay of foreplay!

"How do you like being my girl so far?"

"It's indescribable. I've never had such intense feelings."

In the mirror I could see his satisfied grin.

"That's nothing compared to the orgasm you're about to have."

12

Connor

I slipped Dana's panties over her hips. Light as a feather, the fine fabric fell down to her ankles. Damn, her body was beautiful.

To support her, I took Dana's hand and pushed her two steps forward. Now she stood naked in front of me, and not only physically. Her looks signaled to me that she was absolutely ready to give herself to me. I gently stroked her collarbone, but this time with my own hands. I wanted to feel her, every majestic part of her body. Dana's soft skin was warm and smelled of cloves, and under her tender skin, her muscles tensed at my touch.

I kissed her neck, starting from the ear, down to the shoulder blade.

"I like you," I murmured, not breaking my kisses. "You drive me crazy, Dana."

Damn, I could hardly wait to taste her lust. With no other woman had I ever held back as I did with Dana at that moment. I don't know why, but when her big eyes caught my gaze, all my fuses burned out.

Dana moaned softly, leaving her lips slightly open, which made my beast rage.

Don't lose control! I also covered her other shoulder with gentle kisses, although I wanted to grab her, throw her on the bed, and fuck her as hard as I could. Later, because first I wanted to savor every single moment. I owed it to Dana that I first admired, appreciated and adored her beauty.

Before I unleashed my beast in a suit on Dana, however, I had to make one thing clear.

"If you say stop, I will stop. Do you understand?"

Dana nodded. "Yes."

Actually, I had a bigger system and a safe word, but Dana seemed so inexperienced that too much information would only confuse her. One stop was enough to start with, after all I was only giving Dana a taste of what was to follow later, if there was a later at all. It was possible that Dana would go into shock at the sight of my beast or want to run away. There was no guarantee that she would stay, even if deep inside, I hoped she would.

I shook my thoughts from my mind, because there was only the here and now, right now there was only Dana, me, and my fucking hard erection.

"Open your legs a little more!" I commanded. Dana obeyed and spread her legs a bit, then I grabbed the inside of her thigh and pushed her legs apart one last bit.

"Keep stretching your back, I want you to stand completely straight!"

Immediately Dana straightened up, full of grace and pride, like an Amazon.

"Good girl," I praised her posture. "Now put your arms up."

Gently, I grasped both her wrists and guided them upward, interlacing her hands at the back of her head.

"I like you even better that way."

Dana smiled proudly at me, she obviously liked that I liked her. Very good, that's exactly how it should be. That was exactly the prerequisite for everything I still had planned with her.

The mere fact that I was standing in front of her in my tuxedo while she was naked had led to a natural power imbalance. There was no question who was now in charge. No one had any doubt that I was a dominant man, and she was a submissive girl. By holding her position, Dana had understood and accepted that.

I kissed her. First soft and sensual, then the passion between us ignited, and our, never-ending kiss, became fiercer and more intense. Our tongues touched, caressed and tasted each other, while a deep growl escaped my throat.

Damn, I sounded like a hungry wolf, my beast was starting to make itself known.

Dana kissed well and tasted even better. I don't know if it was minutes or hours, but as we breathlessly pulled away from each other, I rubbed my lower lip in bewilderment, trying to remember Dana's taste. Never before had a kiss felt as meaningful as this one. Dana's looks signaled to me that she felt the same.

I traced the outline of her lower lip with my thumb tip, and Dana automatically opened her mouth so wide that I couldn't resist. Her mouth felt warm and moist, the tip of her tongue licked gently over my finger.

I moaned softly. For the fact that Dana seemed so reserved, almost virginal, she did her thing damn well. It drove me half-crazy how she licked my finger. Harder and harder until she sucked on it, I could hardly wait for Dana to repeat that with my cock as well.

"You're doing very well," I whispered.

Then I pulled my thumb out of her mouth, only to exchange it for my index and middle fingers so that I could penetrate her mouth even deeper. Her full, soft lips closed tightly around my fingers. I wonder how much she could take. Could I sink my entire manhood into her mouth? At the thought alone, my erection pressed painfully against the fabric of my tuxedo.

I continued to enjoy her mouth, giving in to the fantasy that it was my hard erection fucking her mouth.

Someday, yes. But not today. Today I would only be able to show Dana a fraction of what I loved. That night, Dana got only a small taste of my proclivities. Enough to show her what was what, but too little to scare her. Nor did I have to chain my beast. I knew I had to go slow with Dana, but I was sure it would be worth the wait. With a little experience Dana withstood my beast in a suit, I even felt that only my beast in a suit could satisfy her deepest and most hidden desires.

Yes, now Dana's exterior seemed as fragile as glass, but underneath was a femme fatale. The insecurity she wore on the outside was just a facade with which she imprisoned herself.

Don't worry, I will set you free.

If Dana allowed me to, I would shake her entire worldview, maybe even have to destroy it and rebuild it, but she really had to be ready for that, and she wasn't. Not yet.

"I want you to stay still until I allow you to move again."

Dana nodded. With my fingers in her mouth, she couldn't speak. I enjoyed my fingers inside her for a few more moments, thrusting hard a few more times, then I withdrew from her.

Dana looked at me expectantly. The blue of her eyes reminded me of the bright sky of a cloudless summer day.

Still wet from her mouth, my fingers ran over her buds, which became even harder under my practiced touches. Her shapely, firm breasts were truly a dream. They fit perfectly in my large hands and thus had the ideal size.

Dana bit her lips with pleasure and suppressed her moan. I took her nipples between my thumb and forefinger and pinched them gently at first, then harder and harder. Dana's suppressed moans grew louder, and when I increased the pressure another time, she winced in surprise.

"Hold still, Dana!" I admonished her. Of course, I made it a point that she didn't hold still, but to my great surprise, Dana bravely held out until I was done working on her sensitive buds. She could definitely take more than she looked, at first glance.

"Well done."

I took a step closer so that I was standing close to her. Her regular, strong breath tickled my skin. Surely Dana's upper arms were now already burning like fire, because this position was one of the most painful of all for inexperienced women.

"It's exhausting, isn't it?"

"Yes," Dana sighed.

"Just a little bit more. I know you'll hate me for it, but if you're willing to pay that price, I'll give you the most intense feelings you'll ever have in return. Believe me, if you go for it, you'll love it."

"I'm not so sure about that."

Her honesty made me smile softly. I gently stroked Dana's cheeks, which elicited a soft sigh from her.

"Pleasure and pain are sometimes close together, the line is so narrow that they overlap in some places."

"This isn't the first time you've done this, is it?"

The question must have cost Dana a lot, so I rewarded her with the truth, even though I didn't usually talk about other women.

The serious look I gave Dana answered her question and no doubt raised more questions that I left unanswered.

Of course, I had experience in what I was doing. More than that, I was not only experienced, I was an expert, an exceptional talent, a legend in my field. I knew exactly what women needed to be truly fulfilled, and I knew exactly what to do to turn pain into pleasure and vice versa.

My right hand slid between her legs. Dana closed her eyes and threw her head into her neck. I could clearly feel her arousal, she was wet and absolutely ready for me, but that didn't mean I claimed it right away. No, I wanted to take full advantage and enjoy this moment as well. The longer I dragged Dana's pleasure in agony, the more intense all her perceptions and feelings became.

"Can you feel how aroused you are?" I asked.

"Yes," Dana sighed.

"And why?" I asked further.

"Because of you."

"Because of me or because of what I do to you?"

"Both, I would say."

"Very good."

Her arms began to tremble, and from her look I could tell that it wouldn't be long before this posture was no longer possible for her, but still Dana was bravely biting her lips and trying to make me proud.

Nevertheless, I kept massaging her most sensitive spot because I just couldn't help it. Her body reacted violently to my touches, her legs trembled with pleasure more and more.

"You may put your arms down now."

Sighing, Dana dropped her arms. Relief was written all over her face. Alternately she clenched and stretched her hands. I was not deterred by this and penetrated her with one finger, which elicited a loud moan from Dana. Her legs were now shaking so much that I wrapped an arm around her body to hold her. Gratefully, Dana leaned against my chest. Damn, she was so wet and tight ... I couldn't help but continue. Dana's breathing was getting faster and more erratic. Not much longer and she would come.

Hopefully screaming loudly and writhing in pleasure...

With a firm grip I grabbed Dana's hips and carried her to the edge of the bed, because her whole body was shaking so much that she couldn't stand anymore. Not that I would have minded her sinking to her knees in front of me, but I had to fuck her now. By God, I almost exploded.

She was lying so sensually on the bed that I just had to muster all self-control not to just throw myself at her.

"I'm going to fuck you for a long fucking time," I said, unbuttoning my shirt and throwing it on the floor.

I allowed Dana to look at me for a moment, then I took off the rest of my clothes as well. When she saw my erection, her eyes widened.

Grinning, I pushed her legs apart and knelt between them. Then I rubbed my hardness between her legs, which made Dana groan. Her lust could not be overlooked - or overheard. Dana stretched her hips towards me, she could hardly wait to be fucked by me.

Playfully I licked over her erect nipples, eliciting another sensual moan from her.

"I'm going to fuck you until you cum for me," I gasped.

Dana bit her lips uncertainly but said nothing.

"What's on your lips?" I inquired as Dana continued to look at me silently. Actually, I didn't ask my subs, because I expected them to address problems on their own. My subs not only had the right to do so, but even the duty.

But Dana wasn't my sub, at least not yet, so she didn't know my rules.

"No," Dana answered hesitantly. "I've just never had an orgasm before."

I eyed her briefly, then nodded. "I'll change that now."

Dana smiled at me, but I could see the doubt in her eyes, but in a moment, I would prove her wrong. Fortunately for her, it was immediately clear to me what Dana was missing to orgasm. Me. Dana needed me to satisfy her darkest fantasies, and she didn't need to ask me a second time.

I pinched both nipples, mostly gently and playfully, but sometimes without warning so hard that Dana reared up her entire upper body. I took my time working her breasts one more time, because I loved how Dana squirmed, moaned and gasped under my skillful fingers.

Only when Dana's excitement had completely disappeared and she had completely adjusted to me, I went further, rubbed my erection against her wet entrance and penetrated her.

You. Are. So. Damn. Tight.

Even when I didn't move, Dana closed around me so tightly that I almost came. Gasping, I enjoyed the feeling of being inside her until Dana moaned loudly, dug her nails deep into my back, and I could barely hold back my beast.

With steady movements I pushed into her again and again. First slowly, to get Dana used to my size, then harder and harder, deeper. With every inch that I fought my way further, Dana became louder.

Again and again, Dana pushed her pelvis against me so that I could penetrate even deeper into her. To increase the effect even more, Dana wrapped her legs around my waist. Yes, Dana really got into it and fucked herself with my cock. Her insecurity had disappeared, which pleased me extraordinarily. I had suspected that deep down, Dana had a dirty, depraved side, but the fact that she broke through the surface so quickly impressed me. By God, I loved Dana for showing me her innermost so quickly.

Our bodies collided, again and again, more and more violently. The heat between us kept rising, but we didn't burn. On the contrary, it became even wilder and more passionate. Dana's moans were sensual and sounded beautiful, just like her eyes and the rest of her body. I loved the way her breasts bobbed along in time with my thrusts.

Damn, Dana was perfect ... and depraved in equal measure. Perfect.

"I want you to come for me, Dana!" I gasped in a throaty voice.

"Then fuck me harder," Dana moaned.

Music to my ears! Dana wanted even more, much more than I had initially given her credit for.

"God, do you have any idea how insane you're driving me?"

Dana grinned at me. Intense. Wild. Enthusiastic.

I was only too happy to comply with Dana's request. She had conjured up the beast, so now she also got the beast, which took no more consideration for her delicate appearance. As hard as I could, I took what was mine. Her center quivered and pulsed, tightening around my erection. I fucked Dana the way I liked best, without pity, without mercy, and the way I needed it right now.

Her breathing became more and more irregular, she gasped with every thrust. Her body tensed tighter and tighter and vibrated. Dana's eyelids fluttered. Her head arched back.

I knew the signs and knew she was about to come.

"Come for me," I commanded a second time. This time Dana was smart enough to listen to me, because ignoring my orders could have bad consequences for her. Dana came. Violently. Her body reared up, and her fingernails dug deep into my back.

I enjoyed the intensity with which Dana welcomed her orgasm. These scratch marks would remind me of our night together in the days to come, no question.

Dana's moans transitioned seamlessly into soft sighs, the wild, strong twitches of her abdomen also bringing me the release I needed.

I pumped my seed into her, then dropped to my side and watched Dana completely surrender to the surges of her first orgasm. Gently I stroked her cheek and praised her. "Good girl."

Dana's breathing slowly returned to normal, but her body continued to quiver for a long time.

"Wow. Was that the beast in the suit?" she asked, gasping.

"No," I replied with a smile. "The beast would have done very different things to you."

"And what would the beast have done to me?"

"She would still fuck you."

With shackles. Clamps. Blows. Candles.

Dana would not be allowed to come as quickly as today when she was under my control. Dana smiled contentedly and closed her eyes. Not a second later she was asleep, I watched her for a while before falling asleep myself.

The next morning, I was rudely awakened when a pillow was thrown at me. Next, a seat cushion flew against my head, followed by my tuxedo shirt from last night.

Dana was naked and jumping around the room excitedly. "Damn it! She's gone!"

I had no idea what Dana was doing or why she was so upset.

"What's gone?" I asked.

"My work uniform! One of the maids must have taken it away with the towels, only my shoes are still in the dressing room. Besides, I should have started working half an hour ago."

I stood up, held Dana by the wrist and gave her a kiss on the forehead.

"Then wear the evening gown until you get a new uniform."

"Can't, I just stand out too much in this dress."

"Then alternatively wear your work shoes and nothing else," I joked.

Shocked, she looked at me, mouth agape. "Connor!"

I continued to grin. Yes, I even found it quite cute how shocked Dana was, she was just too easily upset.

Dana looked at me with seriousness.

"The entrance to your suite and the hallway to the elevator are under camera surveillance," she sighed.

"Really?"

"Yes, we are radioed directly when a guest in the expensive suites leaves the room."

"Wow." The hotel really took its guests' time seriously.

"If my boss sees me, I'm screwed. I don't want to lose my job, quitting, now, is definitely not in my seven-year plan. What about the garage? You could just take me outside in the car."

I sighed softly. "I don't think you can, Dana."

"Why not?"

"Because my private elevator is being serviced today. Shouldn't my boss maid know that?"

The first tears were reflected in Dana's beautiful blue eyes.

Don't cry, Dana.

I don't know why a few tears upset me so much, but they did.

"Oh, God, you've got to be kidding me." Dana put her head back and snorted loudly. She was close to despair, which is why I took her in my arms. Comfortingly, I stroked her blond curls while she pressed her wet face against my chest.

When she had calmed down a bit, she sighed a second time.

"None of this would have happened if the maid had just shaken out the towels like the rulebook says."

"Why is that in your rulebook?"

"Because of Oscar," Dana said with a shrug.

"And who is Oscar?"

"Oh, that's right, you don't know anything about that, every employee here knows the story. Oscar was Ozzy Osbourne's snake. And still is now, I hope. Mr. Osbourne was a guest here a long time ago, and his snake found it quite comfortable between the towels. Then one thing led to another ... and Oscar almost got washed along with them in the laundry."

I laughed out loud. "You really experience absurd things here."

Dana nodded.

"Don't worry, I already have an idea."

"Really?"

"Yes," I answered and went to the phone, where I was put straight through to the front desk.

"Good morning, Mr. Lancester. What can I do for you?" I recognized the voice of the receptionist with the stern bun.

"Please bring me a big breakfast, with lots of fruit and two coffees with hazelnut syrup, cream and chocolate sauce."

Mumbling softly, the receptionist repeated my order. I even heard the ballpoint pen scratching across the paper. "I'd be very happy to. Is there anything else I can do for you?"

I looked expectantly at Dana. "Do you have a friend here who can help you? A friend you trust?"

"Yes, Rebecca Hatfield," Dana whispered to me.

I cleared my throat briefly, then spoke to the receptionist again.

"I would think it would be lovely if that nice maid from yesterday, Rebecca Hatfield, would bring us breakfast."

"One moment, please." Silence followed. Dana would simply explain to her friend on the first visit what had happened, and when Rebecca Hatfield came back for the car, she would have a uniform for Dana, it was that simple.

"I'm sorry, but Mrs. Hatfield is not in right now."

Okay, that was a setback, but no big deal.

"Then have someone else take it upstairs and make sure Mrs. Hatfield picks it up, will you?"

Then Dana's girlfriend wouldn't smuggle anything into his suite, just out.

"Of course, sir. I'll get right on it. Is there anything else I can do for you?"

"No, now I'm happy as a clam. Thank you."

I hung up and Dana's face reflected a wide range of emotions. Fear, uncertainty, concern, but also curiosity.

"Will you tell me how breakfast will help me?" There was also a hint of anger in her concerned tone. Was Dana angry with herself? At me?

Reprovingly, I raised an eyebrow. Under other circumstances, this tone of voice would have caused a glowing, red butt.

Not yet...

"We're going to have breakfast now, then I'm going to call room service and the buffet cart will be picked up again."

"I don't quite understand, Connor."

"You're going to hide in the car, simple as that."

Dana laughed out loud. "Good one."

"I'm completely serious about that. And because the car will be significantly harder to push, you'll need a girlfriend who can keep it all to herself."

Her laughter died away, then she bit her lips thoughtfully.

"This could really work."

"Of course it's going to work," I stated confidently.

Dana grinned at me.

"You wouldn't happen to have a solution for being late, would you?"

Before I could answer, my phone rang, and I looked at the display.

Bad timing.

"Sorry, I have to take this call. You can go take a shower in the meantime."

13

Dana

I stood under the shower and soaped myself for the third time in a row. I felt I had already scrubbed off the first layer of my skin, but I was too upset to stop. Grateful that I had a ritual to hold on to, I picked up the soap a fourth time.

Sorry, I have to take this call. You can go take a shower in the meantime, I repeated Connor's words.

Sure, I had answered. You probably want to get rid of me, I thought.

Not that I thought I could claim ownership over Connor, but secretly I did. For Connor, last night had probably been a one-time thing, although he had made me feel special the whole time.

Yes, last night I had been his girl.

But now it was no longer last night, and I was no longer his girl. Now it was the morning after. In short, the magic of last night had not spilled over into the morning. Quite the opposite! After that magical wedding celebration and the most phenomenal sex in the world, the morning after had been pretty much the lowest point of my life so far. I had a severe affair hangover that hurt not in my head but in my heart, and my head was bursting thinking about my professional future.

I was ninety-nine percent sure that I was starting my last day of work today, more than an hour late and cheeks flushed because last night was still written all over my face. Even if I managed to sneak out of Connor's suite unnoticed, my tardiness could never go unnoticed.

Was it weird that my seven-year plan just passed me by, but my jealousy that Connor preferred a phone call to me somehow felt worse?

Lordy, my dream of owning a sweet hotel was receding into the distance, while Deborah seemed quite tangible. It was killing me that I didn't know for sure if Deborah was on the other end of Connor's line.

Yep, Connor had hit the mark, I was jealous of this woman. Certainly not of her character, and not because of her looks, but I was jealous of the opportunities that were open to her. The whole world was at her feet, but even worse was that she would see Connor again and again at the most exclusive events in the world.

Thinking about how pushy Deborah had been flirting with Connor yesterday, I scrubbed a little harder. Heavens, she had treated me like I was yesterday's air; she had made me feel like I wasn't serious competition.

Was it perhaps also like that? I had been only a simple maid and beyond that only his emergency solution. Nevertheless, I felt sick at the thought that Connor could marry this woman someday, because he deserved better!

Throughout the conversation, Deborah had made more eye contact with her fingernails than with Connor. She had not only been vain, but condescending and arrogant.

I turned the faucet all the way to the left and within a second the steaming water turned to liquid ice. A painful but effective way to cool my mind. I bit my lips and forced myself to remain standing under the ice water until my anger was all gone. It took longer than I would have liked.

Then I got out of the shower, shivering, and wrapped a towel around my body. Back in the bedroom, the whole room was flooded with the scent of coffee; room service had already been here, and I recognized the scents of the in-house coffee immediately.

At the Royal Renaissance Hotel, only coffee made from roasted Ethiopian coffee beans was served.

"This smells delicious," I enthused, following the scent of coffee to the tray on the bed.

"And it tastes even better," Connor added with a smile. He was lying in bed wearing only an open white shirt besides his boxers and looked scrumptious.

Carefully, I lifted the cup that was on the serving cart next to the bed and sipped the coffee, which was garnished with whipped cream and chocolate sauce well beyond the rim. The sweet hazelnut syrup in the coffee was divine!

"This tastes amazing," I groaned.

"You taste even better," Connor grinned. He reached out his hand to me, and his compliment went down like oil. Had I perhaps thought too much after all, and this was more than just a one-night stand for Connor?

I grabbed his hand, followed the call of his lips and kissed it. So intense and sensual as he returned my kiss, I had to mean something to him, I could feel it clearly!

My heart was beating wildly in my chest because maybe I was more than just a girl for one night.

"Yes, you definitely taste better," Connor murmured. Gently, he licked across my lips, down my neck to my collarbone. His tongue left a slight tingle that reverberated many times over in my abdomen.

"We should have breakfast," I said with a sigh, even though I didn't want to have breakfast. I didn't want to get up either, and under no circumstances did I ever want to leave this suite again. But if I wanted to keep my job, I had to do just that.

"Yes, we should," Connor repeated my words. Sensual and wicked.

He let his fingers glide over the huge breakfast. Freshly baked croissants, homemade jam, a small cheese platter, and fresh, chocolate-covered fruit.

Connor picked a fresh grape and held it to my lips. I had never eaten such sweet grapes before.

Next, he handed me a chocolate-covered strawberry. Just as I was about to take a bite, he withdrew the fruit and stole another kiss from me instead.

"Hey! Do you want me to starve?" I protested, pulling a pout.

"No way," Connor laughed, handing me the strawberry. The way Connor handled me felt so beautiful, I wished this moment would never end. Whatever was between Connor and me felt real, way too real to be made up.

For quite a while, we continued to fool around, teasing each other and sharing tenderness. For a brief moment, we forgot that time was actually pressing.

"I should get ready now." I sighed loudly. The realization that it was all about to end weighed a ton on my shoulders.

"Good, then I'll have someone call for Rebecca again. Is she a good friend?"

"My best friend." I smiled proudly. There was no way Beccs was going to let me down, that was as sure as eggs in a basket!

"Excellent. Then your seven-year plan is definitely saved." Connor winked at me and then picked up the phone to send for Rebecca.

"Thank you," I replied softly.

Provided my tardiness is not discovered.

To untangle my stubborn hair, I sat down at the dressing table. Those curly beasts had turned into almost unrelenting knots overnight. Without my special conditioner, which my hairdresser had specially made for me from clove blossom extract, the knots would also stay where they were. The only thing that helped was to knot my hair into a neat bun and hope no one noticed the knots. Messy buns were red tags to Shannon Williams and a cause for admonishment.

With utmost concentration, I took care of my hair until I was distracted by Connor.

"She'll be there in a few minutes."

"Great."

Don't! It shall not end yet...

"I think it's unfortunate that you don't wear your beautiful hair down." There was genuine regret in Connor's voice.

"I have to," I explained. "We can't wear our hair down, and with these knots, a ponytail just isn't possible."

As a maid, there were more duties than rights at the Royal Renaissance Hotel, but everyone put up with them here because it looked pretty good on my resume to have worked here. Besides, the hotel was an integral part of my seven-year plan. I learned from the best what to do, or better, what not to do. But there was one thing I was already sure of: I would value my employees, just as much as my guests.

Connor stroked my shoulders, ending my daydreaming. He nodded understandingly and looked over the mirror directly into my eyes.

"If you were my maid, I'd let you wear your hair down."

"Is that a job offer?" I asked with a grin. It was obvious to me that it was a joke. But something in Connor's look told me he was taking my words more seriously than he should.

"Your loose hair would be the only thing you would wear. Maybe a nice pair of high heels."

Connor reached for the towel I had wrapped myself in and opened it.

"This beautiful body should not be hidden."

Okay. He really meant it.

"Connor, I..." I didn't know what to say or feel. There was so much chaos in my head and even greater chaos in my heart. Connor completely threw me for a loop!

Before I could answer anything, there was a knock at the door.

"This must be your girlfriend. I'll open it for her, then you can get dressed."

I loved Beccs for not having to answer Connor now, at the same time I was sad that everything ended with her appearance.

Connor grabbed his suit pants and disappeared from the bedroom. Shortly after, I heard Rebecca's voice in the entryway. How could I explain the situation to my best friend? And how did it go on with Connor? Did it go on at all?

I quickly slipped into the ball gown, picked up my work shoes, which didn't match the elegant dress at all, and the handbag with my smartphone from the dressing room. In passing, I picked a few more of the forbidden good grapes and smiled when I saw my trophy on the dresser.

"Hi, Beccs. Three guesses what happened!" I greeted her, beaming. My best friend was at a loss for words when she saw me like this.

"Yep, that's right. I found my trophy again!"

"Dana?" Her eyes got huge. The last time she had had eyes that big was on World Donut Day, when there had been 80% off all pastries at Dunkin' Donuts. Or had those been my eyes after all?

"Beccs, I need your help, you have to sneak me out of here or Shannon Williams will kill me." Now I was dropping the ball to save time. Every minute I started working later jeopardized my seven-year plan.

"You can say that again," Rebecca replied. "What are you doing here anyway? In that outfit?"

"It's not what you think." Embarrassed, I looked to the floor. Maybe it is exactly what she thinks after all.

Admittedly, I had no idea what was going on in my girlfriend's head, something like that only happened very, very rarely.

Connor cleared his throat. He was wearing his suit pants, but his shirt was still open. Those tight abs almost made me drool again. Connor's body was incredible. So strong and muscular and masculine.

Heaven, and what Connor had done everything with my body, the madness! Like no man before, this promise Connor had definitely kept. Stylish like a gentleman and at the same time so rough and animalistic that I could hardly pronounce it.

"Dana was my lovely evening companion last night," Connor said.

"WOW! How did that happen?" blurted out Rebecca.

"I asked her," Connor summed up yesterday afternoon.

"Beccs, I don't mean to push, but I should have started work over an hour ago. We should get going," I urged.

"Oh, you only started ten minutes late." Rebecca grinned like a little kid who had done something wrong.

"What?"

"Jenny from the laundry found your key card, radio and about two dozen pieces of candy in a work coat and gave it all to me."

"Beccs, you are an angel! I really owe you, but now you have to get me out of here first."

"And how? Shall I hide you under my dress?"

"No, in the service van." Beccs laughed just as I had earlier when Connor had made the suggestion. Only now it was my look that remained serious, slowly silencing Beccs. She frowned as she looked at the service cart.

"Hmm. Now that I think about it, that could really work."

I turned to Connor to say goodbye. Beccs went to get the car in the meantime, giving us some privacy. But saying goodbye to him, considering that my best friend could still hear everything, was even harder than it already was.

"Thank you for this magical evening." The words flowed tenaciously like honey over my lips.

Should I kiss him goodbye? Give him a hug? Or call him Mr. Lancester again?

"No, I need to thank you for such a lovely evening," Connor smiled. The flash in his eyes signaled to me that he wasn't thinking about the evening, but about the night with me.

"Well, I guess we'll sneak me through the hotel now," I said, rubbing my forearm sheepishly.

"Good luck." Connor winked at me before stepping up close. "I sure hope you're thinking of me every step of the way."

Wow. Connor really knew how to drive me crazy.

"Well, in you go," Rebecca prompted me as she returned with the serving cart. I looked one last time at Connor, who grinned at me and said, "What are you waiting for? Get on your knees."

"You're enjoying this a little too much for my taste," I complained. I then got down on my knees, lifted the heavy white tablecloth of the serving cart and climbed under it. The cart looked much bigger on the outside than it was on the inside. I had to crouch down, but even then, the tops of my feet were sticking out and my back pressed firmly against the underside of the tabletop. Under my torso I wedged the pumps and my new handbag.

Fortunately, I did not suffer from claustrophobia, otherwise the whole plan would have failed. Of course, my position was anything but comfortable, but I could endure it for a few minutes.

I stretched my arm once again under the tablecloth and held my palm up.

"Can you give me another bunch of grapes like that? They're just too delicious," I asked.

"How can you think about food right now?" My best friend sighed; nevertheless, right after that I felt the weight of a big bunch of grapes on my hand.

"If you've tried one, you know what I'm talking about!" I replied confidently.

Quiet smacking, followed by a short groan. "You're right!"

"Told you." I would have nodded in agreement, but my head was wedged between the tabletop, my knees, and my purse.

"Okay, I'll go now," Rebecca said. The car slowly started moving, and I groaned. Logically, the service cart now weighed over fifty kilograms more than usual. I hope the rollers didn't break under my weight! I didn't need a broken service cart on my list of failures.

"Mr. Lancester, it's been an honor. Let us know if you need anything else," Beccs said goodbye in the usual maid's manner.

"Nice to meet you, too," Connor replied. "I'm sure I'll see you around."

Yes, I hope so too.

I saw nothing through the thick fabric, but thanks to my hearing I was not completely disoriented. I heard the door to the room open and close again shortly after. Then Beccs pushed me through the long corridor until we reached the staff elevator.

"Dana? Is there something you want to tell me?"

"Um, nooo?" I dragged out my answer to seem more innocent.

Bing.

The elevator doors opened. I was shaken violently as the rollers were pushed over the edges of the elevator floor. Now that I had to rely only on my sense of hearing and balance, I blanked out all other senses. I felt the movements of the elevator, very gentle and steady, accompanied by a soft hissing sound that I had never noticed before.

"And you just happened to forget to mention yesterday that you were dating the hottest guest in the entire hotel, no, the entire planet?"

"Don't let your hubby hear you say that!" I indignantly said.

"Dana Swanson, don't change the subject!"

"Okay, I was going to tell you. Yesterday I was looking for you everywhere, but then you had to go to Emma and through all the excitement, well, I just forgot. Is everything really okay with Emma?" I asked worriedly.

"Yes, she had skinned her knee while playing, but nothing needed stitches. The shock was still so deep that she couldn't stop crying until I got there. Oh, my little mouse ... wait a minute! Dana, you're doing it again!"

"I would never do that," I replied innocently. "And she picked the rainbow unicorn patch, didn't she?"

"Dana!" reprimanded Beccs with a laugh.

Bing.

Shortly after, it rumbled again, then Rebecca pushed the car along the aisle at a constant speed. As long as my best friend kept silent, I kept my mouth shut, too. Guests could stand in the hallway, and maids talking to themselves didn't look very professional, and maids pushing another maid in front of them in a cart certainly didn't!

"So, are you going to tell me how you ended up dating this incredibly well-built billionaire?"

"As he had said, he just asked me."

"Details, Dana! I need details. As your best friend and partner in crime, I insist on the dirty details, too, all right?" Rebecca was terribly excited. Her voice squeaked in joyful anticipation of my answer.

"I'm not sure where to start."

"From the beginning. where did you first see each other?"

"In his suite," I replied curtly. Admittedly, I was embarrassed to tell her the details of our encounter, when she had warned me against making just such mistakes. Yes, in the highly unlikely event that I would later have children and grandchildren, that would be a great grandma story, but my being a grandmother in thirty years and the reality were two completely different worlds that would probably never overlap.

"Where were you exactly? What did you do? And then? Don't let everything come out of your nose!"

I took a deep breath to be able to answer the volleys of questions.

"I was just in the walk-in closet..."

"Shh! Quiet! Shannon Williams is coming!"

I had never been so happy to meet my boss. Then it struck me that it was the worst possible time of all. If she found me in that serving cart, that was it for my job, and for good. I held my breath and hoped I wouldn't get calf cramps or sneezing attacks.

"Good morning," greeted Beccs over-friendly. The hysteria in her voice could not be ignored.

"Morning," Shannon Williams greeted back. "What are you doing here?"

"This is the serving cart from the suite on the forty-ninth floor. I'll bring it back."

"I didn't know there was access to the kitchen here, too." It hadn't been a question. Still, my boss didn't miss the opportunity to lecture Beccs. "There are only a couple of offices here and the staff locker room," Ms. Williams said in a critical voice.

"Jab. That's right," Beccs replied uneasily. "Where the hell did I put my head!"

"Be careful not to make mistakes like this more often."

"No. I mean, yes. I'll pay attention. I'll make my way back to the elevator then."

"I'll go with you. I need to talk to the sommelier about the non-alcoholic juice accompaniment in the entrecote, they only gave it nine out of ten points, which is unacceptable."

"That's terrible." I could clearly hear the sarcasm in Rebecca's voice.

Entrecôte was one of the hotel's fine-dining restaurants and had held three Michelin stars for years. In total, five of the twelve restaurants had at least one star, something the house was very proud of, but given the high prices, I had never dared to try any of them.

When Rebecca pushed the car back into the elevator, I held my breath. The car rumbled much louder than usual, which my boss fortunately didn't register.

"Say..." Shannon Williams thought for a moment before continuing, "Have you seen Dana? I've been radioing her all morning, but she keeps making excuses. I almost feel like she's avoiding me - or not even here."

"Yes. The last time I saw her was on the forty-ninth floor. I'm sure she'll get back to you in a minute."

I grinned at Rebecca's half-truths.

"I'll just radio them again," Shannon Williams said I heard fabric rustling.

"No!" cried Rebecca. But too late.

"Daaanaaa!" she shouted into the radio in her usual shrill voice.

Since the two radios were only a few feet apart at best, there was massive feedback with high-frequency squealing.

Ouch!

Like long fingernails scratching on the blackboard, only a thousand times louder. So loud that I heard nothing at all for a second. But the worst thing was that I was not allowed to make a sound. No sighing, no whining, I had to bear my pain silently and quietly.

Rebecca groaned loudly.

"Elevators malfunction like this all the time," Rebecca lied. Of course, she knew full well that the feedback was caused by the short distance.

"Really? That's never happened to me before!"

Shannon Williams also seemed confused. "I'll put that on the rules list right away. No more radio in the elevator. You can't put anyone through that!"

"Yeah, sounds great."

"Oh my, how time flies!" Shannon Williams pressed another button. "I'm running late. Tell the sommelier I'll be late, right now I have to take care of Mr. Lancester. Mr. Campbell and I have a meeting with our most valued guest."

Wow. Mr. Calvin Lloyd Campbell – chief executive and son of founder Sir Clinton Campbell, was otherwise rarely a guest at his own hotel, although everyone knew his name and pronounced it with reverence.

"That's great, I suppose," Rebecca said thoughtfully.

"Yes, it is," Shannon Williams replied.

I wondered what they had to discuss with Connor.

The elevator slowed down and the doors opened. Judging by the noise level, we were in the lobby.

Shannon Williams stepped off the elevator, her heels echoing across the marble floor. Just before the doors closed, she paused. "Please remove all flowers on the thirty-eighth floor. One guest is allergic to them and sneezes all the time. I don't know why, but some maid put a bunch of flowers in said guest's suite yesterday. Take care of it, will you?"

Great.

My failed just-try-it-on briefly action had made bigger waves than I would have liked, and my hotel-internal criminal record was getting longer and longer, but at least a duplicate was made from the one earring I still had.

"Of course, I will," Beccs called after our boss before the doors closed again and we were alone. We continued our involuntary journey to the third basement, where the kitchen for the breakfast buffet was located.

"Really intense what's been going on the last two days, don't you think, Dana?"

"You can say that again."

There was quite a lot of activity on the third basement floor. Pots clattered, dishes clanged, people shouted and screamed, and quick footsteps echoed through the corridors. Down there, far from the view of the critical guests, the atmosphere was quite different from that in the public areas.

"I'm going to leave you here for a minute and get you a new uniform, okay?"

"Wait, what?" Before I could object, the car stopped, and Rebecca's footsteps moved away from me.

Unbelievably, Beccs had just left me somewhere in the middle of nowhere.

Then suddenly the car moved again. I peeked cautiously out from under the tablecloth and saw legs as thick as tree trunks tucked into plaid pants and white, half-closed shoes as big as banana boxes.

Oh no, please don't! I didn't know the cooks or assistant cooks particularly well, nor did I know the many kitchen helpers. There were simply far too many employees to know them all personally; I was already having trouble keeping track of the maids.

The chance of my being discovered was greater than I would have liked, and I had no idea what would happen if one of the cooks found me. I was still wearing my cocktail dress, but it was a little too late to pretend to be a guest now. Neither could I just jump out of the serving cart and shout hey, I'm a maid and I'm lost without it being brought to the attention of my boss one way or another. Situations like that spread faster than a California brush fire.

Can this day finally get better now, please?

14

Connor

I'm sorry, Mr. Lancester, otherwise Ms. Williams is very reliable," Calvin Lloyd Campbell apologized to me for the third time in a very short time. Again and again, the hotel manager looked at his gold Rolex and then pushed his black rimmed designer glasses back to the root of his nose.

"Even though Ms. Williams is not here yet, I would still like to talk about my request," I said. The request I had made at the front desk that morning sent ripples up to the executive floor. Now I was made to wait for a vice president. If it hadn't been for a very special preference, I would have disappeared again long ago.

"Of course, Mr. Lancester. What can we do for you?"

"I place the utmost importance on order and cleanliness, so I would like a maid on call," I said.

Of course, I didn't want just any maid, but a very specific one. I smiled at the thought of my girl. Dana didn't know it, but she had made a bigger impression on me than I would have liked. No woman I had ever met had made it to this point. Within one evening, Dana had me under her spell.

Damn, I wanted Dana so bad! I wanted to fuck her, tie her up, spank her bottom, fuck her even harder and possess her.

"I'm sure that can be arranged, Mr. Lancester," the hotel manager replied optimistically. "In fact, I believe our human resources manager already has a similar concept in the works."

"Excellent." I smiled in satisfaction. God, the things I would do to Dana now that I could call her to me on a whim all day long.

"Ah, here she comes at last," sighed Mr. Campbell with relief, pointing to Shannon Williams, who stopped directly in front of us with her head held high. She held a black briefcase pressed in front of her chest like a shield, clutching it so tightly that her fingernails left clear marks.

"Mr. Lancester, Mr. Campbell, I apologize, there was a medical emergency."

"I hope it's nothing serious," I said.

Ms. Williams shook her head. "Allergic shock, but everything is fine now."

"Glad to hear it. Have a seat." I pointed to the empty chair.

"Thank you."

Although Mr. Campbell was at pains to be discreet, the punishing glances in the direction of his deputy did not escape me. "Mr. Lancester would like a personal maid on call."

"What do you think about a personalized pager? That way you can reach the maid easily and quickly."

I nodded. "I like that idea. How long will it take to implement?"

"I'll get right on it."

"Great. I would like Dana Swanson to get the pager, please."

Whenever I spoke Dana's name, I saw her face in front of me. With slightly parted lips and shining eyes, she gave me reverent looks.

"Dana Swanson? Is there any particular reason for that?" Shannon Williams looked at me thoughtfully before noting the name.

"Yes. I like her low-key demeanor, and she does a good job."

I was damn sure that Dana would soon be anything but restrained. Soon I would form a shining diamond from this rough diamond. Just thinking about how I would push Dana beyond her limits made me feel my erection awakening. Admittedly, I loved testing, crossing and pushing boundaries. Obviously, Dana had plenty of boundaries I could cross with her once she was my sub.

"Miss Swanson will be all yours." I was about to stand up when Shannon Williams took a deep breath and slid papers from her folder in front of me.

"Mr. Lancester, if I may, there is something else we would like to discuss with you."

"You have ten minutes."

"I'm putting together the lineup for next year with my sommeliers, not only for the Royal Renaissance Hotel in New York, but also at our other properties. We definitely want to have your name on it next season."

"I am flattered," I replied. My wines and liqueurs were praised to the skies by critics, and rightly so. For my Swiss apple liqueur alone, I had two dozen different apple varieties planted in order to combine them into the ideal blend of fruity sweetness and acidity. It had taken three years to achieve perfection. But what could I say? I was only satisfied with the very best.

"We are mainly interested in wine, more specifically, Cabernet Sauvignon de Música for our restaurants. And possibly a liqueur based on it. You can see the order of magnitude for the different houses in the documents."

Cabernet Sauvignon de Música was the first wine I had produced. The name was a tribute to the theme song of Tetris, Music A, which was known by everyone who had played Tetris even once.

The offer sounded interesting until I saw how many bottles the Royal Renaissance Hotel wanted to order.

"As tempting as your offer sounds, I'm going to have to pass."

Mr. Campbell cleared his throat. "I'm sure we can agree on a good price, Mr. Lancester."

Again, I shook my head. "It's not about the price for me, it's about the quantity. We grow the grapes only in the best locations and thin out the stock on the vines to get a higher sugar content. With these quantities, I could never maintain the quality."

"That's unfortunate," Ms. Williams sighed.

Mr. Campbell finished his Chateau Margaux in one gulp. "Give the offer some more thought, Mr. Lancester, and tell us your terms."

"Of course." But my interests and those of the Royal Renaissance Hotel were too far apart for an agreement. I was not willing to lower the quality of my wine in favor of quantity, not a chance.

Out of the corner of my eye, I saw a woman in a bright pink jumpsuit at the reception desk, which was diagonally opposite the VIP lounge. Only one self-confident woman in New York wore such garish clothes - Deborah. She gestured wildly to a frozen bellboy.

"Now, if you'll excuse me?" I said goodbye formally, because I had no interest in a stiff chat with the hotel manager and the personnel manager. Dana had told me enough about these slave drivers, albeit through the grapevine, to know what sort of person I was dealing with.

"But of course. My pleasure, Mr. Lancester," Mr. Campbell replied.

When Deborah saw me, she put her hands on her hips and let out a sharp scream.

"Connor! What a surprise to see you here!"

"Nice to see you too, Deborah."

I usually only met Deborah at high society events. We hugged briefly, and then Deborah adjusted the Gucci buckle of her ankle-length jumpsuit.

As she did so, she watched with eagle eyes as the bellboys brought their suitcases toward the elevator. "Careful, those are designer suitcases!"

"Remember I mentioned yesterday that I was here?"

"I forgot all about that." Deborah grabbed her head for a moment. "So, you're going to stay here a little longer, right?"

"Yes, until my parents' gala. I promised my mom."

"This is so great! Your parents' gala is always so glamorous," Deborah gushed as she pulled her Ray-Ban sunglasses off her forehead and polished the lenses.

"And for a good cause," I added.

"Do you have a companion? This ... Nadine, no. Sonya? What was her name?"

"Your memory for names is really terrible, Deborah." Deborah just shrugged her shoulders as she looked at me expectantly.

"Her name is Dana and yes, I hope she will join me."

Immediately, I thought of how beautiful Dana looked in evening gowns and imagined myself leading her through the Lancester estate, paying special attention to the secluded pool house or the hedge maze, for an adventurous stopover. Perhaps I could also lead Dana into the sprawling grounds, which now had nothing but the chirping of crickets and the light of the stars.

To be precise, I felt like going to all three places one after the other with Dana. There she would bow to my commands, not because I forced her, but because she had given me this power. I smiled transfigured.

"Hello, Earth to Connor?" called Deborah's attention with a wave.

"I was lost in thought."

"Yeah, I noticed, so now you're taking me out to lunch? I hear the lobster with truffled butter sauce is great."

"Another time, Deborah. I may have another meeting."

"Maybe? You're canceling on me because of someone else's maybe? Shame on you, Connor Lancester." Her lips twisted into a pout.

Sighing, I looked at my watch. "Can I make it up to you with a drink? I'd have some time for that."

"All right, one drink," Deborah grinned. She clung to my forearm and didn't let go until we reached the bar. I don't know why, but Deborah had never acted so agitated and pushy before.

15

Dana

The service cart in which I was hiding was pushed into the large, open kitchen, I could hear it, but especially smell it. It smelled wonderful! Of freshly baked pastries, coffee and boiling jam. Carelessly, my stash rumbled against another car and came to a stop.

Cautiously, I peered under the tablecloth through the kitchen. I saw about a dozen cooks and kitchen helpers and heard a variety of other voices beyond that.

It was loud and hot here. The burly guy who had pushed the serving cart moved away with quick steps, and I dared to exhale in relief. At least I was out of danger for the moment.

What now? I had no idea, so I could only wait for Beccs, who hopefully brought me a uniform. That is, if Rebecca found me here at all. But I couldn't hide in a serving cart in the kitchen all day either.

"Why does this happen to me of all people?" I asked myself in a whisper.

Because you magnetically attract chaos, my cynical subconscious replied.

Yes, the more I wanted to stay out of everything, the deeper I was drawn into the chaos. In any case, I hadn't volunteered to be the mouthpiece for over ninety maids.

I sighed. The more I tried to stay away from problems, the more likely I was to be haunted by them. Okay, I was definitely not innocent in my situation, I had put on someone else's dress in a suite and thought I would just get away with it. Wrong thinking! Karma.

I looked out the other side of the car. There were other wagons next to me, and they were being re-covered one by one. Oh, oh, that was not good.

The two kitchen helpers worked damn fast. Probably because they had to make up carts by the dozen every day. They covered the cart, removed the tablecloth, cleaned the metal frame, and then covered everything anew.

Five more cars until it was my turn. The two women were talking about the latest episode of a soap opera that I only knew from commercials.

Jesus, Rebecca, hurry up!

"Brad cheated on Natasha. With Marc! Can you believe it? With Marc!" the older kitchen help said. Her grating voice seemed even more excited than usual because of the drastic turn of events.

The younger kitchen help let out a pointed cry: "What? I wish I had seen the episode. Stupid shift work! And how did John react to it? Does he even know?"

Four more cars. The voices became louder.

"Well, how about that! He snapped and had revenge sex with June."

"I can't believe it," the younger girl sighed.

I tried to remember the name of the show, to no avail. Something about Gossip. Anyway, the ads I had seen had already announced that there were many dramatic twists in the series.

Only three more cars stood between me and the two women. Actually, I should come up with a plan B and look for a solution, but my brain only used its gray cells to find out what the name of the damn series was.

Two cars. My heart hammered painfully against my chest, and the search for the series title continued. Heavens!

Only one more car and no solution in sight. Even the name of the TV series wouldn't come to mind.

I braced myself for the worst. Only a few more seconds and the two women would pull the tablecloth from the serving trolley and discover me.

Grand Valley Gossip! That was the name of the series. Good, then at least one thing would be cleared up.

The two women were now standing on either side of the car clearing the dishes as they continued to talk about the wonderfully defined contours of Brad and how well he would fit Michael.

The tablecloth was lifted at the corners. I held my breath.

Maybe I could talk the two women down and convince them to keep it to themselves?

Yeah, right. No way.

I definitely offered far too much press for that. A maid in a guest's designer dress hiding in the service cart was at least as big an issue as Oscar the snake had been back then.

The tablecloth was raised so that my legs and arms were completely visible from the outside. Maybe they wouldn't even notice that I was sitting in the lower part?

Footsteps approached. A hand crashed so loudly on the metal plate of the serving cart that I winced in shock.

"Hello!"

Beccs' timing had never been better! The tablecloth was dropped again, and I took a deep breath.

"Hello," the older kitchen help replied irritably.

I felt Rebecca press solid fabric against the tablecloth: a rolled-up new uniform, which I gratefully accepted, hoping our little smuggle went unnoticed.

Now I just had to get out of the car to change somewhere undisturbed.

"It's pretty busy in here, in the kitchen," my best friend babbled on.

"Right, so now we need to get back to work," the younger girl said. Her hands gripped the tablecloth again. With her foot, Rebecca kicked promptly in my direction. I stood on the long side, while the two kitchen helpers stood on the two long sides. The kick was a sign that I should climb out, or so I hoped. Cautiously, I stuck my head outside. The coast was clear, and I crawled past Rebecca out of the service cart. Now where to go? I couldn't just get up and charmingly smile and leave the kitchen.

"Wait a minute. Before I go again, you have to tell me..." Rebecca faltered.

"Yessss?"

"Um, I need to know where the refrigerators are. I need to get something," Rebecca made up an excuse. "Yeah, right. From the refrigerators, that's why I'm here."

"What do you need? Everything is stored separately here because of allergies, cross-contamination and so on."

Was that a hint from Rebecca that I should crawl into one of the large cooling chambers? Was the coast clear? Or was she just saying what was on her mind out of excitement? I saw the ajar door to one of the chambers directly in front of me. But since there were kitchenettes and sideboards to the left and right, I didn't have a clear view.

"Oh, um. I think it's in the big refrigerator. Right, that one over there."

Rebecca pointed with both hands to a large walk-in refrigerator about ten feet from my position. Yes, the more than exaggerated gesture was unmistakable. I crawled off.

"There's only raw vegetables and leafy greens. Spinach, iceberg lettuce, cabbage. Celery. That kind of thing."

"Yes, exactly. That's exactly what the guest wants, the guest wants fresh celery. A lot of fresh celery, in fact!" Rebecca nodded her head vigorously.

As quickly as I could, I continued to crawl across the rough kitchen floor, my uniform in my left hand, my bag in my right. In doing so, I made sure that my ball gown was not affected. The dress could not help my stupidity and should not suffer more than necessary. Besides, it was the only thing I had as a souvenir of last night.

I came steadily closer to the refrigerated chambers. In the background, I could hear Rebecca talking to the two kitchen helpers about the eccentric wishes of guests.

Only a few more feet! Hopefully, my negative karma had been used up by now. I really didn't need a cook who stumbled and dumped a fifteen-quart pot of fresh pudding or boiled jam on me.

Fortunately, nothing like that happened on my long walk to the cooling chamber. I reached my locker room without any third-degree burns or blocks of knives crashing down on me, and from the looks of it, no one had seen me either. Especially the latter bordered almost on a miracle in this busy kitchen.

Now I wasted no time. I jumped up, peeled myself out of the adorable dress that had survived the action intact and put on my uniform.

With a heavy heart, I rolled up the cocktail dress tightly and stuffed it into the bag. Just as I had tied the cloth belt around me, the door was torn open.

"Rebecca! I am..." I faltered. "Hi!" Standing in front of me was not Rebecca, but a man. Judging by the stocky legs, it had been the guy who had pushed me here. Not only was he very strong in the legs, but his shoulders were pretty darn broad. He was carrying a large wooden box that contained about a dozen salads.

His outer appearance reminded me of bodybuilders who had overdone it with anabolic steroids. His face had an inscrutable expression on it. Jesus.

"What are you doing here?" His voice was deep and scary, definitely had the makings of a good super-villain.

"I wonder about that too," I replied, sighing.

Behind the kitchen helper's broad shoulders, I saw Beccs squeezing past him.

"She's helping me," Rebecca replied. Then she grabbed the first box that was in the room and pushed it into my hand. "You know, there's always a lot of chaos during Fashion Week. The guest on the forty-ninth floor is causing tremendous chaos right now!"

First the potential super-villain looked critically at Beccs, then at me, and his hard features softened. I dared to breathe again. "Yeah, sure. Always something going on here," he replied, shrugging. He moved aside, making room for Rebecca and me. Carrying a box of celery and a box of potatoes, Beccs and I fled the kitchen. We had really made it, even if I felt like a thief for having taken twenty kilos of potatoes.

At the end of the aisle, I set the heavy box down and hugged my best friend.

"Beccs, you've really been a lifesaver for me!"

"I get it," Rebecca grinned. She placed the box of celery next to the potatoes, crossed her arms in front of her chest, and asked thoughtfully, "What do we do with it now?"

"When in doubt, we should destroy the evidence," I said, chuckling and rubbing my stomach. My best friend immediately realized that destroy was the same as eat.

"And who peels all the potatoes?"

"Okay. How about we just put them on hold? Later on, at some point. So, it won't be so noticeable." I looked around. "The best thing to do is just put them there in the corner. No one will find them there."

"Okay. That does sound like a plan. Now, hurry back to the upper floors! We're mighty behind schedule."

"I have a feeling this is going to be a really long day of work."

"Hopefully long enough for you to tell me about all the details!"

Rebecca pressed the button for the ride upstairs. At this time of day, most of the elevators were free because the maids were doing their work in the rooms, and most of the guests who could order something were out, so it didn't take long for the elevator to arrive. At first it had irritated me that it was just as dead quiet in the morning, the time after breakfast, as it was at midnight.

"You said something earlier about your trophy. What was that again? I was too distracted by steel-hard abs."

I laughed. "Connor found my trophy."

"So, he heard you sing? And he still went out with you?" Rebecca teased me.

"Beccs, that's not funny!"

"Yes, it is," she grinned, "and now I want to know everything else. Every detail!"

Because Rebecca still had to place cleaning orders at the reception, we went to the lobby. On the way there, I told my best friend everything that had happened the previous evening. The ball, the music, the dance, my loudly beating heart, and Connor's courteous manner.

"Dana, that sounds really beautiful," Rebecca gushed.

"Oh yeah. Just like a fairy tale, only it was all real!"

"Do you think there could be more to it?"

I thought about it for a long time.

"I don't think so. I mean, he's very nice. And attractive. But also very confident..."

"And don't forget he's a billionaire!" Rebecca grinned up to both ears.

"Yeah, he's filthy rich, too."

"So, what are you waiting for? Throw yourself at him."

"No. I think it was a one-time thing. I was a nice companion, and that's what I got the dress for."

Rebecca narrowed her eyes thoughtfully. Actually, I wanted to keep the details to myself.

"Wait a minute. How did this deal come about again?"

"Well, that was one of those things," I beat around the bush.

"What kind of thing, exactly?"

Beccs chastised me again with a you're-hiding-something look.

"Okay! He caught me admiring the dress. Satisfied?"

For clarification, I held up my bag, which contained the dress.

"And then he just asked you to go to this wedding with him?"

"Yes." I nodded.

"Why do I get the feeling that this isn't the end of it?"

"I'm afraid so. That one night was magical, but I don't think there will be a second." Alas.

I sighed heavily, because of course I wished to get to know Connor better, but I realistically estimated my chances to be zero.

Rebecca shook her head. "This is all so unbelievable, Dana! You were invited to a wedding by a mysterious hot billionaire, you even slept at his place – probably with him, too – and now you're just throwing in the towel without a fight?"

"I'm just a maid, after all, and far too old to still believe in fairy tales. What can I offer him?"

"Hello? Did you even notice the way he looked at you? You were clearly more than just a maid to him. Besides, you're more to me too! Fact is, a guy who collects your lost trophy, finds you again and drags you to a wedding sounds suspiciously like a modern Prince Charming. Something like that screams happy ending! Never heard of laws of physics?"

"I doubt the laws of physics have anything to do with it," I said, grinning away my heartbreak. Still, I pondered Beccs' words as she hugged me and planted a friendly kiss on my cheek.

Of course, I had also felt that there was more between me and Connor than met the eye, a connection we couldn't deny. I had clearly felt that, and judging by his looks, he had felt it too. The way Connor had looked at me, he had to feel the same way!

The elevator doors opened.

"Hmm, maybe you're right after all," I replied to my best friend.

"Of course, I am!"

Grinning, we headed to the front desk so Rebecca could turn in the cleaning order when a loud laugh echoed over to us from the VIP area next to the bar area.

God, I immediately recognized the voice among thousands of voices.

Deborah.

I immediately held my hand in front of the left side of my face and turned my back to the VIP area.

"What is it?" whispered Rebecca.

"That is Deborah Landry. She was at the wedding, too."

"You know her?" Rebecca stared into the VIP section. "Oh, there's Connor, too."

Immediately, my heart began to flutter when I heard his name. I risked a glance over my shoulder and saw Deborah and Connor sitting together in the VIP area laughing. I had no right to do this, but I felt cheated. Bravely, I gritted my teeth and swallowed my frustration.

"She threw herself at Connor like I wasn't even there."

"Yeah, she looks like that, too."

I would have loved to join them, but I wasn't allowed to, or I would be exposed as a maid. That was the best thing for both of us. Connor could save face, and I could keep my job.

Not to mention, Connor was not my boyfriend. So, I didn't even have the right to judge him now or be angry that he was seeing Deborah.

I wonder if he knew how shallow Deborah really was under her tons of makeup. No. For some reason, she was his blind spot.

I pulled Rebecca to me by the shoulders.

"You have to cover me up, so she doesn't see me."

"Why?"

"Because Deborah doesn't know I'm just a maid!"

"No?"

"No! I pretended to be Connor's girlfriend at the wedding. No one knew I was just his maid. I can't let that get around either, or Shannon Williams will kick me out!"

Too many things had clearly happened lately that could lead to dismissal. I took another cautious look over my shoulder. Deborah and Connor were no longer sitting in one of the boxes, but at the entrance to the VIP area.

"We have to leave now!" Naked panic spread through me.

"Okay, okay. Take a breath, Dana. We'll be fine. The stairwell is closer than the elevators. Let's go there," Rebecca said calmly, pulling me behind her.

"How can you stay so calm?"

"You've never been to the grocery store with Emma when Crunchy Crinkles was sold out, have you?"

I laughed. Yes, Emma loved those chocolate chip cookies more than anything, and if Rebecca wasn't careful, her daughter would feed only on them.

Once in the stairwell, I took a deep breath.

"We really need to find out how long Deborah has been here."

"Stop painting the devil on the wall. Maybe she's just visiting Connor?"

"Yes. Or she moved in with him," I replied cynically.

"I guess your optimism knows no bounds today," Rebecca joked.

Although I fought back the grin, I couldn't suppress it. Rebecca rummaged around in her deep pockets sewn into the dress and pulled out my radio and key card.

"Before I forget, here are your things."

"You're a sweetheart. I owe you a huge favor!" I thanked her.

"No," Rebecca shook her head. "That makes us even. You saved my karaoke contest and Emma's birthday."

Rebecca rummaged around in her bag once again. Between her thumb and forefinger, she held something that I could not recognize at first glance. I stretched out my hand flat, and Rebecca dropped the object onto my palm.

That. Can. Not. Be. True.

"You owe me for that! I saw the single earring and thought that a single earring stands out much more than none at all. That's why I kept it."

"Oh, Rebecca." I was on the verge of tears.

"Don't argue with me, Dana. This has got to stop! Nostalgia or not," Rebecca continued to rebuke.

So, I hadn't lost the other earring at all, it had been with Rebecca the whole time.

"Where's the other earring?" asked Rebecca, noticing my contrite face.

"With a jewelry designer at New York Fashion Week."

"For God's sake! What is he doing with it?!"

"Standing model for a duplicate. I thought I lost the other earring on the way to the forty-ninth floor. The thing with Connor ... and all the stress with Shannon Williams. I don't know where my head was either."

Rebecca put her head on the back of her neck and groaned loudly. "Dana, you're a magical attraction to bad luck."

I didn't object, but just took the earring and put it in my purse, which I still carried.

"We should get going. The rooms aren't going to do themselves," I rubbed my throbbing temples. "But first I have to close this bag in the locker."

"Sure, it's on the way. How soon can you get the earring back?"

"I'll try to do it as soon as possible."

Actually, I had no clue how to get the earring back. I had no cell phone numbers, no addresses, nothing. God, what was I thinking?

I had thought ... and hoped, that Connor would make contact again. But from the looks of it, he was having a great time with Deborah. My pride was more tarnished than I wanted to admit, and it felt awful to be replaced and forgotten so quickly.

It had only been one night and actually I had known what I was getting myself into, but still my heart broke a little bit.

"We shouldn't waste any more time," I said and ran up the stairs. Rebecca followed me to the second floor. From there we took the elevator up to the eighteenth floor, where there were employee locker rooms and also a large spare store of fresh linens and towels, cleaning carts, and miscellaneous cleaning supplies that served to restock the other stores.

I pulled the wrinkled dress out of my purse and hung it on a hanger in my locker.

"The poor dress." I pulled the fabric taut, saving what could be saved. For a brief moment, the wrinkles disappeared from the fabric, making the cocktail dress look immaculate again.

"Daaanaaa!" croaked from the radio.

"Damn, that's all I need," I groaned. With a flourish, I closed the locker door and got on the radio.

"Answer it already!" commanded Rebecca.

"Yes, Ms. Williams?" I asked angelically.

"The bed on the forty-ninth floor is to be made."

Connor's Suite.

"I'll take care of it."

"Right now!"

"But of course."

Had Connor actually gone to his suite with Deborah, and now I had to get rid of the evidence of their brief lovemaking? I felt sick, at the same time I tried to tell myself that Connor's bed was simply crumpled, and I mustn't read too much into the situation.

"I'm sorry, Rebecca. But can you ask the girls from downstairs if they can help you? I still owe them for the Easter event."

"Sure, I will. Is making the bed a secret code for anything between you and Connor?" asked Rebecca with a mischievous grin. She raised her eyebrow conspiratorially.

"No, I don't think so," I answered meekly. Then I made my way to the most expensive suite in the entire hotel.

Why was Connor so close to me? He had simply appeared in my life and had taken up residence in my thoughts without being asked. And from there, he seemed to control my entire body. Starting with my heartbeat, moving to my stomach tingling every time I just heard his name.

16

Connor

I leaned back in the comfortable chair, which creaked softly under my weight. It wasn't long before Dana knocked on my door. I would never have admitted it, but I counted the seconds as I enjoyed the smell of my Cabernet Sauvignon de Música, which brought back memories. But it wasn't just the wine that brought back memories; my shirt, which smelled like her, made me fantasize, too. It was as if her radiant eyes were still lighting in the room.

Damn, Dana had managed to make an incredible impression in the short time she had been there. Feelings resonated in me that I hadn't felt in a long time; together with my physical desire for her, it a dangerous mixture. I simply had to see Dana again, I just couldn't help it.

There was a knock at the door.

"Come in," I said and stood up.

Shyly, Dana stepped through the door. Her expression reflected uncertainty. "You want me to make up the bed ... sir?"

Hell, I enjoyed the salutation too much. When Dana called me sir, it sounded so reverent and full of respect. I put down the wine glass and walked toward Dana.

"Yes." My gaze caught her eyes. Dana bit her full, curved lips and bravely held my gaze. No doubt it must have taken great effort for her to return my gaze for so long.

I wonder what's going on in that pretty head of yours right now.

"Good, then I'll get right to work."

Dana smiled briefly, then walked past me, but I grabbed her arm and held her tight.

"Why so formal, fair lady?"

"I'm pressed for time and still have a lot to do," Dana replied curtly. Her voice sounded rushed. Yes, that she had a tight schedule, I took her word for it, but there was more. Her sudden, cool way of turning me away could have nothing to do with the time pressure.

"So?" I asked.

"What?"

"That's what I'm asking you, that's not all, is it?"

"No." Dana turned her face away and, sighed, pulling away to release my hand from her upper arm, but my grip tightened.

You're not getting away from me that easy, Dana!

"I want you to tell me what's going on." My voice was serious, as was my look.

"I'd like to know that, too. I mean, that's exactly the problem. I don't know what's going on between us." Her voice broke and she took a deep breath. "And I don't know if there's anything going on between us at all, or if I'm just imagining it."

Dana was close to tears. Poor thing, she was completely lost in the wind.

"What makes you think that?"

"I'm not stupid, Connor. I know what one-night stands are. I don't think I fit into ... your world."

"That's exactly why I called you. Because I want to find out if you fit into my world. I believe you do, and I wish that you did."

Dana looked at me critically. "What do you mean?"

"I have special preferences. We talked about that yesterday."

"The beast in the suit?"

"Exactly."

"I wish I could fit into your world, too," Dana whispered.

I had never seen a more sincere look, a look full of fear and devotion in equal measure. Her breathing calmed, and I felt her slowly relax.

My grip on her arm loosened. I wasn't holding her back anymore; I was just holding her.

"Then let's find out if you like it in my world," I replied gently. I offered her my hand and led her into the bedroom.

When Dana saw the freshly made bed, she paused. "But the bed is neat, isn't it?"

"Still," I replied.

"Well, well." Dana smiled audaciously. Her dismissive posture was gone, and curiosity remained. I untied the knot of her belt.

"I want to test your limits, I want to push you to your limits ... and beyond."

Dana's body shook. With excitement. With lust. With fear.

"You will hate me for this and love me at the same time. You'll beg me to tear down your boundaries."

Slowly I opened her dress. The heavy fabric slid down over her shoulders onto the floor. Under her dress, Dana wore only panties.

Her breasts lifted gently from her upper body, her nipples were stiff. Every muscle in her body was tense. Despite her insecurity, her upright posture was elegant and regal.

If Dana went this way, I would be the fire in her hell and the salvation in her heaven.

"You don't have to be afraid, Dana. I will take care of you and protect you. Do you trust me?"

"Yes, I trust you," Dana replied. "It sounds crazy, but it feels like I've known you my whole life."

"No, that doesn't sound crazy. You're like an open book to me, where I can easily read any secret, no matter how deeply buried."

Still, I would take my time exploring her boundaries. Building trust was a long, steady process. But for what I was about to do with Dana, trust was essential. Breaking down boundaries without trust was torture, not redemption – even for me.

"All right, we'll take our time. There are still a few things that need to be said, but we'll get to that later. Right now, I'm going to give you a taste of what's to come if you get involved with me."

I took her hand and led her to the bed. Dana immediately understood that she should lie down with her back on the bed. As she lay there, provocative and incredibly sexy, my pants became tight. Dana looked at me expectantly.

"Take your clothes off."

Slowly, Dana pulled her panties down to the middle of her thighs, then bent her legs and got rid of the fabric completely. It drove me half-crazy that she lay naked in front of me but covered her most intimate parts. When would she finally understand how beautiful she was?

At the same time, she looked at me expectantly. Yes, I had some plans for her, but first I had to take care of this senseless wall of insecurity and fear of judgment. This facade, behind which Dana was hiding, would be the first thing I would tear down.

Dana was beautiful, there was no reason to hide her body. Her body was to worship, but she became a goddess only when she understood that herself.

"Touch yourself," I commanded.

Surprised, Dana looked at me. "Don't you want to do that?"

"No. I want you to touch yourself!"

Mechanically, Dana's hands ran over her body.

"Not like that. Touch yourself the way you want to be touched by me!"

Her movements became softer, more sensitive. Slowly Dana let herself get involved in the situation. At first Dana only ran over the beginnings of her breasts until she got used to the strange situation. She pinched her own nipples and moaned slightly. Dana touched herself, apparently feeling herself this way for the first time. I was sure that she would experience many more first times with me.

"Yes, just like that," I said. "Convince me with your body that I should fuck you now!"

Dana sighed sensually while touching herself. Again and again, she looked at me and smiled with satisfaction, because I did not hide my enthusiasm.

With a dark, greedy look, I watched Dana lolling gracefully in bed and smiling seductively at me. She knew exactly what she was doing at that moment. Yes, I was sure that Dana was consciously driving me crazy right now. Maybe because she was already delirious thanks to my previous words and wanted me to follow her? But possibly she had also taken pleasure in simply wanting to drive me insane, because that's what she was doing.

"You've won me over," I said. "God, Dana, I like you so incredibly much."

"And I like what you say." Boldly, Dana bit her lower lip.

Yes, I had crossed the first hurdle. Her insecurity was no longer an issue, at least for the moment. Now I could move on. I went to the wine cooler and took out a large, square ice cube.

The dew dripping down on Dana even before the ice touched her skin made her shiver. From those tiny, ice-cold dewdrops, goosebumps spread in waves all over her body. Her skin looked so beautiful when she shivered. When I brushed the ice cube over her belly, Dana inhaled sharply.

"Cold?" I asked her with a teasing grin. "I'll stop when it's too cold for you."

"No, refreshing," Dana pressed out between clenched teeth. I had hoped that my offer to stop would scratch her pride, because I loved it when women defied me. I needed women with character! I could do nothing with will-less dolls.

"Well then." I ran the ice cube over her belly, and the closer I got to her beautiful breasts, the faster Dana's breathing became. Her hands dug deep into the fabric of the bedspread. When the ice touched her sensitive, stiff nipples, Dana moaned loudly.

"So, still refreshing?"

"Yes! Feels really great," Dana gasped.

"Good, I'm not going to stop doing that until the ice melts."

Alternately, I rubbed the ice cube over both of her breasts. Dana's body squirmed beautifully under my touch. The longer I touched Dana with the ice, the hotter her body became. When I could no longer control myself, I placed the ice cube on her flat stomach and began to unbutton my shirt.

"Hold still. If the ice falls off, I'll get another ice cube."

Immediately, Dana held her breath. The ice cube slid menacingly back and forth on its own dew.

I had unbuttoned half of my shirt, but with each additional button I took more time. Dana stared intently at the ceiling and controlled her breathing with the greatest effort, while I enjoyed the sight.

"You know," I began. "I wanted you for myself from the first time we met."

"Really?" asked Dana, looking me straight in the eye. She bit her lips and tried to stay controlled while fire burned in her gaze.

"Yes. I've had some women, and I've owned some women. But never did any of those women call me sir as passionately as you do."

For a second, Dana smiled proudly. At the same time, she continued to focus her body tension. She was doing really bravely, and I was sure that we both would have a lot of fun together.

When the last button of my shirt was undone, I released Dana and reached for the ice cube. By now, the ice had shrunk by more than half. Dana sighed with relief and relaxed as the ice cube continued to slide over her skin, leaving a wet, cold trail.

"You forgot to thank me," I admonished her.

"For what?" asked Dana, irritated.

"For not having to hold still anymore."

Dana giggled until she saw my serious look, then immediately fell silent. "Really?"

"Yes. But today I will be lenient. The situation is foreign to you. We'll talk more about your rights and responsibilities later, after I fuck you."

Dana nodded. She sighed loudly as I ran the ice cube along the inside of her thighs.

"I'm still waiting," I said, pressing the ice cube harder against her skin.

"Thank you," Dana said quickly. She was silent for a moment, then added, "Sir," uncertainly.

"Good girl," I praised her. When the ice cube was completely melted, I took off my pants. My manhood was hard and ready, I couldn't wait to finally fuck Dana. My cock, which had been pressing painfully against my pants the whole time, saw it that way too.

Dana licked her lips lasciviously when she saw my big, hard cock. I threw the clothes next to the bed and reached for Dana's cloth belt, which I doubled and put around Dana's right wrist. Then I pulled the ends through the loop and turned her arm to the side so that her whole body moved with it, until she was finally lying on her stomach. This allowed me to tie the two wrists together on her back.

"That's how I like you," I moaned, rubbing my manhood against her bare bottom. With the flat of my hand, I slapped her magnificent round ass. Dana gasped in surprise. Her head was tilted to the side, but she still had a good view of me.

A second time, my hand whizzed down, this time on the other buttock. Alternately, I worked on her two cheeks that slowly took on more and more color.

With each stroke, Dana gasped before it turned into a moan.

"You like that?" I asked, and Dana immediately nodded.

"Then say it."

"I like it," Dana moaned. "But it also drives me crazy."

"That I beat you or that you like it?"

"Both. I want to move, to fight back, I want to touch you and at the same time I want even tighter bonds."

"Good."

"Connor? What are you doing to me?" asked Dana fearfully.

"I'll set you free."

My hands had immortalized themselves in red traces for the moment on Dana's skin. In this and many other ways, I would immortalize myself many more times. But Dana's body would not only bear visible traces, no, I would also leave traces that no one else could see.

With my hand, I pushed her legs apart. When I felt her wetness, I moaned softly. I liked how Dana's body reacted to me. A clear sign that Dana was the one. Moaning and orgasms could perhaps still be faked, but arousal could not.

With two fingers, I penetrated Dana and her body quivered. She pushed herself as far against me as she could. God, she was so tight ... so wet.

Actually, I had intended to spank her ass a little more, but it didn't work. The pressure was too great. I felt ready to explode if I did not take Dana now, on the spot. Hard and deep and again and again.

I pulled my fingers out of her and replaced them with my cock, which entered her effortlessly. Dana moaned loudly as my manhood filled her completely. I took her exactly as I had intended. Mercilessly, I thrust my hard cock into her, again and again, deeper and deeper. Dana gasped with each thrust, her eyelids fluttered, and her center pulsed rhythmically. Not long now, and she came.

"Please," Dana pleaded. "Please fuck me harder."

Of course, I was happy to comply with the request. As hard as I could, I pushed. It felt incredible, I was high on her moans, addicted to her tightness.

"You like that? Getting fucked hard and deep? The way you deserve?"

"Yes," Dana cried hoarsely. "Yes!"

I growled with excitement and grabbed her hips so I could fuck her even harder. A glistening film of sweat formed on Dana's back, her body twitched and trembled more and more wildly. She was completely in ecstasy.

Damn, Dana was so horny right now that she would do anything for me to be allowed to come. But now I just wanted to hear her scream; I wanted to hear, feel, see how she surrendered to her climax, which was imminent at any moment.

"Come for me," I whispered. My gentle tone was in stark contrast to the ferocity with which I fucked Dana.

"Thank you, sir!"

God, she is so innocent and so spoiled...

Dana's climax was intense. As tight as she tightened around me, I couldn't help but come myself with pumping movements.

Fuck, there had been a whole lot piled up since last night, which now discharged in a violent orgasm.

I gently settled on her back, kissed her shoulder blade and caught my breath for a moment. Dana's abdomen was still twitching, continuing to massage my manhood, and I enjoyed every single second of it.

When we both calmed down a bit, I untied the knot around Dana's wrists.

"Have I met the beast in the suit now?" asked Dana.

"A very small part of it, yes," I replied with a smile. "How much you will see of the beast is entirely up to you."

Dana smiled shyly at me and covered her body with the bedspread. She was simply incredible. Just now she had screamed wildly and uninhibitedly as we had the most intense sex in the world, and the next second she was innocence personified again.

"Connor?"

"Yes, Dana?"

"How long are you going to be here?"

"As long as I want, definitely until the gala next month."

"That's nice." Dana snuggled against my shoulder.

"Why do you ask?"

"Oh, no reason. I think I should go again," Dana sighed and stood up. "I've been here way too long."

"Dana, you don't know me well yet, I know that. But when I ask something, I expect a real answer. So, why did you ask how long I'm going to be here?"

Dana looked at me guiltily as she put on her dress.

"Because I like to know beforehand how long this is going to last between us."

"And you think once I leave, it's over?"

Dana nodded. She put the belt, with which she had just been tied, around her waist.

"I'm just a maid, what can I offer you?"

"More than you think." I stood up and walked close to her. "You are great, you have character and a beautiful body. You're a rough diamond that just needs to be shaped and polished to make the most beautiful facets shine."

Dana lowered her gaze to the floor, but I lifted the tip of her chin with my index finger.

"Tell me why you really doubt, Dana," I asked seriously, but my voice was soft and understanding.

"I don't know why I can't resist you. Maybe because I don't want to. Your attraction is incredible, Connor. But I don't want to be a plaything you have short-term interest in. I don't want to be a petty number on your list of conquests."

"Shh." I interrupted Dana, putting my index finger to her lips. "When did I make you feel like you were just a toy or a number?"

"I saw you with Deborah earlier. The two of you looked so familiar..."

I laughed. "That's why you were so unsure earlier, isn't it?"

"Yes," Dana sighed.

"I assure you, I only have one girl at a time, and I choose wisely."

"And do you have a girl right now?" asked Dana.

"I'm not sure. Although she is wild and uninhibited in bed, at the same time she is very insecure."

"Sounds like you need to draw them out." Dana smiled.

"True. But I can only do that if she tells me when something is on her mind. I can only take her beyond her limits if I can trust her to talk to me. When the tide comes in, a dam can easily break if you shore it up in the wrong places."

"I think your girl can trust you enough if you give her the time."

Good. Very good. Dana had decided, and I kissed her. Long and intense. Her lips were so soft and sweet that I never wanted to break away from her again, so Dana took over for me. She slowly detached herself, albeit reluctantly.

"I've got to go, Connor. There's so much to do, and Rebecca's been covering for me all day. I can't leave her hanging now."

"Yes, I understand. I can talk to ... what was her name? That assistant manager who also takes care of the employees."

"Shannon Williams?"

"Yeah, right. I could talk to her about more staff," I offered.

"No way!"

"Why?"

"The last time a guest suggested more staff, there was overtime for all of us. Too few staff equates to laziness and bad work for the bosses. It's tight as hell, and there's no time for anything else, but we all get our jobs done. No matter how good your intentions, it wouldn't end well."

What a messed up personnel management. I had no idea why Dana was doing all this to herself, but I had the utmost respect for her.

"I understand."

"Thanks for trying, I appreciate it. How do you know the assistant manager, anyway?"

"I had a business meeting with her and the director this morning. She was late because she had to take care of another guest because of an allergy or something."

Dana's smile was gone from her face, as was all color.

"I hope the meeting went well?"

"It went pretty well for me, but not so much for management."

"Because she was late!?"

"No, because the offer didn't fit. Why do you ask?"

"Ms. Williams is sure to take her frustrations out on us again. Especially ... combined with the allergic reaction, it's too much. She hates it when things don't go according to plan." Dana took a deep breath. Her features relaxed, and she forced herself to smile. "It'll be fine."

"I'm sure they will. Heads won't roll."

"I'm not so sure about that. I've kept Rebecca waiting a really long time," Dana said.

"Speaking of which, my mother is still waiting for an acceptance letter for the gala. As my girl, of course it's your duty to accompany me."

"Really?" squealed Dana with delight. Then she cleared her throat and put on a more serious face but kept grinning. "I mean, of course I'm going to accompany you to this gala."

"Very well, I will tell her. But I have to go now too, my appointment in the city is waiting, and I have some things to do."

Actually, I should have been on my way by now, but it was more important to me to extend my deal with Dana.

"Okay. When will I see you again?" asked Dana. She looked at me with a sugary sweet gaze and irresistible lashes.

"How about tomorrow?"

"I'd love to. When do you want me to come over?"

"I'd say let me surprise you," I grinned. "I'll let you know, don't worry."

Dana looked at me expectantly. I didn't know what I was going to do with her, but by tomorrow, I was sure I'd think of one or two things.

17

Dana

I took cover behind a tall laundry cart. Again. Since my shift started four hours ago, this was my third time hiding from Deborah Landry, who went through the hotel like I went through my kitchen when I was hungry. Every single time, Deborah was glued to her pink, diamond-studded smartphone, bellowing her shrill voice across the hallways. It was impossible not to hear any of her conversations if you were on the same floor with her.

Have you heard this? Do you already know about that? Do you already know...

Yes, in the world of the rich and beautiful, there was obviously a lot to report. Sometimes it was the cousin's shoes, sometimes the hairstyle of the uncle's girlfriend. Basically, some accessory bordered on visual assault. Sometimes it also happened that the yoga instructor or the personal trainer had the impudence to be more physically fit than their clients.

Deborah's heels thundered across the carpeted floor toward the elevator, right past me.

Actually, I just wanted to take the used sheets outside, but since Deborah was a guest at the Royal Renaissance Hotel since yesterday, my work became unnecessarily complicated.

Maybe I should just talk to Deborah and explain the circumstances to her? Maybe her first ... and second impression had been deceiving, and she was actually the nice, young friend Connor saw her as.

"Oh, Virginia! You're so funny again," Deborah giggled. "You weren't at that event the other day, by any chance? Yes, the very one where Darlene Boyle fell down the stairs because her heel broke off. That was so embarrassing! Yeah, I would have loved to have seen that too."

Nope. I was right, it was Connor who was very wrong about her.

Snorting, I rolled my eyes. How could she ridicule an accident that sounded quite painful? Compassion obviously didn't exist in Deborah's world. It wasn't until Deborah had disappeared into the elevator that I went back to the suite I was finishing up.

There, I reupholstered all the pillows, fluffed them up, and then arranged them on the bed. Then I wiped the dust off the tables and dressers and vacuumed through.

Actually, I had a break now, but I insisted on having all the suites on the 36th floor ready beforehand. I owed the preliminary work to Rebecca because she had covered my back for so long yesterday. And then there was also this inner restlessness because Connor hadn't called yet. I don't know what he was up to, but with every minute I waited, I got more and more nervous. It was all so exciting and unusual! In my normal, quiet life there was finally variety and a really attractive, charming man.

I was his girl. My abdomen tingled again when I thought of his words. The tingling spread and displaced individual doubts that arose – we hardly knew each other, even if the feelings were so intense, as if we had known each other forever.

I locked the finished suite. Now there was only one room on this floor. Room 4601. Deborah's room.

"Daaanaaa," Shannon Williams' voice boomed through the radio.

"Yes, Ms. Williams?"

"Please come to my office. We have something to discuss."

"I'm coming," I replied and made my way to the assistant manager without any detours. Deborah's room could wait.

Shannon Williams' office was on the first floor so she could keep an eye on everything, as she always said. Anyone who knew my boss knew that she actually wanted to control her employees.

The door to Ms. Williams' office was open, yet I stopped at the threshold and knocked.

"Come on in, Dana."

"Thank you."

Shannon Williams was not alone in the office; standing next to her was a middle-aged man in a tailored suit and thick horn-rimmed glasses. My boss sat in her wide crocodile chair and beckoned me to join her.

"Good afternoon," I greeted them both.

"Henry Hayward, pleasure to meet you," the man introduced himself.

"Dana Swanson, I work here as a..."

"She's the maid who speaks for everyone else. Our face to the staff, so to speak," Ms. Williams interrupted me, stood up, and closed the door.

My boss had already interrupted me so many times that I had learned to stay calm and smile away the anger.

"Very well, then, we can begin," said Mr. Hayward. He lifted a black leather case onto the table. It clicked, then he flipped the top of the case up. Unconsciously, I stood on my tiptoes to be able to look inside the case, but the view was denied me. I just felt like I was in a James Bond movie. Whatever my boss was about to do, it couldn't be good.

"Dana, there are some things to talk about," Ms. Williams officially opened the conversation.

"Of course, I hope I can help."

"Oh, certainly!" she replied pointedly. "First, I need you to find out for me who put flowers in Mrs. Greenwood's room. She has a pollen allergy."

"Oh dear." My shock was not feigned. "Is it bad? Is she okay?"

"Of course she's fine, it's just pollen! She just had to sneeze a bit and move to another suite. But it's a matter of principle, that's why I almost missed an important business meeting yesterday!"

"She moved to another suite?" I inquired. That was all I could think about right now. After all, I had to return the jewelry. "Um, I mean ... does Mrs. Greenwood know anything about the maid?" I hope not!

Ms. Williams took out a pair of glasses from the case. They were plain, square, and matte black. Her gaze shifted back and forth between my face and the glasses.

"No, unfortunately, she didn't. She was able to narrow it down to a female maid, but you'll figure out who that was. Won't you?"

Certainly not.

"I'll do the best I can."

"Great. Would you mind putting on the glasses?"

What is this now?

Irritated, I accepted the glasses and put them on.

"No, take it off. Way too intrusive."

Confused, I put the glasses down again and was handed another pair by Ms. Williams. Again, the lenses were set in black frames, but the rims were much thinner.

"No, absolutely not, way too vulgar!"

What the hell?

Ms. Williams handed me a third pair of glasses.

"Better already, but still not perfect," Shannon Williams said thoughtfully. "Oh, you seem to have made quite an impression on Mr. Lancester."

When Connor's name came up, I held my breath.

"Did I?" I asked cautiously.

"It seems like he didn't want to have a personal butler."

Guests on the top floor were always provided with a personal butler who took care of all their needs.

"Oh, no?"

My boss handed me the fourth pair of glasses. This time with round frames, in a dark blue. Ms. Williams clearly shook her head before the glasses had even touched the bridge of my nose.

"No, he insisted on a personal maid."

"Did he?"

"Yes. He's either pretty clumsy or has a clinical obsession with cleanliness."

Or he wants the maid.

While I was putting on Mr. Hayward's next pair, Ms. Williams waved a small device in front of my face.

"That, my dear, is a pager."

"But I have a radio, right?"

"Not just any pager, Dana! The personal pager for Mr. Lancester. He wants his own maid? He'll get it, it's that simple as a guest at the Royal Renaissance Hotel."

"Okay." So that's how Connor was going to check in. I had to hand it to him, he was damn creative. I hesitantly picked up the pager and after a quick inspection, put it in my left side pocket.

Expectantly, the optician held another pair of glasses in my direction. "Go ahead."

I put on the shiny red lacquered glasses.

Critically, Shannon Williams looked at me. It was clear to me that these glasses were one of the ugliest I had ever seen, but Ms. Williams took a little too long for my taste to come to the same conclusion.

"Next."

Slowly, Mr. Hayward became more restless because he was probably running out of glasses.

Shannon Williams sighed, then casually said, "Oh, the elevators for the employees will be serviced and repaired in the next two weeks."

"So, we get assigned an elevator for the guests?"

"No, not quite," the deputy service chief replied with a shrug.

"What do you mean?"

"That you have to use the stairs during that time period."

My jaw dropped and all the alarm bells rang in my head. I systematically went through the hotel floor by floor. Okay, the day-to-day chores would run normally. Vacuum cleaners, linens, cleaning carts, and all that stuff were in separate storage rooms on each floor, replenished every day. But what about the maids who worked on the upper floors? Were we supposed to walk thirty floors and more?

"Ms. Williams, for us to take the stairs for the next two weeks is not possible," I said thoughtfully. Silently, I hoped my boss didn't rip me a new one for contradicting her. At the same time, I was calculating in my head how many miles a day I already covered as a maid without the lack of elevators.

"Why not? Exercise keeps you fit."

I would have loved to go for the neck of my boss for these words. As if my job wasn't hard enough already! Instead of telling my ignorant boss off, I took a deep breath and searched my gray cells for a solution. At least we had occupational health and safety on our side, because I happened to have the thick manual lying around at home. For quite a while, it had been my unromantic, dry bedtime reading – and that was one of the reasons why I almost unanimously became the spokesperson of the other maids.

Who would have thought that knowing almost all the rules and laws that were relevant in the industry really paid off?

"Ms. Williams, I really don't want to sound rude, but we need the elevators. For catering and for room service. The wait times would get much, much longer. I'm afraid that's a real inconvenience for a lot of guests."

If you wanted to convince the management, you had to think like the management. The higher the level of satisfaction, the greater the profit. I had understood this, and perhaps it helped me to improve the working conditions for me and my ninety-plus female colleagues. I fired off more arguments: "All the maids will move around a lot more and sweat a lot more as a result. So much so that no deodorant or perfume in the world will be able to mask the smell. Not to mention that the new dress code would include red faces and tousled hair!"

"Stop, that's enough!" interrupted Shannon Williams. "That's right, you're right. Let me think for a minute and put on these glasses here."

Yep. A few disheveled hairs and sweat stains were just as big a nightmare for my boss as having to walk forty flights of stairs for me. I should definitely keep that argument in mind for future meetings.

I accepted a pair of plain glasses and put them on.

"Oh, she looks delightful," Shannon Williams gushed. She turned to Mr. Hayward, relief written all over his face.

"We'll take those! We'll start with a small order ... say, thirty pieces? Only minimal changes would need to be made, but we'll discuss that later."

Thirty pairs of glasses? What the hell for? What's the point of all this anyway?

Mr. Hayward nodded. "Yes, that should be possible. Give me a month."

"Excuse me?" I interrupted. "What did you want me to try on the glasses for?" Now I really had to suppress my burgeoning anger. The problem with the elevator ban still existed, and my boss was only interested in fashion!

"I want to increase the effectiveness of my employees."

"With glasses?" I asked critically.

"Glasses with camera surveillance."

"You want to spy on us?"

I was speechless. My boss had a pronounced compulsion to control, but that she wanted to introduce such measures was unbelievable. Was this even legal? I had only seen surveillance cameras in glasses in movies; as far as I knew, there were no precedents for such things.

"Oh, spying is such a negative word. No, I wouldn't want that, of course. That way we can find out which jobs are wasting time unnecessarily."

"We work effectively, quickly, and well," I defended the work of all the maids.

"You can prove that to me with the glasses then."

Well, I couldn't do anything with sweat stains and loose strands here.

"What does the director say?"

"Nothing yet. I want to test a few prototypes first and get statistics done."

I nodded, stunned. I had no words to describe what I was feeling at the moment. My boss's paranoia was no longer a case for the HR department, but for psychiatry!

It beeped twice. It took me a second to realize the sound was coming from my pocket. Connor's pager! My stomach tingled expectantly as I picked up the device. The digital display panel read only: 4901. Presumably, the pager had been set to display the room number from which the pager was radioed.

I wonder if this was also a prototype to be spread across multiple rooms and floors?

"This is Mr. Lancester," I said.

"Well go on then. Shoo, shoo!"

"I think I'll practice already and time it until I get to the forty-ninth floor. Let's see how long it takes me and let's hope it's nothing urgent." Now I didn't worry about my tone. The elevator ban was idiotic, and I made no secret of that anymore.

"Okay, you win, if you have to walk more than ten floors, they may use one of the rear guest elevators."

"Me and all the other maids."

Ms. Williams looked thoughtfully at the floor. "No, the others can take the stairs."

Fuck restraint!

"I'm the spokesperson for my female colleagues, I'm not just demanding this for me, I'm demanding it for everyone. Either we all use the elevators if we have to walk more than five floors, or I will walk too."

Shannon Williams sparkled at me angrily, but also with a hint of respect.

"I'm not used to you like this, Dana. I appreciate your effort."

I was amazed at myself. I had never been so confident and clear with Ms. Williams. I wondered if that had something to do with the fact that Connor was waiting for me, and I could have been with him long ago.

Ms. Williams placed her hand noisily on the table.

"Fine by me. Anyone who needs to walk more than seven floors may use an appropriately designated elevator to do so."

"Thank you, I'll go see Mr. Lancester now."

Anger still blazed in Shannon Williams' eyes. "In the future, I expect you to return to your old restraint. Are we clear?"

"Of course."

Such threats are not to be misunderstood.

I thought about it on the way to the top floor. How was I supposed to explain to my colleagues that this was a victory? Having to walk seven damn floors was sheer horror for me, too.

There are occupational health and safety laws for this kind of thing!

Yes, there were laws to protect workers. There were workers who took these laws seriously and were fired all the time, and there were workers who kept quiet and saved their jobs.

Life just wasn't a wish-fulfillment concert. The only thing that gave me some relief was my tangible seven-year plan. At the end of that plan, I would be calling the shots myself, and unlike Shannon Williams, I would not lose my humanity for more profit.

I knocked on the door to Connor's suite, and he promptly opened it for me.

"Nice, you got the pager," Connor said with a smile.

"Yeah, or I wouldn't be here, I guess," I replied with a shrug.

"Come on in. I have something for you."

Connor pulled me inside, closed the door behind my back and gave me a long, passionate kiss. Greedy, demanding, his tongue invaded my mouth as he pushed me against the door.

It's hard to believe that Connor was so composed one second and going wild over me the next.

"I've been thinking about you all night and what I'm going to do to you. I can hardly contain myself at the thought of how sensual you're going to scream," Connor murmured. Another kiss followed.

I got weak in the knees and would have collapsed if Connor hadn't held me. When we finally broke away from each other, Connor led me into the large living area. The windows were open, and the white satin curtains blew back and forth in the light breeze.

"Was that kiss what you wanted to give me?" I asked, still out of breath.

"No, something else." Connor walked over to the table and lifted a small, velvet-covered box. "A gift for you."

"Connor ... there's no need for that." Smiling, I shrugged off whatever he wanted to give me. I didn't want jewelry. I didn't want clothes, and I didn't want luxury. All I wanted was Connor, his charm, and his beast in a suit.

"Not even five minutes here and already you want to contradict me?"

I faltered, then silently looked down at the floor so as not to make my situation worse. Wordlessly, Connor flipped open the box. Inside was a beautiful silver bracelet with small charms attached. Carefully, full of awe, I ran my index finger over the filigree bracelet.

"Wow. This is beautiful," I gushed.

"You're beautiful!" retorted Connor. "You're special, Dana, one of a kind, just like this bracelet."

"What do the little tags mean?" I was curious.

"The dress represents our first meeting," Connor explained with a smile. "And the clef represents our first dance. The mask symbolizes your mask, which you will drop entirely for me." His face grew more serious, and I took a deep breath. Connor had that look again. Gloomy, dark, animalistic. "And the compass represents your safe word: mayday."

"Mayday?"

"I'm almost certain you'll never need it, but just knowing there's a way out gives you a lot of peace of mind."

Wow. His raspy voice left goosebumps. Was I crazy for feeling that Connor's arms were the safest place in the world?

My fingers slid over each pendant attached to the bracelet.

"What does the padlock symbolize?"

"That means you are mine now. You are my girl. You will love me for what I do to you, and you will hate me for it. I will take possession of you and thereby free you. I will show you the deepest abysses so that you can taste the sweetest heights. You will kneel before me and be proud in your humility. And you will find salvation in your torments. All you have to do is say yes."

God, I was so attracted to Connor, to his charm, his calm, his dark side, that I couldn't help but say yes. I wanted to give myself to him, more than anything else in the world! I didn't know exactly what was in store for me, but I knew Connor would take care of me.

"Yes," I replied, my voice quivering with excitement. "I want to be yours."

"Good girl." Connor smiled gently, then took the bracelet out of the box and placed it around my left wrist. "You're mine now."

Now there is no turning back.

18

Connor

Full of anticipation, I stroked the leather whip while watching Dana with relish. With a feather duster made of ostrich feathers, she cleaned the suite under my attentive gaze. She wore seductive lace lingerie, knee-length nylon stockings and forbidden high heels.

"I've had that fantasy for quite a long time," I said with a grin. I made no secret of the fact that I damn well liked what I saw.

"And do I meet the expectations of your imagination?" asked Dana, without interrupting her work.

"No, you outdo them by a mile."

Although Dana hid her face behind the black duster, I knew she liked my compliment because her posture became prouder. I stood behind Dana's back and gently stroked her shoulder blades with the crop. She paused briefly until my reprimanding snap spurred her to continue.

"I like you, Dana."

"I like that you like me," she replied sheepishly.

"And what else do you like?" I asked, because I wanted to know more about Dana, and what was going on in her pretty head. Actually, I wanted to know everything about her. Her favorite perfume, what had shaped her life, her favorite movie, where she would like to travel, the dreams she pursued, and what fears she had. I wanted to know every little secret she was hiding from me.

"You want to know what I like?"

"Yes."

Dana thought about it for a moment.

"I'm addicted to Ben & Jerry's, in need of harmony, and I love country music as much as heavy metal."

Amazing, I couldn't imagine this shy, delicate creature among all the rough, black-haired metal fans at all.

"And what are you afraid of?" I asked. Dana hesitated briefly, then turned to me and looked me straight in the eye.

"I'm afraid of careless drivers, always take criticism way too seriously and..." Dana bit her lips together.

"And?" I asked expectantly.

"No, I can't tell you that."

"Yes, you will." My gaze was unmistakable. Only if I knew Dana's fears could I protect her from them or help her conquer them.

"You're going to think I'm crazy." Dana sighed.

"What I think you are, how I see you, and what I do with you is my decision." My features softened, and I gently stroked a blonde curl from her face.

"You are my girl. You can tell me everything that's on your mind. For what I have in mind for you, I also need to know your fears. You can trust me, and, in return, I will show you my world."

Dana nodded and took a deep breath. "I know. So ... I'm afraid of yawning with my mouth open in public."

Okay. That's really ... special.

Actually, I had expected all sorts of things. Spiders, perhaps, or fear of flying, the fear of pickpockets or thunder.

"Told you." Dana shrugged, defiance resonating in her voice.

Actually, a red-hot butt would have been due for that look, but I was far too interested in how Dana had come to be so afraid.

"Why?"

"A long story. The short version: When I was in school, a classmate stuck his finger in my mouth while I was yawning, and I was the laughingstock of my classmates for weeks after that."

I smiled at her, clasped Dana's chin between my thumb and forefinger, and opened her mouth. I ran my thumb over her full, soft lips before entering her mouth. "Are you scared now too?"

Dana shook her head and relaxed, closing her eyes. I ran over her soft, wet tongue, eliciting a soft moan from Dana.

Without warning, I withdrew my hand and took two steps away from her. Shocked, almost reproachful looks met me. Jesus, I loved such looks.

"Good, now let's get to the rules you should know."

"There are rules?"

Dana looked at me innocently.

"Rules you have silently agreed to, and duties you have long since followed."

"Will you tell me more?" Dana tilted her head and leaned against the dresser she had just dusted. I immediately lashed out with the crop and slapped her left thigh.

"Let's get right to the first rule. If I order you to do something, anything, you will do it until I allow you to stop. I make the rules and give the orders, and you will happily follow without questioning them." My soft voice was a harsh contrast to the firm slap Dana silently accepted. But she immediately jumped up to continue dusting the dresser.

A second time the crop whizzed on Dana's body, this time it hit her right thigh.

"Rule number two, you should thank me for everything I give you. And it would be better for you if you apologize for transgressions."

After the third stroke, Dana paused briefly and took a deep breath before resuming her work.

"Thank you, sir!"

"Good girl."

I watched Dana's face closely from the side, she bit her full lips and concentrated completely on her work and my voice. Very good.

"Rule number three: stop, quit, and no are words I will not respond to in certain situations."

"That's what the safe word is for? Mayday?" asked Dana.

"Exactly. Remember it well, because it will be the only word that can slow me down then. If it becomes too much for you, use it, but you should know that I know your limits and realize when you abuse the power of that word."

Dana nodded thoughtfully, not letting up on her work.

"As a fourth rule, I expect absolute honesty. I will always tell the truth and I expect you to do the same. I. Hate. Lies." My expression remained serious. I feathered the soft leather crop back and forth in my hand, lunged, and let it whiz through the air with a hiss. There was no more beautiful combination than the cutting hiss of the crop and the reactions that sound evoked. Although the whip never touched Dana's skin, she flinched slightly each time, bracing herself for the next blow.

"And the last rule for now, but the most important one: you are mine. You are my girl. You don't belong to anyone else. You will not take orders from anyone else, and you will not be fucked by anyone but me. Do you understand?"

"Yes," Dana whispered.

"And are you okay with that?"

"Yes," she answered louder.

"Good girl."

Dana's light blue eyes reflected pride and anticipation but also uncertainty. The latter was unnecessary. I was her lifeline, no matter where I led her, and I was her parachute, no matter into which abyss I pushed her.

"Connor?"

"Dana?"

"Does the last rule apply to you?"

Now I understood where Dana's insecurity came from. It was not the fear of the unknown, but something completely different.

"You're my girl, and as long as you're my girl, you can be sure that my full attention is only on you."

Dana exhaled in relief. Everything that needed to be said had been said. She now knew what she was getting into, and a soft smile rested on her lips that made her look forbidden and innocent. God, that look alone made me want to fuck her all the wilder, all the kinkier. My stiffened cock saw it the same way, but it had to wait a short while.

"Do you have any questions?"

"I don't think so."

"If you do think of something, we can always talk about it."

"Thank you, sir." Dana looked at me with devotion.

Damn, my beast in the suit tugged at his chains, which were dangerously under tension. I lashed out with the crop, and a second one appeared right under the first red welt on her thigh. Dana bit her lips together and suppressed a moan.

"When I give you a task," I began, "you perform it until I say otherwise. I will not repeat myself a third time."

"Understood," Dana answered hastily and continued cleaning. She carefully cleaned the cabinets, chests of drawers, and display cases under my supervision.

Again, the crop whizzed down on Dana. Beautiful welts on her splendid butt stood out.

"For what?" asked Dana almost defiantly.

"Because I like it," I replied. "And because I can."

Dana nodded and endured the next blows with composure. She didn't let on anything, but I could see the flaring anger in her eyes, which of course I was aiming for. I motivated Dana to rebel, so that I could punish her even more severely. Thus, I killed two birds with one stone; Dana dared to come out of her shell, and I could live out my dominant side. My blows became firmer. Dana gasped with everyone. It didn't take long until Dana's entire backside was glowing. For having no experience at all, she was doing pretty damn well. Determined, Dana stared ahead, paying attention only to her work. She definitely wanted to impress me, do everything right, and not disappoint me. I didn't let on yet, but I was already pretty proud of her.

Brave girl.

The red welts on her skin looked like a work of art – and I was the artist who had created it.

"I must confess that I'm surprised at the amount of restraint you have in getting your butt spanked."

"I like it," Dana replied thoughtfully. "Very much so."

I smiled in satisfaction. "You have absolutely no idea how crazy you're driving me with this."

Damn it, there was no way Dana was going to find out how much power she really had over me. Beneath her crumbling facade, she hid a hungry nymphomaniac just waiting for me to unleash my beast on her. A dangerous, highly explosive mixture that would go supernova on contact. With unpredictable scale, loud bang and devastating fire – I could hardly wait for the moment to happen.

"On your knees!" I commanded. Dana followed my command immediately. She sank to the floor, and I took the duster from her.

"When you kneel down for me, your legs need to be further apart." I slid a hand between her legs, which she willingly spread. "That's it. I want to be able to touch you here whenever I want."

I massaged Dana's most sensitive spot through the fabric of her panties. Dana moaned softly and her head tilted back with pleasure.

"And your hands should be on your thighs with your palms facing up. That's it. Make sure your back is straight."

After I corrected her position, Dana's posture came pretty close to perfection.

Already I knew that Dana was a special sub. Sure, some things would take great effort and time, but that was a small price to pay for what we both gained.

Attentively, I watched every movement of her body. Every twitch, every slump and every bad posture were punished with blows on her upper arm. While I walked around her again and again and examined her wonderfully submissive posture, Dana followed me with her gaze.

"Actually, your head should be lowered, and your gaze turned down, but I want you to look at me. I want you to see how well I like you."

Dana smiled.

From the dresser drawer I fetched a battery-powered, matte black vibrator. The elongated device looked inconspicuous but had quite a bit of power. The vibrator had three levels. The first level was for warming up, the second level provided great excitement, and the third level literally forced women to orgasm. I turned the device on at level one, and the motor hummed softly. First, I let the vibrator slide down from her belly button to give her a taste of what was about to happen between her legs. Dana gasped softly long before I reached her most sensitive spot.

"Oh God!" Dana's reaction when the vibrator found its destination was unmistakable. The first, involuntary twitches followed immediately.

"Press your legs together!" I commanded. Dana closed her legs and held the vibrator in position. She moaned with pleasure and arched her head back.

"Remember your posture!" My admonishing voice made sure that Dana returned to her basic position. Her moans became louder and louder, and her legs began to tremble.

What this part would do to her only at level one...

"As my girl, my sub, not only do you have to come out of your shell, open up to me and face new challenges, sometimes you have to do the exact opposite."

Dana gazed at me with a questioning look. Her breathing was rapid and her soft, sensual sighing turned into loud moaning.

"Sometimes you have to take a step back, too, like right now."

"I don't quite understand."

"You will in a minute."

Full of anticipation, I undid the button of my pants and freed my erection. Hard and stiff, it pointed right at Dana, whose mouth was at a perfect height. With my left hand, I enclosed my manhood and massaged myself so that my erection became even harder before I penetrated Dana's mouth with it.

"I won't allow you to come until after the blowjob."

"Okay," Dana answered nodding and pulled the vibrator out from between her legs. She had not yet realized the problem with it.

"The vibrator stays between your legs."

Now it clicked. She looked at me with big, questioning eyes. Her gaze was heartwarming.

"I don't know if I can do it," she said meekly.

"The harder you try, the faster you may come."

"Thank you, sir!" Her eyes blazed with anger. Perfect.

Willingly Dana opened her mouth and let me penetrate her. Her full lips gently nestled around my hardness, not too tight, not too loose, just right. Again and again, I thrust into her warm, wet mouth, penetrating a little deeper each time.

God, her mouth is insane!

With the tip of her tongue, she additionally licked and massaged my member.

"You're doing a good job," I praised her. My manhood became even harder inside her. When I grabbed her by the hair of the back of her head, I helped determine the pace and depth. Dana willingly let me guide her. Only when my tip pressed against her throat came slight resistance. Dana's moans were suppressed by my cock, deep inside her.

"Show me how deep you can take my cock in your mouth!" I growled.

Piece by piece, Dana let my manhood slide deeper into her throat. Her body was trembling more and more, she surely couldn't hold back her orgasm for long. but neither could I.

I buried my hands in her long blonde curls and pulled her head further and further towards me. Only when the tip of her nose touched my belly, when I couldn't sink my cock any further into her, did I stop.

Damn, that feels so good.

When I let go of Dana, she reflexively pulled her head back and took a deep breath. Without command, without warning, Dana took my cock a second time as deep as she could. My beast in the suit raged.

Dana's mouth, her tongue and her wild look drove me crazy. Actually, I had intended to take my time, I wanted to see how Dana squirmed, fought against her orgasm and begged me to come after all.

But she did a great job. So, well that I couldn't help but come. Now.

My grip on her hair tightened, I thrust hard several times, fucked her throat as deep as I could and came inside her. Dana kept eye contact the whole time.

It looked so good with my manhood inside her, I enjoyed the view as I pumped my gold down her throat.

"You may come now," I gasped, and her eyes sparkled at me gratefully. I let my cock slide over her lips and watched Dana reach her well-deserved climax. Release was written all over her face, and she looked beautiful as she came. Graceful and proud while maintaining her posture almost perfectly.

"Well done." I smiled at her. Then I helped her up from the floor and carried her to bed because her legs were as soft and yielding as rubber.

"Rest a minute. I'll take a shower in the meantime."

I would have loved to lie down in bed with her and stroke Dana's blonde curls out of her face, whisper in her ear how beautiful she was and what I wanted to do with her, but my schedule got in the way.

"Okay," Dana replied. "In the meantime, can you hand me your cell phone?"

"What do you want with it?" I asked.

"Type in my number so you can call me outside of my working hours." Dana tilted her head to the side and smiled sugary sweet.

"Alright, if you ask so nicely." I took my iPhone from the desk, unlocked it and gave it to her.

"I'll be right back."

I disappeared into the bathroom and got ready in no time. I had finished showering even before the water heated fully. I dried my body only superficially before I wrapped the towel around my hips and went into the dressing room. On the way there, I watched Dana, who was still typing away on her cell phone. When she saw my critical look, she said with a grin, "It's a very long number."

"You should get ready to get out of the room before I do, not that you'll get in trouble with your boss."

"You're right." Dana rolled over in bed, sighing. Then she climbed out of the huge bed and got dressed. As a farewell, I wrapped both arms around her torso and kissed Dana profusely.

"It was a feast for me," I said with a grin.

"Yeah, it was ... nice," Dana replied sheepishly.

"Nice? I'll show you what nice is in a minute!"

Without warning, I threw her over my shoulder. Although Dana struggled violently, drumming her hands against my back and kicking her legs against my chest, I continued to hold her and spank her with my free hand.

She screamed and laughed in equal measure. "Connor! Put me down!"

Only after a few more strokes, on her sensitive ass, I let her down again.

"You really should pay more attention to your choice of words."

"I'll watch for it, sir!" Dana laughed.

"And you may call me sir more often."

She lost her grin instantly. She was so cute when I upset her. Paradoxically, when Dana took off her clothes, she also gave up a large part of her insecurity, and vice versa.

"We'll talk about that tomorrow. I have to go now."

"All right ... sir?"

Silently, I smiled at her, because I wanted to give her pretty little head something to think about when I wasn't around.

Maxine was already drinking her strawberry Frappuccino with extra cream and extra sprinkles when I reached Sweet & Savory. Actually, I would still have been on time if a moving company had not parked in the second and third rows on West End Avenue. All traffic heading toward Central Park had come to a standstill because of it. But, now I was here and could fully concentrate on the affectionate teasing of my sister.

"Hello, sis."

"Hey. Glad you came after all," Max said with a cynical undertone.

"I'm just a busy man," I replied. Then I waved a waitress over to me to order a latte with hazelnut syrup and whipped cream.

"You weren't stopped by your new girlfriend, were you?" Maxine looked at me conspiratorially.

"No, movers parked in the middle of the street."

"I see." My sister's suspicious look remained.

"Before that, though, I was with Dana."

Max raised her brows. "Really?"

"Yes, really."

"Hmm. What was her eye color again?"

"Dana's eyes are blue. Like a cloudless sky on a summer day, to be exact."

Maxine faltered. A waitress brought my order, and Max obviously used the time to think. Yes, my sister knew me damn well, her distrust of Dana was not surprising. Actually, my family never saw a woman twice. Thinking that it felt like Dana might be the last woman I'd have to introduce to my family, I paused briefly before taking a sip of my scalding hot latte.

Damn, it was still a bit too early for such thoughts. We hardly knew each other!

"So," Maxine began. She sipped her Frappuccino twice more before continuing. "You really met Dana at the hotel?"

The interrogation continued without mercy. I took a napkin from the dispenser and spread it out in front of me.

"Yes, we met at the hotel."

I folded the opposite corners together, smoothed out the fold, and then turned the napkin over.

"Connor Lancester, I know you! You're hiding something. I can tell."

"Yes, you're my sister, of course you know me, and no, I'm not hiding anything," I said with a shrug.

"I knew at first glance that Dana was not an actress or escort. She was far too friendly and down to earth for that," Max further concluded.

In the meantime, the folded napkin had become an origami swan, which I looked at contentedly. Origami was soothing, and concentrating on folding the thin paper napkins was better than having to look at my sister's critical face. Maxine was a hyper, impatient person, along with her great self-confidence a dangerous mix.

The interrogation went into a second and a third round, in vain my sister searched for weak points, nevertheless she did not give up. My secret was actually safe, yet I decided to let my sister in on it. When it came down to it, she had been my accomplice since our young years, and I could trust her.

"All right, I'll tell you, Max." I took the next napkin from the dispenser.

"I'm all ears!" Excited, Maxine leaned forward.

"Dana and I, throughout the evening, have not lied to you once."

"Go on," Maxine urged me. Anyone who knew me a little better knew that I always told the truth. Sometimes I kept a few details to myself, but I never lied.

"We met at the hotel, only she's not a guest there, as you and mom suspected, but a maid."

Maxine opened her mouth to a soundless cry. "Wow, how romantic! Tell me more, I want details!"

I told my sister the story in fast forward, and Maxine's eyes got bigger and bigger. Of course I left out the part about the bedroom. That was nobody's business, but I shared all the other details with my sister.

"She's really great, and I can imagine more coming of it," I finished my explanation, setting another origami bird down in front of me. By now, the swan had a flock of kindred spirits around it.

"You? You want a firm commitment? Hear, hear! Connor Lancester is entering into a real relationship."

"Connor Lancester may be getting into a relationship," I corrected my little sister.

"Whatever's going on with Dana, don't mess it up. She seems really good for you."

I nodded. Maxine leaned across the table and whispered conspiratorially, "You have my blessing. I like her."

"Oh, then I'm lucky again."

"Oh Connor, you really have no sense of romance!"

No, I really did not.

"Your relationship is like a modern fairy tale ... like Cinderella!" continued Max, gushing. "Clearly a cosmic sign that your relationship is well and truly starred."

"Since when do you believe in modern fairy tales?"

"Ever since I saw you with Dana."

I kept silent, because I could not contradict her. I don't know why, but I wished that my sister was right.

Max ordered a raspberry crumble muffin, which the waitress brought over immediately. The muffin looked really delicious, just like everything at Sweet & Savory, and smelled even better.

Maxine gleefully took a bite of the oversized muffin. With a curious look, she gazed at me and asked, "So you're really coming to the gala?"

"Yes, we're coming. Dana is hiding it, but she's incredibly excited."

"Of course, it's all new to her."

Maxine took another big bite.

"Not only that is new for Dana..." I said thoughtfully. Did she still think of me with every step?

"What do you mean?"

"Oh, nothing, I was just thinking out loud."

"Anyway, I thought it was a shame you left so quickly," Max mumbled, her mouth half full. "Mom would have loved to talk to Dana longer."

"I believe that right away. After Dana and I danced, we were both pretty tired, so we went back to the hotel."

"Oh, now that you mention it. How did the conversation go? Did you ask them if they were interested in the best interior designer in the world?"

Damn, I knew I had forgotten something.

"They really just wanted my alcohol, but I turned them down, the circulation was too big."

"So, they said no to me?" Maxine raised her eyebrows.

"Well, not exactly," I said, shrugging my shoulders.

"You didn't ask her at all, right?"

"Yes, I was going to ... but Deborah was suddenly standing in the lobby, and I wanted to say hello to her."

"Deborah? Deborah Landry?"

"Right."

Thoughtfully, Maxine looked down. "So that's why she was grilling me about you. Logical. So she came to see you?"

"No, she changed hotels. The cleaning products at her previous hotel had caused an allergic reaction."

"Oh, really? Because of an allergy, yeah right." Max rolled her eyes dramatically.

"What are you trying to tell me, Maxine?"

"That you are the smartest person I know, but when it comes to women, feelings and modern art, you are an idiot. An absolutely hopeless case!"

"Da Vinci, Monet, Michelangelo. These were great artists whose works I appreciate. But smearing yourself with finger paints and rolling around on a piece of canvas is still self-therapy at best, but not art!" I defended my views. I appreciated classical crafts, not just paintings. Strictly speaking, I was an artist myself, combining new and old alcohols and creating something new and better from them. Every good cook was an artist, every musician. In my eyes, anything in which you recognized attention to detail and effort was art. But not something like this!

"That's what I'm talking about, Connor." My sister sighed. "Your sensitivity is abysmal. In fact, you're absolutely blind to operations. Listen, whatever Deborah is up to, nothing good can come of it, okay?"

"We're just old friends, nothing more." Deborah and I had known each other for quite a long time, though not very well. We had run into each other regularly at parties until I spent more time abroad with my companies.

"I don't think so. She really squeezed me to find out where you were staying," Max continued to complain.

"I don't know what's going on between you two, but don't drag me into your catfight!" I growled.

"There's no catfight. After Deborah had all the information she wanted, she got on her broom and zoomed off," Maxine said saccharinely.

Whether I wanted to or not, I couldn't help grinning. My sister's quick wit was always refreshing.

"Oh, sis." I sighed. How was I going to make my little sister understand that she had absolutely nothing to fear from Deborah?

"It's okay, I have to go now. The handmade furniture from France has finally arrived, and I promised the Monroes I'd bring it right over. Trust me, this is going to be by far the most beautiful doctor's office in all of New York!"

"Definitely," I replied. My sister was talented as hell. People were lining up to get advice from her.

We stood up and I put a fifty dollar bill on the table.

"Well, I have to go too then, I have another appointment at Fashion Week."

"You and Fashion Week?"

"Not quite. I have an appointment with Josh."

"Josh Anderson is at Fashion Week this year? How do you know?"

"He told me at the wedding."

My sister punched me in the chest, "Why didn't you tell me about this?"

"I did. Now."

"Idiot." Max snorted loudly. "What are you doing with Josh at Fashion Week?"

I smiled. "I have commissioned some jewelry that is now ready."

"For Dana?"

"Yes."

"Oh, Connor, you got hit harder than you'd like to admit. I'm so happy for you!" My sister hugged me tighter than I was used to from her.

"Yes, she definitely impressed me," I replied.

"See? That's something like a real declaration of love with you!"

Damn, my little sister was right.

19

Dana

Although I knew I was in Connor's suite, I had completely lost my bearings. The black silk scarf that Connor had tied around my eyes blocked out all daylight. He had put it on me when I entered the suite and led me up to the bedroom. The darkness had heightened my other senses. I heard every one of Connor's footsteps, and his aftershave enveloped me. When he stood close enough to me, I even thought I could feel his body heat on my bare skin.

Soft leather cuffs nestled around my wrists and ankles. But since these were not yet connected by a chain, I could move my arms freely. I wore only these leather cuffs and my pride, nothing else.

Connor's footsteps stopped, he stood close to me and gently breathed a kiss on my lips. He grabbed my wrists and pulled me to him.

When my arms were fully extended away from my body, he turned my palms upward. I clearly felt the weight of the leather cuffs.

"Stay like that," Connor commanded, then moved away from me. Metal or sheet metal rattled softly. Then he came back toward me. Eagerly, I waited to see what Connor had in mind for me. I nibbled my lower lip in anticipation and listened into the silence.

Something cold touched my left palm. Hard and smooth and not particularly heavy. An empty tray, I was pretty sure. Shortly after, Connor placed a second tray on my other hand.

"How long can you balance those trays?"

The two, round trays didn't weigh much, and I wondered if I could underestimate the difficulty of the exercise, because so far, his commands seemed pretty simple.

"Ten minutes, maybe fifteen minutes," I replied confidently. I wondered if there was a catch somewhere.

"That's very optimistic," Connor said. There was genuine surprise in his voice. So, there was definitely a catch. But I probably couldn't correct my stated time anyway, so I kept quiet.

Suddenly the left tray became a little heavier, then the right one. Connor seemed to be balancing apples or oranges on it, because the trays kept getting heavier in turn. I don't know how much fruit was stacked on the trays, but I knew for sure that I couldn't hold the weight for five minutes.

"Now what?" asked Connor, in a soft, loving voice. "How long can you last now?"

I wasn't going to give up, I was going to make Connor proud and endure whatever he told me to. Connor had been right in everything he had promised me. Never in my life had I felt so free, so safe and so desired.

"I'll hold out as long as you tell me to, sir!"

Connor growled softly. "What a delightful answer."

I heard Connor walk around me again. Then the whip whizzed through the air. The whip had not touched my skin but was probably intended more as a reminder that it could hit my body at any time.

"Then let's see how long you'll last, and in that time repeat the rules I listed yesterday."

I nodded. "Yes," I pressed out from behind clenched teeth. The trays were weighing heavier by the second.

"Every time you repeat a rule incorrectly or drop an orange, you will be punished. Understand?"

"Yes, sir."

"I love it when you call me sir," Connor said.

I smiled. Connor was really incredible. This mixture of charm, strength, and dominant sensuality was incredible!

The tip of the crop gently stroked my arms. So unexpectedly that I almost dropped the entire tray, but at the last moment I found my balance again.

"Rule number one?" asked Connor.

"You give the orders."

"Very good. And rule number two?"

"I thank you for that," I replied tersely. I focused entirely on balance and the burning of my arms.

"And how?" echoed Connor.

"With joy!" I almost yelled.

"Exactly. And are you having fun now, too?" His voice was rough and dark.

I thought about it for a moment before I could answer, because the answer to that question was anything but simple.

"I'd call it more like anticipation," I replied. "Of what's to come after this."

"You're surprising me with some really beautiful answers today, Dana."

His praise did me good, damn good even. Full of pride, I mobilized all the strength I had to keep the trays balanced, but my hands were shaking more and more. This would not go well for much longer.

"Rule number three?" Connor snapped me out of my thoughts.

"You only stop when I call the safe word. Mayday."

"You're doing great, Dana."

"Really?" I doubted Connor's statement, because he could hardly miss the trembling of my arms.

"Yes. I like the way you try so hard for me. The way your whole body shakes and quivers, and the way you bite your lower lip as you approach your limits."

The crop stroked again over my bare skin, from the shoulder blades to the hip. The soft leather was followed by tingling goose bumps that spread all over my body.

Groaning softly, I put my head back and then it happened. From the left tray several oranges slid to the side, the weight tilted so that the tray slid to the side and all the oranges fell to the floor.

Damn!

I angrily bit my lips so that all my intended curses would remain unspoken. I had expected blows, but nothing happened. Connor got down on his knees next to me and picked up the oranges that had fallen to the ground.

"Sorry, sir." I hoped to soften my punishment a little.

"The fourth rule?" he asked, throwing me completely off my game.

I had understood correctly that there was a penalty for each dropped fruit? Should I remind him of that? No, I'd rather not.

One orange after another was stacked back on the tray.

"I will not lie, ever."

"Right."

More and more weight weighed on the trays. Connor had placed oranges not only on the left tray, but also on the right. There were definitely more oranges than before on the tray.

If I had known that before, I would have preferred to demand blows. A few welts were nothing compared to my aching arms. They burned like fire! But I said nothing and took my punishment silently.

"Let's get to the last rule" Connor prompted me.

"I belong only to you." At these words my abdomen tingled violently.

"Good girl."

His words made up for all the pain I was feeling. I thanked him softly.

"I was actually expecting more oranges to fall off you."

"It almost sounds like you're disappointed," I stated.

"Right, I had thought of such nice punishments for you," Connor murmured.

"What a shame," I replied a touch too cynically.

"Dana, honey. You forget we're playing my game, with my rules."

I swallowed. I had actually forgotten that. All there was around me was darkness, Connor, and this almost unbearable pain. Maybe also my pride, which forced me to keep balancing those damn trays.

Connor moved away from me, and I tried to listen to his footsteps, which I could not. He seemed intent on hiding any sound that might give him away. It wasn't until he was close behind me again and his hot breath touched my neck that I knew where Connor was. His arms reached around my torso and suddenly, without warning, he pressed two ice cubes firmly onto my nipples.

I moaned loudly, winced and had all the trouble to keep my balance. It cost me all the concentration, all the strength I still had. My body shook violently, and I could barely control the gasps that began.

"Cold?" teased Connor, just like last time.

Son of a bitch!

"Yes." This time I didn't begrudge him that satisfaction but made do with the truth. The radio in the living room buzzed. I turned my head to the side.

"We're not done here," Connor admonished me.

"I know. But I have to check in. Shannon Williams penalizes anything over a ten-second response rate."

With the flat of his hand, Connor slapped my butt hard. I struggled to balance the blow so that no other orange fell to the floor.

"Is that how disobedience is punished?" asked Connor smugly.

"It would be nice."

Now I could finally set those damn trays down, or better yet, angrily hurl them against the walls.

"All right, wait here and hold your position, I'll get the radio for you."

Crap! Could have worked.

Still, it was a blessing when the two ice cubes stopped melting away on my stiff buds. I exhaled with relief.

Connor came back and held the radio close to my mouth.

"You nod when you want me to hit the switch and a second time when you're done," Connor said. He didn't even begrudge me the daylight for that brief moment.

I nodded. It cracked briefly. "Hello? What's up?" I asked, then nodded again.

"Dana. I need your help. Right now," Rebecca gushed.

"What happened?" I tried not to let my voice indicate what Connor and I were doing.

"The suppliers for the laundry have gone on a warning strike, there will be no more fresh towels today!"

"And our in-house laundry can't fill in for the time?"

Of course, the Royal Renaissance Hotel had its own small laundry. But about ninety percent of the blankets, covers and towels the hotel had cleaned outside.

"Yes, they do, but they need all the people they can get to fold the towels. Can you help?"

Could I? Expectantly, I turned my head to where I suspected Connor was.

"Can I help? It sounds really serious."

"Of course," Connor replied.

It crackled again. "I'll be right down."

I waited for Connor to take off my blindfold and trays, but nothing like that happened.

"How long are you going to be there?" asked Connor curiously.

"Hmm," I pondered aloud. "I'm guessing between two and five hundred towels to fold, so about an hour."

God, my arms weighed as heavy as lead. Like burning lead!

"Good, then I want you to bring me some fresh towels right after."

"Yes, sir."

"I think you should continue to think about me in the meantime," Connor said. Then, unexpectedly, a slight but steady ache spread from my sensitive buds through my entire body.

"Yes, it really does look great on you." His voice was throaty and deep.

Great. Now not only my arms were on fire, but also my nipples. Finally, Connor took both trays from me, and I let my arms drop down. At first the relaxed position was even more painful than the previous position, but I didn't care. Not a second longer would I have been able to hold those damn silver trays.

After Connor audibly set the trays down, he opened my blindfold. I blinked as the bright daylight blinded me.

Connor stood behind me, grabbed my shoulders, and turned me toward the large mirror on the dresser.

"Don't you think the nipple clamps look great on you?"

I silently looked at my naked upper body in the mirror. Small, inconspicuous clamps were attached to my nipples, with two small, decorative balls hanging from the end of each.

I wonder if I could really stand those things for a whole hour.

"Yes, but ... I don't know if I can take it," I openly confessed my concerns.

"Then you'd better hurry." Unabashedly, he played around with the silver balls.

"Yes, sir," I replied, giving Connor a defiant look. His grin widened even more, and he casually tucked his hands into his pants pockets.

"I'll wait for you here then and figure out how I'm going to deal with your outrageous behavior."

I bit my lips before I could say anything else stupid, so I just nodded and then got dressed in a rush to head to the in-house laundry to help Beccs and the others.

Some would have described the laundry, which was in the basement, more as a Finnish steam sauna, and I smelled the panic that had broken out there from afar.

"Thank God, Dana!" shouted Rebecca from a corner. She was standing in front of a wide, very long table, folding one towel after another in a chord. All around me, angry laundresses swarmed, unloading clean towels on the table and exchanging them for folded towels.

"Wow, things are really happening here," I marveled. The understatement of the year! The laundry was working to capacity and any help was welcome.

I stood next to Rebecca and folded the large bath towels as well. My arms ached every time I folded a towel lengthwise, and my breasts when the towel was folded widthwise. With every movement, Connor was with me, just as he had guaranteed.

"You just came from the top suite, didn't you?" asked Rebecca.

"What makes you think that?"

"Because you're so radiant."

"I'm beaming? The heat here must have gone to your head," I laughed out loud.

Rebecca said nothing but looked at me with a reproachful look. That's exactly how she looked at Emma when she did something wrong and got caught.

"So, were you in the top suite or not?"

"Yes, I was."

A sharp cry. "I knew it! There's something going on with you and Mr. Jackpot! Is it serious?"

That's exactly why I didn't want to say anything, at least not here. More than half of all the washerwomen had stopped working for a brief moment to be able to relate Rebecca's scream.

Great.

"Okay, I'll tell you everything, but not here! Later!"

"I don't think I can stand it!" nagged Rebecca. "After years of abstinence, every flirtatious glance is a real sensation. And now, of all times, you withhold all news from me."

Rebecca pulled a pout as she folded more towels.

"So, abstinence is a pretty strong term, don't you think?"

"When was the last time you had sex, huh?" The question came like a shot from a pistol.

Today? No. That was probably more foreplay, the sex hopefully still came.

"Yesterday," I answered proudly and put my hands on my hips, at the same time stretching my chest forward. In this way, I gave my statement even more meaning. A fatal mistake, as it turned out, because the straightening of my breasts shot an intense pain through my body.

Don't let anything show! Take a breath.

"Not with Connor, silly. Before that!"

I thought about it for a long time. Way too long. "This doesn't matter at all, okay?"

"Gotcha," Rebecca grinned triumphantly.

"Okay, I give up." Then I leaned forward and continued in a whisper, "He talked to Shannon Williams. I have my own pager for his room so he can call me directly to..." I wasn't sure how far to go into detail. "To get things done."

Rebecca got wide-eyed. "Then he's either very clumsy or totally infatuated with you."

"Yeah, I guess it could be."

"Dana Swanson. You can't answer yes to an either-or question."

"Why not?"

"And you can't counter my request with a counter question!"

"Yet, I just did." Yes, I enjoyed putting my best friend on the rack a little.

"Let's be clear. Is there something serious going on between you?"

"I think so, yes," I cheered. Saying it out loud had something solemn, great and triggered euphoric feelings in me. So euphoric that I even forgot my nipple clamps for a moment.

"Oh, I'm so happy for you!" Rebecca threw the half-folded towel on the table and hugged me tightly. So tight, in fact, that my nipple clamps were dangerously affected. This intense feeling brought tears to my eyes. I bit my lips to stifle a scream. Hopefully Rebecca didn't feel the metal parts through the cloth uniforms.

"Oh, Dana. You're actually crying," Rebecca noted when we had detached from each other. Smiling, I wiped away the tear for which Beccs was more or less responsible.

"Yeah, the Connor thing is pretty intense," I replied. To distract myself from my pain and to avoid any more painful hugs, I held my wrist up and showed Rebecca the bracelet he had given me.

"This is beautiful, it must have cost a fortune!"

"It's a one-of-a-kind piece, made by Josh Anderson. He's exhibiting here at Fashion Week," I said.

Rebecca's jaw dropped. "Wow."

Then we devoted ourselves again to folding the towels. New helpers kept coming to the laundry, so that the towel shortage soon became just a towel shortage.

Every second, Beccs, I, and dozens of other laundresses, maids, and even receptionists were folding towels of various sizes.

"Almost done! Then we can finally go to break!" Rebecca shouted euphorically. Murmurs of approval.

Now I found myself in a dilemma. I didn't want to stand up Connor or my colleagues. Putting my feet up and having a well-deserved coffee sounded tempting, but getting rid of those metal clamps around my throbbing nipples sounded almost more tempting.

"Daaanaaa," Shannon Williams called over the radio.

"Yes?"

"A glass broke in room 3601."

"I'll take care of it right away." I sighed loudly.

So, my supervisor had decided for me that my either-or became a neither-nor.

"Go ahead and take your break without me, sorry guys," I said goodbye.

"Us too!" replied Rebecca.

"And thank you for your help," one of the washerwomen said. Further encouragement followed from the whole group.

"You're welcome."

On the way to room 3601 I equipped myself with a vacuum cleaner, a broom and dustpan.

It was not uncommon for glasses to break. Dozens of glasses were broken every day at the Royal Renaissance Hotel. Champagne flutes and wine glasses were particularly susceptible because of their thin stems.

I knocked on the door of the room.

"Come in!" a nasal, female voice answered.

No, please don't!

Had I perhaps misheard him? No. I could immediately identify that derogatory tone. Great. In a moment, everything would blow up in my face because I had been recognized by Deborah Landry!

"Today, please," Deborah grumbled through the door.

Stay calm and maintain dignity!

I entered the suite, the room was divided into two, with a nice, spacious living room and a separate bedroom with a large bathroom. Deborah was lying crossed legged on the sofa, her back facing the door. I could see nothing of her beyond her feet, which were clad in pink, oversized fuzzy shoes. Deborah was way too low on the couch. Only a few individual curlers and a smartphone held in the air were still visible.

"Over there," Deborah said, pointing to the liquor cabinet, in front of which lay a broken champagne glass.

"I'll get right on it, Miss Landry," I replied in a disguised voice. But Deborah was fortunately so busy with Snapchat and Instagram that she wasn't paying attention to me at all. I set to work when Deborah's phone rang.

"Jennifer! Finally, I've been trying to reach you for hours! What? No. I can't believe it!"

Deborah didn't make a big secret of her conversations, the way she yelled into her smartphone.

At least the champagne glass had broken at the stem, which meant two parts without big splinters, which meant that I only had to stay in the lion's den for a short time.

"Did you hear that Cathrine Porter dumped her boyfriend after he gave her new boobs?"

First World Problems...

I took the two broken parts, threw them into the trash and generously vacuumed the surrounding carpet. My movements were rather sparse, to spare my nipples a little, because every movement, meanwhile even every breath, left pain.

"Hello, I'm on the phone here!"

"Excuse me, I'm already done," I replied calmly. Normally I always remained calm with such guests, but Deborah drove my pulse up just by her presence.

Deborah giggled. "No, not yet. Even though I walk around this damn hotel all day, I haven't seen him once again. But believe me, I'll show him what he's missing."

I became alert, even though I didn't want to eavesdrop. Okay, actually I wanted to, even though I knew it wasn't right. Still, I took my time now to eavesdrop without getting caught. Slowly, I left the apartment and picked up a few scraps of words, the context of which was not clear to me. For that I would have had to understand Deborah's interlocutor, but I could have sworn that Deborah was talking about Connor. I felt it exactly. But I was his girl now, me and no one else!

"Hold it, hold it!" shouted Deborah.

What a fucking bummer.

Had she recognized me after all?

"Yes?" I asked, peering through the door.

"There's a tip on the table. It would be rude if you didn't take it."

Yes, I had seen the two dollars on the table.

"We are not allowed to accept tips. Directed by management."

"All right," Deborah murmured. She held out her arm and waved. "Then you may go."

How nice.

As I closed the door, Deborah jumped up from the sofa in horror. "What, really?" Our eyes met for maybe half a second before I closed the door.

I held my breath and did not move an inch. Breathing heavily, I listened at the door. Deborah continued to talk on the phone and was just blaspheming about the bankruptcy of an acquaintance.

Lucky!

If Deborah recognized me, she would not take it quietly. She would confront me with the fact that I was just a maid, a second-class citizen and had no place in elite society. Something like that, probably.

When I had regained my composure, I left room 3601 behind me as quickly as I could. Even now, no dismayed Deborah ran after me.

Arriving at the elevators, I hesitated. Actually, I wanted to press the button for the upper elevators, after all I didn't want to keep Connor waiting, when I realized that I had forgotten the clean towels for him. Snorting, I put my head back and exhaled loudly.

20

Connor

Impatiently I looked at the clock, Dana was late. Lateness was a serious mistake that my previous subs had usually only made once.

This gives extra points.

At least Dana punished herself every moment of her tardiness, by those pretty looking intense clamps that reminded her that she was mine.

I decided to accommodate her a bit, literally.

For that, I just had to find a way for Dana to be in the same elevator with me, no easy task, after all, there were dozens of elevators in the Royal Renaissance Hotel.

Anyway, I thought of a solution. In an emergency, I bribed the receptionist to take all the other elevators out of service for a short time.

When I arrived on the first floor, I saw a small group of kids in the lobby playing with each other. Jackpot.

The group consisted of three boys and a girl, all around ten years old. The girl was wearing a designer skirt, while the boys were wearing tailored suits. They were discussing whether cornflakes tasted better crunchy or soggy. Crispy.

"Hey," I greeted the kids, who immediately eyed me critically. "Do you guys feel like helping me with a prank?"

Now their eyes sparkled curiously. No matter how businesslike these miniature adults might seem, they were children after all.

"It depends," the girl replied shyly.

"And it costs!" one of the boys added seriously. He was wearing a gray suit that made him look like a much undersized businessman. I had forgotten what damn tough negotiators kids could be.

"Okay. I'll tell you what I need your help for first, and then you tell me the price."

"Agreed," the same boy replied businesslike.

"You go to the elevators and stop at each floor until you get to the top." I estimated the rough time the elevators would take and added, "And the same goes for the way down."

"Oh, that sounds fun," the girl giggled.

"Absolutely," I encouraged her.

"A thousand dollars." My God, this kid was tough as nails.

I pulled my wallet out of my pocket and checked how much cash I had with me. I usually paid for everything with my credit cards because it was easier and more efficient than carrying around a wad of bills.

Okay, I would even trust the boy to have a card reader with him specifically for such purposes. I had exactly one hundred dollars in cash.

"You've got to be kidding," I said seriously. "One hundred dollars. That's all."

"No way..." The boy was interrupted by the girl. "DEAL!"

Satisfied, I pulled the one hundred dollar bill out of my pocket and handed it to the girl, who accepted the bill with a smile. The girl definitely had less experience with money than her friends, good for me.

"Are you crazy? That guy just screwed us out of ninety percent!" the boy reprimanded her.

"And if he had gone to other children, we wouldn't have any money now!" the girl defended herself defiantly.

"There are no other kids here at all!"

I cleared my throat. "Tell your parents you're going to play in the elevator now, and then we're off. Take all but the elevator on the far right, will you?"

"Business is business," the miniature businessman grumbled, stomping off with his friends.

I got into the only free elevator, leaned against the wall and pulled my Gameboy out of my jacket pocket. As I did, I thought back to my first hard-earned money. I must have been about the age of those kids when I had offered private tours of my parents' bourbon factory. The concept had been so well received that those tours still exist today, just under different leadership.

Again and again, I went upstairs, but the ride always ended on the first floor, where else?

By the time I had cleared the ninetieth row of Tetris and the geometric shapes were racing down, Dana was finally standing at the elevator door, looking at me with huge blue eyes.

"Excuse me, sir. I'll take the next elevator to bring the towels," Dana stammered. "But that might take a while, all the other elevators are stuck on the upper floors and moving sluggishly. Kids, I guess."

Dana was so cute when she didn't know what to say.

"I know," I replied with a grin. "Get in, I insist."

"How do you know they're children?" Dana entered and examined me with an irritated-critical look.

"I gave them a hundred dollars for it."

Dana raised her eyebrows indignantly, but nevertheless she got in and turned her face toward the doors, which were closing.

"How are your nipples?" I asked as the elevator started moving.

Blushes of shame rose to Dana's face, and she bit her lips.

"What, are the elevators monitored with microphones?"

Dana shook her head. "No."

"Good, then you can answer me."

"I hate those things," Dana sighed.

"I can well imagine that. Tell me, where does the camera hang?"

"Right above the elevator doors," Dana replied without looking. "Will you take the clamps off me soon? Please, I can't take it any longer."

"As soon as we get to my suite. I promise."

She sighed with relief. I put the Gameboy back in my pants pocket and took off my jacket. Then I took a step forward and stood in front of Dana. When my jacket touched her body, she flinched briefly.

In case someone was monitoring the camera, it looked like I was standing in front of it, completely relaxed. But in reality, I was rubbing my jacket in pretty sensitive places. Dana left her legs as they were, she learned quickly.

"I can't wait to fuck you," I murmured.

I pressed the jacket tighter against Dana, who was now sighing softly. "Me neither."

"You dutifully left the clamps where they were supposed to be, so now you get to tell me how you want me to fuck you."

Dana thought about it for a moment. Surely, she was looking for a position where her strained breasts could rest a bit, but there were hardly any options.

"I, um ..." Dana moaned. She could barely contain herself. "Preferably in bed."

I smiled. "So, what else? What else?"

"I want to see your face," Dana whispered.

"Why?"

"Because I like the way you look at me."

"And how do I look at you?"

"Full of enthusiasm and full of greed. Determined to take what you want."

I growled in satisfaction. Damn, I could hardly wait to finally take Dana. Was it just me, or was the elevator getting slower and slower the longer we talked?

I wondered how slowly the elevator went for Dana. She felt with every breath that she belonged to me, while she was trapped here with me.

When we finally reached the top floor, I led my girl straight to the bedroom.

"Take off your clothes," I ordered. Dana immediately complied, moving the fabric around her torso but very deliberately and carefully. Her nipples were reddened and even a breath of air must have felt like a whip. Of course, I had chosen clamps for the beginning that exerted only weak pressure compared to other models, but after more than an hour even hardened ones reached their limits with them. Naked and full of expectation, she stood in front of me and looked at me.

"Clasp your hands behind your back."

Slowly, she bent her arms back and crossed them as I had shown her. I touched the dangling silver balls hanging from the clamps. She inhaled sharply.

"Now get on your knees."

I loved it when Dana knelt in front of me, her eyes downcast, her chest out and her back perfectly arched. Admittedly, I liked the sight so much that Dana would continue to spend a lot of time on the floor in the future, but now she was kneeling in front of me, because otherwise the pain would bring her to her knees. Dana was not yet prepared for this kind of pain, pain that was beyond anything she had ever experienced before, but I was sure that she could withstand this pain, otherwise I would never have put the clamps on her. Once Dana got over the first agonizing seconds, the most intense orgasm ever was waiting for her.

When I touched both clamps, Dana held her breath.

"I want you to breathe!" I commanded. "Take a deep breath now."

Dana needed a few seconds to overcome herself before she complied with my command. She took a deep breath and meanwhile I released the two clamps. Dana writhed in pain, and I pressed her tightly against my shoulders to support her. Tears ran down her cheeks, but she put up a brave fight.

"Well done," I praised her.

"For that," Dana faltered, then took a deep breath. "For that, you owe me the best sex of my life."

Amazing. In the first moment I thought she would need much longer to recover, and in the next moment, Dana even assigned a task for me, which pleased me extraordinarily. Despite the unaccustomed pain, Dana had not forgotten her pride, but had put aside her insecurity.

"I don't owe you anything, you were late," I replied softly, then brushed a few blonde curls out of her face. "But you should still thank me."

Dana looked at me. Half thoughtful, half defiant. God, how I loved that look!

"Or would you like to work with even stronger nipple clamps tomorrow as punishment for being late?"

"Thank you, sir!"

"Good girl. You will always say thank you in the future without me having to ask you to."

Dana nodded. After a while, there would be a few more rules waiting for Dana, but I wanted to introduce these rules slowly, so that Dana had enough time to get used to them. All the rules at once would only lead to excessive demands, and to her messing everything up.

"Now get on the bed so I can fuck you!" I growled hungrily. But my beast was not wearing a suit for nothing. I helped her up like a gentleman and offered her my hand. Although Dana didn't let on – and I gave her credit for that – her body was still in intense pain.

My hard erection pressed against my tight pants. I hated it when my hardness pressed against fabric, which happened to me quite often lately, thanks to Dana.

With a jerk, I stripped off my pants and boxers and lay down in bed with Dana. Gently I ran my finger from her wrist over her upper arm to her collarbone.

Dana's skin was so soft that I could caress it all day long. From the collarbone I wandered over her side, further down to her most sensitive spot. Her wetness excited me even more. Determined, I pushed her legs further apart and knelt between them. With my thumb, I continued to massage that sensitive nub while two fingers penetrated her. Dana moaned and stretched her hips invitingly towards me.

"Do you actually have any idea how insane you're driving me, Dana?"

"Yes," she gasped, "the exact same thing you're doing to me!"

I tasted her excitement and her passion.

"Say you're mine!" I ordered, murmuring.

"I'm yours."

Dana said these words with respect and sincerity, better than in any imagination, in any possible fantasy. None of my subs had ever said those words with so much feeling, because there was a significant difference between Dana and her predecessors.

Dana was real, as were her feelings and her desires – and my feelings for her were just as real.

Without warning, I penetrated her. Dana had had the choice to decide how I should take her, she could have said anything. Hard, deep, fast, animalistic. Slow, sensual, loving.

But she had kept silent and thus left me the choice. Therefore, I fucked her the way I liked it best, mercilessly hard and deep.

Damn, it felt so good! She was almost forbiddingly tight, and with each thrust it closed tighter around my hardness. Dana moaned loudly and pressed her hips tightly against my pelvis. Her fingers dug into the blanket, and her breathing was rapid.

Hard, harder, and even harder, I thrust into her. Dana's moan was sensual, a loud-and-clear sign of her approaching orgasm. I was almost ready too, had been since earlier. God, the idea of how she had had to work with her clamps, how she must have tried to compensate for every movement and hide the pain, drove me half mad. Her breasts bounced along with each thrust, a delicious sight.

"How did the clamps feel?"

"Very painful, but kind of humiliating too," Dana moaned.

"Did you like it?"

"Yes," she sighed.

"So, you like being humiliated by me?"

"Yes, sir."

My erection became even harder and filled her tightness even further. With every push, I came closer to the redemption, which I did not want to postpone. For this, Dana had made me just too horny.

"Come for me," I whispered in her ear.

Dana's eyelids fluttered, her body tensed, and her moans became more and more animalistic. I drove my body to peak performance, my muscles became hard as steel and stood out clearly visible. With a greedy look, Dana watched my muscles flex, her eyes alternated back and forth between my upper body and my cock fucking her. Her tender body was shining with sweat. With Dana it felt so incredibly good, so different from before. Better.

The orgasm burst over both of us like a sudden storm on the high seas. Violent, overwhelming, gigantic. You thought you were prepared when the waves came over you, but it wasn't like that. I was absolutely not prepared for the feelings Dana triggered in me.

Exhausted, I dropped down next to Dana and tried to catch my breath.

"Yes," Dana gasped. "The clamps were worth it for that."

"Don't say that too loud," I replied with a grin.

"The clamps were worth it for that!" exclaimed Dana. She grinned at me challengingly.

Such an adorable little beast!

"Haven't you had enough yet?"

With a strong jerk, I turned Dana onto her stomach and spanked her ass with the flat of my hand. At first, she just giggled, but when my strokes became harder, her laughter turned into moans. One blow followed the other until her ass glowed red. Only then did I let go of her. "There, that's enough for now. Let's save this fun for later."

"Too bad," Dana replied. It was clear that Dana liked her role as a sub. Her curiosity was getting the better of her, and she was opening up more and more to what was to come. Yes, we were both going to have a lot more fun.

"Oh dear," Dana exclaimed, startled, as she looked at my wristwatch. "I've got to go, or I'll be late!"

"Too late for what or who?"

"I have an appointment in Central Park."

Now I was curious, Dana hadn't said anything about a date.

"With Sam Anderson."

"How nice. You guys hit it off at the wedding, didn't you?"

"Yeah, she's really nice, and she had an earring made for me, so, a duplicate."

"I think I know which earring you mean."

"Right. That's the one," Dana replied with a pained face. "I recovered the original twin though, so she doesn't have to make a replacement after all, but stupidly I had already given Sam the other earring by then."

"Sounds adventurous."

"Oh yeah. I swear there's a curse on those earrings," Dana said with a serious face. I didn't believe in curses or any other supernatural phenomena, I was too rational a thinker for that. Quite apart from that, another topic occupied me more.

"What time do you work tomorrow?" I asked.

"I'm on late duty, why?"

"Can you take tomorrow off?"

"During fashion week? No, we can't do that."

"How annoying. I'd like to have you to myself all day and all night tomorrow," I growled.

"What did you come up with?" asked Dana curiously.

"This is a surprise. But I'm sure you'll like it."

I didn't want to reveal what I was up to yet, because if Dana knew what was coming, it would spoil the surprise.

"Would it be enough if you had me all morning and the following night?" asked Dana with a flirtatious look and stood up.

"If I have to," I growled. Of course, I respected that Dana took her job so seriously, but I had to admit that I didn't understand her loyalty, especially under these working conditions.

From the top dresser drawer, I pulled out a small box and gave it to Dana.

"I have another memento for you, so you won't forget our last ... more serious conversations."

Curious, Dana flipped open the velvet box and her blue eyes began to light up.

"Wow, these are beautiful! Thank you so much," Dana gushed. Directly she held her bracelet next to the small pendants.

"The feather," I began, and was interrupted by Dana. "The feather duster."

"Right. If you interrupt me again, I'll keep spanking you."

"I'm asking for it, sir!"

My reproving look put her back in her place.

"And the little balls are to remind you of today," I said.

"And what's the deal with the pineapple?"

I grinned. "Exotic fruit. An orange would have been too boring, I thought."

Dana smiled at me with that one smile that every man longed for. A smile full of love, warmth and affection. Real, honest feelings.

"The pendants are really beautiful."

I helped her to attach the small, filigree unique pieces to her bracelet.

"I'm sure there will be some memorable moments to come."

"If the trend continues, I'll soon need a wheelbarrow to carry all the memories around on my wrist," Dana said with a grin.

"Then I'll pay you a butler to do just that."

We both laughed. Unimaginable, Dana was the perfect mixture of friend and lover. Advantages that I had never been able to enjoy in combination before.

Dana gathered up her underwear, but I held her by the arm and took the fabrics from her.

"You'll save more time if you put your uniform on right away," he said.

"And what about my underwear?"

"I'll save those for you."

She picked up her uniform and put it on. On her lips was a gentle smile, perhaps even with a hint of shyness.

"Also, I have something else for you. I want you to wear it when I pick you up tomorrow. You're also welcome to wear it to your meeting in Central Park. Yes, I think I would like that even better." I picked up the big pink bag that was next to the dresser and handed it to her. I had seen this dress at Fashion Week and had known right away that it was made for Dana's body.

"But you can give it to me tomorrow, or won't you be there tomorrow?"

"I'm leaving the hotel tomorrow," I said.

"What? Why?" Dana looked at me in shock.

Because I'm a fucking free spirit and I can't help it.

21

Dana

You're checking out of the hotel tomorrow?" I asked incredulously. The bombshell Connor just dropped took my breath away.

"Yeah, I need some variety," Connor replied.

Wow.

Now the only question was whether there was just a spatial change for Connor or whether it was a major overhaul, including a new wife. I imagined dozens of scenarios of how Connor would transfer and leave me in a moment. But then would he have given me more gifts and had unique pieces made to remind me of certain moments?

No. Yes. Maybe. Emotional chaos to the power of ten!

Maybe parting gifts? Heavens! I took a deep breath.

"And what about us?" I asked cautiously, afraid of the answer. My heart was hammering painfully against my chest.

"What about us?"

Ouch. I would have liked to strangle him for that question.

"What about us when you move out?"

Now Connor seemed to have noticed my concern. Finally! He grabbed me by the shoulders and pulled me close to him. Full of passion, he kissed me and captured my lower lip with his teeth. That kiss said everything I needed to know, and I allowed myself to breathe again.

"Nothing changes between us," Connor said as we broke away from each other.

"I think that's nice." I sighed in relief and smiled at him. I should definitely keep my emotions under better control. As extreme as I had reacted, however, I just couldn't help it with Connor. By now, Connor had become important to me, so much that just the thought of rejection hurt. Jesus. Either the thing ended with a very unlikely wedding, or with a broken heart.

Don't drive yourself crazy!

"And where are you moving to?" I asked curiously.

"Close." Because he grinned and dodged my question, he probably wanted to keep it a secret. Was that why he wanted me to take a day off? Because he wanted to show me his new domicile? Connor pointed to the bag, the contents of which I still didn't know. "Go ahead and take a look."

I was insanely curious and was only too happy to comply with his request. I put the bag on the bed, literally tore it open and reached for the white fabric inside.

It was a knee-length white summer dress, with the softest fabric I had ever held in my hands. The dress was tightly cut at the waist, and the matching wide leather belt was a perfect match.

"Oh, this is beautiful. I'm already looking forward to wearing it after I get off work," I enthused. Connor handed me a shoe box that contained matching lace-up Roman sandals. The leather had the same embossing as the leather belt. The items had definitely been handmade. A beautifully die-cut paper attached with a brown cord confirmed my suspicions, it was from an Italian designer.

"I don't know how to repay you." All the expensive gifts Connor gave me made me uncomfortable, because I didn't want anyone to think I was with him just for the money. I didn't care about his money at all!

"That's what you do. You pay with your looks, your smiles, and your sensual cries," Connor replied. His dark eyes sparkled at me, full of desire.

"You should go now," he growled. "Otherwise, I'll fuck you right back."

"Yes, sir," I purred deliberately provocative. I adjusted my uniform and kissed Connor one more time.

"I'll pick you up tomorrow after work, all right?"

"Yes. But I really have to go now."

"I know," Connor replied, then escorted me to the door.

"I can't wait to see you tomorrow," I said goodbye.

"Tomorrow is going to be a beautiful day, I know that already."

As I walked through the door, Connor stopped me once again.

"Wait, one more question!" It sounded urgent, his voice was serious.

"Yes?"

"Your cornflakes. Do you prefer to eat cornflakes crunchy or softened?"

Okay, Connor looked way too serious for a trivial question!

"Softened of course, in milk with cocoa!"

Connor screwed up his face. "Softened cereal is for people with thirds."

"No, for connoisseurs and people who like it quiet. Loud noises in the morning are terrible," I justified myself.

"And eating without resistance, too," Connor replied with a laugh.

"So you like it unruly? I'll keep that in mind." Grinning, I headed for the elevators because I was in a hurry. There was no way I was going to stand Sam up after she bailed me out, even though she was in the middle of Fashion Week chaos. Things were always rough, stressful and wild behind the scenes.

As quickly as possible, I went to the employee locker rooms. I had finished work, completed all my tasks, and for the moment there were no bottlenecks anywhere. I didn't meet a single colleague on the entire way, and that was good. That way, I didn't have to come up with an excuse for the bag I had taken from Connor's suite.

There was no one in the locker room either, even better. After all, Connor had robbed me of my underwear. Of course, I had spare clothes and underwear in my locker. Black underwear that would cast unsightly shadows under the white fabric of the summer dress. And in a hoodie with a worn out hem and long jeans in the middle of summer, I didn't want to go out the door. So, I had no choice but to follow Connor's advice and put the dress on right away.

It flattered my figure without being too bulky because it was loose and airy on my skin, while the leather belt emphasized my waist. The shoes went perfectly with this outfit! I estimated that I was wearing three months' worth of fabric right now, maybe more.

Just as I was closing the locker door, I heard the scratching of the radio, followed by Shannon Williams' standard tinny call, "Daaanaaa!"

To be on the safe side, I looked at the clock again. Yep, I had been off work for a quarter of an hour and could leave the house with a clear conscience. Or could I? Just the thought that my boss had another one of her crazy ideas made me feel sick. Who else, if not me, could possibly dissuade her from these dangerous ideas? That's right, no one.

I gritted my teeth and hoped it was just broken glasses or dirty linens as I opened my closet once again.

"Yes?" I asked.

"Ah, good you're still here. I need you in my office."

"Is it important? I'm already moved and on my way to a meeting."

"Yes, it's very important!"

"All right, I'll be right there." I sighed.

"Very good!"

"But I'm not going to fucking change twice," I said without pressing the button on the radio. I wouldn't stand out in the hotel in a dress like that.

On the way down, I imagined what plans our deputy management had. Tracking devices for all employees implanted in the skin? Microphones sewn into the fabric? I would also trust her to take fingerprints, DNA and skin samples just in case.

I knocked on the closed door.

"Come in," Ms. Williams called out.

"Here I am," I said curtly. Hopefully my boss would get to the point just as quickly so that I could reach my appointment at least halfway on time.

"Fine, let's get right to it..." Shannon Williams faltered briefly when she saw my dress. "Oh, I didn't realize you had so much style." Yes, even praise from my boss always sounded like an insult, which is why I didn't thank her. "Let's get back to the subject at hand." She got up from her leather-covered office chair and walked around the table. "These glasses with a camera still have to be approved by the works council. In return, I want to put all the functions through their paces. I want to convince the works council that these glasses will be a revolution for the hospitality industry!"

More likely a huge step backwards.

Bravely, I bit my lips so as not to say anything wrong. Nelson Mandela, Mahatma Gandhi, Martin Luther King. They were revolutionaries. Do-gooders. But Shannon Williams was just neurotic and regressive.

"I still don't think it's a good idea," I said seriously. "It could be misunderstood by staff and by guests. Discretion is paramount at the Royal Renaissance Hotel, after all."

"And we will continue to maintain that discretion. These recordings will only be handled internally and will not be revealed to the public at any time."

"There are hackers who can outsmart such programs with ease, and perhaps there are security people who could sell recordings to the press," I indicated.

"Don't worry about that, I have assigned a security team for that. You are only responsible for the maids."

"And what exactly do you want me to do?"

Shannon Williams picked up a piece of paper from the table. "Sign this."

I accepted the letter, which was drafted by the in-house lawyer. I made slow progress in the difficult-to-understand legalese, but I read everything carefully, including the fine print. In summary, not only was I supposed to give up my privacy, but on top of that, I was supposed to agree to surveillance. This was a fist bump against my human rights.

Of course, I did not agree with the surveillance! But if I did not sign today, I would lose my job; that was as sure as an Amen in church.

"Is something wrong?" inquired Ms. Williams when I hesitated.

Remember your seven-year plan!

"Is this all really sanctioned?" I hammered out. "It really seems..."

My boss interrupted me. "Either you sign this, or I'll find a new advocate for the maids. Are we clear?"

Wow. Those were pretty damn strong words that I would have loved to rebel against, but I pulled myself together. If I signed the stupid note selling my soul, maybe I could sabotage the glasses action in such a way that the project was thrown to the wind.

"I need a pen," I said.

Immediately I got a silver fountain pen with which I signed the paper.

"When will the glasses be ready?"

"Not for long, Dana. I'll let you know when the time comes."

"Good." So then I had enough time to read up on this kind of technology and put the camera in the worst possible light. I had declared war on my boss in my mind.

"If you don't mind, I'm going to go to my appointment now." It was not a question, but a request to let me go.

"Of course. I'm glad we're getting along so well." Shannon Williams pretended to be confident of victory. As proof of our friendship, she waved the signed paper in which I had signed my soul over to the hotel.

Sometimes I wondered if all this trouble was worth it for a good resume. I could certainly learn something at the second best hotel in town.

It was only a stone's throw from the Royal Renaissance Hotel to the Central Park Zoo, where I had arranged to meet Sam. Nevertheless, I was almost half an hour late. As an excuse, I had bought a big box plus two coffees at Donut Duke - the Dunkin Donuts for rich people. Although there was no line in the store, the box, consisting of nine different donuts, had taken more than ten minutes to arrive because they had all still been lovingly garnished. In a rush, I hummed mantra-like don't spill the coffee, don't spill the coffee to myself and rushed to the entrance of the park in front of the Central Park Zoo.

What a stupid idea to wear the dress already! Just the thought of a drop of coffee getting on the precious fabric made me break out in a sweat. No idea what Connor had planned for me tomorrow, but I wanted to look perfect for it.

Sam, who was standing at the entrance to Central Park, waved when she saw me.

Please do not be angry!

"Hi Sam! Sorry I'm late, I didn't get out of the hotel sooner."

Sam looked relieved and laughed. "Oh! I was worried you'd be gone again! I was more keyed up than I thought, too."

In her hands, Sam also held a large box of macarons and two coffees to go.

I joined in the laughter. What a coincidence that we were both late! And an even bigger coincidence was that we wanted to apologize in the same way. Were we perhaps something like sisters in spirit?

A gust of wind made me shiver and then panic, because the light fabric of my dress blew with it. For my taste, the wind exposed my legs a bit too far. One more tiny bit and half of Central Park would have seen that I wasn't wearing any underwear. Help!

I was looking for a way to escape the wind. Somehow, I had to get rid of my donuts as soon as possible so I could hold on to my dress! On such a sunny summer day, the park was packed with joggers, picnicking couples, and frolicking children. Almost all the park benches were occupied, but near a large chess board I saw a free park bench and ran towards it.

"Let's sit over there!" I called out to Sam, who followed me in a rush. Only when I reached the shade of the old oak tree that stood directly in front of the park bench did I slow my pace.

Together we sat down on the wide wooden bench and put the coffee mugs next to us. On my lap I opened the donut box and secured at the same time so my airy little dress from the wind. The donuts were covered with various chocolate and sugar icings, garnished with powdered sugar and colorful sprinkles and pearls. Some of them were filled with puddings, creams, or other sweets. They looked as different as they tasted, but they all had two things in common. First, they looked good enough to eat, just like on an advertising poster, and second, calories in the high, triple-digit range.

Sam grabbed a donut with white chocolate and silver sprinkles.

"Thank you so much, they look really great," Sam thanked him, biting into them with relish. "Hmmm! And they taste even better!"

At the same time, she held the box of macarons under my nose, and I didn't think twice. I chose a pink one filled with strawberry jam.

"Wow, delicious," I gushed. They were by far the best macarons I had ever eaten in my life. The pastry was crispy on the outside, soft on the inside, and the cream filling was beautifully fruity.

Together we snacked on one pastry after another.

"God, these donuts are really sweet as sin. I love them!" gushed Sam.

"Yeah, I have a hard time saying no to sweets, too." Immediately I had to think about my stash of sweet tooth in my side pockets, and the hoard in my locker, and the not-so-secret stash at Rebecca's. I concluded that maybe I should reach for healthy fruits or vegetables more often.

"What do you bring to Prague when you're late?" I asked curiously. I had heard a lot about the Czech city, but knowledge from a real local was worth much more than any postings or postcards.

"Homemade cakes and pies, but now we also have the big American chains."

"Homemade pies sound great."

"Yes, I often bake cakes myself with fruit from our own property."

My eyes grew huge. "A garden of my own, how beautiful!"

"No, not exactly a garden, the trees are in our paddocks."

"Paddocks?" I asked. Actually, I had expected Sam and Josh to live in a stately mansion, not on a ranch; after all, they were designers, not cowboys.

"Yes. Jewelry is Josh's big love, mine is horses. I just love those animals, and I love working with kids. Thanks to Josh, I was able to fulfill both dreams at once."

"That sounds beautiful. I think it's great that you guys are balancing everything and then having this perfect marriage! How do you do it?"

Sam thought for a moment, her face turning serious. Then a smile followed and finally she replied, "We had our ups and downs, pretty deep downs in fact, but we trusted each other, held on to our love and in the end it all worked out."

"I hope to be able to tell stories like that when I grow up." Yep, I was officially extremely envious of Sam, who was living a storybook life.

"I'm sure he did. The way Connor looked at you..." Sam grinned conspiratorially without finishing her sentence.

"Yeah? How did he look at me?"

"He's never looked at another woman like that before."

I swallowed. Sam looked serious, and there was no reason for her to lie. Nevertheless, I had to follow up.

"Really?"

"Yes, really. Josh and Connor have been friends for years, and he visits us from time to time when he's traveling in Europe."

A great feeling spread from my heart over my whole body.

Never looked at another woman like that before.

"Say, Sam. Did you bring the earring?"

"Oh, yeah. Wait a minute!" Sam rummaged around in her purse and pulled out a small velvet pouch. Only now had it occurred to me that I hadn't talked to Sam about the earring at all, even though it was the reason we were together. With Sam, it was just pretty easy to talk about God and the world. Admittedly, I had never believed that there were still people among the rich and beautiful who, despite all the money and success, still remained as down-to-earth as Sam. Connor was grounded too, but in a different way. He still knew exactly what power he had, but he did not exploit it.

Sam opened the bag, which was tied shut with a cord, and dropped the contents onto her hand. Two identical earrings. "When you called, Josh was already done, so now you have a spare in case he gets lost again."

"Oh, if I had known that ... thank you so much!"

"No, I have to say thank you! With all the stress, coordinating and those terribly spoiled models, it was a real treat for Josh to do what he really loves."

I looked closer at the two earrings. Every single detail matched. The only difference was a small blue rubber attached to the end of one plug.

"Um. Which one is the original?" I asked uncertainly.

"The earring with the rubber is the duplicate."

"Unbelievable, Josh is really brilliant!"

"Yes, he is," Sam gushed. Her eyes sparkled in love. Her eyes fell on my bracelet, and she grinned.

"What about the bracelet?" I asked. With eagle eyes, I searched for the cause of Sam's grin.

"Every single one of these little pendants are unique to Josh. I remember it well, Connor came to see us specifically at Fashion Week because of it. And I think you know Connor well enough to know that he hates the whole chemical perfume smell to death," Sam replied.

"Really? Wow. Now, I love this bracelet even more!"

And so does Connor.

"I think there were a few more pendants Josh made, but I could be wrong," Sam said thoughtfully.

"No, I can well imagine that Connor still has a surprise or two for me."

The butterflies in my stomach danced samba, so excited was I for the upcoming time with Connor.

"Without surprises, it would be pretty boring, too."

"That's true. Although I must confess that the jet-set life doesn't appeal to me at all," Sam sighed. "My stable, my horses, and a trip to the theater are quite enough for me."

"Yes, during Fashion Week everyone in the hotel goes crazy too. Actually, the whole city!"

While watching a couple of dogs trying to catch butterflies flying around, we destroyed all the pastries.

Two strong coffees and what felt like a million calories later, we ended our meeting. Sam was firmly scheduled at the event and still had a lot to do, and I wanted to treat myself to a bubble bath after the stressful day.

"Thank you for a lovely meeting. New York does have its quiet corners after all," Sam said goodbye.

"Yeah, you just have to know them and then hide there so the stress doesn't catch up with you," I said. "Thanks again for your help."

"Always happy to do it again."

We hugged amicably, then Sam hailed a cab while I walked toward midtown Manhattan. The bubble bath had to wait, the butterflies in my stomach needed some more run. Anything else would have been a waste on such a beautiful summer day. And from 5th Avenue I could go home by bus, cab or subway.

The whole walk I pondered what Connor had planned for me tomorrow. It would be quiet in the hotel, boring. I missed the secret game between us already, even if my nipples were of a different opinion. On the other hand, Connor had certainly thought of something that would make up for his absence from the hotel.

Connor Lancester, what are you up to?

22

Connor

Impatiently, I waited for the receptionist to confirm that I had been checked out, but the computer system was just less than cooperative.

"I'm heartbroken, sir, so can I maybe buy you some champagne or coffee while you wait?" the receptionist asked me politely.

"No, don't bother. I'll just wait," I replied, annoyed. I pulled my cell phone out of my jacket pocket. I hadn't received a message from Max yet either, although she had wanted to get in touch half an hour ago. Was nothing working today? I sent her another text message.

Is everything done?

My sister didn't answer, and she lived in symbiosis with her damn smartphone. I had already prepared several lectures in case she got behind schedule and therefore couldn't keep her promise to deliver on time.

"Sir," a different receptionist discreetly called attention to himself. "If you'll just sign there, please? Then everything will be taken care of."

I accepted a pen, signed the paper, and returned both.

"Thank you very much. I hope you enjoyed your stay at the Royal Renaissance Hotel."

"I did, thank you."

I left the hotel and Dana was waiting for me at the fence in front of the main entrance, as arranged. She was wearing the dress I had bought for her at Fashion Week, and she looked delightful, irresistible. Her blonde curls blew over her shoulders in the summer breeze. When Dana saw me, her radiant smile was brighter than the morning sun.

"Good morning," Dana greeted me, beaming.

"Good morning, sunshine. You look beautiful."

Dana looked down at herself shyly, and her cheeks turned rosy. "Thank you."

I gave her a gentle kiss on the lips, but she flinched.

"What's going on?" I asked.

"Well, the hotel ... the cameras." Dana tilted her head toward one of the security cameras that monitored the entrance.

Ah yes, those stupid rules at the hotel. On the other hand, I thought it was cute how Dana tried to abide by all the rules, no matter how nonsensical they were. Maybe I should make some rules like that too, just to see her face, conflicted between pride and insecurity. I imagined Dana silently biting her lips to keep from crying out her horror or crossing her arms behind her back so she wouldn't attack me with them. Yes, I would like that.

"So, I'm not a guest anymore. So, the regular police can't arrest you," I said with a smile. A second kiss followed, which Dana enjoyed this time.

"Right, you're absolutely right, so what are you up to today?"

"I already told you it was a surprise," I told her with a conspiratorial expression. Then I handed her my arm, and Dana hooked up with me. Together we strolled through Manhattan to Central Park.

Actually, my destination was in the other direction, but I had to stall for time. Of course, I could risk it and possibly everything would be fine, or I could lead Dana into the middle of a major construction site.

"I'm really excited," Dana said expectantly. She put her head back and enjoyed the sun's rays, which made her eyes shine.

"Me too," I grumbled honestly. My cell phone vibrated. Finally! I picked up without checking the screen to see who the call was from. "Yes?"

"Hey Connor, everything is taken care of. Just took a little longer because one of the shipments got stuck in customs."

"Great, you're the best!"

"Yeah, I know, but I also know it's going to be too dark for Dana," Maxine grumbled.

"It's not dark, it's modern!"

"Yeah well, whatever, just don't say later I didn't warn you, all right?"

"Thank you, sis."

"The bill plus rush charge is coming." Max laughed, then hung up.

Dana looked at me questioningly.

"Maxine did something for me that was related to my surprise for you."

"Wow, you really brought out the heavy artillery when your sister is involved," Dana said thoughtfully. "You didn't plan anything ... huge, though, did you?"

"No, I don't think it's huge." That I had a different definition of huge because of my lifestyle, I kept quiet for the time being. Anyway,

Dana had long known that I thought on a different scale. Now I led her to my destination without any detours. We stopped in front of the door of a huge high-rise building. From my pants pocket I pulled out a silk scarf that Dana already knew.

"What are you going to do?" asked Dana anxiously.

"I don't want to spoil your surprise," I murmured and blindfolded her. I clasped Dana's hands and carefully led her straight ahead.

"Connor? We're not going to..."

Dana was so cute! I smirked at her unspoken thoughts.

"No, I'm not going to fuck you on the open road."

I moved closer to her ear and whispered, "If I'm going to fuck you in public someday, I want you to watch. I want you to see all the looks, all the excitement, all the fantasies they will have because of you."

Dana's body shook, and she threatened to trip.

"I was going to say blind cow, but I like your suggestion better, I think."

Smiling, I put my arm around her waist so I could support her better. She was light as a feather in my strong arms.

I opened a front door and led Dana directly to the elevator.

"Almost there, now it's just upstairs," I murmured as I pushed Dana into the open elevator, which immediately made its way to the top floor.

Once there, Dana allowed herself to be steered without resistance, which made it pretty easy for me to direct her to where I wanted her.

When we reached the middle of the loft, I let go of Dana.

"Ready?"

"More than ready!"

I removed the blindfold. "You can open your eyes now."

Dana blinked to adjust to the bright daylight, then looked around.

"Where are we?" she asked curiously, spinning around.

"In our apartment."

"Wait, what? Our apartment?" Dana stopped abruptly. Her eyes grew wide.

"Yes, you heard right. That's our apartment, just three blocks from the Royal Renaissance Hotel."

"You bought us a loft?" asked Dana incredulously.

"Yes. I want you with me as often and as long as possible. You're my girl."

Dana walked through the large, open living area that led directly into the kitchen, and I followed her. There were panoramic glass walls everywhere, offering a great view of New York.

Her gaze lingered on the wall in the living room, in the center of which hung her trophy, framed in gold. "You displayed my trophy like a work of art?"

"That's right," I replied with a smile, knowing how much that trophy meant to her.

"That's so sweet of you," Dana gushed. She kissed me, then Dana ran on, to the other end of the apartment, where the bedroom was.

"Wow, this is so huge. So much space just for the two of us?"

"Do you like it? Maxine decorated it to my liking."

"Oh yeah, it's great!"

Ha, take that Max!

"It might be a little gloomy, but you can make up for that with some bright ceilings and more lamps," Dana said casually.

Damn! Touché Maxine, touché.

I pulled a bunch of keys out of my pants pocket and handed them to Dana.

"This is your bunch of keys. This key here is for the front door, and this one is for the apartment door … this is the key for the garage, and this key … will take you straight to heaven, or hell, whichever I want."

Dana bit her lips in anticipation. "And where is the lock to unlock it?"

"I'll show you." I took her by the hand and led her past the bedroom. Hidden behind it was a staircase to a higher floor. These stairs led up to the inviting rooftop terrace with grill, infinity pool and semi-covered sitting area if you went to the left. And if you stopped at the door to the right, you entered my favorite four walls. The game room.

In this room, there was only Dana, me, and the power imbalance between us.

"Go ahead, open it," I urged her.

Uncertainly, Dana selected the appropriate key and inserted it into the lock. It was easy to recognize, because the bronze-colored, playful key stood out quite clearly from the shiny silver precious metal keys. She opened the black door and stepped inside.

"Did Maxine do that, too?" asked Dana sheepishly.

"No. It's the only room in the house that only you and I are allowed to enter. No one has ever seen it except us."

I had set up the playroom before Maxine had even set foot in the apartment.

Impressed, Dana let her gaze wander around the room. Yes, at first glance my playroom had to be overwhelming. For every girl I'd ever had, I'd built a separate playroom that always matched her preferences. But with Dana's playroom, I had outdone myself. Soft light fell into the room from various small lamps, bathing the black wallpaper with red baroque prints in mystical light. The door itself was padded with black leather; no one outside this room would be able to hear screams, no matter how loud Dana was. Her screams were all mine.

There was a St. Andrew's cross on the walls, with a leather cuff hanging from each end. The room also had a leather love swing, a closet full of vibrators, dildos and plugs of various sizes, and a large king-size bed with leather cuffs hanging from the ends as well. Next to the bed was a wide leather chair from which I could watch Dana intensely in the future while she would kneel in front of me. Rings hung on the walls, distributed at different heights, to chain Dana in every possible position. Just as I liked it, and what I felt like. In addition, whips and crops of various structures and lengths were attached to a rack. The floor was covered with soft black carpet, which absorbed noise, muffled footsteps and did not chafe knees so quickly. The latter was most important. In addition, the large room held other large equipment that would make the heart of any dominant man beat faster.

Dana didn't say anything but strode through the room as if she were a stranger who had no business here. Yet she was the soul of the room, the reason for its existence.

She opened the drawers hesitantly, as if a predator might jump out. I grinned. There were no predators in the drawers, no monsters. But things that drew out my very own beast. Restraints, ropes, clamps, candles, vibrators, dildos, plugs.

"Today you get to choose how we're going to play," I promised.

"With a lot of things, I don't even know what they're used for," Dana whispered shyly.

"Don't worry, you will know the purpose of each thing sooner or later."

"I'm sure you know," Dana smiled conspiratorially.

"Now pick what I'm going to drive you crazy with."

Dana pointed unerringly to the black St. Andrew's cross. "With that."

Perfect. My hardness throbbed against the fabric of my pants and waited for the St. Andrew's cross to be used. Damn, Dana wouldn't be leaving this room anytime soon today. Chances were good that my beast in the suit insisted on dealing with my girl for the next three days straight – and I didn't mind.

"Why do you want it to start?" I asked curiously.

"Because I know how it works."

"Aren't you curious what else this room has in store for you?"

I walked close to Dana and embraced her waist from behind. My breath tickled the back of her neck, and I felt her shiver. Even in the pale, warm light, I could see the trail of goose bumps spreading across her skin.

"Yes, I do, but with the cross, I know what to expect ... and I like that."

"Do you like the idea of being tied up there? Defenseless and completely at my mercy?"

"Yes." I saw how much effort it took Dana to tell the truth.

"Good."

I let go of Dana and went to the door.

"Once this door is closed, you are my slave, and I am your master. As soon as you enter this room, you will kneel in the middle of the room and wait for my orders. Do you understand?"

"Yes, sir," Dana replied. She sank to her knees and rested her palms on her thighs, just as I had shown her. With her eyes lowered and her posture perfect, she looked down at the floor.

"Good girl," I replied and closed the door.

Dana looked so innocent in her white dress, while the room around her was pure sin. I sat down on the comfortable leather chair and eyed Dana. I just couldn't get enough of this sight.

"I want you to pick at least one more thing. Something you don't know."

"Yes, sir."

Dana stood up and opened the individual drawers again. It took her a long time before she took out an object with a considerate look. Her body obscured my view of the drawer, then she went to the crop holder on the opposite side and pulled out a paddle.

"Show me what you picked out!" I commanded.

Dana walked over to me. Her gaze switched back and forth between my face and the floor. I nodded and Dana went back to her knees. In her hands she held the paddle and two balls connected by a string. The love balls had a modern design and shimmered red metallic. But the paddle in her hand irritated me. Was Dana really so inexperienced that she had never seen such a wide leather whip?

"You've never seen a paddle before?"

"Yes, I have, I just don't know what this is," Dana replied. She held the love balls up by the string.

"Then what did you take the paddle for?"

"Because I want to be chastised by you with it." Dana smiled shyly, but passionate fire burned in her eyes.

"Yes, you should definitely be chastised if you don't carry out simple orders," I admonished her.

"I thought we were playing by my rules today?" Dana dared to grin in victory.

"Not quite, darling, but if you want the paddle with you today, please do. That can be arranged."

Dana smiled with satisfaction. Still. She had no idea how much more strenuous the love balls were about to get. Yes, those cute little balls didn't look very threatening, but they had it in them! I held out my hand, which Dana accepted. First, I undid the wide leather belt around her belly, then I took off her summer dress and laid it over the back of the leather chair. I almost thought it was a pity to see her naked right now. In the dress, Dana looked innocent like an angel, with a sinful, fiery mind.

By the shoulders, I pushed her to the cross until she touched the wood with her upper body. The tip of her nose touched the wall until she turned her head to watch me. First, I took Dana's left wrist and guided it to the leather cuff. The wide leather strap was padded and designed to support Dana's entire weight. With her right wrist, I did the same.

Lovingly, I kissed her neck and took her skin between my teeth, played my tongue over it, varied with the pressure and so elicited Dana's first sensual moan.

With my knee I pushed her legs further apart. Dana's lust manifested itself wetly between her legs.

Like the wrists before, I now tied Dana's ankles to the ends of the cross with the leather cuffs. I took two steps back and examined my finished work. Dana's slim body cut a really good figure in this position. Her muscles were tense, and she breathed deeply in and out. Her legs were spread wide, and her ass looked damn inviting in this position.

In my hands I warmed up the love balls Dana had chosen. It was the set with the smallest balls, which were about the size of golf balls.

"These are love balls," I explained. Thoughtfully, I looked at the toy while Dana watched me out of the corner of her eye. From her position, she couldn't see much. Good thing, that would further increase her excitement.

"How do they work?" gasped Dana.

"Oh, that's easy," I said. With my hand I grabbed between her, widely spread, legs. I moaned softly when I felt her wetness while I massaged her most sensitive spot with circular movements.

"I'm about to put these two balls in your hot little cunt and you don't have to do anything but keep them inside you."

Dana moaned at my words. I inserted the first bullet, which intensified Dana's moans, followed shortly by the second. Dana bit her lips, continued moaning through her closed mouth, threw her head back with relish.

Dana would still barely feel the small weights, but I knew that this effect would not last long.

"For now, it will seem like no hard task, but believe me, with each passing minute, the weight of those balls will double for you," I announced.

Then I took the paddle. I let the black leather whip hiss through the air until it unerringly hit Dana's ass. A loud crack, followed by sensual moans. A second blow followed and landed slightly offset above the first blow.

Dana squirmed in her bonds, seeking support in them, and by her look I could see that she now understood what it was all about. The third stroke landed below her round cheeks on her thighs. Judging by her reaction, Dana had to be much more sensitive there than on her magnificent buttocks.

One stroke after the other followed, always a little offset. So long, until her whole ass shimmered reddish down to the thighs. Now that her skin was so well supplied with blood, Dana would react even more sensitively to my treatment.

"So, are the bullets getting heavier yet?" I asked.

"Yes, they are, very heavy in fact," Dana gasped. When she saw my warning look, she quickly added, "Sir!"

"Very good," I said. Again, I lashed out and covered her ass with firm strokes. God, I loved the sound of the paddle cutting sharply through the air, and I loved the sound of the paddle hitting her soft, rosy skin.

But most of all, I enjoyed her immediate reaction to it. The soft sigh she tried to suppress and the way she clawed at her bonds was a real feast for me.

Her red butt was a true work of art. Proudly I looked at the work that I had created.

"How many more strokes can you take with those love balls?" I asked.

Dana went inside herself and her whole abdomen trembled. For never having worn love balls before, Dana was doing pretty damn well. No matter what Dana's response was, no matter how long she lasted, I was damn proud of my girl.

"I don't think very many."

"Dana, honey. By now you should know that I appreciate concrete answers," I growled. My voice sounded dangerous, threatening.

"Excuse me, sir! Twelve strokes," Dana replied immediately.

"Twelve strokes," I repeated her answer. I agreed with that, except that I would have guessed ten or fifteen strokes. The number twelve must have been the first number that had appeared in Dana's head under pressure.

"You count along loud and clear. When you've done it, I'll fuck you as a reward."

"And what happens if I don't make it?" asked Dana cautiously.

To keep the tension high, I ignored her question and lashed out. No punishment I would name was as threatening as what Dana's imagination came up with. There was no better motivation.

"One!" Dana's look became serious. She didn't ask another question. Good. I wouldn't answer any more questions for her for the moment anyway.

The next blow followed.

"Two ... Three! ... Four! ... Five!"

Her enumerations turned more and more into screams. With each blow, the blows became a little harder. Dana bit her lips, it must be damn exhausting to keep up so much body tension now.

The next three strokes slapped her butt. I wonder if Dana regretted bringing the paddle into play by now.

"NINE!"

The ninth blow was the firmest so far. Dana gasped for air. I took the time to look at her red-hot ass, which contrasted in color with her pale complexion. With the edge, I traced the contours from the shoulder blade down to the back of her knees.

Dana moaned, whimpered. Waiting for the last three strokes was worse than the strokes themselves.

"Ten!" Dana's voice trembled. Her pleading eyes sought my gaze, silently asking for release, but I was merciless.

Again, I took an agonizingly long time before I lashed out for the next blow. The penultimate blow would hit her plump ass even harder than all the blows before.

"ELF!"

Dana squirmed in the restraints, but bravely maintained her body tension. I had the greatest respect for her stamina.

"Just one more stroke, dear. Then you've done it."

"Yes," Dana gasped.

But I didn't want to put her out of her misery so quickly. I wanted to show her clearly that I had her in the hand. I determined everything that happened in this room, just as it was in my mind.

Bravely, Dana withstood my gaze.

Good girl.

Dana was really into her role, her soft sighing was music to my ears. The muscle play of her trembling body was beautiful to watch, and I enjoyed the moment even more for a moment, then I gave Dana the release she silently begged for.

The final blow made Dana's entire body quiver. "Twelve!"

Not a second later the love balls fell to the floor with a dull sound and Dana let herself fall exhausted into the bonds.

Tenderly I pushed her hair aside and kissed her neck.

"You did very well, Dana, I'm proud of you." I covered her shoulder blades with more kisses, and Dana sighed heavily.

"You were really brave, so now I'm going to fuck you as a reward."

"Thank you, sir."

I opened my pants and freed my erection. Damn, I wanted to fuck her exactly as she stood in front of me. Through all the effort Dana was now nice and tight for me, even tighter than usual. I inhaled sharply at the thought, rubbed my cock briefly against her wetness, then penetrated her. Tight couldn't begin to describe how Dana closed around my member. Fucking tight! Forbidden tight!

Dana moaned out and stretched her ass out to me as best she could in her position. With each thrust Dana got even tighter and the contractions of her body were enough to make my erection even harder.

"You feel so good," I murmured against her shoulder.

I licked over her salty tasting skin. The next moment, I buried my teeth in Dana's skin, pulled on her, bit harder. So hard that Dana gasped loudly. She tried to squirm and escape me that way – but there was no escape for her. Dana was my girl; she belonged only to me.

"May I come?" cried Dana breathlessly. Her body was electrified, glowing, burning.

"Yes, come for me." How could I deny her an orgasm when she asked for it so enthusiastically?

Dana came, screaming loudly as she squirmed in her bonds. Her pulsating body, her violent trembling, and her sensual moans gave me the rest. As hard as I could, I thrust, eliciting a few more heavenly cries from Dana. Then I also surrendered to my climax. Jerking, I came inside her, squirting deep inside Dana while I continued to enjoy this incredible tightness.

"Will it always be like this?" she asked, gasping, and at the same time, smiling beatifically.

"Every game we play will be different," I replied thoughtfully.

"And what about the feelings that come with it? Will I always feel this good at the end?"

"Yes," I promised. What else was I going to plunge them into abysses for if the depths promised no flight of fancy?

23

Dana

While I pushed the laundry cart through the aisles, I told Rebecca in a whisper about this morning. All the while, I could think of nothing but Connor. His dark brown eyes, his defined six-pack, and his raspy voice echoed in my head.

With every single step I felt the soreness in my middle. Muscles that I had never known existed before! Connor really put it on that I felt him with every step.

"He really bought you an apartment?" asked Rebecca incredulously.

"Well. He bought an apartment and gave me the keys," I replied. To hide my sullen look, I glanced to the side. Beccs was my best friend, but I still concealed from her that I had looked at the name tag on my way out.

LANCESTER was written on it in big letters. My name was missing, and I felt kind of blindsided by that sign. I tried to distract myself with the fact that maybe Connor had just forgotten, but it didn't really work.

"And what about your apartment?"

Yes, about my apartment. Beccs just had to point that out.

"Well. It'll be cleared out by tonight, I guess."

"What?" cried Rebecca in horror.

"Shh! Not so loud!" I admonished her to be quiet.

"Sorry." Rebecca took a deep breath. "Isn't this all moving a bit too fast?"

"Yeah, kind of, but this thing between Connor and I is something serious. I've never been this serious before." My looks left Rebecca in no doubt as to the genuineness of my feelings. Still, I had to admit that the sweet idea of sharing an apartment had a bitter aftertaste because Connor had simply gone over my head. He expected me to move in with him as a matter of course, and to break my old apartment's lease within a day.

Well, I wasn't really attached to my one-bedroom apartment with the best view of a backyard complete with a huge advertising poster for canned soups, but it was a matter of principle! Did Connor's dominance go that far beyond the bedroom? Was I also his submissive, obedient girl outside the playroom? I had to accept all his decisions with a smile?

"I want to know everything about the loft!" blurted out Rebecca, once her initial shock was over.

"It is huge, very modern, with a fully equipped kitchen and huge bedroom. In the big bathroom, there is a rain shower with massage jets, and on the roof terrace, there is a pool. A freaking pool where you have a wonderful view of the city, Central Park, and the Royal Renaissance Hotel."

Plus, a game room with equipment that could drive everything and everyone crazy.

"Wow. I need to come visit you guys as soon as possible," Rebecca marveled.

"Absolutely! Bring Emma and Tom and we'll have a pool party with Hawaiian necklaces, big sunglasses, and colorful cocktails."

"Sounds really great."

Slowly, my anger at Connor's decision over me dissipated. If I told him how I had felt about it, I'm sure he would understand and ask me first the next time I made a big decision. I'm sure he would.

I pushed the laundry cart to the end of the hallway and then unlocked the first suite on the left. No one lived in this suite for the duration of the elevator maintenance, it was only used as temporary storage because the standard storage was bursting at the seams; there was not enough space.

"Done!" I rejoiced. The level of madness of Fashion Week was dropping with every show that ran. Everyone, including the city itself, was slowly but surely catching their breath. Now at dinnertime, it was very quiet anyway because most of the guests were having dinner or had appointments outside the hotel.

"Good, now there's just one more thing to do!" Beccs put her hands on her hips, put on her conspiratorial face and looked at me seriously.

I grumbled out loud. "I know, but I don't know how!" Thoughtfully, I pulled the earrings out of my pocket and looked at them. I had suffered a thousand deaths because of these damn little things, even though the owner, Mrs. Greenwood, had not been aware of their disappearance at all. Kind of unfortunate, but definitely a plus for me.

"Well, it certainly won't work with flowers," Rebecca began.

"No, besides, I can't just walk into the room because she might recognize me."

"Do you even know what room she moved to?"

"Yep." I dug around in my side pocket and found a piece of paper between a whole-grain apricot bar and some wine gums, which I waved around triumphantly. It was the very first thing I had researched when I came on duty. "She got an upgrade and is now on the forty-third floor. Room 4319."

"Hmm, how about a fire alarm or a cobra in the next room that snaked into the ventilation system?"

"No, we have to be more subtle. Much more subtle! We don't want to cause mass panic and throw the hotel into chaos, Beccs. We just want to get that earring back."

"Easier said than done, Miss Aggravation."

"Hey!" I sparked at her with a raised index finger. "You took the second earring out of the box!"

"After you put on the jewelry!"

"Okay, okay, you win." I rolled my eyes, and we both fell into quiet laughter.

"Thanks. I may have gotten a little too carried away, too," Rebecca admitted.

"A teeny bit, maybe," I replied. At the same time, I held my thumb and forefinger close together, as if I were holding a pin.

I had been racking my brains for the last few days about how I could bring the earrings back, but all previous plans failed even in theory. Either I was discovered or didn't even make it to the jewelry box.

"So what now?"

"I don't know." I shrugged. "It's a shame Connor's not here, I'm sure he'd have a plan – a pretty crazy one probably, but also ingenious enough that it could work."

"Like last time?"

"Exactly, just like last time."

I didn't like it at all when my best friend started muttering. "Just like last time."

Beccs sparkled at me with that scary-crazy look she only had when there was only one piece of chocolate cake left at the buffet, but three people interested. Oh, now the doorbell rang, and I knew exactly what my best friend was up to.

"No! No way, Beccs!" I refused to even think about that possibility.

"Come on, why not? It's worked before, and we don't have anything better."

"The fact that it worked out the last time is bordering on a miracle. We could have been busted in so many places that I don't even want to think about it anymore. I still feel like a criminal because of it!"

"Dana Swanson, most wanted maid for illegal misuse of a service cart." Rebecca giggled out loud.

"Stop making fun of me so shamelessly!"

"Make me!" Rebecca laughed even louder.

"Okay, I'll think about our Trojan chariot, you win!" I snorted defiantly, but for Beccs it was still a victory.

"All right, let's go over our only idea so far in detail."

"We're going to the forty-third floor, or rather you're pushing me there," I began.

"So far, so good. So far, a solid plan, I think."

"Then we get caught by Shannon Williams and lose our job."

"Wrong. What would she be doing on the forty-third floor anyway?"

"I don't know. Okay, so we'll just make it to Mrs. Greenwood's room and then get caught by her." Once again, my optimism was boundless. Not.

"Wrong!" my best friend corrected me again. "I'll distract her while you put the earring back."

"Still, this plan is not safe, we should come up with something better."

"When does she check out?" Beccs asked.

"Morning." I moaned like a scared dog.

"Then today is our last chance, tomorrow morning at the latest when she's packing, she'll notice that one earring is missing, and then all hell will break loose."

"I know." My best friend was absolutely right. "But we still don't know how to get to the suite."

"We'll just bring her a bottle of champagne, it's that simple."

Granted, Rebecca's plan was pretty good, so I nodded.

"All right, let's bring the earring back. After all, our Trojan chariot has a success rate of one hundred percent, so what could go wrong?" I said to encourage myself.

"Very good, that's my best friend talking! Let's go!"

Together we went to the forty-third floor, where, as on every other floor, there was a storeroom in the first room on the left, containing everything I needed for my work as a maid. Just before the elevators were serviced, we had thoroughly restocked each storeroom. Anything needed beyond that had to be hauled up the stairs, and I could gladly do without that. Especially now, when I felt the sustainability of these damn love balls with every single stair step.

Once on the forty-third floor, Beccs and I caught our breath for a few minutes and went over the plan again. A plan full of gaps, pitfalls and unanswered questions, but better than nothing.

I wonder if my books survived the transport unscathed? And all my furniture?

Jesus. The movers would not only transport my furniture, but also all my underwear, including the clothes I only wore away from the public. I had not thought about that at all.

"How discreet do you think movers are?" The question haunted my mind so loudly and presently that I had to spit it out.

"Huh? What makes you think of movers now?" asked Rebecca, irritated.

"Movers, Beccs. What do you think they do when they find, say, spicy stuff?"

"Oh, come on Dana, what would they find with you? You're boring!"

"Hey!" I protested.

"Sorry, you know what I mean. "Beccs gave me a kiss on the cheek.

"Maybe that's where my bathing cave is? Or something else really weird from my secret double life that you don't know about?"

"Then I'm sure they'll be discreet with your bathing cavity."

Grinning, I pulled a serving cart out of the corner, and Beccs placed a new floor-length tablecloth over it.

"What kind of champagne are we going to buy Mrs. Greenwood?" asked Rebecca. Her hands wandered over the large wooden crates that held a small selection of the most popular varieties.

"One I can afford," I said with a sigh. Of course, I paid for the booze out of my own pocket, sort of as a tuition fee; my guilty conscience simply wouldn't allow anything else. Not to mention, Shannon Williams would turn all the maids inside out if even a ten-dollar champagne was missing from an inventory.

"How about this?" Rebecca handed me a bottle.

It was a champagne Blanc de Blancs, and the logo looked expensive.

"Whew, that's seventy-five dollars!" In my head I calculated how many Ben & Jerry's that was.

"I don't see a cheaper one here, but another for three hundred and one for eight hundred and twenty-five dollars."

"All right, that one then," I snorted.

I said goodbye in my mind to a lot of ice cream, with chocolate shavings, caramel pieces, pickled fruit or brittle. Even the comforting thought that all those sundaes wouldn't end up on my hips didn't build me up much.

Rebecca put the champagne in a champagne cooler, placed two champagne glasses next to it, then lifted the tablecloth.

"Get down!" she commanded, in a commanding tone I had heard several times before today, albeit in a completely different context.

"Yes, ma'am," I replied with a grin. Then I hid under the wagon. Today it seemed even tighter and lower than last time, but I remained brave.

"Let's go," Rebecca said. She opened the door, then the car started moving. It wasn't very far to Room 4319; it was in the first third of the hall.

Through the heavy fabric of the tablecloth, the sounds came through to me only muffled.

I wondered while waiting why these suites were still called rooms even though they consisted of several rooms.

Rebecca knocked on the door, called out, "Housekeeping," and a moment later she was invited in.

"Good afternoon Mrs. Greenwood," Rebecca greeted politely once again. The car was still rolling. We had discussed that Rebecca would push me as close as possible towards the bedroom so that I could climb out and put the earring back.

The car stopped and the fabric was lifted slightly on one side. That was my sign!

"I bring a little treat from the house," Rebecca explained cheerfully.

Carefully, I lifted the fabric further and got a brief overview. I found myself directly in front of the open bedroom door. A stone fell from my heart. Only now had the thought occurred to me that the door could have been closed.

Silently, I climbed out of the serving cart and crawled like a ninja into the bedroom. Heavens, if the action went well, it was a great story to show the grandchildren what a cool grandma I was, but if this action went wrong, it was a story that couldn't be glossed over in any job interview in the world.

"Oh, how nice," Mrs. Greenwood replied. "I'd like a glass right away, please."

"I'd love to."

I could hear the cork pop softly. Only a few more feet to the jewelry box. A few tiny feet, and I would be rid of the damn earring!

There was only one problem, from the floor I could not see the box. If I just dropped the earrings in, Mrs. Greenwood would see a change at first glance. Nothing would be missing, but it would still arouse her suspicion.

"A glass of champagne Blanc de Blancs. Cheers." Rebecca handed Mrs. Greenwood the glass. Afterwards, Rebecca clasped her hands behind her back and waved at me.

I didn't have time to think about it, so I had to act, and act now! I decided that the safest thing to do was to simply pull the box off the dresser and put the earrings back where they belonged.

No sooner said than done. I pulled the box off the dresser with my fingertips. As I did so, Rebecca gave me a warning look. "Hurry up," her lips said silently.

My relief was great when I held the heavy box in my hands. Stupidly, I had underestimated the length of the lid, which caught on the edge of the dresser and made a thudding sound. What a bummer!

I held my breath and didn't move an inch.

"What was that?" asked Mrs. Greenwood.

"Excuse me? What was what?" Rebecca played dumb. She spread her fingers as wide as they could go – a sign that I shouldn't move.

"Well, that ... sound?"

"I didn't hear a sound, Mrs. Greenwood."

Rebecca waved her hands in panic. What the hell was that supposed to mean? Do nothing? Hurry up? Anything in between?

I trusted my instincts and put the earring back in the box as quickly as I could.

"I'm sure the noise came from the bedroom," Mrs. Greenwood murmured thoughtfully.

"Well, I didn't hear anything," Rebecca replied. She turned, stared at me insistently, and whispered, "Get out!"

Ha, good plan, Rebecca. Where the hell?

I put the box back on the table and crept to the front door. When I reached the car, I lifted the tablecloth up and was already halfway in when it started moving.

"Move this cart to the side, I want to check. The window is open, not that anything has been broken." At the very moment of her command, Mrs. Greenwood pushed the cart aside herself.

Sheer panic rose in me as Mrs. Greenwood rushed past me into the bedroom. If Mrs. Greenwood had run half a foot further to the left, a fall over my feet could not have been avoided.

My heart was beating so loudly that I was afraid it could be heard. Actually, it didn't sound like a heartbeat, more like the hammering of a woodpecker; that's how fast my heart was beating!

After the initial shock, I took my chance to climb back into the car unobserved.

"Hmm, I guess it wasn't anything after all," Mrs. Greenwood stated. There was almost something like disappointment in her voice.

"All right, I'll leave you the champagne," Rebecca said goodbye.

"Oh, no, take it away again. This little glass ... was enough for me, the champagne is not quite to my taste."

In order not to protest loudly, I bit my lips. I had just bought this woman a seventy-five dollar champagne and she threw it away after half a glass?

"All right, have a great day," Rebecca said sweetly.

Then she pushed the serving cart out of the suite back into the storage room. When Rebecca closed the door, I just plopped myself out of the cart.

"Oh. My. God! I can't believe that actually worked, Beccs!"

I felt great. Adrenaline and endorphins raced through my body. I jumped up and hugged my best friend.

"Of course it worked, we make a hell of a team, like Mulder and Scully," Beccs cheered.

From the open cabinet, I pulled out two champagne glasses and poured generously of the champagne Blanc de Blancs. "We should celebrate."

Rebecca accepted one of the glasses, and we toasted together. "Cheers!"

The champagne was just bubbling in the glass, which could only be a good sign for its great taste. Couldn't it? Far from it. I had to pull myself together not to spit the liquid back into the glass.

"Ugh. This is the most disgusting thing I've ever drunk in my life!"

Rebecca's expression also reflected disgust.

"Yes. Gag! Gross."

"I think, actually, Mrs. Greenwood is due an apology."

"I can't believe how calmly she reacted!" snorted Rebecca.

"There you see it again, good taste has nothing to do with the price," I stated soberly. Then I went into the bathroom and poured the contents of my glass, as well as the rest of the bottle into the toilet.

Heavens, I just flushed seventy-five dollars down the drain, what a waste!

I shook the thought away from me. That had not been a waste, but the price I had to pay for my stupidity. But now everything was all right again. I was finally rid of the cursed earring, and with it, hopefully, the curse it had brought.

"What do you say we celebrate our victory at O'Riley's? You can get bile-bitter champagne and stale beer there, too, and much cheaper," Beccs suggested.

The bar was very close to the Royal Renaissance Hotel, and Rebecca worked there regularly.

"Sure, I totally dig the homemade chicken wings there!" I enthused. Almost every good pub in New York had a specialty. A single dish, a special sauce, a secret blend of spices. A meal that put everything else to shame and got you hooked right away. At O'Riley's, it was the chicken wings with a chili marinade made from an old family recipe.

"Very good. Then you can tell me all about this gala you're going to!"

"Your sensationalism knows no bounds, Beccs."

"Who would I be if I didn't probe until I knew every little detail?"

"A normal person with tact?"

"Exactly!"

We both laughed.

"Okay, okay. You win. Then come on, let's call it a night before Ms. Williams comes up with anything else to spoil our celebratory mood."

"Daaanaaa," Rebecca mimicked our boss, a little too well for my taste.

I took a deep breath. Everything was fine now, the earring was with its rightful owner, the hotel was quiet, and my relationship with Connor couldn't be going better.

Everything was good, maybe too good to be true.

24

Connor

May I help the most beautiful lady of this event out of the car?" I asked with a smile.

"But of course, I can't refuse a wish from the most handsome man at the event."

With a seductive look, Dana accepted my hand and got out of the limousine. Her heels were forbidden high and emphasized her endlessly long legs excellently.

Damn, I just couldn't get enough of Dana. Her eyes and her smile shone with the starry sky around the bet.

"Can you believe how fast time has flown, Connor?"

"Time passes very quickly when you're having fun," I replied conspiratorially, then led Dana up the grand stone staircase to the mansion. She had to gather her floor-length dress to avoid stepping on the pink fabric of the chiffon dress.

Ever since she put on that sleeveless dress, I couldn't stop staring at her. Around the torso, the dress was tightly cut and emphasized her breasts, just like her feminine waist. To all the guests at the gala, my evening companion would look like a royal princess, and only I knew what Dana really was – my girl, my angel, my whore! Christ, I really had to pull myself together, so as not to bend Dana over the railing here and now and turn her princess look into an I-was-fucked-hard look.

"Say, isn't there another way? These stairs and shoes like this are potentially deadly."

I had purposely taken the employee driveway because I didn't feel like waiting in my limo for most of the gala because of a few press photos at the entrance.

"Believe me, once you see the long line of cars outside the main entrance, you'll thank me. It can take hours for the last car to pull up."

Dana stood on her tiptoes, trying in vain to survey my parents' vast estate. "You're right, I guess."

"Right, that's why we use the staff entrance, I want you to enjoy every second of this gala."

Dana beamed at me. "That's really nice of you."

"It was worth it for that smile alone."

But the uneasy feeling that Dana had triggered in me, because of the stairs, would not go away. Without further ado, I rummaged through the chiffon fabric until I grabbed her legs, then I threw Dana over my shoulder.

"Connor! You can't keep transporting me like a thing just because you feel like it!"

"You should know me by now and know that I can and will when I feel like it."

Dana didn't even try to rebel at first, but just snorted loudly until we reached the top step of the stairs and I carefully set her down.

"Good girl. But you still owe me twenty strokes for the protest."

Dana held her breath, swallowed her anger and smiled, a discussion would have only earned her more blows. Instead, she looked around briefly, just to make sure no one had seen us, then looked at me questioningly.

"Will Josh and Sam Anderson be here?"

"No, they went back to Prague shortly after Fashion Week. Josh just restructured his business, so it needs a little more care than usual."

"Oh, what a shame, I would have liked to thank him in person." Dana sighed heavily.

"For the bracelet?"

"No, for the earring. Without Sam's help, I would have had another heart attack from all the excitement."

I remembered the earring and its lost counterpart when Dana had first encountered me in my suite.

"Yeah, the earring thing." I grinned because I had upset Dana so much then.

"Oh, you wouldn't be grinning like that if you knew the whole story," Dana blurted out. Not a second later, she covered her mouth guiltily with both hands.

"Yes?" I asked smugly. "Well, tell me about it."

Dana stopped for a moment and looked thoughtfully at the floor. Her face reflected many emotions, from excitement to concern.

"Hmm," Dana began thoughtfully, but faltered again. I took her chin between my thumb and forefinger and lifted it. With that, I forced Dana to look me straight in the eye.

"Just put it out there," I urged her.

After a deep breath, Dana nodded.

"It was an accident, okay? I was just going to try on the earrings for a minute, then I got distracted and forgot to return one of the earrings. When I came back, its twin was gone. Beccs had found it. We could have placed it back there the next day, but by then I had already given Sam the earring for a copy."

"Quite adventurous," I said, still grinning broadly.

"Getting those two earrings back to the suite was adventurous. I felt like a ninja in a Trojan horse, or better, Trojan service cart!" Dana buried her face in both hands and sighed loudly. "I don't know why I magically attract chaos."

"It may have something to do with your obsession with wearing other guests' things," I opined.

"It's not an obsession or anything perverted! I just like to imagine being someone else sometimes."

"Why would you want to be anyone else?"

"Sometimes I just don't like the standard Dana. Insecure, clumsy, chaotic."

"And what about my girl? She's elegant, sensual and getting more and more confident."

Dana bit her lips, her rosy cheeks giving way to a deep shade of red.

"Yes, I think I quite like the playroom Dana," she replied with a smile.

"Good, you know I'm going to punish you for not being honest with me from the beginning, right?"

She looked at me rebelliously, at the same time with a serious look, until her features softened again.

"Yes, sir."

"Is there anything else I should know?"

"No."

I eyed Dana seriously and tried to notice every little movement in her face. When Dana looked at me from below, with her big, light blue eyes and her slightly open mouth, I could hardly control myself.

When I didn't say anything, Dana added, "I really didn't, I swear. I haven't tried on anything else since the dress, and by God, the earrings got me in so much trouble, I finally get it now."

"Good girl." Then I led Dana to the adjacent gardens where the gala was being held. With the considerable number of guests, there was no other option but to hold the celebration outdoors.

The paths were marked with lanterns, fairy lights and torches. Arranged bouquets were everywhere, and soft chirping of crickets mingled with the delicate tones of some strings. We followed the music.

"This is insane," Dana marveled. "And you grew up here?"

"Yes, together with Max. We were constantly on each other's heels, especially on rainy days."

"How did you guys manage to do that? The whole of Central Park would fit in here comfortably! In your house alone!"

"No, dear, not quite."

When we reached the entrance to the garden, we stopped for a moment so Dana could soak up every impression. We stood to the right of the villa and the house for the employees behind it. Small open marquees were spread across the lawn, but there were also small round tables under the stars. Red carpets had been drawn through the garden like a grid so that the female company would not have to do without their high heels.

Although it was still early, many guests had already arrived, strolling through the garden, standing together in small groups or dancing to the soft orchestral music.

"Wow, it's all like a fairy tale."

I smiled and offered Dana my arm, which she gratefully hooked into.

"My sister really has a knack for this, not all celebrations of this kind are so beautifully arranged."

Slowly we strolled to a small pavilion at the edge of the garden, from there we could easily observe the emerging hustle and bustle.

"This is where I discovered my passion for mixing and experimenting with beverages."

"Really?"

I nodded. "Yes, Maxine had thrown a tea party for Mum and me, and I mixed together all the fruit juices I could find."

"And that tasted good?" Dana screwed up her face about the way Maxine did when she tasted my first, extremely unsuccessful, Lancester mix. I laughed out loud.

"No, it was absolutely awful, but that's what got me interested."

"Wow. So, I'm getting a private tour of your childhood right now?"

"You could say that."

"I want to know more!" she urged me.

"Trust me, my mom will tell you so much more, your ears will bleed."

Dana giggled, then leaned against one of the pavilion's ivy-covered support beams. "I'm sure it was wonderful growing up here."

"It was," I confirmed. "But enough about me, how did you grow up?"

Dana had talked very little about her past, and I wanted to change that.

"Mainly, I grew up in New Orleans. My grandparents had a cute little boarding house there."

"A small, cute boarding house suits you much better than such a swanky, cluttered giant mansion."

"You think so?"

"Yes, a person with character needs a place with character," I replied with a smile.

"And this has no character?"

"No, that's just bragging."

"But you have character," Dana protested.

"I don't live here either," I replied with a grin. I put my arm around Dana's shoulder and kissed her forehead. Dana's past kept me busy for quite a while.

"Why do you want to work at the Royal Renaissance Hotel?" I asked.

"I want to learn everything I can from the best so I can stand on my own two feet later."

"I see." For a moment, I considered speaking my thoughts aloud. "I don't think you're in as good a place with them as you think, then."

"Oh, so now you're an expert in the hotel industry, too?" teased Dana. I could tell she was pretty passionate when it came to her profession.

"No. But I don't have to be an expert to know that between Carrara marble, sterling silver and high-carat diamonds, there's little room for passion."

If I had learned one thing in my career, it was exactly this. A good wine only becomes something perfect when you bring passion into play. Before that, it's just an average drink with no deeper character. It's not only like that with alcohol, it's also like that with art or music, in gastronomy, just everywhere in real life.

Only true passion creates a character. I could also only fathom Dana's true character when passion was involved.

"Without passion, we are nothing," I concluded my thoughts.

"Wow, I think I need to let that sink in," Dana muttered.

"How about a drink for the lady?" I asked, already standing up before she answered.

"Gladly."

I led Dana to one of the many small islands where bartenders stood and could satisfy almost every wish. I ordered a sparkling wine for Dana and a non-alcoholic fruit punch for me. Both drinks contained frozen fruit instead of ice cubes. I had insisted on this because ice cubes watered down the taste of everything, Max agreed, though for looks, not taste. Since I was sixteen, ice cubes had not been used at parties hosted by my parents.

Here and there I let myself get involved in short conversations, during which I proudly introduced Dana as my evening companion. She was much more relaxed than at the wedding, but that had also been a case in itself.

"Connor, where is your family anyway? I thought they were hosting the event," Dana asked thoughtfully.

"That's right, and at this kind of social event, it's part of being late as an organizer."

"Really?"

"The waiters, bartenders and musicians are entertaining us splendidly, aren't they?"

"Right."

The darker it got, the brighter the lamps, candles and fairy lights that were spread throughout the garden shone. Dana couldn't get enough of it all and watched the entire event with enthusiasm.

"I feel like a princess from a Disney movie," Dana gushed.

"Then I guess I'm your handsome prince and savior in need."

I stepped closer to her, took her hand and placed it on my swelling erection.

"And I am at the same time the beast from which you should be saved."

Dana stifled her moans by biting her lips. Unfortunately, I didn't get to whisper any more depraved things into my girl's ear.

"Hey bro, hey Dana," Maxine greeted us.

Undecided what Dana should do with her hand on my hardness, she cleared her throat. In order not to embarrass Dana further, I took a step to the side. Dana immediately clung to her champagne glass as if it were her life preserver on the high seas.

"Hey, sis," I greeted Max with a kiss on her forehead. She was wearing a light blue silk dress that flattered her slender, tall figure.

"Hi, Maxine, you look great." Dana and my sister greeted each other like old friends.

"How did your conversation with the CEO go?" I asked. After I had smoothly forgotten to ask for an appointment for my sister at my first meeting, I had organized a second meeting shortly afterwards.

"Stop it, that ship has sailed. We have completely different opinions when it comes to aesthetics, there's nothing to be gained from it," Maxine said, shrugging her shoulders.

Even if she looked innocent and cute at first glance, she was a tough businesswoman on whom everything rolled off.

"They don't know what they're missing," I said anyway, for the sake of decency.

"So, Dana? How do you like your apartment? Connor said you were thrilled?" Maxine changed the subject. With narrowed eyes, she eyed Dana, like a tough cop wanting to hear a felon's confession.

I took the floor. "You decorated the apartment just perfectly! Didn't she, dear?"

There was no way I was going to begrudge my sister the satisfaction of knowing that my apartment was a touch too dark for Dana's taste. I hated it when Maxine looked at me with that I-told-you-so look.

"Yes, it's so huge!" enthused Dana. "And after a few lamps and white upholstery, the loft shines beautifully."

"Aha!" Maxine pointed her index finger at me accusingly and poked it against my chest several times, "I told you, it's too dark!"

"Oh! Well, I didn't mean it that way, of course," Dana tried to save the situation. "I didn't mean to offend you, Maxine. You did that beautifully, and..."

"It's okay Dana, I thought it was too dark too," Maxine replied sugary sweet.

After that, her gaze snapped back to me. Demandingly she stretched out the flat of her hand, "Give me the coal."

"All right." I sighed and pressed a hot-off-the-press five hundred dollar bill into Max's hand. Of course, the few dollars didn't hurt me, but Max's triumph did. The symbolism of my defeat was underscored when Max folded up the bill with a grin and let it disappear into her cleavage.

Dana scratched her neck in irritation. "I feel like I missed something."

"No, you didn't," I said with a smile. Just as Maxine was about to object, she saw Dana's bracelet.

"Wow, what a gorgeous bracelet!"

"Yeah, I love it too. It's from Connor," Dana gushed. She held out her hand to Maxine so she could examine it more closely. This was the moment I wanted to get drunk, too. Of course I loved my sister ... and Dana too, but I just wasn't cut out for that kind of talk. I decided to leave such conversations to womankind and take a token walk to the bar, but a hand on my shoulder prevented me from doing so.

"Mr. Lancester, what a pleasure to see you here." Through the Spanish dialect, I could immediately place the voice. Justino Olivera, who kept quiet about his new fermentation process.

"Nice to see you too, Mr. Olivera. This is my sister Maxine, and this is my beautiful evening companion Dana," I introduced everyone together. "How's business?"

Not that I was really interested, Mr. Olivera didn't want any cooperation, so he had become uninteresting to me as a businessman. Possibly, however, he did reveal something about the process I was so keen on, so I stopped.

"Our cue!" said Maxine exaggeratedly. She grabbed Dana by the wrist and pulled her to one of the set-up bars, which stood between two large tables covered with canapés.

"Whew! Is that okay with you?" Dana asked, but already let herself be pulled along.

"Of course, but you shouldn't make a habit of letting women kidnap you at events like this." I winked at her. Then my girl had disappeared into the crowd, leaving an emptiness inside me that I could hardly describe.

25

Dana

Maxine pulled me once across the garden until we stopped a bit offside at a bar, where Max grabbed two champagne flutes. I insisted on a sparkling wine with lots of orange juice, however, because I wanted to remember every single detail of this wonderful evening. This evening was like a dream, and I wanted to hold on to it forever, come what may!

"There, now show me that bracelet again!" commanded Maxine.

"I'd love to." I proudly held out my wrist to her. Ever since Connor had given me that bracelet, the urge to show it around had been immense. I would have loved to put it on a billboard and run it as a continuous advertising loop during the NBA. I would have loved to show off Connor's gift to me to the whole world!

"It's really beautiful and pure handmade."

"Yes, it's from Josh Anderson. I was hoping to thank him again in person. He did something else for me. Unfortunately, they left shortly after Fashion Week."

"How unfortunate. But as often as Connor is in Europe, it won't be long before he makes a side trip to Prague, too, then you can visit them there," Maxine said as casually as if it were the most normal thing in the world to spontaneously hop on a jet and fly to Europe.

For me, it was already half a world trip to take the train to New Orleans to visit my parents.

"Really? He would take me?"

"Sure, you're his girlfriend."

My heart leapt for joy. Connor had called me a friend in front of his sister. As in girlfriend. As in relationship. His girl.

Now it wasn't the bracelet I wanted to show off to the whole world, but the man at my side.

Maxine looked at me expectantly, I had to say something, but my thoughts were dancing samba and I just couldn't sort out the chaos in my head. Heavens, Connor introduced me as his girlfriend!

Maxine's lips moved, but I didn't hear a word, my heart was beating way too loud.

Smile nicely, nod and hope it wasn't a question, Dana!

"Do you really think he would take me to Europe?" I don't know what else Maxine had said after that, but the question burst out of me as I struggled to break free of my caramel syrupy thoughts.

"Sure, why not?"

I was beside myself, but my euphoria was tempered by the fact that I never had more than two days off at a time, and vacation at the Royal Renaissance Hotel was as non-existent as worker protection. Anyone who had vacation or overtime had it paid out, that was an unwritten law.

"Well, right now I probably have too much to do," I stammered to myself.

"Where is there much to do?" asked Maxine critically.

"At work." I left it as a vague statement to keep all my options open. After all, I had no idea how much Connor had actually told his sister about me. I didn't want to get Connor in trouble, any more than I wanted to get myself in trouble. Not tonight, anyway. Everything was so perfect.

"Don't worry, Connor told me everything." Maxine winked at me conspiratorially.

Really everything? Or did Maxine just think that? Uncertain, I bit my lower lip. Of course, it could also be that Connor's sister knew nothing, but suspected something and wanted to trick me that way.

"Did he really?" I asked another time.

"Sure, he told me every detail of your first meeting."

Damn, Maxine was far too sparse with her information in my opinion. Did Maxine know the truth or not? I risked the jump into the cold water – with a life jacket.

"And you don't mind that we presented you with a slightly altered version of our first encounter?"

Maxine laughed out loud. "Believe me, if I cared, you would have noticed long ago." Real madness sparkled in Maxine's eyes. Yes, there was no doubt that she had a strong personality.

Maxine's madness disappeared, and she grinned broadly at me. "Besides, I think your seven-year plan is pretty exciting; it shows some real business acumen."

Okay, if she knew about my plan, then she also knew where I was standing right now. Full of relief, I sighed loudly. "I'm glad that's off the table."

Now the evening could be even more relaxed because I didn't have to think about what I could and couldn't say. Not only was I the worst liar in the world ... it was also one of Connor's fixed rules. Because of his opinions, words, and rules, moral, almost mundane things, suddenly became something sacred that I adored.

"Dana, I must confess that this makes me like you all the more."

"Yes?" I squinted my eyes.

"Sure. The fact that you just said yes without knowing what to expect, without even knowing a single person, is pretty brave. You did my brother a very big favor by doing that." She leaned forward conspiratorially. "You're the first person he's brought to two events in a row."

Wow. I was the first? Was it presumptuous to hope that I was also the last to take Connor to multiple events?

"The first one?" I repeated with a gasp.

"You should breathe again!" said Maxine with a worried look.

I took a deep breath. "I'm fine!"

"Good, I was getting worried."

Maxine had just told me that I was the first woman Connor was really interested in, and she expected that to roll off me like water? The Lancesters really were crazy – in a way that I liked.

Maxine toasted me. "Here's to last firsts."

"Cheers."

While I drank a small sip, I listened to the small orchestra that was playing Vivaldi's Spring.

Maxine had a new glass brought to her with another sparkling wine. I admired how sober she still seemed. I wondered if most of the guests here were more or less basic immunized because they drank gallons of alcohol at such events.

"You really made an impression on Connor," Maxine continued, which almost made me choke.

"Yes?"

"Of course, or he wouldn't have given you such a personal gift. Believe me, he brought a lot of women here and not a single one of them wore anything unique."

"How many women?" I asked uncertainly, not quite sure I really wanted to know the answer.

"Many." Maxine's eyes grew huge. "A hell of a lot!"

"Interesting." I hadn't pegged Connor as a playboy at all, rather the opposite in the way Connor presented himself to me. In my eyes, Connor was a true gentleman who sometimes liked to put women over his knee, in a very classy way.

"Interesting," I murmured another time. Then I put my lips thoughtfully to the rim of the champagne glass.

What if Connor went back to his changeable one-woman-a-day diet? Maxine saw my insecurity suddenly spreading through me.

"I'm one hundred percent sure we'll see each other again at the next event."

"I hope so, too."

The event was picking up speed. Dozens of quiet conversations echoed through the huge garden, which was packed with hundreds of guests. Just thinking about what the hosting must have cost made me dizzy.

To somehow distract myself, I set my glass down on one of the nearby bar tables and plucked at the leaves hanging out of a large bouquet.

"These are really beautiful," I gushed. "Everything here fits together so perfectly! The tables, the blankets on them, the fairy lights and flowers, the music. It must have been a lot of work to organize."

"Yes, it was, but thank you for the compliment," Maxine replied.

It took me a second to realize that Maxine had arranged the party. I don't know how I could have forgotten, even though Connor had told me earlier.

"Wow, you did that?"

"Yes. So, I didn't tie those bouquets myself, but I took care of the decorations and the tables. The catering is traditionally always done by Connor and my parents sponsor various stuff for higher donations."

"Wow." That was all I could say. Connor had told me that Maxine was a good decorator and had made a name for herself, but Maxine was about the same age as me. While I had just barely graduated from college and was now slowly and laboriously climbing the ladder as a maid, Maxine had long been at the top. She had achieved things that I had not even dared to dream of.

"Oh, come on, it's just a little garden party," Maxine waved it off. Had that been false modesty or was she serious? My urge to explore was aroused.

"And what else have you arranged?"

"I'm involved in the big Texas Derby, which is kind of like football for the elite. But mostly I furnish the homes of super-rich actors and other celebrities."

Now I was really hooked. "Whose house are you taking care of right now?"

"Hmm, actually I'm pretty discreet about that unless my clients mention my name on their own."

"Oh, come on, don't keep me in suspense! Please, please, please," I pleaded.

"Okay, I'm just taking care of Bonnie Buckley and Ted Sylvester's joint mansion in LA."

"Oh. My. God." I hyperventilated. "Bonnie Buckley! I don't think I've ever been so jealous!"

"You want to know who I'm jealous of?" asked Maxine. She took a step closer to me and whispered, "Jason Momoa and Chris Hemsworth's personal trainers. Heavens, those bodies make me drool instantly!"

We both laughed out loud. "Yes, they are definitely to be envied," I agreed.

Connor didn't have a personal training assistant, but the way he trained, he didn't need one. He motivated himself, pushed himself to his limits, and just the thought of his naked, sweaty torso shining in the sunlight made my abdomen tingle. The muscle play under his flawless skin was a real feast for the eyes.

"Dana? You're drooling." Maxine giggled. She had caught me daydreaming, and I winced guiltily.

"Oh, whoops!" Reflexively, I wiped my mouth with the back of my hand, then said the first thing that went through my mind. "You were talking to Connor earlier about the Royal Renaissance Hotel, do you have a job there?"

"No, not exactly. I wanted to – a job like that would be a challenge, but they weren't interested."

"What a pity. So then the guests will have to continue to be bludgeoned by all the heavy pageantry."

"You said it! Best service or not, the hotel needs a decorative overhaul."

"Well, maybe in a few years they'll ask you for help when the hotel runs out of guests."

By this I meant not only the expensive but stylistically old style, but also the methods of Shannon Williams employees with surveillance camera glasses, I could only shake my head in bewilderment, next came surely listening microphones in dental fillings and implanted tracking devices in the neck.

"Well, and then I'm going to decline, because that's when I happen to be, um, shopping. Time. Oh, time always runs out so unexpectedly."

Maxine said it so seriously and professionally that I had to giggle.

In the crowd, I spied Connor talking animatedly with Mr. Olivera. The top button of Connor's shirt was undone, and in my mind, I continued to undress him. There was a gentle smile on his striking face, and as he looked thoughtfully to the side and returned my gaze, my entire body quivered. The butterflies in my stomach fluttered wildly and excitedly, I felt like I was about to take off. In all my life, I had never felt like this, especially because of a smile.

I couldn't deny it, I was head over heels in love.

"Hello, Earth to Dana!" Maxine waved her hand in front of my face.

"Sorry, my mind was racing."

"Yes, that was you, again. And you were drooling, again! And there's no naked Chris Hemsworth over there, just my brother," she joked, then her expression suddenly became very serious. My heart stopped when I thought her death stares were directed at me, but Maxine wasn't looking at me, she was looking behind me.

"Great, bitch on eleven."

Immediately I looked to the side, curious as to who had incurred Maxine's wrath, and sighed heavily when I saw my nemesis strutting around as if the gala was dedicated to her.

"Oh crap, I forgot and left my garlic necklace and crucifix at home, today of all days," I said, holding my breath. For a moment I had totally forgotten that I was at a glamorous event and this kind of cynicism would be better served on a girls' night out with Beccs.

"Believe me, you won't get rid of such demons even with holy water blessed by the Pope himself," Maxine replied dryly. "I like your sense of humor, by the way."

"What humor?" I asked seriously.

"Just that kind."

We watched with critical glances as Deborah immediately grabbed two champagne flutes and eyed the company disparagingly. She wore a sky-blue, floor-length dress adorned with diamonds on her upper body.

"Do you know Deborah better?" I asked.

"Well, not very well. Her parents have a big sand mining company."

"Sand mining company. A good word for Scrabble, I should remember."

"Yes, but it's not as cute as it sounds. They steal sand off African coasts, destabilizing the entire area and thus destroying entire coastlines, the home of thousands of animals and plants. These are really mafia-like structures in some cases."

My jaw dropped. "That's terrible!"

"Her mindset reflects nothing else. Deborah Landry is rich, arrogant, obnoxious, but worst of all, she's had the hots for Connor for years."

"I knew it!" So my jealousy was legit after all, and worse was to come. Deborah parted the crowd like Moses parted the sea and came straight for Maxine and me. Great. This was exactly what I had been missing.

"Maxine Lancester!" cried Deborah hysterically. "What a pleasant surprise to see you here!"

"I live here," she replied dryly, and I suppressed my giggle.

"Ah, that's right. I forgot you still lived with your parents," Deborah teased back. Ouch.

I was simply ignored by Deborah, just like last time. Good thing. With this woman, my impulse control just stopped, one wrong word and her extensions were on the floor. Breathe deeply!

I admonished myself to be calm, for I did not know myself to be so prickly.

"Excuse me for a moment, I have to do something. I'll be right back," Maxine said goodbye.

Nooo! Do not go away!

I almost felt a little betrayed because Maxine left me alone with my competition. Sadly, I watched her walk purposefully toward the orchestra.

"So ... Joanne, nice party, right?" Deborah turned to me.

"Yes, wonderful." I didn't even correct Deborah at first because I didn't want to embarrass myself. Of course, Deborah had deliberately addressed me by a false name, but I didn't begrudge her the success of this condescending teasing.

"Where did Connor go? Did he just leave you here?"

"He's big, he can take care of himself," I replied.

What the hell was Maxine doing over there with the conductor of the orchestra? She was talking. Great! Did this have to happen right now? Didn't Max have time for a chat with the conductor later?

Deborah took a step toward me and eyed me narrowly.

"I recognized you," Deborah said.

Immediately, my pulse shot up. Panic gripped me and it became increasingly difficult to breathe. As best I could, I tried to shield my emotions from the outside world. I did not want to give Deborah this satisfaction.

"Yes, we know each other from the wedding."

As long as there were no facts, the presumption of innocence applied to me.

"Not here, but at the Royal Renaissance Hotel."

"I see."

I looked longingly at Maxine, hoping she came to rescue me, but Maxine was far too fixated on the conductor to notice anything about my plight.

"Not as a guest," Deborah added icily.

What a fake snake.

I bravely swallowed the heavy lump that was stuck in my throat.

"So what?" I asked.

"Does Connor know about your, shall we say, less than glamorous life?"

"Of course, that's how we met."

The corners of her mouth twitched slightly. The first movement I had ever seen in Deborah's Botox face. Even chewing her gum didn't make any movement, so I must have really surprised Deborah.

"Anyway, I know Connor, and I know you're just a nice pastime for him. A toy he'll throw away after he uses it, like dozens of toys before it."

Now my panic had turned to anger. Good. Because I needed the flaring anger to say what I wanted to say, no, what I had to say, to settle the matter with Deborah once and for all.

"Does he always buy a loft for his toys?"

Again, the corners of Deborah's mouth twitched. Ha! This small, minimal twitch was almost something like a reward for me. A triumph. A blow that had hit home.

Take that, Deborah!

Deborah pulled another piece of gum out of her Gucci handbag, untied the pink paper around it, and popped the strip into her mouth. Smacking her lips, Deborah now chewed a lump of gum as big as a ping-pong ball.

"Listen, sweetheart," Deborah said. "You're not in his league, and you'll never be able to play there."

"I guess that's up to Connor," I replied. Still, Deborah had managed to sow the first doubts in me. Damn it!

"Yes, and eventually he'll finally realize that I'm the one for him! Not some run-of-the-mill cleaning lady."

"So far, it's one to zero for the cleaning lady." I purposely used Deborah's wording as I showcased my handmade bracelet in a conspicuously unobtrusive way that did not go unnoticed.

Shock was written all over Deborah's face, her lips screaming a soundless cry. A moment later, she regained her composure and looked through the crowd. "What if it comes out that Connor Lancester, son of the Lancester dynasty, is dating a mere maid?"

Connor was above such things! Wasn't he? Yes, probably.

I looked to Maxine for help. Without her quick wit, I would lose this fight! She just pulled the five hundred dollar bill out of her cleavage and handed it to the conductor. Nodding contentedly, she shook his hand, then returned.

"Sorry, I just had to make some arrangements there," Max apologized. She nudged me lightly with her elbow and whispered, "Trust me, it'll be worth it!"

I had no idea what Maxine meant, but it didn't matter. The battle was fought, and Deborah had won. Before I could say anything, Connor appeared behind me and wrapped his arms around my waist.

"Well, ladies? Are you having a good time?"

"Delicious," Deborah exulted.

I said nothing, but turned around, clasped Connor's prominent jaw with both hands and kissed him uninhibitedly, with a hell of a lot of tongue action. It took quite a long time for anyone standing around, but that's exactly what I had intended. Quite apart from wanting to get one over on Deborah, I needed the kiss, Connor's confirmation that I meant something to him too.

As we breathlessly broke away from each other, Connor looked at me in surprise, which made my heart beat faster because it was joyful surprise. I smiled at him, then looked down at the floor, embarrassed because I had no idea if such a kiss at an elite fundraiser was too much of a good thing. Either way, the kiss was a statement to Deborah, to myself, and to the world. That Connor had not denied me that kiss.

Deborah took the floor again, "Very well, I'll mingle with the crowd."

She toasted Connor and Maxine, then eyed me with a razor-sharp gaze.

"And you, my dear, I'm sure I'll see again at the hotel."

This was not a statement, but an ice-cold threat that ran cold down my spine.

"All right," I replied, but what I really wanted to say: I hope I will never see you again!

Deborah turned and left. At the same moment, Maxine gave an inconspicuous sign to the conductor, and the music immediately changed to the Imperial March, which somewhat irritated some guests who lacked context. I, on the other hand, immediately understood what Maxine had arranged and had to grin while Maxine held her stomach laughing. Nevertheless, the seeded self-doubt took root and infiltrated my good mood.

When Deborah realized she was the punch line of Maxine's joke, she briefly raised her middle finger in our direction as she stubbornly continued walking.

Maxine patted me on the back. "That was the best investment of my life!"

"Yes," I answered. At the same time, I smiled bravely so as not to let my bad mood show, because otherwise Deborah would have won.

Connor's gaze switched back and forth between Maxine and me.

"What have you two been up to?"

"We? Nothing," Maxine squeaked excitedly.

"Dana?" Connor raised his brow the same way he did in the playroom. That look made me weak at the knees. No, not quite. Soft knees were the wrong word. I wanted to sink to my knees, back straight and hands in my lap, waiting for his orders.

"We were talking about girl stuff." That wasn't a lie, it had been girl stuff. Still, I felt like a bit of a fraud, because Connor must have understood the term to mean something else. But I knew Connor liked Deborah for some unfathomable reason, so I didn't want to tell him about this incident at all. His gaze continued to rest on me.

Maxine raised her glass in the air, getting Connor's attention.

"We gossiped about jewelry. About the chunky decorations at the Royal Renaissance Hotel, about Europe, and about actors with washboard bellies. With damn hot bodies..." Maxine purred. She did not finish the sentence but left it to all listeners to do it themselves.

"Okay, that's enough," Connor relented with a smile. "And what about the orchestra spontaneously playing the theme song of probably the most famous super-villain in the world?"

"I guess it looks that way," Maxine said sweetly.

"So, if this had been a prank, it would have been a really good one."

Jesus, I knew exactly what Connor was up to. Don't fold, Maxine!

"Hmm, may well be."

I saw Maxine's will grow weaker by the second.

"I don't know how I could have topped that in our sibling competition."

Maxine sighed loudly. "Yeah, okay, I admit, I put the orchestra up to it."

Connor grinned. "I'm not really surprised, yet I would have expected more professionalism from you."

"Say that Madame-I'm-something-better," Maxine defended herself.

Connor looked at me. Crap. I had hoped that I was the impartial Switzerland in this discussion who could stay out of it.

"Yes?" I asked innocently.

"Don't you think my sister should take this fundraiser more seriously?"

Oh no, I was caught between the fronts and had no idea for whom I should take sides. Of course Connor was right, but so was Maxine!

"I'm staying out of it!"

"No, you won't. I want to hear your opinion," Connor urged me in no uncertain terms.

"I agree," I replied with a sigh, but when Connor nodded in satisfaction, I took a deep breath. "But only thirty percent!"

"Ha!" blurted out Maxine. "Also, let me remind you that – strictly speaking – you sponsored the orchestra."

"You're impossible, sis." Connor shook his head, but there was a grin on his lips that he couldn't suppress. Then he put his arm around my hips and pulled me close. "I'll keep that thirty percent thing in mind."

Heavens, why did his threats only trigger such flights of fancy in me?

He gently ran his hand through my open curls, his brown eyes radiating sensually. I enjoyed his gaze.

"Would the most beautiful woman of the evening like to dance?"

"Yes, with the most beautiful man of the evening," I replied with a smile and took his hand.

"All right, I'm going. This is getting too cheesy for me," Maxine said, feigning seriousness. "Enjoy your evening!"

"We will."

I took Connor's tone very seriously, although Deborah's voice, despite everything, echoed in my head.

Was I, Dana Swanson, a sugar-addicted, bumbling maid dogged by bad luck, good enough for Connor Lancester, billionaire businessman and sex god with the world at his feet?

26

Connor

How long had Dana been waiting for me in the playroom?

I looked at my watch and smiled with satisfaction. Dana had been waiting for me for twenty minutes, in provocative underwear, kneeling and with perfect posture.

Heck, as I looked out at the New York skyline from my living room chair, I imagined Dana impatiently waiting for me. With each passing second, she found it harder to maintain her perfect posture, but I knew she wouldn't move an inch.

Not because Dana couldn't, but because I hadn't allowed her to. It was as simple as that. Everything I didn't explicitly allow her to do in the playroom was automatically forbidden. A simple rule that was easy to understand, but difficult to implement.

Twenty-five minutes. I had never made Dana wait that long, and to be honest, I enjoyed it more than I should have. Jesus, I loved having so much power over Dana! As my trust and love grew, so did Dana's boundaries. By now, Dana had become acquainted with most of the toys in my playroom.

When I felt I had left Dana to her thoughts long enough, I got up and went to her.

As expected, Dana knelt, with perfect posture, in the middle of the room, with her back to the door. This posture was the first thing Dana had learned, and very lasting.

The only thing that bothered me about this visual work of art was Dana's dull look. She didn't seem to be focused, but in thought, as she had been for the last few days. Although she denied it, Dana could not hide the fact that she was beside herself. Sooner or later, she would have to confide in me what was going on, but I didn't push her, especially in places where she felt she owed it to me.

"Well, darling? Is it exhausting?" I asked, and Dana's thoughtful expression disappeared instantly. She smiled at me gratefully because I no longer left her alone with her thoughts.

"Yes, sir," Dana answered me proudly. She did not let the slightest effort show in her voice.

Like a wolf, I stalked around her, consuming her body with greedy glances.

"What do you want me to do with you today?" I gave her the choice.

"Anything you feel like," Dana replied. She watched me closely out of the corner of her eye.

"You've been a pretty good girl lately, too good maybe." I spoke softly and carefully. In the playroom, it seemed appropriate. In my little dark shrine, there where I paid homage to sin and Dana was my goddess who served me.

Dana stood up. Unasked. Without permission.

"Why are you getting up?" My voice sounded rough and dangerous.

"I'll give you a reason to punish me," Dana replied with a smile, then picked up a flogger. With an innocent expression, she played with the dozens of leather straps hanging from the handle. Now Dana was really into it.

"What a good, naughty girl you are," I murmured. My girl was driving me especially crazy again today. I took off her flogger, grabbed her by the hips and pulled her close to me for a passionate kiss. Through her slightly parted lips, I penetrated her mouth with my tongue, licking over the tip of her tongue and tasting her sweet innocence. Dana gasped softly. Her eyelids fluttered sensually, and she pressed her body tightly against mine, deliberately rubbing against my hard erection.

"Take off your clothes," I commanded as we disengaged from each other.

Dana obeyed to the word. Elegantly she opened her black lace bra with red decorations, then she took off her underwear until she stood naked in front of me. Seductive. Full of anticipation, I took the black leather cuffs from the dresser and handed them to her.

Dana looked so beautiful when shackles adorned her wrists and ankles. That's why they were part of almost every game. It almost felt like the restraints had become a part of Dana. Actually, the leather restraints belonged in the drawer, but for my newly developed preference, they were always within reach on the dresser.

Dana now wore nothing but the black leather cuffs and her proud humility.

Smiling, I went around my girl one more time, then opened a drawer and took out a silver rod with two hooks on both adjustable ends. Just the thought of fixing Dana's ankle and hand cuffs to it at the same time drove me half mad.

Dana eyed the spreader bar curiously as I led her to the bed.

"Bend forward, beautiful!" I commanded.

Immediately, Dana propped herself up on the mattress with her hands and leaned forward so far that her back bowed with a seductive hollow.

I knelt behind her and attached the bar to her ankle cuffs so her legs would stay spread whether she wanted them to or not.

Dana didn't fight back, which was advisable, because Dana had indeed been a good girl for far too long, and it tickled my fingertips to finally be allowed to punish her. Hell, I burned for punishment and, along with pleasure, I used everything against her that she offered me.

"You better hold still now," I warned Dana before working her petite back with the flogger. She moaned softly and welcomed my strokes as she stretched her seductive butt further up – what a sight!

The fine leather straps whipped across her back, a little harder with each stroke, but Dana dutifully held still. The flogger moved further and further down until the first welts appeared on her ass.

Each time I lashed out, the leather cut through the air with a loud hiss. Together with Dana's gasps, moans and sighs a unique composition that made my erection even harder. Dana was clearly more sensitive on her legs than on other parts of her body, because her soft sighing turned into a loud, animalistic sounds when the leather hit her thighs, but even now she bravely held her position.

Admittedly, I was playing a wicked game with her. With each blow, my strokes became firmer, while at the same time her skin became more sensitive. Dana stifled her screams by biting her lips. I was merciful and gave Dana a short break to catch her breath.

The red, fine lines that stretched across her flawless body were almost like a map of our trips to the playroom. Reverently, I stroked Dana's hot body with the flogger, my hand following shortly after.

Her thighs were spread so invitingly wide that I could not resist stroking my fingers over her most sensitive spot. Wetness had accumulated between her legs, and I moaned with satisfaction. Dana sighed softly, as I penetrated her with two fingers.

So warm ... and humid ... and tight.

"I love it when you get this wet for me."

Damn, Dana's arousal was like a drug to me and the more I got of it, the more addicted I became to it. I took it with my fingers and massaged that one, very special spot that made Dana explode within seconds. Her abdomen twitched and she visibly found it hard to hold her position.

"May I come?" she asked quietly, almost shyly.

"Not yet," I replied softly. A stark contrast to my hard-thrusting fingers. Dana became louder and louder, her whole body trembled.

"Please, sir!" she screamed.

Not yet, darling. To make it easier for her, I withdrew my fingers from her and gave her a kiss on her shoulder blades instead. Her big green eyes looked at me punishingly.

"You'll have to be able to hold out a little more for me before you can come."

Dana nodded silently. I knew exactly that she had to muster all of her self-control right now in order not to yell at me or beg me to come after all. I was merciless in that respect.

"Yes, sir." Anger blazed in her gaze, which she could not hide. I couldn't blame her, because I had just cheated her out of her orgasm, yet I put on a cautionary face that didn't stop Dana from continuing to stare at me.

There was so much fire in her eyes that I had the feeling she was about to ignite my suit.

So, Dana, you want to play with fire? You can have it!

I lit one of the long, red candles that were not just for decorative purposes on a chandelier. They were a special manufacture from skin-friendly wax with a low melting point.

While the candle burned down, I grabbed Dana, whose big doe eyes fixed me. Again and again, her gaze darted back to the candle with which she was about to make acquaintance. I had saved the hot wax for a suitable moment, which had now come.

"You will dutifully hold still until the candle has burned down enough for me to use it."

"Yes, sir."

I guided Dana's arms upwards, then continued to work Dana's backside with the flogger. Not as hard as before, but not exactly gentle either, because I loved how Dana's body quivered and her beautiful breasts bobbed along slightly with each stroke.

Due to the spreader bar Dana had to balance every blow with her upper body, her whole body was electrified.

"That must be pretty exhausting," I murmured smugly. At the same time, I knew exactly that Dana could endure much more for me, just to please me.

"Yes, it is," she replied softly.

She was my girl, and I was so fascinated by her humility that I could not take my proud eyes off her.

"It's very tiring," Dana improved herself. Her legs were trembling. She wouldn't last long in this position, because she had to keep correcting her posture. After a few more strokes, I stopped and stepped close to Dana. I felt her body heat and her hot, fast breath.

"You have a choice, Dana," I whispered, then left a meaningful pause.

"Either I keep hitting you with the flogger – standing up – or else, we're going to get to the candle – lying down."

Dana's gaze switched back and forth between the leather whip in my hand and the candle. Earlier, she had looked at the candle as if it were something dangerous, sinister, now the candle seemed to her more like a salvation.

Dana let her gaze rest on the candle, with that she had made her choice. Good. Now I was going to give her a good going over. I got down on my knees in front of Dana, kissed her belly and then threw Dana over my shoulder to carry her to bed.

Tenderly I covered her arms with kisses before I fastened them to the top of the bed frame. Now Dana was completely helpless at my mercy, nothing could save her from my beast. The beast was merciless, and the beast took what it wanted. Always.

"Close your eyes," I commanded. Dana obeyed, albeit reluctantly. It was one thing to deprive her of sight with a cloth or blindfold, but quite another to simply forbid her to see. It was more intense because she still had an option, only the prohibition stood between the desire to do it and the doing itself.

"Good girl," I praised her and picked up the candle, which had now burned down far enough. Before spreading the hot wax on Dana's body, I dripped some of it on my wrist, just to make sure the burning point was really low enough.

Perfect. The wax wasn't hot enough to cause burns, but still hot enough that I could drive Dana crazy with it. The thought of Dana writhing under the heat and pleading for her orgasm pleased me.

With this little burning thing I would now elicit the most beautiful sounds from Dana, but first I wanted to torture her a bit with her expectations of it.

Slowly and tenderly, I stroked over her body with my free hand. From her ankles to her wrists, I did not leave out a single spot.

Every time Dana thought that the hot wax was about to drip down on her, she winced slightly. She looked beautiful, so innocent, but Dana hadn't been that for a long time. Since our first night together, I had corrupted her in every possible way – and corrupted women were the most beautiful in my eyes.

Finally, I released my girl by tilting the candle over her arm. The first, small drops hit her skin, ran down her arm a bit until they cooled and solidified again.

Dana sighed softly.

"How does it feel?" I asked. At the same moment, I let wax drip onto her other arm, just in case she had forgotten the feeling again.

"Strange. First very hot, almost unbearable, and then a moment later..." Dana searched for the right words.

"You want more of that all of a sudden?" I finished her sentence.

"Yes," Dana answered softly. Her voice quivered and sounded reverent, at the same time rough and demanding.

I gladly complied with the request. Little by little, I covered her arms with the red wax.

In Dana, a wide variety of feelings just had to collide with each other. That was what I did best. I mixed things. Black and white. Pain and pleasure. Love and hate. Things that were actually clearly separated by a line suddenly had infinite shades, and the dividing line disappeared. And suddenly you asked yourself new questions about things you already knew the answer to.

Every time I did just that with Dana, I knew she would have to question everything she had ever known before, and some things would suddenly become crystal clear.

On her breasts, Dana was particularly sensitive to the wax, her hands digging deep into the leather cuffs as her breathing quickened.

She looked beautiful when she squirmed in pleasure like this. And with each hot drop, Dana turned a little more, knowing that the wax was only further distributed on her body. When her arms and upper body were almost completely covered with wax, I placed the candle on her lower leg. From there I wandered piece by piece upwards.

"If you're already reacting like this with your beautiful breasts, I wonder how intense it will get in other places."

Dana bit her lips.

The wax spread over Dana's thighs and ran down the sensitive insides. By now the entire sheet was full of wax, but that only perfected the sight for me.

So hot...

The closer I came to Dana's most sensitive spot, the greater her tension became. Resistance was impossible for her. Her hands were firmly fixed to the bedposts and her legs were held in position by the spreader bar. She held her breath, that was all she could do. Dana could only hold still now, wait for the pain and endure it for me.

I loved the little tremors that twitched through her body and how hard Dana strained to keep her fluttering eyelids closed. Her little heart was beating so hard that I could almost hear it.

"How can you stay so level-headed while I'm on fire like this?" asked Dana.

"Years of practice. Believe me, my darling, otherwise I would have been all over you long ago."

Only a few more inches until the wax touched her thighs where her skin was most tender. Meanwhile, the elongated candle had shrunk by more than half. In fact, it was now just a large, burning stub that I held between my fingers.

Dana already had to prepare for the most extreme feelings, but I wouldn't go that far today, which didn't mean that I would let her in on it right now. I played with her fears and expectations for a while.

"I love it when I make a work of art out of your body," I said murmuring.

"I'm yours, and you can do whatever you want with me," Dana whispered devotedly. "I like that I'm your work of art today."

Damn. At these words, my beast, my rough and wild side, gained the upper hand. I put the candle back in the candlestick, took off my suit and knelt over Dana. First, I freed her left arm from the bedpost, then her right. But only to attach it to a small eyelet on the spreader bar. So, Dana had to maintain the only position possible for her with these restraints. Her arms were stretched upwards at waist level, as were her legs.

The inviting view of Dana's most intimate parts made me growl softly. Not that Dana had any other choice, but I loved it when she showed herself to me.

"You may open your eyes again now, Dana."

Despite the warm light in the room, Dana blinked a few times until she got used to the brightness in the playroom. She looked more closely at the spreader bar to which her wrists and ankles were tied. Curiosity and excitement were mixed in equal measure in her gaze. Almost invisible were her movements to get herself into a more comfortable position, but I had immediately unmasked Dana's body. She tried not to let on how difficult and exhausting the position was for her.

"Comfortable?"

"Yes, sir," Dana replied. Provocatively, she looked me straight in the eye.

"What was that about lying, beautiful?"

"That screams punishment." Dana grinned.

If Dana knew what other positions she could be forced into by a spreader bar, she would stop laughing, but all in good time.

Now I would fuck my naughty little girl. I could think of nothing else. There was only my hard cock, her tight little cunt and the fire between us. This hot sight, how ready, how wet Dana was for me, was it for me.

Growling, I knelt between her spread thighs and thrust my hard erection into her without wasting time. I thrust again and again. I grabbed her spreader bar and allowed myself to get completely lost in my ecstasy, because that was exactly what I needed and what Dana craved. Damn, Dana always gave me exactly what I had been looking for all my life, and I hadn't even asked for it.

Dana was the one woman I could chastise and punish however I wanted, and she adored me for it.

Dana was the one woman I could fuck so hard and deep that she cried out in pleasure.

Dana was the one woman I loved outside of the playroom.

I slowed my pace, my thrusts were now no longer hard, but sensual and still just as deep. I sank my erection in her small, tight femininity.

"God, Dana, I just can't help myself with you."

Dana said something, but the words kept changing into moans. Nevertheless, I felt exactly what Dana wanted to say. In such moments, no words were necessary to know the definition of her feelings. Then the orgasm burst over Dana, and she gave herself to me without restraint. She tightened even more, sucking like a vice around my erection. Moaning, my head fell back.

Fuck! This feels so fucking good.

Where had this woman been hiding from me all these years?

I thrust a few more times, enjoying the tightness around my hardness, then I withdrew from her. With rapid pumping movements, I continued to massage my erection. I wanted to see my gold on her body and thus further perfect my artwork of welts and wax.

Moaning, I poured myself onto Dana's body. She was still breathing heavily and irregularly. Nevertheless, Dana did not miss the opportunity to look at me furtively. Her eyes slid down me, over my sweaty upper body, the tense abdominal muscles to my twitching, half stiff member.

As aroused as I still was, Dana really shouldn't go for it. Unlike me, she still had obligations today.

"You should only challenge me to a second round if you can take it," I said admonishingly.

"Excuse me, sir," Dana purred. She lolls and deftly directs my gaze to her center.

"My God," I growled. "You're really going for it."

"Maybe." She smiled coquettishly.

"I'll spank you for that later, over and over again. I'm going to get horny on you and drive you crazy until you beg me to finally take my cock in your mouth." My voice was quiet but radiated incredible authority. Power.

I loosened the leather cuffs from the spreader bar, freeing Dana from her uncomfortable position.

"But not until you get back from work."

"Then why are you telling me now?" asked Dana.

"Because I know you'll be thinking about it all the time," I smiled knowingly.

"Right. Or I could just call in sick, and we'll spend the day in the playroom." Judging by Dana's face, she meant it. Odd. Actually, for

Dana, the job was the central focus of her life, even though we had hardly talked about it lately.

"Do I have such a bad influence on you?"

"No, you just spoiled me," Dana replied with a smile. A moment later, her face turned serious again. "It's just that lately, I'm not so fond of the Royal Renaissance Hotel. That's all."

"A lot of stress?"

"Yes, you could say that. There are just guests who like to drive poor little maids crazy."

"I like to drive you crazy, too."

"No, this is something completely different. With you, I like to be submissive, but with this kind of guest, it's just humiliation. You know? I just want to be able to save face, but right now that's pretty hard." She sighed heavily. Poor little thing. I wish there was some way I could help her.

"Is that why you're so silent?" I asked, even though I already knew the answer.

Without answering, Dana grabbed my watch that was on the dresser and cried out.

"Oh dear! I should hurry." She jumped up and ran barefoot to the dressing room, one floor below. Her bare feet echoed on the black marble floor. After putting on my suit, I followed her. Although I arrived in the dressing room only a few minutes after her, I barely recognized the room. Dozens of dresses, shirts, and shoes lay scattered throughout the room, and in the middle of them knelt a distraught Dana, burying her face in her hands.

"What's wrong?" I asked. Comfortingly, I put my hand on her bare shoulder.

"I don't have anything to wear."

"And what about all the clothes around us?"

"These are not my clothes."

"Of course they are, whose clothes would they be otherwise?"

Dana looked around and shrugged. "Yeah, you bought them for me, but they're not my clothes. Do you understand? My clothes are packed in boxes somewhere in the basement below us, just like all the other stuff."

I was no expert in women's analogy, but it was obvious that it wasn't about the clothes.

"I can get everything upstairs if you want."

"That doesn't change anything, either!"

"What doesn't it change?"

"Having a closet full of Prada, Gucci and Versace doesn't change the fact that I'm a simple maid."

I still had no clue what Dana was talking about or what the problem was.

"That's not true, Dana. You're smart, pretty, and funny. You're my girl."

"But is that enough?" Dana stood up, although she turned her face away from me, I saw a haze of tears on her eyes.

"Dana, look at me," I ordered sternly. Dana obeyed, but seeing her so upset almost broke my heart. I took her in my arms and stroked her hair.

"I will never belong," she sobbed.

"You belong to me, and that's all that matters."

"Do your parents feel the same way? Your sister? The fine company you surround yourself with? Deborah?"

Her questions sounded like accusations. Slowly, I guessed what Dana was really upset about.

"Of course."

"So you told them about me?"

"Max knows, and obviously you guys get along really well anyway."

"And no one else knows?"

"I haven't had a chance to tell my parents yet. But my mom loves you whether you were a maid or a millionaire heiress. She doesn't care, all she wants is a big, happy family."

Dana bit her lips thoughtfully. "Deborah knows about it."

"So what?" I didn't know what Dana was trying to tell me.

"She doesn't think I'm good enough for you."

"Did she say that?"

"Yes, more than clearly, actually," Dana replied defiantly.

I raised a brow and examined Dana closely. Whatever had happened between the two of them, it had visibly affected Dana. That must have been the reason for her strange behavior, but Dana could have told me that earlier.

"Maybe you just misunderstood."

"No, her words were really more than clear." Dana glared at me angrily.

"And even if she did say that, so what? Since when do you care so much about other people's opinions?"

"Because this isn't just about me, it's about us!" replied Dana indignantly.

"Yeah, I got that."

"But nothing else."

"No, nothing else," I answered honestly.

"And that's the fucking problem!"

Dana grabbed the pink dress closest to her and put it on.

Silently, I waited for Dana to explain herself.

"Am I good enough for you?" whispered Dana. She didn't dare look me in the eye.

"Of course. I prove that to you every day!" What made Dana think that wasn't the case? I had bought a damn apartment near her, I was dishing out tenderness and spankings in equal measure, and until a few minutes ago, I had believed that everything was fine between us.

"Then why did you only introduce me as your escort at the wedding?" asked Dana. But she didn't give me time to answer but shot right after the next questions.

"Why does the damn name tag on our apartment only have your name on it? And why don't your parents know the truth?"

Dana could no longer hold back her tears. I would have taken her in my arms again, but Dana fought off all attempts. Therefore, I leaned against the door frame and waited until she had calmed down a bit.

"Connor? I don't know how I'm going to manage being a part of your world if you don't make me feel that way."

I could change the stupid name tag right now, call my parents, and then scatter Dana's belongings all over the apartment, but I knew that didn't solve the problem. All of these things were just an excuse, pent-up anger fired outward because of a burst valve. If only I could find the damn valve.

"Maybe you really should call in sick today so we can work this out." I pulled my smartphone out of my pocket and offered it to her.

"No." Dana shook her head. "I need to do some thinking first, and so should you, before we start throwing things at each other that we'll regret later."

Those were her last words before she disappeared from the room and then from the apartment. What remained was silence, confusion, and me.

What the hell had just happened?

27

Dana

Although my tears had long since dried, I could still feel them. Even the guests at the Royal Renaissance Hotel looked at me more pityingly than usual today, if I was noticed at all.

Fortunately, most do not pay attention to maids.

At the moment, my cynicism was screaming the loudest, right up there with my guilty conscience. I knew I had treated Connor unfairly, after all, he had no idea about Deborah's performance at the gala.

But he should have known!

Would it have changed anything? Maybe. If I had just left at the gala without giving Deborah even a second of my attention, I certainly wouldn't have any doubts now. Neither about my relationship, nor about my status, nor about myself.

My stomach tightened when I thought back to my first fight with Connor. Actually, I should have had the strength to tell Connor what was going on. Connor was so understanding that he would surely have taken my feelings and fears seriously.

And there it came, the worse attack of conscience of all time. I felt terrible because I had yelled at Connor for no reason and would have loved to drop everything and apologize to him immediately.

"Daaanaaa," Shannon Williams called indistinctly over the radio. It rushed and crackled louder than usual. Maybe I should change the batteries.

"Yes, Ms. Williams?"

"In my office!"

"I'll be right there," I promised.

If someone had told me this morning that I would be happy about Shannon Williams absurd tasks, I would have declared the person crazy. But yes, somehow I was glad today that my crazy boss had a task for me. Something that offered variety and took my mind off things. Today, I definitely needed distance from my confused feelings.

Since the elevators for the employees was working again, everything in the hotel went back to its usual course. At least, something felt normal.

The door to Shannon Williams' office was closed, so I knocked twice and then waited for permission to enter.

"Yes, please!"

I stepped inside. At first glance, I saw that Shannon Williams was beaming with joy. Not a good sign, my boss was never in a good mood unless she was able to implement one of her super-villain surveillance plans. My next glance was at my boss's desk, which was full of eyeglass frames, and I knew why she was beaming. She was really pulling off the camera-glasses thing.

"So, the board did approve the glasses?" I asked cautiously.

"Not yet! But he will, believe me, he will." My boss beamed with enthusiasm.

"Sure," I replied, barely hiding my sarcasm. But Ms. Williams was so euphoric that she didn't notice anything, not even her obvious loss of reality.

"Come on, Dana. Put on your glasses," Ms. Williams demanded.

"Sure." I stepped toward the large desk on which lay dozens of black eyeglass frames.

She picked up one of the models and handed it to me.

"The glasses look quite outstanding, don't they? They complete the service outfit," she observed.

I accepted the frame and put them on. They felt unfamiliar.

"Well. I can't quite say yet, until I see the combination," I replied, as I kept looking over the rim of the glasses. The rimmed lenses didn't alter my sight, but still my framed field of vision was unusual.

"Oh yeah! Right!" From the top drawer, Ms. Williams pulled out a hand mirror and handed it to me.

"Wow, intense." That was the first thing that went through my mind. The thought that followed was weird. Everything that came after was somewhere between outlandish and totally deranged. Not to mention, the outfit absolutely didn't work; stylish one-of-a-kind glasses and washed-out one-piece didn't match in any possible universe.

"And these glasses now record everything I see?" I asked.

"Yes, as soon as the house technician, together with security, have installed all the technical stuff."

Sure, the technical equipment, the monitors, and hard drives had to be housed in the security service rooms. Not only did the security men monitored the garages, parking lots, and hallways, but now they also had to watch my colleagues. Such a thing could never go well, but I didn't protest any further, because there was no point. I had to somehow put the project on ice in a different way.

"Well, I'll get back to work," I said.

"Why don't you come back half an hour before the end of duty so we can evaluate the results together?"

"I'd love to," I replied sugary sweet.

As the door slammed shut behind me, I loosened a thick strand from my braid. Now a blond curl dangled back and forth in front of the camera lens, which was mounted on the left side of the frame. I also adjusted the frame several times and left a few fingerprints on the camera.

That was a good start, wasn't it? Maybe Rebecca had another idea to manipulate the test phase further. Today we were assigned to the lower floors. The lower the room number was, the less basic the cleaning staff was. The rooms were significantly smaller, as were the beds, and the number of bathrooms shrank dramatically along with them. In return, the number of rooms tripled.

On the way to the fifth floor, I lowered my gaze at each guest. I felt uncomfortable secretly recording people. I was definitely not turning into a good secret agent.

The radio crackled. "Dana, a glass broke in Room 3601."

Silently, I repeated the room number. *Room 3601 – Deborah's Room.*

Even though Connor had long since left the hotel, Deborah had stayed there. But since the gala, I no longer made a secret of my job, I had stopped hiding in the corridors or inventing excuses to avoid the thirty-sixth floor. But I still didn't want to enter Deborah's room.

"I'm really busy right now," I lied, hoping the camera wasn't yet transmitting images that could expose my lie.

Endlessly long silence. Would another maid be willing to do the job? I silently prayed that one of my colleagues would cross my path and take over this unpleasant task.

"That can wait. You seem to make quite an impression on the guests."

I narrowed my eyes. *What does she mean by that?*

I had a really uneasy feeling, so I thought about insisting that I felt sick. But I didn't.

"I'm really busy, I'll ask Rebecca to do it," I tried one last time.

"No, the guest insisted on you because you were so nice last time."

Of course.

"I'll be on my way." I sighed, because I had no other choice. If I had turned down the request now, sooner or later, it would lead to my resignation. Still, I was afraid of what was coming. Deborah Landry had definitely planned an ambush. Damn, that was all I needed. If only I hadn't argued with Connor, then this wouldn't be so bad. I could listen with my head held high to whatever Deborah had to say.

By the time I reached room 3601, I had chiseled myself a neutral expression; it wasn't perfect, but it still gave me some security. This expression didn't have to last long. If I hurried, it wouldn't take two minutes to clean up the pieces.

I knocked on the door and was invited in by Deborah not a second later.

"That took a long time," Deborah immediately complained. Today she wore a mint green skirt and a white blouse. Her outfit was topped off with a gold belt from Chanel.

"I'm here now," I replied calmly. Such reproaches were heard from maids every day, and I could easily deal with them.

We had a first-class staring contest. Deborah seemed to be thinking, then finally opened her mouth to say something.

"Nice glasses, Josephine. I didn't think you had that much style."

I remained silent. What could I say? That the thing was a new spy gadget for employees?

With a quick glance, I skimmed the floor looking for the broken glass. Directly in front of the bar was a broken scotch glass. Even without looking closer, I could see that the glass had been vandalized because it had shattered into hundreds of pieces.

Without waiting for Deborah's request, let alone an order, I set to work picking up the pieces.

I wonder if the camera was broadcasting live in the meantime. At least it didn't record my face, which I had a hard time controlling.

"We need to talk about Connor," Deborah began.

"No, we don't," I replied as I picked up the large shards by hand and tossed them into a plastic trash can.

Deborah cleared her throat. "I'm sorry, but I think I misheard?"

"I'm not going to talk about Connor," I repeated myself. Neither did I want to talk about my relationship with Connor, nor did I want to fight about it with Deborah. I was Connor's girl, and that wasn't going to change anytime soon, whether we fought or not!

"I wonder if the hotel management knows how rude their maids are."

I took a deep breath, then let go of the pile of broken pieces and stood up.

"As a maid, I am behaving absolutely correctly toward you, Miss Landry. But I certainly need not and will not behave like a friend after our encounter at the gala. Above all, I will not fight a battle I have long since won."

Anger blazed in Deborah, her blood boiled, and the blush of anger was clear even under the blush.

"I wouldn't be so sure of victory if I were you. You have no idea who you're messing with right now, Dana." Deborah spat out my name as if it were bile.

"True, and I don't care." Outwardly, I acted unimpressed and calm, but inside I was celebrating my quick wit, courage, and strength that I had just demonstrated.

Take that, Deborah!

"Shit, I'm so gonna fuck you up. I'm going to crush this puny existence you call life under my heels and spit on it!" Deborah was really picking up speed now, showing her true colors. Hopefully the damn camera had recorded it! I would have loved to run to security right now to secure the footage and show it to Connor! But I took myself back and continued to concentrate on Deborah.

"It must be a pretty lonely life you live. With so much envy and resentment," I stated soberly. What good was the fattest bank account in the world if you had no friends, no family with whom to share all the joys of life?

Knowing full well that Deborah would have loved to stab me in the back, I turned away from her to suck up the remaining glass splinters. Triumphantly, I grinned to myself, while Deborah was about to explode with rage behind me. Admittedly, Deborah's rage was like a drug to me, one I wanted more of. And beyond that, I was in control. As long as the vacuum cleaner was running, Deborah had to keep quiet.

Painfully, Deborah bumped my shoulder and disappeared into the bedroom. I was almost a bit disappointed how cowardly Deborah had suddenly retreated. Did the wounded pride have to lick its wounds?

Anyway, now I didn't mind vacuuming the carpet even more carefully than usual.

It wasn't until I couldn't drag out the sucking any further that Deborah came back and leaned against the doorframe, grinning with a mischievous glint in her eyes.

"You shouldn't gloat too soon," Deborah said slyly. So she had already found a new way to attack me. But if the attack looked just like the last one just now, I guess I didn't have to worry. I could handle a jostle.

"The carpet is cleaned now, Miss Landry," I said coolly, then left the room.

Oh. My. God. Did that really just happen?

Only now did I notice how violently my heart was beating. All this time I had felt so calm, so superior. But now I felt how rattled I had actually been.

Then I realized what had just happened in Room 3601, and my breath caught.

Damn, I'm screwed!

Even though I grudgingly admitted it, Deborah could really destroy my life. If Deborah came clean with Shannon Williams, I was definitely screwed. I had broken dozens, maybe hundreds, of house rules during Connor's presence as a guest.

Yes, the house rules were not laws and breaking them was not a crime, but there were still consequences – termination.

I had the uneasy feeling that this was my last day as a maid. And if I couldn't talk to someone about my problems right away, I was in danger of bursting. I pulled the radio out of my pocket and hit the send button. "Rebecca?"

"Present!" she promptly radioed back.

"There's a sheet shortage on the thirty-third floor."

"Oh dear! I'll be right there!" my voice sounded scratchy and worried. Rightly so. It was my secret code for: Help, the world is ending! and other similarly serious problems.

Help! SOS! Mayday ... oh, Mayday.

"Thank you, Beccs."

The laundry room on the thirty-third floor was something like my disaster shelter or my secret superhero base. Rebecca had declared it that ages ago. For all the other maids, it was just the laundry room on the thirty-third floor.

I wonder if my glasses were already recording. Just a moment ago, I had wished that everything was on tape, but now I didn't mind a loose contact or a short circuit, because I felt so damn watched. If these glasses were soon part of the standard basic equipment, paranoia and more paranoia were the order of the day for maids.

Anyway, I couldn't leave the glasses on, or my secret shelter wouldn't be a secret much longer, but I already had an idea for that.

On my way to the employee elevator, I made a small detour to the nearest employee restroom. I opened the door, then took off my glasses and put them in my side pocket. There they were well stored between the forest honey gummy bears and strawberry cream candies.

Next, I turned off the radio and then went to my secret meeting place. The plan was perfect, no one would suspect anything. If they asked later why I hadn't put my glasses back on, I could just say: Oops, forgot!

I was already expected by Rebecca.

"What's wrong?" it shot out of her even before the door had fallen back into the lock. Her face reflected sincere concern.

"Beccs, it's awful. This whole day has started off pretty damn bad," I began. Okay, actually it had started brilliantly, with a delicious breakfast followed by multiple orgasms before I had even entered the playroom.

"Out with it!" demanded Rebecca.

"Connor and I had a fight because of Deborah. Because of what she said. God, how I hate that woman! And I think she's trying to get me fired. I was just in the room with her."

"You were what!? How did that happen?" asked Rebecca, horrified.

"She threw a glass on the floor and had me come up."

"You are not serious."

"Yes, she did, she tried to make me look bad again."

"She didn't make it, though, did she?" Rebecca's expression tensed, and her hands were clenched into fists. It almost looked like Rebecca was about to throw a punch at any moment.

"No, I stayed totally cool, so cool that Deborah almost exploded. But I think by doing that, I just made it worse." Despair spread through my insides. I wish I had just shut up!

"You'll have to explain that to me in more detail."

"If Deborah spills the beans, I'm fired. I'm one-hundred-thousand percent sure she's going to spill."

"She's not serious! And what does Connor say about it? Have you talked to him yet? Surely, he's on your side?"

I bit my lips.

"Connor and I got into a fight before work."

Rebecca put her head back with a moan.

"You're not serious, are you? You had a fight over that goat?"

I nodded and bravely swallowed the first, burgeoning tears.

"What did Connor say exactly?"

"Not what I wanted to hear," I snorted. But just because I didn't want to hear it right now didn't mean his answers were wrong, did it? Bullshit!

He should have protected me. That was his duty. I was his girl.

"But the thing that needed to be said?" asked Rebecca cautiously.

"Maybe," I grudgingly admitted.

Deep down, I had to admit that my best friend was right. Until just now, I had only looked at everything from my own point of view. To him, Deborah was not a beast, not a monster, she was simply the spoiled daughter of rich parents who were friends with his parents.

"Maybe," I repeated my own words, "maybe I really was a little too emotional. I'm just so afraid of losing him!"

And suddenly I realized why I had reacted so extreme. I loved Connor. I loved him very much, and I didn't want to lose him to someone like Deborah. No, actually, I didn't want to lose him to anyone. I was his girl, and I was going to stay that way for the rest of my fucking life!

"Do you think you guys can talk about this again?"

"Yeah, I think so. We didn't yell. Well, Connor didn't, at least."

"There you go, then I'm sure things will be settled soon, and tonight you'll be laughing about it. He doesn't want to lose you either, I'm sure of it."

Rebecca's words were a balm for my soul. Now the argument with Connor no longer weighed so heavily on my shoulders. The pressure on my chest, the feeling that I could no longer breathe, decreased, but did not disappear completely. Rebecca also noticed my thoughtful expression.

"Is there anything else?"

"What am I going to do if I get laid off?"

"I'm sure Connor will just buy out the Royal Renaissance Hotel so you can work here again," Rebecca said with a laugh.

"And what if..." I couldn't bring myself to finish the sentence. At the same time, I tried to convince myself that it was just a silly little argument. A tiny little argument that didn't mean anything. A tiny thing that would surely have evaporated by tonight. Hopefully!

I shook my head and pushed all thoughts away, then eyed my best friend.

"Oh, never mind, there are more important things to take care of right now."

"What?"

"Those stupid glasses with camera are here," I whispered. Actually, whispering had not been necessary, but it seemed appropriate.

"Really? Let me see!"

"Not here," I continued to whisper. "Out in the hallway. I think we're already on the air."

"Wow. It's like Big Brother!" said Rebecca, fascinated. With a touch too much euphoria for my taste.

"We need to make sure this is never approved."

"We could go to the police." Rebecca shrugged her shoulders.

"Your pragmatism is honorable, Beccs. But reporting the employer sends our job security into negative territory."

"What if we leak it to the press? Anonymously and stuff, of course!"

"I had thought about that, too, but it would probably cost us all our jobs. If discretion is in doubt at the most discreet hotel in town, who's going to come here?"

"We'll figure something out, you bet we will. And you and Connor will be okay, you're both big enough already. You can handle it." Beccs winked at me.

"Thank you." I hugged my best friend and gave her a kiss on the cheek. "If it wasn't for you, I would have lost my nerve."

"That's what best friends are for. Now we should get going, the carpet in the twelfth floor hallway is waiting for our attention."

"Sure," I replied with relief. Now every step seemed like flying, that's how relieved I was. Just before the elevators, I pulled my glasses out of my pocket and said, "We're going on the air in three, two, one!"

Rebecca giggled softly but couldn't hold back her laughter any longer when she saw me wearing the glasses.

"Dana, you look like a professor!"

I was almost flattered by the compliment, but then Rebecca added, "In an adult film." Ouch. After that, Rebecca imitated a passionate blowjob that made me laugh.

"If you keep making fun of me like that, I'll make sure you start wearing a pair of these things tomorrow!"

"Oh no!" Rebecca continued to moan. I shook my head and averted my eyes from my best friend who was cutting one typical porn grimace after another.

"Oh, almost forgot," I reminded myself, pulling my radio out of my pocket and turning it back on. Now that my little secret council session in the laundry room was over, I had to be available to everyone again.

Rebecca had calmed down by now, and we took care of the carpets on the lower floors together.

One thing was clear to me now. There was nothing that could stop me, and there was nothing that could destroy my relationship!

"Daaanaaa!"

"I'm coming," I replied with foresight. No answer came, strange, but not further suspicious.

The time with Rebecca had flown by, and just then, Rebecca and I had stocked up the cleaning carts with cleaning supplies.

"Do you have psychic abilities by now?"

"No. But she wants me to stop by just before the end of my shift to talk about the glasses."

Rebecca's gaze switched back and forth between me and my wrist.

"But we don't get off work for another two hours."

Okay. That was a little strange after all.

"Maybe she was looking through the recordings and she noticed something? Or there are no recordings at all because the technology doesn't work yet."

"Well. You'll know in a minute," Rebecca said.

"Yes," I replied. "But I don't have a good feeling about this."

"Just let me know if you need backup in the lion's den."

"Will do!"

While Beccs had both fingers crossed for me, I walked into my boss's office with an uneasy feeling. The uneasy feeling intensified when I heard excited voices through Ms. Williams' half-closed office door. A hysterical voice howling like a hurt puppy dog and Ms. Williams trying to calm them down in a similar high falsetto. Cautiously, I peered through the crack.

Damn, damn, damn!

I wanted to turn around, but Ms. Williams had already seen me through the door.

"Dana, I'm glad you're here so we can resolve this messy situation!"

"Of course," I replied professionally. Then I looked at Deborah, who was standing in front of the desk, completely distraught. Her makeup was completely smeared.

"Yes!" shrieked Deborah. "That's the thief!"

She pointed a raised finger at me, and my heart stopped short.

"What? I don't quite understand," I replied as calmly as I could, even as panic spread through me. So, this was Deborah's plan? To accuse me of stealing?

"You stole my brooch!"

"I didn't steal anything Ms. Landry."

Now Shannon Williams stepped in.

"But you were in Room 3601 today, weren't you Dana?"

"Yes, because a glass had broken there. I cleaned the room and left."

"Lie!" it burst out of Deborah.

If Deborah had known how close I was to pouncing on her with battle cries, claws, and a full body effort, she certainly wouldn't have screamed like that. But she felt superior. Superior.

"Hmm," Ms. Williams thought aloud. "Dana, what do you say to the allegation?"

"That I have nothing to hide, you're welcome to search me. Me, my locker, whatever you want." I had done nothing wrong. Even though I hated the thought of strangers rummaging through my things, it was the only way to prove my innocence. And I was innocent, damn it!

"Well, clean out your pockets," Shannon Williams said calmly. Her expression was serious, but clearly she didn't know what to make of the situation. This situation was unprecedented at the Royal Renaissance Hotel.

"Yes, clean out your pockets!" repeated Deborah, hissing, as if she were a vicious echo of my boss.

"Good." I reached into my side pockets and pulled out first the radio, then a handful of wild honey gummy bears, followed by a couple of individually wrapped candies, and a piece of sherbet that must have been in my side pocket for weeks. I laid it all out on the table.

"My goodness, Dana. I hope for your sake you have supplemental dental insurance, with all that sugar," Ms. Williams marveled, and I had to stifle a grin.

"No brooch," I said.

Shannon Williams nodded thoughtfully. Her gaze was still shifting back and forth between my hips and my snack stash, and I thought I saw a hint of envy on my boss's face. Clearly, Ms. Williams forgot that I ran several miles a day at the hotel.

"I have to give you a warning, you know that. Do you? Eating in the suites and hallways is prohibited."

"I know, but that's why I only eat gummy bears here, they don't melt or stick," I smiled innocently.

"That wasn't all the pockets!" growled Deborah.

"Oh, right," I replied. Reflexively, my hands shot to my breast pockets, which I never used.

Don't let all this be true! Please just be a bad dream!

I wished to wake up from my nightmare, but this was no dream, no illusion, no imagination. The round, hard thing in my breast pocket wasn't either. It was really there.

When I didn't respond further, Deborah acted on her own and pulled the brooch, which she must have placed there herself, out of my breast pocket.

"This is my brooch! A rare family heirloom, in my family for generations and priceless!"

Guilelessly, Deborah slammed the family heirloom on the table.

"I ... I have no idea how that got in my pocket," I stammered.

"Dana, the evidence is against you."

No, no, no!

I hoped that my boss would not say the next words.

"I'm going to have to fire you without notice."

My seven-year plan immediately and irrevocably went up in flames.

"Very good!" jeered Deborah.

"And as for you, Ms. Landry," Shannon Williams continued, "should you wish to press charges, we are happy to do so. Discreetly, I hope."

Charges? What? I thought I had misheard. Was I now supposed to go to court for something I hadn't even done? In the worst case, even to jail?

Deborah growled thoughtfully. Her sadistic gaze fixed on me. Yes, she enjoyed seeing me suffer.

Within seconds, my entire future passed me by. With immediate dismissal for theft, not a single hotel, restaurant, or anyone else would hire me. If my boss went through with it, I was a branded thief. Nobody hired thieves because nobody wanted to risk potential thefts.

How could this happen? Wait, I knew how it could happen.

"I can prove my innocence," it shot out of me, pointing to the glasses.

Immediately, as if stung by a tarantula, Shannon Williams jumped up from her seat and grabbed my shoulders.

"Remember the contract you signed!" she whispered. She then turned to Deborah. "Ms. Landry, we've wasted enough of your time already. Unless you have another request, I don't want to keep you any longer."

"Good, you'll be hearing from my lawyer," she said businesslike and disappeared from the office with an overly broad grin.

Karma may not come when ordered, but karma always comes!

My eyes fell on the brooch, which still lay on the table. So, Deborah had tricked me with this super precious family heirloom. Clever, because I couldn't prove my innocence, because the thing with the glasses wasn't as compliant with the rules as my boss might have wished. And we both knew that!

"She slipped me the brooch, I swear. I can prove that with the camera, too!"

"No, the camera isn't recording anything yet," Shannon Williams said quickly.

"You're lying."

I was perhaps the worst liar in the world, but I saw through other liars just as quickly.

"Look, Dana. I really like you, and I certainly don't want to fire you." With a sigh, my boss looked thoughtful but didn't finish her thought. So I did.

"But you still have to do it even though I'm innocent?"

"Yes, unfortunately, I have the reputation of the hotel to think of. Deborah Landry will give us hell if she finds out you weren't fired. And what do you think will happen when the press gets wind of this? A theft at the Royal Renaissance Hotel! Far too scandalous."

"So that's it?" I asked with tears in my eyes and an aching stomach.

"I'm sorry, yes. All I can do for you is a small settlement. I'm sure I can find a discreet solution with Ms. Landry."

Should I be grateful to my boss for that now?

"I don't know what to say." I was truly at a loss for words.

"You don't have to say anything. Leave the goggles and radio here, clean out your locker and take the uniforms back to the laundry."

"Thanks for nothing," I said and left the office.

"Daaanaaa!" shouted Ms. Williams after me.

The termination had at least one positive thing. I would never again be called so shrill and drawn out.

"What?"

"Think about the contract you signed. Do yourself a favor and just let it go."

If I was going down, why not take the Royal Renaissance Hotel with me? Probably because I was in a small canoe and the hotel's lawyers would sink me mercilessly with a destroyer without a single person noticing. I had lost my hope as well as my job.

I could at least mend fences with Connor, because I couldn't lose him too. Otherwise, I was really lost.

28

Connor

I sat in the loft, headed for my next record in Tetris, and thought. The afternoon faded into evening, passing me by like the cool summer breeze through the open window. Just as cool as Dana was earlier in the bedroom.

I didn't understand the women.

What made Dana think that she wasn't right for me? If I wasn't serious, I probably wouldn't have taken her to events, bought us an apartment together, and postponed my next trip to Europe for a month. For no other woman in this world had I felt the way I felt about Dana. Heavens, no other woman in the world had I ever felt for! Dana was my girl, dammit. Maybe she didn't fully realize that yet.

Thoughtfully, I poured myself a Macallan Scotch. The aromatic, delicate smell of the Scottish masterpiece calmed my thoughts.

What was I supposed to do with Dana? How should I deal with her after the quarrel? How would she react to me? Questions over questions.

My pragmatic side wanted to just drag Dana into the playroom, spank her, which would quickly lead to wild, uninhibited make-up sex, but after that, the matter just wouldn't be settled. Whatever Dana's problem was, I couldn't solve it in my playroom.

I cannot solve all the problems with sex.

So what then? I was bad at that. Relationships had never been my thing, but for Dana, I wanted to try. In my eyes, make-up sex was more effective and lasting – much more honest – than words could ever be, but I was a man with no idea if the same rules applied to Dana or if she preferred words.

I finally decided to compromise on both trains of thought. First reconciliation sex and then, if the elephant was still in the room, I could talk about her.

The door banged loudly as it crashed into the lock. I immediately jumped up, clenched both hands into fists and reflexively held them in front of my upper body. Then I remained in my attack position for a moment until I realized that Dana had just kicked the door in like a swat team.

She was leaning with her back against the front door, her expression agonized. When our eyes met, she did not say a word. All warmth and radiance was gone from her face. If I had to describe her in one word, despair would come closest to what I saw.

Was I the reason for that? I'm a fucking idiot! I clenched my teeth tightly and looked at Dana urgently. I felt bad when I saw Dana like this. No, bad wasn't the expression at all – I felt like shit!

To her left and right were two large paper bags. They were not shopping bags, but simple brown paper bags.

"Dana, what's going on?" I asked.

Slowly, my muscle tone eased, and I let my arms hang to my sides.

"You're back early. Did you get off early?"

She said nothing, just continued to stare at me. Her eyes filled with tears and her beautiful, full lips trembled. Poor girl.

Hatred crept up inside me, hatred for the person who had hurt her so much, hatred for myself. For me, the argument earlier had been nothing more than a disagreement. No end of the world, no end of anything, but for Dana; it seemed to have been far more disturbing.

Or something else had happened, something I could have protected her from. No! From which I should have protected her!

"God damn it, talk to me," I growled.

Dana winced, then looked down, unsure and scared.

Fuck. I didn't want to talk to her that roughly, but I hadn't been able to hold back. Not when something was making such a lasting impression on her.

I went to her and looked at her, at least at the sad little heap of misery that was left of Dana.

Was it me? Was I to blame?

A tear ran down her cheek and I caught it with my index finger. Dana sighed when my finger touched her skin, her hand gripping my wrist. At first, I thought she was going to push it away from her, but the opposite was true. She buried her face in my palm. She was looking for my closeness, my tenderness, and my protection.

Now, I knew that the argument earlier had absolutely nothing to do with her pain. Tenderly, I kissed her wet cheek and tasted her salty tears.

Dana didn't want to talk, I understood that, but I needed to know if she was okay, if she was hurt, if...

"Are you okay?"

I examined her briefly, looking for clues, for torn clothing, dirt or blood. Full of relief, I found nothing of the sort. More and more tears ran down Dana's cheeks, and I pressed her tightly against my chest, while my strong arms shielded her from the cruel world outside.

"I'm with you," I whispered in her ear.

I carefully stroked Dana's soft, curly hair and let her cry. At first, it was just quiet crying, but soon there was no stopping her harsh sobs. She didn't have to hold back either. I held her tightly in my arms, protecting her from all threatening dangers.

She cried unrestrainedly, and her sobs ached in my chest. I needed to take away the sorrow that weighed her down, that threatened to crush her.

Only when Dana's tears slowly dried up and her breathing became calmer did I say something.

"Whatever happened, it's over now."

"That's the problem," Dana sobbed. "It's over!"

"What's over?"

"Everything! My future, my job, my seven-year plan. It's all gone."

I glanced at the large bags Dana had dropped. Inside were no new clothes, no shoe boxes, just some everyday clothes, photos, and other odds and ends.

"You quit your job?" I asked in shock.

"No, I was fired," Dana said bitterly. Anger sparkled in her eyes, drowned by new tears. Dana Swanson, model maid, polite and courteous, was summarily dismissed?

"Why?"

"Because I allegedly stole! But I can actually prove the opposite on video!"

"On video?" I repeated her last words. I tried to sort out Dana's chaotic thoughts, but I didn't succeed.

"Do we have an echo here?" asked Dana desperately, then she bit her lips and looked at me sadly. "I'm sorry, Connor. I didn't mean to yell at you. I've just never been treated so ... unfairly."

"It's all right. Now tell me what happened," I whispered. I gave her a gentle kiss on the forehead. A small, meaningful sign of sincere acceptance of her apology. Dana wiped the tears from her face, took a deep breath, and told me, "I signed a contract a few weeks ago to keep quiet, but I can't keep quiet any longer."

Dana gave me a cryptic look.

"What kind of contract are we talking about here?"

"Our assistant manager wants to provide all maids with camera goggles."

I frowned. "In no possible world would any kind of council approve that, let alone the management. Privacy is a fundamental law."

Dana nodded. "I've tried. But it doesn't matter. The glasses can prove my innocence. I didn't steal anything, Connor! I really didn't."

Now Dana was crying again.

Damn it, I wanted to storm the hotel right then and there to bring those responsible to justice! No one was allowed to do this to my girl, no one!

"And what did your boss say? Does she believe you?"

"Well, unofficially, yes, but the official version is hard to prove without the video because the pin was in my pocket."

"We'll find a solution. I promise." I looked deeply into Dana's eyes with a determined expression.

While I was stroking Dana through her fragrant hair, I was already thinking of solutions. Lawyers who bombarded the hotel with threats, warnings and claims for damages, or journalists who could publish reports. For that, I just needed to know every single detail.

"Tell me, Dana, have you been trying on jewelry again?" I asked. The very second I said the words, I regretted them. I hadn't really wanted to put it that way; now my question sounded sharp, almost reproachful.

"No, of course not!" Dana pierced me with a reproachful look that I undoubtedly deserved.

"I just had to make sure, Dana."

"Wow, thank you for your confidence." Her words sounded bitter. She brushed my hand aside and walked sideways past me. At last Dana had moved away from the front door, but unfortunately for the wrong reasons. Just then she ran away from me.

She only stopped at the living room table, where the Macallan Scotch still stood. She took the glass and drank it empty in one go. Without relish, she downed the five-thousand-dollar Scotch to numb herself. Dana poured herself the next glass from the bottle, drank it empty again. When Dana raised the bottle for the third time, I put my hand on the neck of the bottle and pushed the bottle back onto the table.

"That was enough."

"Right, you're right." She put her head back, sighed for a long time, and then looked at me questioningly.

"Why does Deborah hate me so much? What did I do to her?"

"Deborah? What does she have to do with this?"

"She got me fired," Dana sobbed.

"Because of Deborah Landry?"

What had I missed between the two women? Or had Maxine set something up? My sister had never made a secret of the fact that she didn't like Deborah.

"What other Deborah would it be? She slipped the brooch into my pocket when I was in her room." Seeing my questioning face, she added, "Because she broke a glass! Even if I had wanted to take it, I was never even near that brooch."

Dana buried her face in her hands. "If she turns me in, I'm screwed. No one wants to hire a thief."

"It won't come to that. I will talk to her," I said thoughtfully.

"Really?"

"Of course, she won't turn you in. Don't worry about that. I'll talk to her, and you two should really have a clarifying conversation together."

"Tell me, are you crazy?" Dana jumped up from the couch angrily. "Deborah ruins my life, and you're talking about forgiving her?"

Now the conversation was going in a direction I did not want to go at all. No matter what I said now, everything would be used against me. But I couldn't put up with her tone either, my pride wouldn't allow that.

"Watch your tone," I growled.

"Fuck no! We're not in the game room, and this isn't a game. This is real life, Connor. I liked my life the way it was."

I ignored her provocation. She was upset, I understood that, but I could not remain so calm and understanding for long.

"I'm talking to Deborah, what else do you want?"

"That you're talking to her for the right reasons!"

"And what is that supposed to mean, please?" I growled.

"She wants you, Connor. She wants to be your girl. Make her understand that she's not, and that you don't want her," Dana's voice broke.

"I only want you," I replied.

"Then show me that, too, damn it."

"What do you think I do all the time, Dana?"

"You insinuate that I took the brooch. For whatever reason, but you didn't believe me. You accuse me of picking a childish fight with Deborah. Jesus, you don't even realize how much I've suffered at Deborah's hands lately! At the hotel! The hiding and everything."

I said nothing, just glowered at her and didn't move an inch. I had the feeling that we were playing with pots and pans in a minefield. But Dana obviously had more to say, so my speechlessness seemed fitting, almost polite.

"You dress me up in expensive clothes, but that doesn't change the fact that I'll never be like the elite just because I look like them. You buy me a loft, but only write your name on the doorplate and have all my stuff packed in boxes in the basement. You take me to beautiful parties, but only introduce me as your escort. Not as your girlfriend. Not as your love. Not as your sub."

Dana lost herself in her anger, and feelings burst out in her that she must have suppressed for a long time.

"Damn it, Connor! You say you love the way I scream, the way I moan. You say you love fucking me hard and deep. But you never whisper in my ear that you love me. Only what you do to me."

Dana was right. Not that I had intentionally outshone her, but damn it, she was right. I just couldn't bring myself to say it. Not now, not like this.

I love you.

I was such a fucking idiot.

"Sometimes I don't think I deserve you at all, Dana."

Her look told me that those were not the words she would have liked to hear.

I love you.

Did my pride have to get so rebellious now of all times? Three simple words.

"Yes, I think so too," Dana said. Her expression seemed so sad, so tormented, that I would have liked to take her in my arms again. In my arms, she was safe from the rest of the world. Only from myself, I could not protect her, because I was the reason why she cried so much, although I was supposed to be the one who dried her tears.

Dana cupped her hands in front of her mouth as if to keep herself from saying words she might later regret.

"Say you love me!" commanded Dana.

"You know that. You're my girl."

Suddenly, Dana's expression became completely rigid, emotionless. As if everything had been frozen in a matter of seconds.

"That was the wrong answer," she said, walking back to the door.

"What are you doing?"

"What does it look like I'm doing? I'm going."

"Don't you dare," I growled, but Dana ignored me, my tone, and my command.

"Dana!"

I wanted to go after her, grab her by the shoulders and trap her body between me and the wall, look her in the eyes and tell her that she just made the biggest mistake of her life. I wanted to dry her tears with hot kisses, whisper in her ear the words she craved so much. I wanted to drag her by the hair into the playroom and punish and fuck her until she lost her mind. Spankings. Fucking. Spankings. Fucking. Again, and again and again.

But I did nothing of the sort, I just stood there and watched her. My pride paralyzed my whole body and even paralyzed my mind.

Dana opened the door and walked through. Everything went as if in slow motion. For a second she hesitated and stopped, waiting for me. I could hear her little heart breaking as the silence didn't fade. I knew exactly how it felt because it was shredding my heart too.

When the door slammed shut, it felt like silence cut through my entire body. Dana had left, and the room filled with emptiness and pain. Dana had left, and she had taken my heart with her.

"I love you, Dana. Hell, I really love you."

29

Dana

Resignedly, I dropped my spoon into the empty Ben & Jerry's cup. Rebecca's gaze fell back and forth between me and the huge empty container of ice cream I'd been scooping up since arriving at Rebecca's house.

"You wouldn't happen to have another one of these, would you?" I asked.

"No, we weren't prepared for you to come, or we would have bought a year's supply," Rebecca replied cynically.

"Hmm, I'd rather be somewhere else right now, too," I grumbled. Beccs had painfully reminded me why I was here with her in the first place, instead of in my apartment. But as it was, I was homeless now.

"Sorry, I actually meant it differently."

"I know." I smiled conciliatory at my best friend. No one could blame her for the fact that I could eat a huge sundae within minutes, or that my love life was a total mess.

"Don't you have brain freeze?" asked Rebecca, awe resonating in her voice.

"Yes, I do, but I'm a masochist."

Rebecca laughed, and I let my best friend think it was a joke.

"Shannon Williams is losing it," Rebecca changed the subject.

"Oh yes, please tell me more about my former boss who cold-heartedly kicked me out."

"Sorry, Dana, you're going to have to get through this."

"Why? Because you're a sadist?"

"No, I'm not a sadist, but fine, let's talk about Connor."

"All right, you sadist," I said, sighing. "What happened at the Royal Renaissance Hotel after I got kicked out? And before you answer, I'm getting that secret Crunchy Crinkles stash you've been hiding from Emma, or there's nothing keeping me here." I over-emphasized my last words theatrically, like a diva, which elicited a giggle from Beccs.

"Whew, you've become a tough negotiator. Connor's business acumen has rubbed off on you, huh?" Rebecca climbed out of the nest of pillows and blankets I'd built for myself on the sofa and went into the kitchen.

Not just his sense of negotiation.

Strictly speaking, Connor had not only given me new senses, but also robbed me of all my other senses at the same time.

I longed for his masculine tart-but-warm scent – sandalwood.

I longed for his fingers to brush over my skin.

I longed for his deep, soft voice, with which he whispered things in my ear.

I longed to see his strong body, his brown eyes.

I longed for the taste of his sweet lips.

In my thoughts there was only Connor. My heart beat only for him, and all my senses obeyed him better than me. Every single fiber of my body longed for Connor!

"Hi. Earth to Dana!" Rebecca interrupted my train of thought by rattling a half-full box of Crunchy Crinkles in front of my face.

Like a viper, I swooped in seconds and claimed the crunchy cornflakes that looked like colorful mini donuts. Then Beccs handed me a bowl and I dumped a generous portion of the cornflakes into it.

"The chocolate loops are missing!" I noted in horror. The little crunchy loops had different flavors. Chocolate, vanilla, strawberry and lemon. I was convinced that the combination of all the flavors made Crunchy Crinkles a success.

"Well, what can I say? I'm just a sadist," Rebecca replied with a grin. "And chocolate is just the best, so they go on the plate first."

"Hmph," I said munching after popping a handful into my mouth. I was missing the chocolate flavor, which is why the taste was imperfect, just as I was without Connor.

Had I overreacted? No. Okay, possibly I had, but whether I had gone too fast or not, Connor could have stopped me, but he did not. That was a fact. He could have held me, yelled at me, begged me, done anything, but he hadn't done anything.

Rebecca cleared her throat. "What are you going to do now, Dana?"

"I don't know," I replied, perplexed. Except for the clothes I was wearing, my cell phone and a wallet with no cash, I had nothing. My apartment had been cleared, lease cancelled, and all my belongings were in the basement of Connor's apartment.

"Trust me. Another day or two at most and Shannon Williams will be on her knees begging you to come back!"

"What makes you so sure?"

"That you were fired spread within seconds, and so did certain rumors about secret cameras. Williams is freaking out because the phone hasn't stopped ringing, and there's a whole bunch of employees lined up outside her office door. There's been chaos with orders and a couple of employees must have filled out some order slips incorrectly."

"But I've only been fired for one night."

"Right, and wrongly, all the maids know that. Also, the laundresses from the laundry, and..."

I interrupted my best friend. "Are you sabotaging the hotel? Because of me?"

"What, we didn't! We're just so damn disoriented and lost without you!"

I was moved to tears that my best friend and my colleagues stood by me like that. But even together, we didn't stand a chance against Deborah. The guest was always right, period.

"That's so sweet of you, but please don't risk your job because of me. This is all unfair enough," I sighed.

"No! They should know what they had in you," Rebecca protested.

"Maybe it's not so bad," I tried to make myself feel better about my situation. After all, I had only lost my job, not my future. All doors were open to me.

Stop, who am I kidding? Life is not that simple.

I knew I was fooling myself. Deborah had done it, she had won the battle, and I had lost everything I had ever cared about.

In any case, I could forget about my career in the hotel industry; no one wanted to hire thieves, and no one was interested in the motives. As so often in society, everyone got a stamp of approval.

Woman. Man. Young. Old. Healthy. Sick. Small. Big. Fat. Thin. American. Foreigner.

The stamps left no room for anything else, certainly not personality.

Back to the topic at hand, I was finally able to take some time off to visit my parents. Due to the strict working hours and the few vacation days, I hadn't seen my family for months.

"I haven't been to my parents' house in New Orleans in a long time, and now I will have the time."

"That sounds like a plan," Rebecca said. But she didn't seem all that convinced. Of course she wasn't. I was unhappy with my plan and could hardly get up from the couch. How was I supposed to travel across the country?

It wasn't that I didn't want to see my parents-I loved my parents-but that was only a short-term goal, not a long-term strategy.

The emptiness inside me was crushing. What the hell was I supposed to do with my life? By day I had sacrificed my time to the hotel and by night I had devoted myself to Connor. Both were now parts of my past.

Rebecca looked at her watch. "Tom and Emma should be back any second. So either we hide the Crunchy Crinkles again, or you're going to have to share them."

"Mine," I growled, wrapping my arms tightly around the large package.

"Okay, okay." Rebecca raised her hands placatingly.

"Good, then ownership would be settled now," I said, smiling. I loosened my grip on the package and held the open side in Beccs' direction.

"No thanks, I only like the chocolate ones."

"You have to eat them together, all the flavors at once, only then it's like a revelation!"

"Dana Swanson, the culinary prophetess has spoken!" shouted Rebecca across the room in awe.

"Idiot!" Giggling, I took a handful of Crunchy Crinkles and threw them at Rebecca.

"Oh no! I have incurred the wrath of the prophetess. Mercy! Gnaaade!"

God, I loved my best friend for the fact that we could always laugh together. We were like an old married couple who were there for each other in the good times, but especially in the bad. Rebecca was a huge support for me, and I hoped I was just as good a support for her when things were bad.

"You really are the best friend anyone could ask for, Beccs."

"Well, if that's the case: There's another karaoke event next week, and there can never be enough singers." My best friend grinned conspiratorially.

"No way!"

"You're still welcome to join me."

"Sure, I'd love to."

"And you know you're always welcome here, right? Stay here until you figure something out." Rebecca's voice was soft and caring, like a mother comforting her child with soothing words. I took a deep breath, and my vision blurred through a new veil of tears.

"Thank you, I really appreciate that."

"Of course, you're family."

"Somehow this whole situation will work itself out, won't it?" I had to ask.

"Yeah. I mean, you can always do worse, but look on the bright side. If you work off all that bad karma right now, by the time you're thirty you'll have used it all up, and nothing will stand in the way of your life of sunshine and happiness!"

"Thank you, now that was exactly what I wanted to hear. Not."

"You're welcome!" Rebecca pulled me close and hugged me tightly. "That's what best friends are for."

I could not suppress my grin. Maybe Rebecca was even right about that, at some point I had to have balanced my bad karma. Either that, or the world was the most unfair place in the entire universe.

"So now you're going to tell me what happened with Connor and you, all right?" Rebecca had put on her inquisitive face. With that look, she looked like a professional journalist who could get even the most secretive politician to point out the skeletons in his closet.

"I don't know exactly what happened." Sighing, I tried to sort out my thoughts.

"But nothing irrevocable, right?"

I swallowed the huge lump in my throat that was now heavy in my stomach.

"Dana?"

"It's over," I whispered.

"Really?"

"I think so."

Rebecca took me in her arms again.

"Oh, I'm so sorry for you guys, you were so perfect."

"Yeah, that's what I thought, too, and then, bang! Everything blows up in your face."

"I swear to you, Dana. Tomorrow morning I'm going to dump green waterproof paint into all of Deborah's shampoo and soap bottles so everyone can see what we already know!"

"Or we could just do nothing and not waste energy," I argued.

"Ah! Reverse psychology, very good! We'll let her stew until she looks around every corner, is paranoid on every phone call, and jumps at every little sound, wondering if we're about to take revenge."

Okay, that wasn't what I meant, but it kept Rebecca busy making more plans. That was better than having to talk about Connor, because just thinking about him made my heart hurt like crazy.

Damn, I'd love to go back to the loft, drag him into the playroom and lock us in there forever. Far, far away from the cruel reality. But did Connor even want that? I doubted it. I probably meant nothing to him, or he wouldn't have let me go in the first place.

Nervously, I played around with my bracelet. Actually, I should have taken it off, but it was too early for that. I wasn't ready to show the world that Connor and I were no longer together. I gave in to the illusion that I was still his girl until I took off that bracelet. The shackle that tied me to Connor's life and that I had put on myself. The bracelet was both a shackle and a lifeline, even if now only painful memories were attached to it.

Rebecca looked at me conspiratorially. "And if you talked to him now, do you think you could work it out?"

"If Connor wants something from me, let him come to me!"

"Hmm. Do you really think so?"

"Yes. If he loved me, he would have said it and shown it."

"And he didn't?" asked Rebecca thoughtfully.

Now I began to ponder. Rebecca had slyly pushed me into an abyss, which I now had to face.

Damn traitor.

Regardless of whether I knew Rebecca only wanted the best for me, I just hated my best friend for it.

A loud bang echoed through the apartment, as if a door had been ripped off its hinges.

"Mom! Aunt Dana!" cried Emma euphorically.

"Hello, my darling," Rebecca greeted her daughter, who immediately jumped into her arms.

"Emma! How was it at practice?" I asked with relief. I was glad that now Emma was the center of all conversations and no longer ... never mind. For the past few weeks, Emma had been a part of the Junior Cheerleaders, which was put on by the school to get kids excited about getting more exercise.

"Great! Look!" Emma proudly presented a colorful band-aid, with the imprint of dozens of little kittens, on her left shin.

"Oh dear, what happened there?" Concern flashed across Rebecca's face.

Tom, Rebecca's husband, joined in the conversation. Emma dashed up the stairs almost twice as fast as her dad.

"Our big one was at the top of the pyramid."

"What, and I wasn't there! Oh, they grow up so fast!"

"And if Brenda hadn't been so wiggly, we wouldn't have collapsed!" snorted Emma.

"That's why you're wearing that giant band-aid with baby kittens?"

Emma nodded. "But an Indian knows no pain!" At this, she looked meaningfully at her father. Surely, she had learned this idiom from Tom, who could rarely be ruffled.

"But I'm sure an Indian is hungry too, right?" asked Rebecca.

"Yes!" Immediately her eyes darted to the box of Crunchy Crinkles and the full bowl resting on my lap.

"Here." I held out the box to Emma, but when I saw Rebecca's reproachful look, I immediately withdrew the cereal. "I mean ... candy only after dinner."

"And you had dinner without us?" asked Emma, disappointed. She let her gaze wander over the couch. Empty candy wrappers, scattered gummy bears, and the family pack of Ben & Jerry's were impossible to miss. I was sitting in the middle of a candy massacre of my own making. I had also talked myself into a corner from which there was no escape, so I jumped up and headed for the kitchen.

"Who's hungry for mac and cheese a la Dana?"

"Yay!" Emma rejoiced.

Tom followed me and said, "I can take over if you'd rather talk to Rebecca."

Full of understanding, almost a touch too compassionate, he looked at me.

"It's okay." Then I leaned forward and whispered, "I'll be quite happy to escape their cross-examination for a moment until my thoughts are sorted."

Tom grinned knowingly, then went back into the open living room while I raged in the kitchen, preparing dinner. Out of the corner of my eye, I contemplated the family life that Beccs was in. Laughter. Giggles. Serious conversations. Chiding. To my best friend, the sweetest girl in the world, and Tom, this was just another day. The sun was shining, everything was perfect, and the world kept spinning ... but it was spinning without me. Everything was different for me today. Now, amid people I loved, I felt more alone than ever before. I had lost everything; it was all gone, and I had also lost the last hope for a happy ending. The realization hurt, but not as much as the thought that Connor had left me, my seven-year plan had fizzled out, and that Deborah had robbed me of the last bit of dignity I still possessed on my last day of work.

Everything was lost.

30

Connor

"Connor Lancester, you're a fucking idiot," Maxine reprimanded me. Her reproachful look pierced me, until the served blueberry pie from in-house production made her more conciliatory.

"I know that myself, Max."

"Good." She pulled out her smartphone, turned her back to me and said, "Smile."

I didn't even bother. Ever since Maxine discovered Snapchat, she's been spamming the internet with everything in sight, even if no one remembers the picture in a few minutes.

Sighing, I stirred my latte macchiato with extra hazelnut syrup and cream and thought.

"If you women didn't hide your feelings and desires in cryptic messages, but just said what you wanted, there would be a lot fewer problems."

"So, am I to blame for your stupidity? Or Dana? Or do you mean the female gender in general?" She pointed the tines of her pie fork at me accusingly, and I raised my left eyebrow.

"I don't even know why I told you about it in the first place," I growled. Yet I hadn't mentioned a single word about the incident at the hotel.

"But I know. You don't want to bathe in self-pity, you want to win Dana back!" Maxine nodded with conviction. "You just don't know it yet."

Do I want that?

Thoughtfully, I folded an origami crane from a napkin and placed it in front of me. Even the damned paper bird stared at me reproachfully, at least that's how it seemed to me.

Damn, I missed Dana more than anything else in the world. Would I trade everything I had for Dana? Fuck, yes. I was that serious!

"I love her," I said for the first time.

"Then tell her. Show her!"

"No, the train has left the station." I sighed softly, making sure that at least the crane wasn't left alone. "Besides, if Dana had been serious enough, she would have come forward by now."

Maxine groaned loudly. "Sometimes women run away, too, because they hope to be caught again."

I thought back to the evening when Dana had left me and how she had hesitated for a moment. She hadn't paused to say anything, but because she had been waiting for me. My God, Maxine was absolutely right, I was a fucking idiot.

"I broke her heart. I don't know if I can ever make it up to her."

Not only was Dana's heart broken, mine was too. She had torn it out of my chest when she left. Only her sweet, flowery scent on the sheets had remained. Everything else was gone, her laughter, her warmth, her bright eyes.

Damn. No woman in the world could ever give me what I really needed again, only Dana could. Only with Dana by my side was my world perfect.

"If you don't do something, you'll never find out, and you owe that to Dana."

"You're right."

"Of course I am." Maxine grinned at me, then her smile slipped, and the corners of her mouth tipped grotesquely downward.

"What's Deborah Landry doing here? Is she stalking my Snapchat profile?" she pressed out between clenched teeth.

"No, I have a date with her," I replied, looking at the clock. Deborah was much too early.

"You what?"

"I need to clear something up with her." If I wanted to find out what had really happened at the hotel, I had to listen to all sides. When Deborah saw me, she immediately came to our table.

"Connor!" For the first time, I noticed how pointedly she yelled my name when she saw me.

"Hello Deborah."

And for the first time I noticed how disparagingly she looked at my little sister.

"I actually thought we were ... undisturbed."

Maxine gave Deborah an even more snide look, but it had never escaped me before. "Ditto."

Immediately I was attacked by both women with death stares. Probably it would have been better to hold my two meetings in different places, because I had actually known how difficult the situation between Deborah and Max could be. I was also slowly coming to understand why my sister felt the way she did. If even a fraction of what Dana had told me was true ... Damn. Where did I even get the idea Dana hadn't told me the truth? It was a rule, one that Dana had always taken seriously. Not once had she betrayed my trust, and besides, she no longer had any reason to fantasize about someone else's jewelry – I had made her fantasies come true.

"Please sit down, Deborah, I have something to discuss with you," I said seriously.

Deborah tugged her extravagant dress into place, then sat down and ordered a café au lait with two sugars and nonfat milk.

"That sounds very serious. What's so important to talk about?" Deborah asked curiously. At that, she gave me a blink that other men would kill for, but not me. At last, I had recognized the spectacle behind her thick facade.

"I want you to rethink this Dana thing."

"What thing?" Deborah acted innocent, but Maxine's ears perked up.

"Connor? What did I miss?"

"I'll explain that to you later," I said with an urgent face. Reluctantly, she nodded and bit her lips together.

Deborah bent over and rested her chin on the back of her hand. As she did so, she literally forced me to stare into her ample cleavage. "I'm all ears."

I averted my eyes in disgust. Damn, how could I have been so blind over the years? How had I been able to see friendship where there was only cheap desire? Interest that came from greed? How could I have ever doubted Dana?

I would have loved to get up and leave, but I couldn't because I had to settle the damage that Deborah had caused. Nevertheless, I swore by God and all that was holy to me that I was speaking to Deborah Landry here and now for the last time.

"Withdraw the charges you are seeking against Dana. You know it's not right."

Deborah's eyes grew big. Maxine's grew even bigger. But a warning look from me was enough for Maxine to remain silent.

"Aaah, we're talking about your ... ex-girlfriend?"

I clenched my teeth.

"We're talking about my girlfriend," I corrected.

"Well, that's not what a lot of people are saying."

"I expect three things from you. One, just stop your games, two, leave Dana alone, and three, stop bombarding the hotel with possible lawsuits."

"Uh, Connor, you can get really angry!" Deborah poked my chest with her index finger. Obviously, she had not yet understood the gravity of the situation.

"I will not withdraw my charges. The brooch was a family heirloom!"

Hell, I was on the verge of losing my temper. I wanted Deborah's whole world in ruins; I wanted to do to her what she had done to me and, especially, to Dana! But I stayed calm, because I owed that to Dana. I could torch Deborah's world when Dana's wreckage was cleared.

"You know about the video goggles, right? I'm sure they'll be used for evidence."

"What kind of glasses?"

Jackpot.

"The glasses Dana was wearing were equipped with a camera lens, which is now standard hotel equipment, so the theft should have been recorded."

"You're kidding." Deborah fiddled with her designer dress, and she was seized with unease.

"Do I look like I'm kidding?"

"No."

"Good. Now listen to me carefully, because I'm only going to say this once. Withdraw your lying accusations, they can be refuted. Apologize for being wrong – publicly and so remorsefully that a few tears will run. Also, you will never exchange a single word with Dana or me again, do you understand?"

"But Connor? I didn't mean any of that!"

"Yes, you did."

"Fuck yeah, Deborah! You're a fucking beast!" Maxine interjected.

Deborah narrowed her eyes and gave Max a death glare that rolled off her.

"I did all this just for you! You know I would have been the better choice! I'm rich! I am–"

"You're a terrible person," I interrupted her in a calm tone. "You know I could end your life of luxury with a snap of my fingers."

Deborah pressed her lips tightly together, knowing full well that I could really do it.

"But I'll let you live your messed up life if you clear Dana's reputation."

It cost me a hell of a lot of strength to appear so cool and uninvolved on the outside, when I was almost exploding on the inside. My veins pumped lava through my body, and it roared loudly in my ears.

"Please, I'm way too good for you anyway," Deborah hissed. "I can't believe I was even so ... emotional over an unimportant maid."

She jumped up and rushed out of the café and with it out of my life. Hopefully for good.

Maxine looked after Deborah, then her face snapped back to me.

"What a bitch!"

"Yes," I growled. A bitch who had successfully sabotaged my relationship. My only really serious relationship I had ever had.

"Why didn't you tell me about this before?"

"Because I wanted to talk to you about Dana, my feelings about her, not Deborah," I thought out loud. "Fuck. I'm really an idiot."

"Jab. You can say that again and actually you shouldn't pass on your idiot genes at all. You're really lucky that Dana can compensate for that," my sister said dryly.

"You know our genes are almost identical, right Maxine?"

"Almost. Except I just inherited the non-idiot genes, just like Mom's voluminous hair! You inherited the idiot genes and Dad's penchant for booze and quiet."

"Oh, is that so?"

"Yes!" Max stroked through her black, chin-length hair, the tips of which flew in all directions.

"You also inherited Mom's foul mouth. So did her caring nature, albeit in a weird way."

Maxine tilted her head and smiled. "True. So, how are you going to win Dana's heart now that you've defeated the dragon?"

"With your help," I replied. The solution to all the problems was clear in my mind, I just needed a few helping hands to get everything rolling as quickly as possible.

"Well, because of the caring genes, I guess I have no choice, right?"

"Do you have a pen and paper here?" I asked.

Maxine nodded and pulled out a small drawing pad and a pencil from her purse. On the first pages were detailed drawings of a living room with a fireplace. This was followed by a conservatory and a bedroom in the same country house style.

Very fancy, but I couldn't focus on that right now. My highest priority was Dana, I had to win her back at any cost. My whole body was screaming for her, and my heart continued to beat only with protest without her. Without Dana, I was nothing. Why hadn't I realized that sooner? I loved her with all my heart.

I love you, Dana.

The next time I saw Dana, I wouldn't hold back the words, no, I would shout them out to the whole world, fly it across the sky with an airplane banner, and have it tattooed on my chest. Hopefully, it wasn't too late.

"I have a plan," I told her as I filled a blank page with a list. "But for that, I need you, sis."

When the list was finished, I handed the pad back to Maxine. Her eyes grew big.

"Wow, I think you need more like twelve sister hearts for that."

The list was quite long, but I knew the work was worth it.

"If anyone can do it, you can."

Maxine narrowed her eyes, her gaze shifting back and forth between me and the list.

"Hmm. Pretty daring, but if the stars align and I start right now..."

"Can you make it in no time. Shall we say by the weekend?" I finished her sentence, leaving no room for negotiation. Every day that passed without Dana was a day lost.

"Are you crazy? How am I supposed to do this in such a short time!"

"You're the best, if anyone can do it, you can, Super Max."

Maxine rolled her eyes, but I knew I had long since won with that argument. Maxine was without question the best in her field, and she never missed an opportunity to prove it.

"Fine, all right, but it's going to cost extra."

"Good."

I pulled my gold credit card out of my wallet and slid it over to Maxine.

"I don't care how much it costs. The main thing is to get it done as quickly as possible."

"Good, I'll get right on it then. I think I have something in mind. Anyway, I'll keep you posted, all right?"

"I insist."

We got up, I settled the bill, and together, we left the café. Before Max got into her limousine, I took her in my arms.

"Thank you, Sis, it means a lot to me that you're helping me."

"Sure, little brother, we are a family; we stick together, come what may." She gave me a kiss on the cheek. "What are you doing now?"

Meaningfully, I pulled my smartphone out of my pocket and held it up.

"I'm going to set up some meetings."

As I walked through the lobby of the Royal Renaissance Hotel, I caught myself looking for Dana for a moment. *Dana's not here, idiot.*

When I had expressed the wish for a meeting yesterday, the management of the hotel already complied with my request. Of course, I was a valuable customer and a damn successful businessman, and successful people were not kept waiting.

"Mr. Lancester, it's good to have you here," Ms. Williams greeted me. When she held out her hand to me, I shook my head. This woman was a monster in a designer suit. She had gotten Dana fired, not to mention I had witnessed how unglamorous things were behind the curtains.

"I'm glad you could arrange a meeting so quickly," I said coolly. Brief horror appeared on her face, then she regained her composure and her gaze fell on the small briefcase I was carrying.

"May I take the case from you?"

"No thanks, I'd rather carry it myself." Inside that leather case was Dana's pardon, at least I hoped so.

"Please follow me." Ms. Williams led the way and ushered me into the office of the store manager, Mr. Campbell. Together we entered the business room.

"Good afternoon, Mr. Lancester," the hotel manager greeted me. "Please sit down." He pointed to the chair that stood in front of his heavy office desk and across from him.

"Thank you."

I sat down, and Ms. Williams stood off to the side, facing the hotel manager more than me.

"Have you changed your mind?" the CEO asked without mincing words.

"No." I leaned back and paused meaningfully. The hotel manager's eyes grew wide, then I continued, "But I have another offer for you. One that I think you'll like."

"Well, let's hear it, Mr. Lancester."

I put the briefcase on the table and opened it. Dozens of documents, contracts, reports and statistics appeared, which I pushed over to the director and waited.

Mr. Campbell read through the papers carefully as he kept looking up at me.

"And these are notarizations?"

"But of course," I assured the director. "You're welcome to have everything cross-checked by your own lawyers."

The director gave the papers to his deputy.

"Assuming we agreed, and assuming everything worked out as described in theory, what would you want in return?" Mr. Campbell looked at me critically.

If I had been presented with my own contract as a businessman, I would be just as doubtful, my deal was just too good.

"I am only an intermediary in this case. I want no commission, no royalties. Nothing like that." Then I pulled another paper out of the briefcase and presented it to the hotel manager.

"I just want you to sign this."

I watched Mr. Campbell's reactions closely as he read through the document that cleared Dana of all charges. A perfect job reference for a perfect employee. With this recommendation, signed off by the director himself, Dana would be cleared of all charges and would have no problem getting a permanent job anywhere. Not that my plan called for such a thing, but I knew how much a clean resume meant to Dana.

"Dana Swanson? That maid we were talking about the other day?" the director asked his deputy.

"Yes, sir."

I cleared my throat. "The trouble was caused by a guest, and you know it as well as I do." Glances. Silence. Tension. No one said anything. While I looked seriously at the deputy, she exchanged meaningful glances with the director.

"Well," she said, "before that, she was pretty exemplary, always on time and reliable."

"And don't forget this once-in-a-lifetime deal. It's a deal that I'm sure other hotel managers would be scrambling for."

The hotel manager was struggling with himself. "And you can guarantee me that the Olivera Distillery will also agree to this deal?"

"I guarantee that."

"And how can you guarantee that?"

I smiled confidently. "Because I spoke to Justino Olivera personally about it. And if you'll be patient for a moment, you can discuss the finer details with him in person right now."

The two businessmen, both Mr. Campbell and Mr. Olivera had the same ambitions, nothing stood in the way of a deal. Fortunately, both sides were looking for potential partners, that had been my luck.

Not a moment later, the phone rang. Perfect timing.

Mr. Campbell picked up the phone and nodded. "Send him up, please."

From his breast pocket, Mr. Campbell pulled out an engraved fountain pen, removed the protective cap, and signed Dana's job reference in sweeping handwriting.

"Here you go." Mr. Campbell handed the document back to me. I quickly pulled it to me and packed it safely in the briefcase.

"Thank you."

I could hardly suppress my euphoria, and I couldn't wait to give Dana the paper that proved her innocence. With this letter, she could work anywhere, and if she didn't like any other hotel, I would buy out the damn Royal Renaissance Hotel.

"I guess we're done with all the business then, and you'll want to take a moment to prepare for Mr. Olivera," I said goodbye.

"Thank you, Mr. Lancester. It has been my pleasure. You have my utmost respect for your unselfish acts of kindness."

I nodded to the hotel manager. He didn't have to know that I hadn't acted altruistically – I killed two birds with one stone. I got Dana back and, thanks to the million-dollar deal between the hotel and the

Olivera Distillery, I had the promise of being allowed to produce one hundred liters of rum myself using their process. I wonder if Dana liked Cuba.

On both sides, I had gotten the best deal possible. I had everything I wanted, without any of the obligations that everyone preferred to refuse.

Ms. Williams still accompanied me outside.

"Listen, Mr. Lancester. If you see Dana ... I'd be willing to give her back her old post. In fact, after Miss Landry clears everything up – that terrible mix-up – I'd be delighted! Would you please give her the message?" She looked at me ruefully.

Like hell I will.

I certainly wouldn't throw Dana into that lion's den again, because my girl didn't deserve that.

"Could you please call one of the maids to the front desk for me?" I asked.

She frowned. No idea why almost all my wishes caused frowns in this hotel, where there were only extravagant wishes.

A bathtub full of champagne? No problem.

A room full of penguins? But of course.

A certain maid? What?

"Of course," Ms. Williams replied grudgingly, because I had passed over her request.

In case Dana really wanted to work here, I had to extend my deal with the hotel manager and make sure Dana got her crazy supervisor's job. Of course, the resignation could have been part of the deal, but I wasn't sure it would work out that way, and I wanted to play it safe. Dana needed a clean slate for her seven-year plan.

"Who may I page?"

"Rebecca Hatfield. Tell her it's about a very important event."

Ms. Williams nodded. "Of course. I'll send the maid to the front desk right away."

"Thank you."

Without further words, we parted ways. She went back to the hotel manager's office, and I took the elevator to the lobby. There, I leaned against a side wall from which I had a perfect view of the reception desk and pulled my Gameboy out of my side pocket while I waited.

Before I had even cleared the first five rows, Rebecca was standing at the front desk looking around.

To my regret, I didn't have a good relationship with Rebecca yet. Although she and Dana were best friends, she only dropped by a few times for a short visit. But of course, with a job like that, it was almost impossible to balance family, free time, friends, and everything else. Until recently, Dana and Rebecca had seen each other every day at work, for years. Such things melded together, logically. That's why it was even more important that Rebecca understood my plan, because I was something like her mortal enemy right now, because I had broken her best friend's heart.

When Rebecca returned my gaze, she gave me a nasty glare.

"What do you want?" She crossed her arms in front of her chest.

"I want to talk to you."

"Sure, do I look like I'm aligning myself with the enemy? Forget it, Connor."

She stared at me with hostility, and I couldn't blame her. Hopefully she understood that I had noble intentions and would leave no stone unturned to win Dana back.

"I want Dana back, by any means necessary."

"Why?"

"Because I know she wants me back, too."

Rebecca raised a brow and eyed me critically. Her arms remained crossed in front of her chest, not a good sign. "And what makes you so sure of that? You know Dana will hate me for it if anything goes wrong."

"We need each other to make our world perfect. I fucking love her. Dana proved to me that she does, too."

Rebecca nodded thoughtfully. Now she let her arms hang down, which made her whole posture seem less hostile.

"Assuming – and I'll say this very clearly – assuming I believe you, how are you going to win her back?"

"I need your help for that."

Rebecca's face was streaked with doubt, and I understood that. She was right. If my plan backfired, Dana might never forgive her best friend, but if it worked – and by God, I hoped it would – Dana would be eternally grateful.

"I'm sorry, I can't risk it," Rebecca said with a sigh, leaving me standing alone in the lobby. But her serious facade was cracking, and if I hit the right notch, maybe I could get Rebecca on my side. Giving up was not an option,

"Rebecca, wait!" I ran after her and grabbed her by the shoulders. Looking deep into her eyes, I offered her a perfect view of my troubled soul.

"Face it, you fucked up. Over, out, finished. I couldn't stand it if you hurt Dana any more. Do you have any idea how fucked up she is?"

Yes, of course I knew that. I felt the same damn way! Including feelings of guilt that put salt in my wounds, because I was to blame for the whole situation.

"Without you, my whole plan will fail," I said. It took all his strength for me to speak loud enough. I was so tired...

"So?"

I took the last chance I had.

"Listen to my plan, and then think about it again, okay?"

"Why do you want to tell me about your plan? I could tell Dana. All of it. Or none of it."

"If you don't help me, it's all over anyway and you can tell her whatever you want."

Rebecca sighed as she rolled her eyes. "Alright, you have five minutes."

I wasted no time but let Rebecca in on every detail of my plan to win Dana back. Could I ever make up for breaking Dana's heart?

I could never forgive myself if I didn't.

31

Dana

Hot, hot, hot! Hectically, I hopped through the kitchen while balancing a hot cake tray on much too thin potholders.

I desperately searched for a free spot for the two-hundred-degree baking sheet, but the entire kitchen counter was full of bags of flour and sugar, bowls of separated eggs and other baking ingredients. And the kitchen table was blocked by four finished fruitcakes and a three-tier cake.

The heat burned more and more through the cheap potholders, and I started to gasp.

When the front door was almost ripped off its hinges, I almost dropped the tin.

"Hey, we're back!" announced Beccs.

"Mommy, it smells like cake!" exclaimed Emma excitedly. "Aunt Dana baked a cake!"

"Not just one," I called from the kitchen, preparing my best friend for the sugar shock to come.

When the searing heat began to burn my fingertips, I had no choice but to set the baking tray down on the floor because I had no better alternative.

Emma ran excitedly, and still wearing a street shoe, into the kitchen. Rebecca followed her, and her face was priceless when she saw the chaos around me.

"Oh my god. What happened here?"

"I'm afraid I happened."

I blew a loosened curl out of my face and smiled charmingly at Beccs.

Admittedly, it was huge chaos, and I had no idea how it had come to this. Actually, I just wanted to bake a simple apple pie, according to one of Grandma's old recipes, and then the baking had distracted me so much from my grief that I had taken refuge in a true baking mania. The apple pie was followed by a crumble cake with blueberries and a strawberry cake with vanilla pudding. In between the cakes I had dedicated myself again and again to the three-tier chocolate cream cake, which was still not quite ready. The decorations were still missing.

I had scurried to the little store on the next corner a total of three times to buy egg and flour supplies over and over again. The salespeople there must have thought I was crazy by now, but what didn't one do to escape one's sorrow? At least for a little moment, I had been able to forget everything.

"Wow, these look great," Rebecca marveled at the cakes.

"Please, help yourselves," I offered.

"For once, before dinner, but only because they look really yummy," Rebecca said, giving her daughter serious looks.

"I want the one with strawberries!" Emma jumped in the air with joy, and her sweet, braided pigtails bobbed along.

I took three cake plates from the cupboard and spread huge pieces of cake on them. Together we went into the open living room and sat down on the couch to watch the children's news together with Emma, which she insisted on every day.

"Man, this cake is really delicious, you should bake for us more often, Dana."

"Thank you."

"Maybe you could start a pastry shop too? Now that you've escaped slavery."

I sighed loudly. "That was just therapeutic baking."

"Did it help?"

"Yeah, totally good," I lied, torturing myself into a smile. Ever since I'd pulled the last sheet cake out of the oven, Connor had been omnipresent again. So my newfound form of therapy wasn't particularly sustainable.

God, how could this man have so stubbornly lodged himself in my mind? He was still there ... he was never gone.

"You are the worst liar in the world," Rebecca stated matter-of-factly.

"I know, and I don't want to talk about it, okay? How was work?"

"Great!" replied Rebecca a touch too quickly.

"You're not a very good liar either," I remarked.

"I guess so."

"So, what all happened at the Royal Renaissance Hotel today?"

"Oh, nothing spectacular. Nothing that would interest you in any way." Rebecca shrugged her shoulders. She was hiding something, that much was certain, I just didn't know what yet.

"Why do I feel like something totally spectacular happened?"

"I don't know. Maybe you stuck your head too deep in the oven and now you're having heat stroke? Hallucinations and stuff."

I eyed my friend critically. There was no doubt that Rebecca had a secret. But before I could get to the bottom of my best friend's secret, the doorbell rang, and I winced.

My first thought: Connor!

My second thought: Tom had forgotten the keys.

My third thought: Please, please Connor! No, please not Connor!

Rebecca went to the speakerphone, frowning. Whoever it was, Rebecca knew nothing about it. Good, at least I could rule out a weird we're-there-for-you surprise party. Beccs hit the buzzer and threw herself back on the couch.

"Just Tom, he forgot his keys again."

"I almost had a heart attack because of your husband," I said. Then I stuffed a big piece of cake in my mouth to further numb my grief.

"Really?" Beccs looked at me with huge eyes. "Were you hoping someone else would be at the door?"

"No!" Yes, I had. Oh, I didn't know exactly what I had hoped. My feelings were a mess, and I had long since lost track of them.

"Admit it, you miss Connor!" my best friend prompted.

"Now where do you get Connor from?" I asked.

"Because it's unmistakable that you were thinking about him."

"Not at all."

"Yes, you were!"

"Hey, the news is on!" Emma interrupted us with a precocious look, silencing us.

"Just admit it, Dana!" Beccs continued our discussion in a whisper.

"Yes, okay. I've been thinking about him, even though I don't even know if I'd have anything to say to him. Are you happy now, you tease?"

"I am." Rebecca pricked a large piece of strawberry with her fork. "Maybe you'd just have to listen to him?"

I thought about Rebecca's argument, but her solution was somehow too simple. Life was that easy only in Hollywood movies and romance novels, but not in real life.

Therefore, after a long consideration, I shook my head. "I don't think he has anything to say, otherwise he would have done it long ago."

Listlessly, I poked around on my cake.

"Um, did you forget that you're hiding in my apartment and your phone has been turned off for days?"

"And did you forget that Connor is Connor. He would have found a way long ago if he really wanted to."

"Oh, come on, Dana, maybe he made a mistake just like you did. You both just made mistakes that you regret."

I narrowed my eyes and looked deeply into Rebecca's eyes. "When did you join Team Connor?"

Placatingly, she raised her hands, interrupted the gesture for another piece of cake, and said, "I'm not. I'm just saying ... maybe Connor is sorry?"

"Don't bullshit me, Beccs," I replied, shaking my head. Of course I wished Connor back. But I had to face reality and accept what was coming. I wanted Rebecca to see it that way, too. As my best friend, it was her duty to curb my utopian hopes and knock them out of my head entirely, not to plant new hopes in me. Except...

"Have you talked to Connor!"

"Me!? No!" Rebecca shook her head violently.

Tom entered the apartment. I had to interrupt my cross-examination for a moment.

"Hello, ladies," he greeted and took a deep breath. "It smells good in here."

"Hey Tom. There are some cakes in the kitchen, help yourself," I greeted him.

"You don't have to tell me twice!"

Tom disappeared toward the kitchen, and I resumed my cross-examination. "Rebecca, I want an answer!"

Loud clatter. Followed by a male scream and a dull bang. We immediately jumped up, while Emma had long since been on her way to the kitchen.

Tom was lying on the floor with his face contorted in pain, and he had his left foot stuck in the yogurt and cherry sheet cake I had placed on the floor to cool.

"Oh God, Tom! I'm so sorry!" I apologized. Rebecca, meanwhile, got down on her knees to examine Tom more closely. At first glance, he looked unharmed.

"Hm. I guess you can't save the cake," Tom growled. He stretched his foot upwards and individual cherries and cake crumbs fell down.

"Are you okay, honey?" asked Rebecca.

Tom gave all his limbs a quick shake, then rubbed his head and nodded. "Yeah, I guess so. Better than the cherry pie, anyway."

I could have slapped myself for my negligence for completely forgetting about the cake on the floor.

"Tom, I'm sooo sorry!" I sobbed.

"It's okay, nothing's broken," Tom reassured me. He freed himself from the cake tray and took off his cake-stained shoe and sock.

"I once heard yogurt is good for your skin," Tom laughed, and Rebecca and I laughed along.

"I'm off to the bathroom to freshen up then."

"You do that, honey. Dana and I will clean up the mess here."

I grabbed a paper towel and used it to collect the larger chunks of cake while Beccs took care of the tray. Emma, still giggling, went back to the TV.

"If there's one thing I don't miss at all about my job, it's something like this," I said.

"Speaking of work, I got a part-time job super spontaneously." Rebecca's eyes sparkled.

"Oh, great. A good deal?"

"Absolutely, and I thought maybe you could help me. You know, get you back around people. Remember your seven-year plan, it doesn't get done on the couch."

I snorted. "I don't care about the annual plan! You know I don't care about people or parties."

"And that's exactly why I want you to come with me! I don't want my best friend to become a loner who collects cats and swears off men forever."

"Oh, Beccs. Stop painting the devil on the wall. It's never going to escalate that badly."

"Uh-huh, and how many hundreds of cakes are going to be sitting around here tomorrow? You absolutely-not-crazy-cake-baker?"

As always, my best friend was right, but I didn't want to go outside. Out there, the danger that some man would show up and suddenly rip my heart out of my chest increased massively. I didn't want to do that to my heart a second time.

"Dana Swanson, if I don't get you out the door, I'm going to call Vincent McMiller to run you out of the house with his finger."

"You wouldn't!"

"You want to go for it?"

"All right, you win, I'll help you."

"Very good, now what are we going to do with all this cake? Eat it?"

I counted up in my head how many cups of sugar I had consumed and shook my head abundantly. In front of me were tens of thousands of delicious calories.

"Hmm, probably shouldn't do that to my hips."

"Dana? You do know you've been eating at the hotel all day. Right? Gummi bears, candy, and various other stuff."

"That's different," I defended myself, curling my lips into a pout.

"Ah. Sure. Gummy bears and cake are two completely different things, of course."

"Yes. That piece of cake would never fit in a side pocket."

"That's your rule of thumb for candy? That they fit in your pockets?"

"Exactly. It has to fit in my pocket and not melt or stick. Does the soup kitchen behind the park actually still exist?"

"Yes, I think so. Why?"

"I think they could do significantly more with two cakes and a three-tier cake than we could. Besides, we still have half the strawberry cake."

Rebecca nodded thoughtfully, then smiled. "A nice idea. Yes, let's do that! I'll get a transport box out of the van really quick, and then we'll jet right out, okay?"

"Actually, I wanted to enjoy my solitary existence until the end of the week, but if I have to..."

"Yep, it has to be!" Beccs grinned triumphantly. She then took the key for the van from the board and disappeared.

I sighed. On the one hand, I was infinitely grateful that my best friend made sure I didn't fall into a deep hole, but on the other hand, a deep hole wouldn't be so bad. Far, far down in the dark, everything would be perfectly clear, and there were no Connor Lancesters running around there to break my heart! At the same time, I had no idea how life would go on without Connor. Since he had left, I was missing something. Neither cake nor Beccs nor the Royal Renaissance Hotel could fill the void he had left. Only Connor himself could do that, and what he did with me ... in the playroom and beyond.

Mayday.

Although I had never spoken the word, it had been the most precious word I knew. Stupidly, I could not stop my thoughts from whirling with it. Heavens, Connor still had more control over my body than I did, which I enjoyed very much – in fact, I still wanted him to.

Maybe I should call him or go back to his loft and talk to him? Maybe Rebecca was right, and Connor missed me too? Yes, or maybe he had long since gotten over me. With Deborah. At the thought of the beastiest beast ever, as Maxine would call her, I brushed the thought aside and became angry.

That damn beast had taken everything that had ever meant anything to me, and Connor had let it happen! Connor had betrayed me, that was the bottom line.

Now I suddenly didn't want to crawl into a hole anymore, on the contrary! I wanted to show the whole world that I didn't need a man at my side. Everything I needed, I already had. Friends who picked me up and a family who loved me. I didn't need anything more in my life, at least that's what I tried to tell myself.

"Ready?" Rebecca pierced my thoughts. She packed one cake after another into a large Styrofoam box.

"Yeah, sure." I pushed myself off the kitchen counter and followed Rebecca outside into the big, wide world. Into a city full of hustle and bustle and noise; a city where you were lost without directions, and no one cared.

Who am I kidding? I can't do without Connor!

32

Dana

I steered the van away from the main road, which proved to be quite difficult during rush hour. I had no chance to park even near the Royal Renaissance Hotel, especially not a van with excess length.

According to statistics, there was a one-in-nine-hundred-and-sixty-thousand chance of being struck by lightning. The chance of dying from a shark attack was one chance in three-point-seven million. Getting a free parking space in New York in a van just under six feet long was somewhere in between.

Geez, why had I even let myself be talked into picking up Rebecca after hours? Because Tom needed the little car to pick up Emma from cheerleading practice after his shift was over, that's why. Oh, and then there was the teeny tiny little matter of Beccs' being late to her super-spontaneous party that she was supposed to organize and was forcing me to attend in order to finally detach myself from my hillbilly aspirations. When I spied a free parking space in a side street, I pulled a movie-like emergency stunt, including squealing, smoking tires. There was a loud crash and rumble in the back of the car as some of the stacked boxes fell over. A quick sideways glance was enough to assess the damage – it looked as if a unicorn had just exploded.

I almost jumped up from the driver's seat, but to do that, I had to get the car off the road first, dozens of motorists behind me agreed with a concert of horns.

I turned into the side alley and parked Beccs' van before taking a closer look at the damage I had done.

Sighing, I realized that it wasn't just one little unicorn that had exploded, but a whole herd of unicorns!

Garlands, glitter confetti and flowers were everywhere, arranged by Beccs according to a system I had no idea about. But my sense of order forced me to do at least some damage control. There were also a few boxes that were only half dumped, so I put those up first. I felt a bit like a detective, retracing tracks and drawing conclusions.

First, I sorted the garlands by color, no problem, but with all the glitter confetti it became more difficult.

As I was sorting, it struck me that Beccs must have added quite a bit to her budget, because while quality was important to her, she had never used such expensive decorations before.

The decorations were in gray, silver and pink, even the confetti and balloons. Surely in the locked boxes were still napkins, tablecloths and flowers in the same shades.

Either it was a baptism or ... an engagement or wedding party.

I immediately put my job as a detective on hold. Was Beccs seriously taking me to a fucking wedding? No, my best friend would never do that to me. At least, I hoped not. And if she did, I would kill her myself!

As quickly as I could, I gathered up the items and threw them into the nearest boxes, completely eliminating the evidence of the existence of happy couples.

Admittedly, whoever ordered the decorations showed good taste. I would have chosen the same colors and style for my wedding reception, without a doubt.

At the thought of Connor and I ... my heart skipped a beat.

Slowly but surely, the floor of the van could be seen again, and a short time later, everything was packed back into boxes. Including my frustration.

Then I left the car and headed straight for the Royal Renaissance Hotel. Beccs would never find me here, no chance, and thanks to rush hour, there was no way I could stop in front of the hotel and just collect them.

With a cool wind blowing around my champagne-colored pleated skirt and giving my steps more momentum, I made quick progress. I had also opted for a white blouse and mid-height pumps, neither too festive nor too casual. With this, I could show up at any kind of event.

A few yards before the hotel, I paused to watch the bustle of bellhops frantically hoisting suitcases out of a limousine, while an elderly guest with a beard that went down to his chest was greeted by one of the doormen.

Gritting my teeth, I had to admit that I missed my old workplace. Not the stupid rules and regulations or my supervisor, but the atmosphere and the nice conversations with the other maids and sometimes with guests. Yes, I missed it more than I wanted to admit.

A little distance from the entrance, I paced for quite a while. Again and again, I cast impatient glances at my wristwatch, because Beccs should have shown up twenty minutes ago. Sure, overtime was nothing unusual, but Rebecca had other obligations as well, not to mention she still had to fill me in on whether we were arranging a wedding or if I was mistaken.

Beccs left me alone with these thoughts for an agonizingly long time, and to make matters worse, Shannon Williams also ran into me. The normally composed and self-confident deputy seemed rather distracted and stressed today. Her elegant pantsuit was wrinkled, and individual strands were hanging out of her otherwise impeccable hairstyle.

As fast as I could, I turned to the side, but it was too late; she had already spotted me.

"Daaanaaa?"

Oh, what a bummer.

Silently I stared at the floor, because my traitorous boss didn't deserve a conversation with me. She had burned my seven-year plan with a snap of her fingers, and I would never forgive her for that.

"How are you doing, Dana?"

I gave her the silent treatment and pretended Ms. Williams was air.

"What are you doing here? Have you changed your mind?" she continued to probe persistently.

Somehow, I had to get rid of her, otherwise she could no longer guarantee anything.

"I'm busy and I'm here waiting for a friend."

"Oh. And I thought you might have been persuaded."

Persuade? By whom? When?

"Ms. Williams, I'm just waiting for a friend here," I repeated to myself, hoping the destroyer of my dreams would finally disappear.

"I get it. But aren't you interested in your old job at all?"

My old job? The one I had just lost, as well as my faith in humanity?

Even if all the problems suddenly disappeared into thin air, too much had happened at the Royal Renaissance. The next time there was a problem, the hotel would undoubtedly drop me again, like a hot potato, and I didn't want that a second time. I definitely deserved better!

What made Shannon Williams offer me my old job back in the first place? Certainly not out of sympathy. No, that was all thanks to Rebecca, and it was probably partly due to the chaos that no one was able to take over my duties so quickly.

How mendacious and hypocritical!

"I think my priorities have changed a bit," I said coolly. I hated Shannon Williams for letting Deborah just get away with everything that had happened at the hotel. Shaking my head, I wondered how shameless my boss actually was, then I bristled.

"How come you even want to hire me back after everything that's happened?"

Shannon Williams narrowed her eyes. "Wait, Mr. Lancester hasn't talked to you yet?"

Connor? Connor had talked to the assistant manager about me? My heart suddenly beat so loudly that it thundered in my ears.

"No, why should he?" I asked as calmly as I could, yet my voice trembled a little.

Someone touched my shoulders from behind, I flinched and took a step to the side. Even before hopes could spread in me, which gave my heart a stab, I turned around and looked Rebecca directly in the eyes.

"Man, Beccs! You scared me to death!"

"Come on, we have to go," Rebecca urged, pulling me away from the hotel by the arm, not paying attention to the guardian of limbo.

Shannon Williams kept pace and kept talking at me, "Dana, think again, you can have your old job back right now. Right now! With a raise and compensation, of course."

Rebecca quickened her pace as if she wanted to run away from my former boss. Over my shoulder, she called out, "I'm very sorry, Ms. Williams, but we are in a very, very big hurry. Besides, Dana isn't interested."

Okay, on the one hand Beccs was absolutely right – time was pressing, and I had no interest in my old job – yet I felt betrayed because my friend was speaking for me vicariously.

"Hey, I can speak for myself," I protested, stopping and looking my former boss straight in the eye.

"Thank you for the offer, but I decline. A raise doesn't compensate for the injustices you've done to me. I want a job where my work is valued and where I am appreciated as a person. That is not the case at the Royal Renaissance Hotel, where only extravagance and money count, nothing else."

Actually, I didn't realize I felt that way until I heard myself say it out loud. I would rather work in the cheapest motel in the world than in the Royal Renaissance Hotel.

Shannon Williams said nothing more, her mouth wide open in horror, glaring at me with a disappointed expression.

"Have a nice day," I ended the conversation. Then I let myself be pulled along without resistance by Rebecca, who had almost run in the wrong direction twice because she was walking so fast.

"What did Ms. Williams tell you?" asked Rebecca cautiously.

"Not much. She wanted to give me my job back, and she was talking about Connor."

"Oh, really? And what?" Was this Rebecca's hopeful side? Or did she know more than she was letting on? Damn it, what was going on here?

"Nothing direct, just that they had talked about me," I said thoughtfully. "Do you think he talked to them about Deborah, too, and put in a good word for me?"

My heart was beating wildly in my chest.

"It's possible. It would be nice of him, wouldn't it?"

"Don't act so innocent, Beccs. You're in this somehow, I want to know what happened at the hotel right now!"

Rebecca looked at her wristwatch. "My goodness, it's so late already! We have to get going or we'll miss the party we were supposed to arrange!"

"Don't change the subject!" I admonished my best friend, raising my index finger threateningly. "When were you going to tell me you were hosting a wedding, anyway?"

Rebecca looked at me, half grinning and half despairing. "Well. I just don't want you to miss anything in your life, you're too important to me for that. Besides, it's an engagement party, not a wedding."

"Oh, well then everything's fine if it's just an engagement party," I grumbled cynically. "Do you really think I need an engagement party right now? With happy people celebrating their love?"

Rebecca sighed, "Yep, I think you need just that."

"All right, you self-proclaimed expert."

"Dana, deal with it. You're just going to have to get through it, okay?"

"You can just drop me off at the next rest stop."

Beccs looked at me, shaking her head. I snorted loudly and said nothing more.

Well, now Beccs probably had to see my pouting face for the next three weeks.

You'll just have to get through it now, Beccs.

We reached the van. I handed Rebecca the keys and sat down on the passenger side. Because I was still giving my best friend the silent treatment, she turned on the radio so that current music hits vibrated through the van.

Rebecca exited the side street and joined the slow-moving traffic. We drove north through Manhattan, and she kept looking at her watch, frowning.

"Is there a time problem?" I asked, but only half cynically. Of course, I didn't want my best friend to get in trouble for showing up late.

"A little bit, maybe, but we'll get there."

When the new super hit by Bonnie Buckley was played – Wild, Wild Heartbeats – I completely forgot how mad I actually was at Rebecca and instead drummed along on the dashboard to the beat of the jaunty tune.

The longer we drove, the more rural the area became, until we had left the urban metropolis behind us. Where the hell was this event? Beccs usually never arranged anything this far out.

"Where are we even going?" I asked.

"You'll see when we get there. I don't think the place means anything to you."

"So when do we get there?"

"Soon," Rebecca sighed. "You're already asking the same, annoying questions as Emma."

Now Rebecca had elicited my sarcasm.

"I'm hungry! And thirsty too. And I have to go to the bathroom! I'm bored," I enumerated all sorts of stereotypical phrases that children would think of during a long drive.

Rebecca laughed. "Okay, okay! A few more minutes and we'll be there. See that place up ahead? That's where we're headed." She pointed to a small coastal town on the horizon.

My gaze alternated between the hamlet in front of us and the town behind us until the sea captured my view. It was so close that I had the feeling I could taste the salt in the air. Even from a distance, I could spot the typical, rural coastal charm. At the same time, New York was within reach.

"Beautiful, isn't it?" asked Rebecca.

"Dreamy," I said thoughtfully. Somehow, I couldn't get the conversation with Shannon Williams out of my head. Nothing fit together anymore, and Rebecca's behavior certainly didn't clear anything up. But maybe I was just making things up because I couldn't believe that my relationship with Connor was really over.

Maybe I just needed a little distance from everything. A short vacation, in New Orleans with my parents, would be a possibility. Would my parents be disappointed in me when they heard what had happened? Surely...

Rebecca steered the car through town until we stopped in front of a cute bed and breakfast.

"Okay, we'll carry all the boxes into the foyer first, and then we'll take care of the decorations, okay?" asked Rebecca.

"You're the boss," I replied.

"I would be if I paid you." Rebecca laughed and got out to open the rear doors of the van.

The charming guesthouse stood on a small hill on the edge of the village and the sea was so close I could hear it rushing.

"Quit daydreaming, Dana, we're late," Rebecca reprimanded. She pressed a box of garlands into my hands.

"Careful, or I'll go on strike and demonstrate!" I threatened with a grin.

"Oh no, that would be terrible. I would then be forced to break up the demonstration with a water cannon ... or that garden hose over there." Rebecca pointed to a neatly coiled garden hose hanging on a white-painted wooden fence that encompassed the entire property.

The guesthouse was painted the same white and was in the center of a beautifully landscaped garden. God, this idyllic spot was perfect.

Later, when I had collected enough money and experience, I wanted to run a boarding house just like the one Grandma and Grandpa had. A small villa, designed and managed with love – just like the one we were standing in front of right now, organizing a dream engagement party.

Except for a gardener who was tending to some wild roses, I saw no one. No guests, no potential bride, no one.

"Hello!" Rebecca waved at the gardener. He waved back and then pointed to the open front door. "Great, thanks!"

The entryway was lined with a small wooden porch that held dozens of blooming flowers. Most of the flowers bore white or pink blossoms, in the style of the decorations Rebecca had brought with her.

Together we lugged one box after another into the large foyer, whose floor-to-ceiling windows offered a beautiful view of the garden and the sea.

The longer I stayed on the property, the greater my urge to visit my parents in New Orleans. My homesickness became almost unbearable. At the same time, I caught myself memorizing the small details with which the boarding house was so lovingly decorated. The stucco was beautifully engraved, timeless pictures hung in the golden picture frames, and the upholstered furniture invited me to snuggle in.

My stomach contracted painfully the more time I spent here. Everything, really everything, looked exactly as I had always imagined it. The same furniture, the same style, the colors, the flowers, everything. It was as if someone had put my dreams on paper, and yes, I was beastly jealous of the one who owned the boarding house.

"There!" groaned Rebecca loudly, setting the box down in front of her. "That was the last box."

"That's all my back could have taken," I replied, panting and rubbing my aching loins. Beccs nodded in agreement.

"All right, let's get this mess in order." Rebecca roughly sorted the boxes. Not only the foyer, but also the dining room next door were to be decorated. The dishes were already in place, and judging by the number, it had to be a small, romantic party. Suddenly, I didn't feel comfortable here at all. Everything reminded me of Connor and what we could have become.

"What should I do now?" I asked. I was dying for Rebecca to give me all kinds of work to do so we could leave as soon as possible.

"Hold on." Rebecca left the foyer and returned a moment later with a large bouquet of flowers, which she pressed into my hand.

"You could take the bouquet to the bride-to-be's room, on the second floor. Just up the stairs, you won't miss it."

Rebecca grabbed a stepladder and began hanging the garlands, leaving a few inches of space to the ceiling so the stucco would continue to show.

I gritted my teeth, because I definitely didn't want to go into that room. Into all the others, yes, but not this one cursed room. My broken heart could not take so much happiness and love now.

"Can't I just hang any garlands or set the table?"

"There is only one ladder. I'll take care of the table at the end, the dishes still need polishing."

"Then I'll do that," I suggested.

"No!" screamed Rebecca. There was a hint of hysteria in her voice. She cleared her throat briefly and then continued speaking more calmly, "I mean, the bouquet really needs to go in the room now. The guests are about to arrive, and then we can't show our faces in the honeymoon suite. That would be rude!"

Ah, damn!

I sighed. "Fine, but you know I hate you for that, right? Dragging me to an engagement party. Now."

"And I know you don't mean it," Rebecca replied smiling graciously.

Directed by Rebecca, I had no trouble finding the honeymoon suite. The whole damn way there, starting from the stairs, was strewn with petals.

Whoever the potential groom was, he had a real romantic streak. This place alone screamed romance. The well-chosen decorations were another sign of his good taste. Although I hated the circumstances, I wished for the groom that the bride said yes. Anyone who went to that much trouble was worthy of being loved.

This realization softened my pain somewhat. Nevertheless, I felt like a burglar when I reached the suite.

Out of decency and habit, I knocked and waited before entering the room.

The suite was spacious and as stylishly furnished as the rest of the guesthouse. The large windows offered a magnificent view of the sea. The entire floor was covered with flower petals, and there were hundreds of lit candles on the cabinets and tables.

I envied the woman whom this was all for. Yes, I was jealous of a stranger I knew absolutely nothing about. Shaking my head, I placed the bouquet of flowers on the only free table, which was right next to the large four-poster bed.

On the bed was a beautifully arranged dress of white silk, gorgeous and expensive.

"You don't leave anything to chance, do you?" I asked.

Even though I felt like an intruder and my past spoke for me, I looked closer at the dress.

Look only, do not touch!

Memories became present. The last time, my daydreaming had almost cost me my job. But if I hadn't worn that dress then, I might never have gone out with Connor. My broken heart ached, and inevitably I wondered if I would turn back time if I could.

Something caught my gaze that I had not noticed before. Next to the dress was a single earring. I smiled at the coincidence; that it seemed so familiar. Everything here reminded me of my first encounter with Connor. The dress, the earring, even the scent of sandalwood was in the air.

God, how I had been drawn to Connor from the first moment, his warm arms and that fire that had ignited my passion. Connor had taught me so many things. Hell, Connor had shown me my deepest desires that I had repressed for so long.

"If you only knew how sorry I am for everything," I heard Connor whisper. Heavens, he still possessed all my senses. Now, I not only smelled him, but I heard him as well, only I couldn't feel him.

I took one last look at the dress and the earring, then started to retreat. As I turned, I ran into a wall that hadn't been there before. Strong and hard, masculine smelling – with a hint of sandalwood. Oh God, it wasn't a wall, it was Connor, keeping me from falling over with his strong arms.

After regaining my composure, I staggered back two steps.

"Connor? What are you doing here?"

"The only right thing to do."

"I don't quite understand..." I began. But when Connor took my hand in his hands, I held my breath. Before he had even said a single word, I had to blink away individual tears. My whole body was going crazy, I was getting hot and cold at the same time.

God, I had missed his hands on my body so much.

"You're still wearing my bracelet," Connor said with a smile. Reverently, he stroked the small charms with his index finger.

But of course I was still wearing the bracelet. I was his girl after all. At least for a time. A time that I associated with the best memories of my life, but also with the worst.

"Dana, I was an idiot, a fucking moron, and I finally realized it. I hope the realization doesn't come too late."

"Yes, you were an idiot," I repeated before my voice broke.

Connor nodded. Now, for the first time, I dared to look at his face. He looked tired, but also full of hope. His brown eyes locked onto me, full of affection. No question about it, he meant it.

"I've made unforgivable mistakes in the past, but I still hope you can forgive me so we can have a future together." Connor smiled, half-pained, half-hopeful.

I had never seen him so desperate. Not even once.

Of course, I forgive you, was the first thing that went through my mind, but for some reason I kept silent. I just stood there and stared at Connor in disbelief.

What do you think that future would look like? And they would live happily ever after? Probably not. Especially not if Deborah had her way. Besides, I didn't even know what my life would look like tomorrow. I no longer had a job or a goal, and with no prospects, I lacked the drive to even think about the next hour of my life.

"Connor, I don't know if I can take this again. You broke my heart."

"And when you left, you took my heart with you," Connor replied. With his thumb, he wiped a tear from my cheek. His words began to mend my broken heart. Slowly, but I could feel my heart and soul healing.

"So many obstacles have been put in our way that I can hardly look forward."

"Don't worry, I will build you a castle out of these stones that will protect us from everything and lead you wherever you want."

I hated Connor for saying exactly what I wanted to hear. It was exactly what I wanted to feel and what I needed to forgive him.

"And what about Deborah?" my voice broke again.

"Gone, and gone for good. She won't turn you in, and you won't have any more problems. I've cleared everything up. Don't worry, she'll never bother us again."

So Connor had been at the Royal Renaissance Hotel after all and had stood up for me there. Now everything was suddenly crystal clear, and I understood why everyone around me had been acting so strangely, namely because of Connor! Heavens, he must have been arranging everything for days.

"Really?" I asked, just to be sure. This was all just too perfect. There had to be a catch. A needle that burst my dream, a hair in the soup, something.

"Really. I love you, Dana, I love you more than anything in the world."

When Connor said the magic three words – twice – my heart stopped for a moment. I was speechless, and my legs went all soft.

Connor turned sideways for a moment and opened the top drawer of the dresser. From there, he pulled out a wrapped gift, about as wide and thick as an envelope.

"What is it?" I asked.

"This is my attempt to save us," he said with a smile. "Open it."

I accepted the gift. It was wrapped in red paper and heavier than it looked. It felt massive and stiff. A picture frame?

Carefully, I separated the paper and pulled out a silver, smoothly polished tablet, about the size of a cutting board. It felt classy, without a doubt, but why was Connor giving me something like this? A silver-plated cutting board?

"Turn them over!" Connor prompted me.

"Oh, whoops." I hadn't even considered that the board had a front, too. My breath caught as I complied with Connor's request. Reverently, I traced the engraved script with my fingertips, which was decorated with vines and scrolls.

Dana & Connor Lancester

"Oh, Connor," I sighed, moved to tears. At the same moment, Connor got down on one knee in front of me. He flipped open a small box set in leather, in whose velvety bed was a silver ring with a huge diamond. Right next to it was a miniature version for my bracelet.

Oh. My. God.

"I give you everything I have. My heart, my dreams, my future, and my thoughts. Dana Swanson, will you marry me?"

33

Connor

So there it was, this one moment that would change my life forever. And the decision of how my future changed was entirely up to Dana.

Unbelievable how right it felt to have someone else deciding over me. Was Dana aware of how powerful she was at that second? Otherwise, it had always been me who had kept control and made the decisions.

I opened the small leather box and had to muster all my strength to keep my hands from shaking. Dana was about to decide on both our futures.

"I give you everything I have. My heart, my dreams, my future and my thoughts. Dana Swanson, will you marry me?"

Dana stood in front of me, tears streaming down her face, and she stared at me with wide eyes. Again and again, her gaze slid back and forth between the door sign and the ring.

"You're asking me to be your wife?"

"My wife. My best friend. My lady. My whore. My girl."

"This is so ... unexpected," Dana sighed. Then her voice broke.

Damn, it felt like she was almost crushing my heart. I remained motionless and tried to hear an answer in Dana's silence.

"Say something," I finally whispered when Dana did not break her silence. Her beautiful face reflected an infinite number of emotions.

"You know, in the beginning I didn't believe that you would really love me. In fact, I thought you would banish me from your life after our first night, and I would have been okay with it," Dana said thoughtfully. "But then you showed me your beast and my secret desires, so dark and sinister that I never wanted to admit them to myself."

"No, they are not dark and sinister. Your desires are radiant and redemptive and beautiful," I murmured.

"Through you. You turn it into something beautiful, Connor," Dana said. She ran her index finger over the engagement ring. A high-carat, one-of-a-kind piece by Josh Anderson, which I had flown in specially from the Czech Republic on my private plane, as was the earring that lay on the bed.

I had wanted to recreate everything as it was when we first met – only much more romantic. An encounter that had changed both our lives so much. Just as this moment could change our lives forever.

I knew in my heart that I could no longer live without Dana; we were soul mates, and Dana had to see and feel that too.

Why don't you just say yes, Dana?

"Connor? You were right. I was jealous of Deborah. I was jealous of her wealth, her influence, and that it could make anything you wanted possible for you." Dana's lower lip quivered, and a tear ran down her cheek. It must have taken a lot of strength for her to admit this weakness to herself.

"No, Deborah absolutely cannot give me what I need, neither with her money nor with her terrible character. All I need is you. You give me everything I need to be happy." I took a deep breath as I looked deep into Dana's sky blue eyes that were shimmering with tears. "Dana, I am a man who has it all. Money, power and influence, but without you, I am nothing."

If Dana didn't say yes soon, I was going to go crazy, that much was certain. I hated her for putting me on the rack like that. Now I was beginning to get an idea of how violently I was driving Dana crazy in the playroom.

"Am I dreaming, Connor? This is all just too perfect right now – you and this boarding house and our romanticized first meeting!"

"No, you are not dreaming, Dana, but until you answer my question, I am in a nightmare," I said thoughtfully.

"I want you to touch me with your hands and make me get on my knees. I want you to be gentle with me and spank me as hard as you can. I want to make great memories with you and get through the bad times with you."

For the first time since I knew Dana, she was saying what she wanted on her own. Not only had I grown in our relationship, Dana had too. Full of pride, I smiled at her as she continued, "I love it when you look at me like that and the feeling it gives me. I want you to look at me like that every day, every single day for the rest of our lives. Yes! I want to marry you!"

No laughter, no matter how sincere, and no moans, no matter how sensual, resonated in my soul the way Dana's last words did.

I want to marry you!

Like a gentleman, I put the engagement ring on Dana's ring finger, but then there was no stopping me. I jumped up, wrapped Dana in my arms and kissed her, so long and passionately, until I had no more air in my lungs. At that moment, I didn't need air, I was breathing Dana and needed only her to live. She made my heart beat; she was the reason it kept beating.

Breathlessly we broke away from each other, and Dana was still crying, but now, fortunately, they were tears of joy, because there was a smile on her lips.

"Say you love me again," Dana begged.

"I love you."

"That sounds so beautiful. It suits your voice when you say it. Say it again."

"I love you with all my heart and soul. I love you!"

Now that I was saying the words, I realized what a fucking idiot I had been. Words had never felt more honest and meaningful, and if I had told Dana earlier how I felt deep inside about her, it could have saved us a lot of trouble.

"I love you too, Connor."

Now it was Dana who demanded a kiss. Sensual and full of tenderness. Her lips were soft and slightly open so that I penetrated her mouth with my tongue. She tasted so good. Sweet and full of longing. Again, we detached from each other only when we were breathless.

It was as if a weight had fallen from my shoulders now that I had reclaimed her.

"You're not a casual guest here, are you?" asked Dana with a grin. She already knew the answer.

"No, not really," I smiled knowingly.

"I really need to show this ring to Rebecca! I have to call my parents too and your parents too! And..."

I put my finger on Dana's lips. "Shh. All in good time. I think we should give Rebecca a few more minutes to decorate properly. There will be plenty of moments and opportunities to celebrate with everyone. All that matters now is that you and I have found each other again."

"I knew it! She was in cahoots with you," Dana snorted almost reproachfully.

"Yes, but I had to convince them for a long time. A very long time, including hours of interrogation. She's a good best friend."

"Yeah, sounds like Beccs." Dana smiled, then her face grew more serious. "So how are we going to pass the time until the festivities can begin?"

"I know something," I said. Then I pulled a pair of handcuffs out of my pants pocket. "Because you're such a good girl, I'm going to let you choose how I fuck you."

Dana tilted her head and bit her lips lasciviously. "Hmm. I'm afraid I've been rather a very, very bad girl lately."

"Well, well. So what do you want me to do with you, bad girl?" I growled and walked around Dana until I stood behind her and kissed her neck.

"My ass hasn't been spanked in ages," Dana whispered. Her body quivered as I grasped her hips and pressed her ass firmly against my stiff member.

"Seems like a good move to me," I murmured in her ear.

"Thank you, sir."

Sir had never sounded more meaningful. Dana's voice breathed soul into lifeless words, giving them deeper meaning.

"Take your clothes off, honey."

Dana obeyed immediately. She unbuttoned her white blouse and then took off her pleated skirt. I took care of the white lace underwear and her pumps myself.

"I missed that sight," I said in awe.

"And I this feeling."

What had I done to deserve this woman? No other woman had driven me so out of my mind.

It clicked as the handcuff around Dana's left wrist snapped into place. Then I led Dana to the four-poster bed and clamped Dana's body between me and the ceiling-high bedpost. Under my guidance, Dana's hands followed upward. Far above her head was a large metal ring, through which I passed the handcuffs halfway, then secured Dana's right wrist to it. Dana had no choice but to stand on her tiptoes. Nevertheless, she smiled at me expectantly while I stroked her arms downward.

Still you smile, darling.

Where my nails touched her skin, they left goosebumps. I massaged her breasts, rubbed my thumbs over her buds, which slowly rose.

"I like seeing you tied up, Dana."

I pinched both nipples firmly and elicited Dana's first, sensual scream. Her body squirmed between my hands and her bonds, but Dana had no chance to escape my grip.

"Damn it, Dana. You have no idea how much pleasure your pain gives me, your pain is a gift to me, never forget that."

"No, sir," Dana gasped.

I let go of her nipples. A short jolt went through her body, then she relaxed. With her big, light blue eyes, Dana returned my gaze, devoted and full of trust.

With my foot, I pushed hers to the side, so that Dana had to spread her legs further. It was a balancing act for Dana, but she looked damn seductive doing it.

"Exhausting?"

"No, rather uncomfortable," Dana replied. Her gaze remained fixed on the handcuffs.

"Oh, has the princess only ever been pampered with padded leather restraints?" I grinned maliciously.

"I'm not a princess," Dana hissed, her eyes sparkling defiantly.

"That's right, you're my whore now."

With my hand, I slid between her legs. I unerringly found Dana's most sensitive spot and rubbed it with circular movements. Moaning, Dana put her head back.

"Good girl," I said. "Accept everything from me that I give you. Pain and pleasure."

"Yes, sir."

I continued to rub her pearl, feeling her wetness and enjoying Dana's soft sighing as I put my free arm around her loins. Her sighing grew louder as I penetrated her with two fingers. She stretched her pelvis towards me so that I could take her even deeper, but I took my time and moved my fingers agonizingly slowly inside her.

"Please," she pleaded softly.

"Shh."

Not yet, darling.

I covered her neck with soft kisses, sucking in her scent. She smelled so wonderful, sweet and flowery and of pure sin.

"Please," Dana continued to whimper.

"If you ignore my order again, I will punish you, and a plug and a massage stick will play a big part in that. Understand?"

"Yes, sir," Dana replied sugary-sweetly, but squinted her eyes at the same time. Dana was putting it on, I knew that. I wondered if she knew that she was playing right into my hands. I wanted to chastise her, beat her, tie her up, gag her, fuck her senseless, and do so many forbidden things to her that it would take me forever to do whatever was on my mind.

"You must not speak again until I give you permission."

Dana nodded. With an unmistakable smile on her lips.

You want to play? Then let's play! My game. My rules. My decisions.

God, how I loved this woman! It was hard to believe how wide Dana's line between submissive shyness and defiant rebellion had become.

She had opened herself for me and had gone with me to the edge of her limits ... and beyond.

I pulled out of Dana, went to the dresser and pulled out a ring gag.

"You are lucky, Dana. Today, I'm actually going to help you follow my orders. Open your mouth."

Dana's gaze slid back and forth between me and the gag, willingly opening her mouth. The large metal ring forced Dana to keep her mouth wide open and the two leather strips I closed on the back of her head kept everything in place.

I ran my index finger over Dana's soft lips and then entered her mouth to show her that I could. I could take her mouth whenever I wanted. Damn, I loved demonstrating to Dana the power I had over her, over her body, mind and soul. Then I penetrated her center again, as slowly and sensually as before, knowing that I was driving Dana crazy with it. That's exactly where I wanted her.

"Now you're helpless against me," I stated. "I can fuck you as slow or as hard as I want, and there's nothing you can do about it. Do you like that?"

I penetrated her again with my fingers. Her look said everything. Dana's eyes always betrayed her, because her face was like an open book for me, in which I could simply read everything, although her thoughts were often as deep as the ocean. I kissed her open mouth and then focused again on my fingers massaging her most sensitive areas. Restlessly, Dana shifted the weight back and forth between her legs.

"It's getting tiring now, isn't it?" I asked gently. Dana nodded.

"You'll have to be patient for a moment, beautiful."

Now I moved my fingers faster, deeper and gave Dana the relief she desperately needed. She moaned throatily through her mouth while she could no longer prevent saliva from running out of the corners. She was damn tight around my fingers, and I imagined how my erection, now pressing painfully against my pants, felt inside her.

Dana's abdomen twitched, and she tilted her pelvis back and forth. Her body shook and trembled as her orgasm became more and more tangible. A second before Dana came, I pulled out of her. Reproachful and angry in equal measure, Dana looked at me.

"As my girl, you should know that you have to earn your orgasm first." I smiled.

I released one of her wrists from the handcuffs and Dana's legs immediately gave way. Only my firm grip around her hips prevented Dana from falling to the floor. Slowly, I lowered Dana to her knees, and when she looked at me so submissively from below with her mouth wide open in invitation, there was no stopping me. Hectically I opened my pants, freed my cock and thrust into her wet, warm throat. Hard and deep, just as Dana deserved, just as she wished for herself. I took her head between my hands, and Dana let me guide her. After a few hard thrusts, I slowed my pace but penetrated her even deeper. I knew I was asking a lot of Dana when I fucked her so deeply, to the hilt, but she endured it for me. She was my whore, my girl, my slave.

Her mouth felt so good, her soft tongue, her hard palate, her hot breath. A dangerous combination that could make me explode within seconds.

Not yet ...

I had just gotten Dana back; I wouldn't give her up so quickly. Damn, I would love to chain her in the playroom and never, never let her go again.

With a firm grip, I pushed my hardness deep inside her, so deep that the tip of her nose touched my belly. Her throat tightened around my tip and stimulated me fucking intensely. At the same time, Dana maintained her eye contact with me, which made my beast rage.

She looked so amazing when she had my cock in her mouth and was gazing up at me. Dana could not give me a more submissive sight.

"Touch yourself," I rewarded her for her look. Immediately, her left hand, which still had the handcuffs dangling from it, moved between her legs. Full of pride, I smiled at her while I continued to thrust into her throat. At first, I restrained myself. I didn't want to release the beast yet, but I had simply locked him behind bars for too long; he could hardly be restrained. To be honest, I didn't want to restrain the beast any longer either. I let go of the beast and it pounced on Dana.

Hard. Wild. Deep. Uninhibited. Passionate. Libidinous. Desiring.

Dana also noticed the difference and continued to concentrate on following all my movements, which was not so easy, because I just took what I wanted. Dana had no choice but to take everything I gave her.

A few more times, I thrust hard, enjoying the sight of sinking my manhood into Dana's mouth, then I exploded inside her, certainly not for the last time today.

As I pulled my manhood out of her mouth, I watched in fascination as my gold slowly dripped down the corners of her mouth onto her breasts and ran down her throat at the same time. With a ring gag, swallowing was almost impossible.

"Good girl," I praised her.

I freed Dana's gagged mouth, which she gratefully closed. I ran my thumb over the corner of Dana's mouth, picked up my semen and put it in her mouth. She willingly licked my finger until there were no more traces of my explosion on her body.

God, how I had missed Dana and this. Now it was her turn, I pulled her up by the arms and looked deep into her eyes. "How do you want me to fuck you?"

Dana stared at my still hard erection and licked her lips.

Heck, I hadn't even started yet, and now that I had Dana back, my stamina seemed endless.

"The way I deserve," she replied with a smile.

Somberly, I glowered at her. A smile was on my lips, followed by a throaty growl. I pushed Dana backwards onto the bed. Like a predator, I climbed over her, kissed her throat, and grabbed her wrists, stretching them upward away from her body.

I wanted to see her face, every single emotion. I loved the look on her face when she came.

Without warning, I thrust and penetrated her to the hilt. Dana was more than ready for me. Even when she'd been tied to the bedposts, she could not deny her desire for me. The wetness between her legs spoke for itself.

Dana moaned out, thrusting her hips at me, and I accepted her invitation to fuck her even deeper. With each thrust, I elicited sensual, loud cries from Dana. Her eyelids fluttered and her breathing became more and more erratic. Dana's entire body was electrified, her muscles tensed, her hands balled into fists, and the madness in her gaze became more and more present. Dana's madness was the air my beast needed to breathe.

It was a paradox. On the one hand I wanted to fuck her forever and never stop, on the other hand I wanted to cum immediately. I decided to compromise. I wanted to share my orgasm with Dana, just as I shared pleasure and pain and the rest of my life with her.

"Come for me!" I commanded.

Dana obeyed me not a second later. Her legs wrapped around my waist, and she tightened so strongly around my erection that I came too. For the second time in no time, I pumped my seed into her body. Together we surrendered to the orgasm that rippled through both our bodies, causing tremors in the other. Damn, those were not waves, those were tsunamis.

I rested my head on Dana's chest to catch my breath. Dana sighed softly, and when I loosened my grip, she wiped a curl from her face.

"Wow, that was..." Dana gasped, searching for the right words.

"Damn good," I added.

"Damn necessary," Dana corrected me with a smile.

"Well, where did that innocent, shy maid go?"

"You spoiled that."

I grinned then kissed Dana.

There was a knock at the door, and I felt Dana wince.

"Hello, everything okay in there?" called Rebecca through the closed door.

"Yes! Don't come in!" Dana answered frantically. Nevertheless, she pushed me off her and covered herself with the bedspread.

"You sure? You've been in there so long, um, how's it going?"

"Hold on, I'm coming," she shouted.

"Again?" I asked with a grin.

"Connor!"

"Oki-doki," Rebecca called through the closed door, but I heard no footsteps.

"How about you go freshen up in the bathroom, honey?"

"Okay," Dana replied and staggered into the bathroom with the handcuffs still dangling from her wrist. Only when I heard the water in the shower did I open the door for Rebecca.

"Well?" asked Rebecca curiously.

"She said yes!"

"Ah! I knew it! Congratulations!" Rebecca shrieked with joy. She hugged me tightly and then hopped back on the spot. She cleared her throat and then put on a business-like face. "Of course, I'll be totally surprised when Dana shows me her engagement ring."

"Of course," I replied with a conspiratorial air. "Is everything ready downstairs?"

"Yes, everything is ready – and by the way, I'm also exhausted. You and Dana are getting married. I still can't believe it!" squealed Rebecca.

"We'll be right down," I said.

"Okay, cool, cool, cool," Rebecca chattered excitedly, as she ran down the hallway like she was being chased by a pack of wolves.

I closed the door behind me, undressed, and joined Dana in the shower.

"What did Rebecca want?" she asked curiously.

"Oh, she was just checking in," I said with a shrug. "It's kind of like those checking WhatsApp messages on first dates to know if your best friend is dating a serial killer or stamp collector right now and needs help."

"Oh well, good to know, good even if Beccs and I never did anything like that," Dana said with a giggle. "But nice that she wanted a sign of life from me."

"More likely from me!" I replied seriously, while I soaped her silky soft skin.

I would have loved to fuck Dana again, but I didn't want to keep our guests waiting, which Dana didn't even know about.

"We should hurry," I said as Dana rinsed shampoo from her hair.

"Why? I'd like to spend the whole day here," Dana answered wistfully.

"Believe me, the one I prepared is much better."

"Better than sex? Besides, you haven't spanked my ass yet." Dana pulled a pout and her eyes sparkled darkly.

I had to control myself so that I didn't grab Dana, push her against the wall and fuck her brains out.

"I haven't forgotten your ass, nor the plug and the massage stick," I whispered in her ear.

"Sounds tempting," she purred, then reached for the soap one more time. Christ, she was going to be in the shower forever if I didn't do something, so I turned the faucet to the other side and in seconds the hot water, whose steam had spread throughout the bathroom, turned into ice-cold water.

Dana cried out, "Connor!"

With both arms I blocked Dana's way out.

"Alright, honey, if you really want to keep showering, go ahead!" I ordered, growling.

Angrily, she sparkled at me. Her whole body was covered with goosebumps and her nipples were so stiff that I wished I had nipple clamps within reach.

Actually, the ice-cold water was also supposed to cool me down, but it had the exact opposite effect.

"Fine, you win, I'm coming with you!" Dana gave up with a sigh. With a triumphant smile, I turned off the water and handed her a towel.

"Very good, why aren't you happy?" I asked with a smile.

"Because I'm a naughty girl."

"And what a bad, bad girl you are, Dana."

After I had dried off, I left the bathroom and waited until Dana had gotten ready. She had all the makeup from the loft at her disposal, and I had also had everything else brought here from there.

By now, Dana had been in the bathroom for more than a quarter of an hour and there was no sign that she would be leaving it any time soon, the hairdryer kept howling anew.

"Dana, we're late!"

"Just a minute," Dana replied, then she finally left the bathroom. Wow. She looked damn seductive with that red lipstick and those long, curved lashes. Her blonde curls hung loosely over her shoulders and her blue eyes shone.

"You look beautiful."

Dana smiled and picked up the beautiful white dress that had fallen off the bed earlier. I helped her into it and zipped up the back.

"It fits perfectly." Dana looked down at herself, beaming.

"But of course, it was made to your measurements."

Dana smiled warmly at me, then her eyes fell on the earring that was also lying on the floor. She picked it up. "That earring looks pretty familiar."

"I know. It's the earring from when we first met. I had it made by Josh because he could still remember exactly what you did."

Dana laughed out loud. "You're never going to let me forget that, are you?"

"No. Never," I replied with a grin.

She put on her earring and sighed. "I'm afraid I didn't bring shoes to match the dress."

"Yes, you did," I replied, walking over to the closet and opening the closet door. Not only were all my things and the things I had intended for Dana in here, but all the boxes from Dana's apartment were there as well. They were on the top floor waiting to be distributed around the boarding house, including her trophy.

"Well, how do I look?" asked Dana. She spun like a ballerina so that the dress spun with her.

"Perfect and now come with me, we're really late." I grabbed her by the hand and literally pulled her out of the honeymoon suite.

"I'm really excited about what can't wait any longer," Dana said. Although she looked away, I had clearly seen her eye roll.

"Twenty additional strokes."

Dana answered nothing, but only grinned contentedly. When we reached the stairs, I heard soft voices and muffled banging. I stopped short and slowed Dana down.

"Close your eyes, Dana. Don't be afraid, I'm holding you!" I commanded.

She closed her eyes, and I led her down the stairs step by step, where all the guests were already waiting to receive us. Damn, I couldn't even think about what would have happened if my plan hadn't worked.

A brief, scrutinizing glance around the room, which was almost bursting with excitement, then I gently stroked Dana's cheek.

"You may open your eyes again."

When Dana opened her eyes again, I gave the signal and the assembled company around her shouted in unison, "Surprise!"

Dana blinked and looked around in amazement. In the meantime, Rebecca had dressed as festively as the other guests I had invited here to celebrate our engagement.

"Oh, Connor. Why didn't you say anything?" asked Dana, close to tears.

"Then it wouldn't have been a surprise anymore," I replied with a smile. Then Dana turned to the guests.

"Mom, Dad! What are you doing here?"

"Celebrating your engagement, what else!" replied Dana's mother.

She embraced her parents, Dana's mother sobbing while her father euphorically stroked both women's backs.

"I really missed you guys."

Afterwards, Dana walked over to Rebecca, gave her a friendly hit against the shoulder, and hugged her. "You knew about everything!"

"I not only knew about it, I even organized it all," Beccs boasted, her chest thrust out. Then Emma took the floor, standing between Tom and Rebecca. "If it's any consolation, she didn't tell me either." She shrugged and tilted her head, which made all the guests laugh. But Emma had made the biggest impression on my mother.

"Oh, what a sweet child! I can hardly wait for you to have babies," she whooped with joy.

Maxine grabbed our mother by the arm. "Easy mom, first comes the wedding and then the honeymoon and then come the grandkids."

"Sam and Josh unfortunately couldn't make it on such short notice, but they firmly promised us they would be at the wedding. After all, they are outfitting the most beautiful bride in the world with wonderful jewelry," I said.

"I can't even put into words how overwhelmed I am."

"You don't have to be. Our hearts beat in time, I can feel it."

Although it was only a small party, it took quite a while for everyone to congratulate us. Dad still couldn't believe I had a real fiancée, mainly because he had lost a sports car to Maxine. Apparently, behind my back, the two of them had kept making bets on what kind of escort girl I would present to my family, at various events.

The female guests lined up to look at Dana's engagement ring, chuckling gleefully. Again and again, they held Dana's hand up to the light, while the quieter male company was content to nod their heads and drink good bourbon.

Again and again, I kneaded a small, oblong package in my back pocket, waiting for the right time to give Dana her actual engagement gift. But over and over, Dana or I got involved in conversations that I didn't want to break off or interrupt.

After the mood calmed down a bit, I took the floor by hitting a champagne glass with a cake fork.

"Excuse me, but I have a few words to say."

I glanced briefly at the silent crowd, then continued.

"I would like to thank all of you. Thank you to Rebecca for organizing the entire celebration and bringing me my bride." I smiled gratefully at Rebecca.

"And thanks to Dana's parents for coming up from New Orleans on such short notice."

I also gave Dana's parents a warm look. I knew how much it meant to Dana and her parents to be able to celebrate together today.

"And thank you mom and dad for finding time to cater on such short notice."

My parents cheered me on, Mom in particular beaming proudly at me.

"I also have to thank my sis, Max, you have performed a true miracle, and it is only because of your efforts that we are able to celebrate here today at all."

Max winked at me, then I went to Dana and took her hand.

"I thank you for saying yes. By doing so, you make me the happiest man in the world."

Dana was so moved that she only nodded but could not say anything. That was not necessary, her feelings were clearer than words could ever be.

"So, to celebrate our engagement, I want to give you this," I said, handing Dana the package.

Curious, she opened it, then looked at me with wide eyes. "A key?"

"Not just any key, it's the key to your pension."

"My pension?"

"Yes, this is yours now." I pointed to the rooms around us.

"That's what the big name tag is for, right?" concluded Dana.

"Exactly," I smiled.

"Wow, I thought that was just symbolic. Maxine. You set it up, didn't you?"

"Yes, but this time he gave me free rein to set it up just the way you like it," Max replied with a laugh.

"It's perfect," Dana enthused.

"No, not quite yet," Dana's father interrupted the conversation, and Dana's mother handed us a small package, about the size of a shoebox.

While I held the box, Dana opened the big bow and lifted the lid. An old bell was revealed, polished to a high shine.

"Is that from Grandma and Grandpa's boarding house?" Dana's eyes filled with tears.

"Yes. We brought you all that was left of it," smiled Dana's mother.

"Thank you!" sobbed Dana. "I thank all of you. You guys are so great, and I love you. Thank you for sharing the best day of my life with me."

"To young love," my father raised his glass.

"Cheers!" everyone else joined in.

I put on a record on an old record player on the wall, and after a short hiss, beautiful classical dance music came on. Then I held out my hand to Dana and asked, "May I ask my fiancée for a dance?"

Dana beamed, and in her blue-bright eyes, I could see myself, smiling and content. I was now a part of her, just as she was a part of me.

"Only too gladly," Dana replied, letting me lead her to the center of the room. I put my arms around her petite body while she rested her head against my strong chest and let me lead her. Silently, we enjoyed our first dance as fiancées.

Just now, I experienced one of those precious moments when you wish it would never pass. But weren't those the moments that made life precious? Yes, damn it, you should enjoy every single moment while you could.

As the song drew to a close, I whispered in her ear, "You make me the happiest person in the world. I love you."

"I love you too, Connor."

34

Dana

Thoughtfully, I let my finger slide over the necklace that stood in the jewelry box on the dresser, right next to my trophy that had changed my life forever. Hesitantly, I picked up the necklace and held it to my neck.

I liked the look and smiled contentedly, my reflection smiling back.

"Yep, Dana, this piece of jewelry goes perfectly with your outfit," I said to myself. Then my gaze was caught by my bracelet, which by now had a whole bunch of charms attached to it. Little trinkets that were associated with precious memories. But probably the most impressive memory was on my left ring finger, where my engagement ring and wedding band were.

I was his girl, his wife, his whore, and I wanted to be all of that for him too. He loved every part of me in his own way, just as I loved all facets of Connor. His gentle side, his erratic ideas, his beast.

I looked at the clock and was surprised at how much time had passed.

Oops, late again!

Although I had settled into the boarding house by now and all the work was quite intuitive, I often sank into reveries that later led to time constraints, which was somehow nothing new. I left my small dressing room, which, like the rest of my private rooms, was on the top floor, and walked purposefully into the garden. Although the sun was still low, the garden was lit up like paradise. The lawn was a rich green, while the flowers and hedges everywhere in the garden glowed in the brightest colors. That it looked so fantastic here was thanks to Alberto, who had been taking care of the garden for more than twenty years and was currently pruning a huge elderberry. The sudden sale had hit him and his wife hard, but I had offered them both to just keep working here. He was a great gardener, and his wife was an equally good cook. The guests loved their traditional Italian dishes.

"Good morning, Alberto."

"Good morning, Dana," Alberto answered me with his typical Italian accent.

"Have you taken care of the bouquet for the arriving guests yet?" I asked.

"Si, si! Arabella has already picked up and arranged the flowers."

"Great, I'm sure the bouquets will be as beautiful as ever."

Alberto nodded at me gratefully, then went on to take care of the elderberry, with which Connor still had great goals. Admittedly, I still didn't understand much about alcohol, but everything Connor served me and our guests tasted forbidden-good.

The foyer of the guesthouse already smelled of freshly brewed coffee and pastries that Arabella had baked herself, as she did every morning. Mixed in was a slightly sweet scent, which came from the red roses that stood in small bouquets all over the place.

Satisfied, I noticed that everything was prepared for the newly arriving guests, perfect, because they had to arrive any moment.

Although our guesthouse had only recently opened, word was already spreading about it as an insider's tip for a short vacation on the East Coast, which made me quite proud.

The small bell above the entrance door announced the arriving guests with a bell-bright sound, and I immediately dashed to the entrance to receive them. As I did so, I took one last look in the large mirror in the foyer to check my appearance one last time.

"Welcome," I greeted the British couple Mr. and Mrs. Holmes. At the Royal Renaissance Hotel, guests were just room numbers with bank accounts, but at my boarding house, every single guest was addressed by name.

"Good afternoon," Mr. Holmes replied politely. He had the air of a university professor and was about retirement age. His wife had hooked her arm around him and was looking around.

"It's so beautiful here and so peaceful!" gushed Mrs. Holmes, who seemed a bit younger than her husband.

"That's why we're here, sweetheart." The look he gave his wife melted my heart. That's exactly how I wanted Connor to look at me twenty, thirty, fifty years from now. So full of love and affection.

"I hope you had a pleasant journey," I inquired.

"Yes, the flight and the time change are just a little tiring," Mrs. Holmes replied wearily.

"That's right," I replied understandingly. "If you'd like, I can take you to your room so you can get some rest. We'll just take care of the luggage later."

"That would be very kind," he replied, hugging his wife tightly. Heavens, they were both so cute that I wanted to adopt them!

I took the last key from the key hooks – all seven suites were now fully booked – then led my guests to the stairs. Although there were only a few rooms, these lacked nothing. There was a huge bathroom, an even bigger bed, and every single room had a great view of the expansive garden or the open sea. In my guesthouse, luxury and attention to detail came together and blended harmoniously.

"From here, you can access the terrace and conservatory, and in the basement, there is the sauna area and a heated pool."

I led the couple up the stairs to the second floor and opened the door for them.

"Here you go, let me know if you need anything," I said with a smile.

Gratefully, the couple stepped into the suite, and I watched their reactions with anticipation.

"Do you like it?" I asked curiously.

"Oh yes, it's beautiful, just like the pictures," Mrs. Holmes said, beaming.

"I'm glad to hear that. Make yourself at home and, if you like, our cook will put together a picnic basket for you this afternoon for a nice picnic in the pavilion or on the beach."

Mr. Holmes nodded. "That sounds good."

I smiled contentedly. "Fine, then I'll get everything ready and let you rest for now."

Back at the front desk, the phone rang – Connor. Still, I picked up the receiver and out of habit said, "Lancester Pension. Dana speaking, what can I do for you?"

"Playroom. Now."

Connor said only those two words, but they were enough to send my body into turmoil. His voice was rough and throaty, then Connor hung up. No, it wasn't Connor, it was his beast that was calling me – and I was only too happy to answer that call. From my abdomen spread a firework of feelings that reached to my fingertips.

Before I left, I put up a sign pointing to the bell and the phone. Usually, Rebecca or Arabella were close enough to hear the bell. Of course, Beccs worked here now, and not just as a maid – we took care of all the rooms together – but also as event manager.

Quickly I left the reception hall, because I didn't want to keep Connor waiting.

Damn, he hadn't done anything to me yet, hadn't even touched me, and yet I felt myself ready for him. More than ready, even.

"Gotcha!" shouted Rebecca from behind. I flinched and stopped.

"Caught doing what?" I asked.

"Oh, I don't know, you just looked guilty."

"I have nothing to hide."

"So why did you flinch?" Rebecca had put on her badass journalism face again, which made me sigh. My best friend just knew me too well.

"Maybe I was going to see Connor for a minute, he just called."

"And what did he want?"

"Good question," I replied.

Spank me, maybe. Tie me up and gag me. There were also no nipple clamps for a long time...

"Is it urgent?" asked Rebecca.

Yes.

"No, I don't think so. Why?"

Rebecca grinned broadly as she presented me with the concept for the next week. "I got the cellist I really wanted for the dinner, oh and this is the menu plan I created with Arabella."

"Reads great, as always," I said, smiling with satisfaction.

"Thanks, boss," Rebecca grinned broadly.

"You know you're not supposed to call me that!"

"All right, boss."

"Beccs!" I put my head back and snorted. "I'm going to go check on Connor now."

"Aye, Aye, Captain!"

Threateningly, I pointed my index finger at Rebecca and put on a serious face, but my facade quickly crumbled, and I could no longer hold back my laughter.

Since the first day, Rebecca played this game with me, and to my astonishment, she kept finding new names to replace *boss*.

"See you then." As I walked, I remembered that I hadn't yet finished my checklist. "Beccs? Would you please still take care of the cloth napkins? They would need to be ironed and folded, no telling how long Connor will take me."

"Sure, you can consider it done already."

"Thank you."

Quickly I made my way to our own four walls. Our playroom was hidden behind the bedroom, and I cautiously knocked on the locked door. In fact, the playroom was larger than the rest of our suite, which wasn't surprising since Connor and I spent more time here than anywhere else anyway, so it only made sense.

"Come on in."

Hesitantly, I entered, and, before I had even closed the door again behind me, I noticed Connor staring at me somberly from his chair.

"You're late," was all he said.

"I beg your pardon, sir."

I got down on my knees, put my hands on my lap and looked at the floor in awe.

"What am I going to do with you, darling? You're always defying my direct orders. You could try harder, or do I really always have to punish you?" murmured Connor. There was no doubt that he enjoyed being in such a powerful position. He stood up and stalked around me like a hunting wolf.

"Maybe your disciplinary measures aren't sustainable enough?" I teased in a deliberately provocative manner. At that, I tilted my head to the side and grinned at him. "You could try a little harder."

Oh wow, he was glaring at me so darkly that my entire abdomen quivered.

This look brought me around the mind. I would have loved to get up and fall wildly over him, but instead I remained motionless on my knees and poured instead, with my lascivious looks, more oil on the fire.

"What a bad, bad girl you are today."

"Yes, sir. I'm a really bad girl."

Connor gave me a tender kiss and whispered, "Don't ever stop being my bad girl, honey."

"Never," I breathed.

I accept everything from you, what you give me. Pain and pleasure.

Get a free copy of my fan-exclusive romance novel *Palace of Pain* over at: https://lana-stone.com/